BLACK SUN
RISING

BLACK SUN RISING

BOOK ONE: PRAETORIAN SERIES

DON MANN *and* JEFF EMDE

Skyhorse Publishing

Skyhorse Publishing books may be purchased in bulk at special discounts for sales promotion, corporate gifts, fund-raising, or educational purposes. Special editions can also be created to specifications. For details, contact the Special Sales Department, Skyhorse Publishing, 307 West 36th Street, 11th Floor, New York, NY 10018 or info@skyhorsepublishing.com.

Skyhorse® and Skyhorse Publishing® are registered trademarks of Skyhorse Publishing, Inc.®, a Delaware corporation.

Visit our website at www.skyhorsepublishing.com.

10 9 8 7 6 5 4 3 2 1

Library of Congress Cataloging-in-Publication Data is available on file.

Cover design by Bar-MD
Cover photos credit: © Adobe Stock

Print ISBN: 978-1-5107-5898-8
Ebook ISBN: 978-1-5107-6780-5

Printed in the United States of America

CONTENTS

PROLOGUE

Mohammad al-Rafah walked the streets of Khan Yunis alone. It was a moonless night and he had to carefully pick his way through the cluttered streets and alleys. It was after 2:00 a.m. on an unseasonably warm spring night and the streets were all but deserted save the odd stray dog or alley cat. This always amazed him. At over five thousand people per square kilometer, the Gaza Strip was one of the most densely populated places on the planet yet it went into hibernation after midnight. There were other places that were denser, of course—Macau, Hong Kong, Monaco—but they had a nightlife. *If it weren't for the Israeli embargo. If people actually had electricity and jobs, this would be a much better place. Instead, they were cut off and isolated. Fucking Israelis and their Egyptian lackeys.*

Mohammad was on his way home from spending the evening with Ameena, his mistress. She was the young wife of a low-level Hamas commander. Her husband worked evenings, which gave Mohammad the opportunity for regular trysts at her house on the eastern edge of the city. He was not in love with her; she was just convenient. He chuckled at the irony of her name—Ameena means "faithful." If only her husband knew. Mohammad surmised the man probably did know but just wasn't in a position to say anything about it. After all, Mohammad was a senior Hamas paramilitary leader with a violent and terrible reputation. His nom de guerre was Alkawbra—the Cobra—and people feared him. Ironically, he wasn't given that name by Hamas but rather by an Israeli settler when he was a teenager. He'd been walking past an Israeli settler's farm when he was bitten by a Saharan horned viper. Thanks to quick intervention from a doctor in the settlement, Mohammad survived and they called him "the Cobra" from then on. Despite owing his life to a Jewish doctor, the incident did nothing to temper his hatred of the Israelis.

The streets of Khan Yunis, like everywhere else in Gaza, were notoriously dangerous. Mohammad always kept alert for thieves who, not knowing who he was, might try to rob him. As he walked, he wrapped his fingers around the grip of the Makarov 9 mm pistol he kept in his pocket. After about fifteen minutes of walking, he arrived at the Al-Rasul Mohamad Hospital in the center of the town. Next door was a police station and the men smoking outside waved to him as he approached. They all knew who he was, of course, and one of the reasons he chose to live there was the added security the police station afforded. He knew he was on Mossad's hit list. It was a badge of honor but also a serious threat.

The Al-Rasul Mohamad Hospital was a glorified clinic. It occupied the bottom two floors of a plain, four-story concrete building with examination rooms, a pharmacy, and offices on the first floor; and two small patient wards and a couple of crude operating suites on the second. There was a walled courtyard in the back with two small outbuildings that served as the hospital's laundry and kitchen. The third and fourth floors were used by Hamas paramilitaries. A handful of soldiers lived on the third floor while Mohammad and his bodyguard, Walid, lived on the fourth.

The entire building was painted white with large red crosses and red crescents on the exterior walls and roof to clearly identify it as a hospital to the Israeli drones and helicopters that routinely flew overhead. Mossad certainly knew Hamas paramilitaries used the building as a base but the thinking was the Israelis would not risk international condemnation by bombing a hospital to kill even a senior Hamas commander like Alkawbra. So far, at least, the strategy had paid off.

As Mohammad trudged up the three flights of stairs to his residence, all he thought about was sleep. Ameena was much younger and she had worn him out. The stairs were dimly lit by a single bulb dangling from a wire above the second-floor landing. As he emerged from the darkened stairwell into his apartment, Walid was not in his bed. He was about to call out when he heard a voice coming from the roof, "Boss, is that you?"

"Yes, I'm back and I'm going to bed. You sleeping on the roof tonight?"

"Yeah, there's a nice cool breeze out here. You should sleep up here too."

"No, I'm good down here." Walid often slept on the roof when the weather was nice but that meant getting up with the sun. Mohammad needed to sleep in so he collapsed on his bed and was soon snoring loudly.

* * *

As Alkawbra drifted off to sleep, about 6.5 kilometers to the northwest a dark shape rose from the inky depths of the Mediterranean Sea. As the small conning tower of the submarine breached the surface, the hatch opened. A man dressed in black and equipped with night vision goggles (NVGs) popped up to scan the horizon in all directions. He softly shouted below, "All clear. No Israeli or Egyptian patrol vessels in sight."

"Any fishing boats?" a voice from within asked.

"Just that fifteen-footer about a klick and a half to the southwest. It's dark. We're good topside."

A couple of minutes later the submarine had surfaced completely with only a meter or so of its thirty-meter long angular hull rising above the calm seas. The submarine was not just black, it was blacker than black. It had a special coating that reflected virtually no light, making it a hole in the ocean. But it wasn't rounded and smooth like most submarines. The part of its hull that protruded above the water consisted of flat slab sides at obtuse angles relative to the water. The purpose was to deflect radar waves in any direction except back toward their source. Between the broadband absorption of its black coating and the angle of its sides, the submarine was virtually invisible to any military sensors.

Aft of the conning tower, a pair of large doors opened on the deck revealing an angled ramp below. Three men emerged and immediately began pulling three large items up the ramp. The first was a large carbon fiber black box about 1.5 meters long by 1 meter wide and half a meter thick. It resembled a large Pelican case except for the two deep holes in its ends. Next came two long narrow shafts with a round hub at one end. Attached to each hub were three two-meter-long scimitar-shaped blades folded parallel along the shaft. The men quickly attached the shafts to each end of the center box. They then unfolded the blades and snapped them into place so they radiated out from the hubs. Completely assembled, the machine's purpose became clear—it was a twin-rotor helicopter. But this helicopter had no room for a pilot or passenger. It was a large drone. The first man grabbed the controller that was around his neck and called out, "Alpha team, you ready?" The other two men were carrying weapons but in contrast to the other equipment attached to their body harnesses, these were distinctly not high tech. Strapped to their chests were old Soviet era AKS-74U assault rifles. These were the shorter special ops version of the modernized AK-74 and fired the same Russian 5.45 x 35 mm round that Hamas routinely used. They were like the one Osama Bin Ladin was always pictured carrying except these were fully suppressed and sported advanced infrared laser sights. In addition, each man carried on his hip a suppressed Russian Makarov pistol. Another person came up the ramp and handed each of them a small backpack. The men slipped on the backpacks and gave a thumbs-up.

"Stand clear. Firing up the drone." The armed men moved behind the man with the controller. The blades of the drone started to turn and within a few seconds it began to lift into the air. It was virtually silent. The drone was electrically powered and the rotors were specifically designed to minimize rotor noise. As it took to the air, a rope maybe fifteen meters long was dangling below it. The end of the rope was split into two two-meter lengths each with a metal ring and carabiner attached. The armed men moved under the drone, snapped their harnesses to the ends of the rope, embraced each other, and were lifted silently into the black night. As they did, one quipped to the other, "This doesn't mean we're going steady."

The drone whizzed quietly toward the lights of the Gaza Strip. It was on autopilot flying a preprogrammed route; it knew where it was going. As they approached the shoreline, the drone gained altitude. Though it was virtually silent and impossible to see in the pitch-black sky, this was a precaution to minimize the chances of being heard or seen. Nearing Khan Yunis the drone slowed and then hovered. The men heard a voice in their earpieces. "Alpha Team. You're above the LZ. Please confirm the LZ is clear."

"Alpha One copies. Give us a second." The men were suspended about twenty meters above the Al-Rasul Mohamad Hospital. The big red cross on the roof made it very easy to identify. As they twisted gently in the wind, they scanned the landing zone and the surrounding rooftops. Alpha Two nudged his partner and pointed. Through their NVGs they made out the form of a man sleeping on a pad on the south side of the roof near the stairs. They also discerned the shape of an AK assault rifle lying next to him. Alpha One gave a thumbs-up to acknowledge. He keyed the microphone on his headset, "Alpha Control, this is Alpha One. We have a single hostile sleeping on the roof, as predicted. We are a go for insert."

The two men maneuvered so as to be back-to-back during the descent. Since they were gently spinning as they neared the rooftop, it was unclear who would be in position to take the shot. When they were about two meters off the roof, Walid started to stir. Alpha One fired two rounds into his chest before he even sat up. A couple of seconds later, they were on the roof and quickly uncoupled from the rope. Alpha Two ran to check on Walid. He was dead but he put another round into his heart just to make sure. Alpha One inspected the roof. There was an old-style TV antenna on a long thin pole held in place by guylines. He quickly cut two of the wires and gently lowered the antenna to the ground. He then placed a flashing IR beacon in the middle of the red cross on the roof and turned it on. "Alpha Control, we are clear for landing. The big red 'X' marks the spot." Seconds later, the black drone dropped out of the night sky right in the center of the red cross on the roof and powered down. "Bird is down. See ya in a few."

The two men crept silently down the stairs. They were happy the steps were made of concrete versus metal or wood. One creak might cost them the element of surprise. The apartment at the bottom of the stairs was dark except for a couple of dim lights from a clock radio and the standby power light from a large flat-screen TV on a table across the room. They were in the living room with the kitchen to their immediate left. Alpha Two entered the kitchen and returned quickly indicating the room was clear. They moved deliberately and stealthily through the apartment. The first bedroom was small and empty. This must belong to the dead guy on the roof. They crept along to the next bedroom. The door was closed, and Alpha One heard soft music coming from inside. He signaled for Alpha Two to move to the opposite side of the door. He gently turned the knob and pushed on the door. As it opened, the AK-74 leaning against it slid noisily across the door before clattering to the ground. In the dead quiet of the apartment, this might as well have been a Chinese gong.

The man sleeping in the bed across the room immediately sat up and grabbed the Makarov pistol on the nightstand. "Walid, is that you?" Before he cleared the fog from his eyes, two 9 mm rounds tore into his chest. The last things he perceived before the light faded from his eyes for the final time were two masked Caucasian men, dressed in black with alien-looking NVGs and communications headsets. Alpha One checked to make sure the man was dead and that it was Mohammad Al-Rafah. He dragged his finger across his throat to indicate the man was indeed dead and gave a thumbs-up on the ID. He twirled his finger in the air to indicate that they should finish clearing the apartment.

Two minutes later they returned to the living room. Alpha One whispered, "Okay, check the stairs leading down and secure 'em." Alpha Two nodded and moved toward the stairs.

Keying his headset mic, Alpha One whispered, "Alpha Control, this is Alpha One. The target is down. Repeat, the target is down. Site is secure. Commencing search for intel."

"Copy that Alpha One. Good job. Finish up and get the hell out of there."

"Roger that."

Alpha Two removed a small claymore mine from his backpack along with a stick-on motion sensor. He set up the mine to take out anyone coming up the stairs and positioned a motion sensor to point down the stairwell to give them advance warning of anyone coming up via a tone in their earpieces.

They then turned their attention to the dead terrorist. Alpha One removed an older iPhone 6 from his backpack while Alpha Two focused on the computer on the floor by the bed. He whispered to Alpha Two, "He's a righty, correct?" Alpha Two nodded. Alpha One activated the fingerprint ID feature on the phone and repeatedly pressed the dead man's right thumb on the "home" button until it registered his thumbprint. The phone had an Israeli number and was preloaded with cryptic text messages and telephone call records originating from a pay phone near the headquarters of the Shin Bet, Israel's internal security service. He then took the phone and a wad of money and scattered them at Al-Rafah's feet. He surveyed the room. It was familiar to him. He'd seen it several times in the images pirated from Al-Rafah's computer. They installed malware on his computer remotely through a jihadi website he liked to frequent. It allowed them to activate the camera and microphone on his laptop remotely. Al-Rafah had also walked around his apartment a couple of times with his laptop in his hand to show Walid particularly gory videos from Syria and Iraq. This allowed them to determine his floor plan in advance. *I should have thanked him for that before I capped him.*

Alpha One covered the door as Alpha Two connected Al-Rafah's laptop to his own tactical computer. "Don't forget to remove our malware. We don't want any of them to find it. These Palestinians are pretty good with computers. Then mirror the hard drive and put it back where it was."

"I'm on it."

Alpha One continued to search the apartment. It was a bachelor's apartment. There were clothes strewn on the floor and a thick layer of dust on anything not used often. He opened an old armoire in the bedroom. There were some clothes hanging up but more simply thrown inside. Poking through the clothes he found a stack of old German hardcore porn underneath. "Figures." He picked up a magazine and was thumbing through it when Alpha Two glanced over his shoulder.

"Five more minutes on the hard drive. What ya got there?" Alpha One showed him one of the magazines. "Ah gross! That shit is just nasty."

"It's always the religious ones." He dropped the magazine on the bottom of the armoire and it made a kind of clunk, like stepping on a loose floorboard. Alpha One knelt down and tapped the bottom of the armoire. The wood was loose. He lifted up a piece and discovered a hollow space below. He shined his IR flashlight inside and made out the edge of a computer. "Hello. What have we here?" He gently removed the computer. It was a newer model Acer. He whispered to Alpha Two. "Looky what I found. How much more room on that mirroring gizmo of yours?"

"Oh, a few terabytes. I think I can squeeze that on. Give me a minute." Alpha One handed the computer to his partner who connected it to his tactical laptop which was already copying the first one. "Uh, this thing has a fingerprint reader."

Alpha One replied, "Give me a second." He took the computer and walked over to the dead terrorist and placed his finger on the fingerprint reader. The computer unlocked. "Okay, here ya go."

Alpha Two commented, "Okay, I'm in. There's stuff on here but not a lot in the grand scheme of things. A couple of gigs, maybe. Won't take but a minute." He then added, "That finger might come in handy later. They'll only need his thumb to unlock the cell phone and it might keep anyone else from accessing the computer."

"Roger that." Alpha One was getting impatient. They'd been on target long enough already. "I'm going to finish up while you do that." Alpha Two gave a nod but never took his eyes off his computer screen. Alpha One walked over to Al-Rafah's lifeless body. *Sorry, buddy, but I gotta, do what I gotta do.* He removed a KA-BAR knife from the pocket of his black 511 pants and snapped it open. He slit the dead man's throat from ear to ear. Reaching into Al-Rafah's mouth, he pulled out the tongue and with a quick slice, cut it off. He then pinned it to Al-Rafah's chest with a pocket knife he found in the nightstand. Finally, he sliced off his right index finger, put it in a ziplock plastic bag, and put it in the thigh pocket of his pants.

Alpha Two said, "I'm about done. A couple more minutes. I'm going to get the other guy. How you doing?"

Alpha One replied, "All done. He didn't feel a thing."

"Don't forget the message."

"Right." Alpha One picked up a dirty sock from the floor, dipped it in Al-Rafah's blood and wrote "KHAYIN"—Arabic for "traitor"—above the bed and stuffed some of the money in Al-Rafah's mouth. *I expect that's how they'd treat an informant.* As he finished, he heard his partner trudging down the stairs with Walid's body over his shoulder. "Put him on the floor near the stairs so it looks like he died trying to defend his boss. I'll put the computer back in the armoire and grab ours. Did you grab his weapon?"

"Roger. And I found our brass on the roof. I'll place it in the stairwell."

Alpha One replied, "Good thinking." He appreciated his partner's attention to detail.

"I'll get the claymore and the sensor and meet you on the roof."

Alpha One took one last quick glance around the apartment. Satisfied that they had not forgotten anything, he disconnected the tactical computer and put it in his backpack. He put Al-Rafah's computer back on the floor where they'd found it and returned the Acer to the hidden compartment in the armoire, making sure it was in the exact same position that he found it before replacing the porno magazines and clothes. He left the bedroom as Alpha Two was heading up to the roof.

At the top of the stairs, Alpha Two scanned the rooftop and the surrounding buildings before exiting. He focused on the bloody pad Walid had been lying on when he was shot. He pointed to it as Alpha One emerged from the stairwell. "We can't leave this here. Doesn't fit the narrative."

"Take it with us. We'll drop it in the ocean." touching the mic button on his headset, he said, "Alpha Control, we're done here. Ready for dust off."

His earpiece squawked. "Copy that, stand clear. Firing up the bird in three, two, one. . . ." The rotors of the drone began spinning and a few seconds later it lifted off the roof into the blackness with only a whoosh of air to indicate it had ever been there. The rope was pulled up with it but then stopped when the two ends were still on the deck, and the two men quickly snapped them onto their harnesses.

Tucking the bloody sleeping pad under his arm, Alpha Two quipped, "Ya know, my biggest fear is that one of these days that thing is going to dust off and just keep going. Then we'd be fucked for sure."

"Ya got that right." Alpha One picked up the IR beacon, switched it off and put it in his pocket. "Can't forget that." Touching his mic button, he said, "Alpha Team ready for dust off." With that, the drone continued its climb, snatching the two men off the roof and spiriting them away like wraiths in the night.

CHAPTER ONE
THE PRAETORIANS

Alen Markovic walked into the small café across the street from Tasmajdan Park in Belgrade and inhaled deeply. He loved the smell of fresh coffee and warm pastries. He signaled to the barista, who immediately started preparing an espresso—Alen's usual. The café faced the park and had a few tables on the sidewalk, but he preferred to be inside where he was less exposed. His usual table was across the room along the wall facing the door but this morning it was occupied. Two old Serbian men were already sitting there arguing loudly about local politics. He had to settle for the small table tucked in a corner just around from the front door. He pulled out one of the rather dainty wooden chairs and sat down cautiously. The small chair creaked under his weight. Markovic was a big man—six foot five and at least 250 pounds. Maybe more now since he hadn't been exercising as regularly as he should. *Alen* meant "rock" in Serbian and people always joked that his parents' choice of name had been prophetic.

Markovic knew the café intimately but double-checked all the exits out of habit—main door behind him to his left (less than ideal), exit directly to the street to his right, and back door to the alley through the kitchen to the left of the bar in front of him. He had left the Serbian Special Brigade only some six weeks earlier. He was a captain but given his age, he should've at least been a major, probably a colonel, but he had a bad habit of speaking truth to power and that wasn't always a good idea in his or any other military. He was vocal about the lack of necessary aggression by his government.

Serbia was still atoning for the sins of the Yugoslav Wars that followed the dissolution of Yugoslavia in 1989. They were now applying for membership in the European Union and the government was very reluctant to take meaningful action—even against terrorists—for fear it might insult the delicate sensitivities of the EU members who must ultimately approve its membership. This, coupled with Markovic's frustration with his promotion prospects and a lack of a meaningful mission, led him to resign his commission. While he didn't regret leaving, he was now kicking himself for not lining up follow-on employment before he did.

Markovic checked his watch; it was 9:58 a.m. He had been seeking work in earnest for about four weeks and had yet to find a position that interested him. There was plenty of work as a bodyguard or "Personal Security Specialist"—which was just a fancier way of saying bodyguard—and one of his old SB colleagues even tried to put him in contact with the head of a local criminal syndicate, but Alen had no interest in work that might land him in jail. Then three days ago he had received a mysterious telephone call from a man he only knew as Lon. He'd first met Lon years before when both were in Kosovo. Lon was a member of the United States Army's elite Ops Detachment Delta, also known as Delta Force. Alen and Lon were on opposite sides of the conflict at the time but not actually shooting at each other. Despite their countries' political differences, Alen and Lon respected each other's professionalism and cool heads which on a number of occasions kept misunderstandings from turning into gunfights. Years later they met again under friendlier circumstances during a joint counterterrorism training exercise in Romania after 9/11. With the earlier political issues now resolved, they struck up a genuine rapport and had stayed in periodic contact ever since.

As Alen sipped his espresso, he heard someone enter the small café behind him. The ensuing footsteps were light and almost catlike yet with the low timbre indicative of a large man. Without turning around, Alen said, "Long time, no see, Lon."

Two big hands clapped him on the shoulders from behind, "Alen, you son of a bitch. How'd you know it was me?"

Alen rose to greet him. "You're right on time, plus you don't exactly walk like an office worker. You expected me to sit with my back to the wall like your famous cowboy, Wild Bill?"

"Well, kinda."

Motioning to the two old men across the room, Markovic said, "My usual table was taken but I still need to keep my eyes on the street."

Lon replied cautiously, "Threats?"

Alen laughed, "No, women! The view is much better from this direction." Both men laughed and gave each other a hug. "So, what brings you to Belgrade?"

Lon replied, "You. I heard you were out of the service. Is that true?"

"Wow, news travels fast—and apparently far. I've been out about six weeks now."

Lon queried, "You mind if I ask why? You're what, forty years old? Kinda young to be retired. You working somewhere else yet?"

Alen laughed, "Thirty-nine actually, but I put in my twenty. To answer your question as to why, I was fed up. There's no stomach for necessary actions any more. I can't tell you how many times we had bad guys in our sights only to have some politician nuke the mission. They are all pussies now. More worried about joining the damn EU than protecting the country. The last straw was a few months ago. We had this scumbag in our crosshairs—quite literally—only to have the mission scratched at the last second. The target was a Syrian ISIS affiliate but he had German refugee status so they wouldn't let us pull the trigger. It didn't matter that he'd killed four people in Serbia. We were ordered to capture him, during which four of my men were wounded. He was turned over to the Germans, who released him on bail! Can you believe it? After that, I put in my paperwork. Given what I said to the Minister of Internal Affairs, they were happy to be rid of me. As for work, I'm still looking. Keeping my options open, ya know? I've had some offers but nothing that piqued my interest. Why, you know someone? You still with Delta?"

Ignoring his last question, Lon smiled and said, "Actually, yes I do know of something. And I think you might be interested."

Alen replied cautiously, "Listen, if you're talking mercenary shit in Yemen or Africa, forget it. The pay is never what they say it's going to be, and I don't want to sit in a foxhole getting my ass chewed on by sand fleas for six months."

"No, nothing like that. This is a new group. Sort of an Interpol for terrorists but without the bureaucracy."

Markovic snorted contemptuously, "Bullshit. There's always bureaucracy. Paperwork, reports, committees, accountings, and ultimately, 'stand-downs' when you're about the pull the trigger."

Lon grinned, "Not this gig. We're managed privately and very well-funded. No politics, no stand-downs. All operational decisions are made by the people on the ground."

Intrigued but still skeptical, Alen asked, "So they're subcontracting out the anti-terror mission. How does that work?"

"Well, I can't go into all the details here, but we've put together an international counterterrorism strike team. We've cherry-picked the best special operators in the world to carry out missions targeting only the highest of the high-value targets; no low-level shit. We have complete autonomy in planning and execution."

"Snatch jobs? Those are always rife with problems."

"Not snatch jobs—eliminations. Once the problem is identified, we find it and eliminate it. No one wants to fill up another Guantanamo. That was a disaster."

Alen nodded, "Yeah, you Americans were stupid for doing that. I get capturing them to get intel but once you got it, you should've put a bullet in their heads. You can't pretend savages are civilized. Now you have to stage a big public trial for Khalid Sheikh Mohammad (KSM). At least you got it right with Bin Laden. Well, as interesting as that sounds, I'm not sure I can just pick up and go work for the US military. I don't even know how that would work anyway."

"This isn't the military."

"Well, I can't go work for the CIA either."

"This isn't the CIA."

"Well, who the hell is it, Lon?"

"Officially, it's a private affair. We have a wealthy benefactor who provides backstopping, logistics, weapons support, everything."

Alen was dubious. "Where do the missions come from? I'm not willing to kill off some oligarch's business rivals."

"There's an informal committee with representatives from several of the top Western intel agencies. It's unofficial—plausible deniability for them and operational efficiency for us. They select and rank the targets. Once they give them to us, they walk away. They have no operational control and can place no restrictions on how, where, or when we do it. "

"Really? So, if you conduct an operation in say, Paris, you don't have to get the approval of the French?"

"Nope. But there's a catch."

"Of course, there is," said the big Serb.

"No 'Get Out of Jail Free' card. We have to fly below the radar and stay there. If we get busted, we stay that way."

"I'd live with that if the mission is a success. What's the pay?"

"Negotiable but we pay around $300K to start—plus expenses. Benefits too."

Alen's eyes widened, betraying his surprise. Quickly composing himself he replied, "That's in the range I was aiming for. Where is this job?"

"Well, clearly, the work takes us where it takes us, but we have training facilities in the western United States and Southeast Asia. Our primary location is here in Europe. Can't say where just yet. The company is registered in the Cayman Islands to keep scrutiny to a minimum and ease the banking. Technically, you can live wherever you want when we're not training or on a mission, but I would pick someplace with a good airport. If you want, you can just live at our European compound. It's up to you."

Alen rubbed his chin in false contemplation. He didn't want to be too eager. "This wealthy benefactor, who is he?"

Lon explained, "I can't tell you that or identify the other members of the team until you're fully on board. All I can say is he is stinking rich and from Texas."

Alen smirked. "Texas. Why am I not surprised?" He had to admit, it was intriguing. He had nothing to keep him in Serbia, not really. His parents were gone and his one attempt at marriage ended in divorce after only a couple of years with no kids. He relished the idea of doing a vitally important job without the inherent political restrictions. He liked and trusted Lon despite the fact he didn't even know his last name. Sometimes you just know about a guy. "Okay, I'll give it a whirl. What have I got to lose?"

Lon reached across and shook his hand. "Great!"

"When do I start?"

"Now. We've already wired some money into your account to cover near-term expenses. There will be a private jet at the Belgrade airport tomorrow waiting to take us to meet the others."

Alen was shocked. "What?" He grabbed his cell phone and checked the balance of his bank account. While he had been talking to Lon, someone had deposited 10,000 euros in his checking account. "Jesus, you weren't kidding, were you, Lon?"

"No. I'm serious; dead serious. Go home and pack a bag." He handed Alen a new cell phone. "I'll call you on this in the morning before I come pick you up but figure on 0700 hours. Pack just what you need and say your goodbyes. We'll be gone for a while."

Alen was still a bit stunned. "Uh, okay. Do I need to bring anything in particular? Weapons? Equipment?"

Lon smiled, "Just some clothes and a toothbrush. We'll provided everything else you might need. I think you'll find our inventory is up to your standards."

"Hey Lon, I know this sounds stupid given what I have just agreed to, but what the hell is your last name? I can't remember."

Lon laughed, "That's because I never told you. It's Oden, Alonzo Oden."

As Lon got up to leave, Alen asked, "This team I just signed up for, does it have a name?"

"The Praetorians."

"Like the Caesars' personal guard?"

"Exactly."

* * *

The Bombardier Global 8000 jet took off from Belgrade at 0800. Lon had been true to his word. He had been waiting outside Alen Markovic's apartment building at precisely 0700 hours and they were airborne exactly one hour later. Alen chuckled. *People riding private jets didn't go through the same security as us peasants.* With a top speed of almost a thousand kilometers per hour, the jet would cover the sixteen hundred kilometers between Belgrade, Serbia, and Larnaca, Cyprus, in under two hours. Alen didn't even ask where they were going until after they were airborne.

Though he tried not to show it, Markovic was very impressed. He had never ridden on a private jet, let alone one costing $50 million. He felt more than a bit out of place. He was wearing cheap knock-off Levi jeans, old combat boots, a black T-shirt, and a black windbreaker. His "luggage" consisted of his old army duffel stuffed with a small toiletry kit, socks, underwear, two more pairs of jeans, a couple of shirts, a set of camos, and a jacket. He would have felt self-conscious had Lon not been similarly dressed. His luggage was just a small green nylon "go bag."

Glancing around the plush cabin, Markovic commented, "Not a bad way to travel but a bit of overkill, don't ya think?"

"How do you mean?"

Subtly probing for more information, Alen said, "This thing has to seat at least fifteen people. Your team that big?"

Lon smiled. He realized what the big Serb was doing. "It seats seventeen, actually. And no, our team is not that big. But we need to haul our gear too. Some of it can be rather heavy. The real reason for this particular model was the range. It can cover 7,900 nautical miles; that's over fourteen thousand kilometers. That can get us pretty much anywhere we need to go."

Alen shrugged. "Fair enough. So long as you're not wasting money."

Lon ignored the comment and redirected the conversation. "We'll discuss all that when we get there. Now tell me, what have you been up to the last couple of years?"

Alen understood what Lon was doing too. He didn't push it further, and they spent the remainder of the flight talking about the old days in Kosovo, lying about the women they had slept with, and just getting caught up.

The jet touched down at Larnaca International Airport in Cyprus at a little before 11 a.m. It taxied to a private hangar at the far end of the airport and stopped. Alen and Lon deplaned and headed straight for a waiting Range Rover. "No customs or immigration?" Alen asked.

Lon smiled wryly. "You already filled out the paperwork. Don't you remember?"

Alen just snorted. He peeked back at the jet. It had never powered down its engines and was already moving back to the taxiway to take off again. "Where are they going?"

"They have another pickup." Approaching the Range Rover, Lon said, "Get in, I'll show you the office. It's our home base, a compound really, but we just call it the villa."

They drove north out of Larnaca following the highway to Nicosia but once they hit the southern suburbs of the capital, they turned west toward Lakatamia. Lakatamia had once been a bucolic rural suburb of Nicosia but as the city grew, it became just more of the urban sprawl. What was unique about the area, though, was its proximity to the old Nicosia International Airport. When Turkey invaded Cyprus in 1974, the airport got caught up in the fighting. After the formal ceasefire, it was left stranded in the UN-imposed buffer zone extending across the island to separate the Greek Cypriot and Turkish forces. While the airport was used as a local headquarters by UN forces, it would never again see a commercial flight and the Cypriots had to build a new airport in Larnaca. The old Nicosia airport became a ghost town, its buildings frozen in time, dusty time capsules reflecting life as it was the day the airport was abandoned in 1974.

Lon navigated through the town working his way farther west until he reached the last road before the UN buffer zone. The neighborhood consisted of upscale homes on large lots. Alen caught occasional glimpses of swimming pools and tennis courts through the fences and hedges as they drove past. Finally, the Range Rover slowed and turned into a driveway at the end of Plotinou Street. There was a three-meter-high wall around the property with tall hedges on the inside which extended even higher. Surveillance cameras covered every inch of the wall as well as the street and surrounding areas. Pulling up to a heavy steel gate, Lon reached over and waved a card over the proximity card reader. After a beep, he punched in an eight-digit code and held his head still as the facial recognition scanner read his facial features. After a couple of seconds, a robotic voice said, "proceed," and the heavy gate retracted to allow their passage.

Alen commented, "You guys don't fuck around when it comes to security, do you?"

Lon chuckled, "Yeah, well, we have our reasons." They drove into the compound and parked in front of the house. It was a large, two-story, pale yellow stucco building with an orange terra-cotta tile roof. It was very similar to other villas he had seen in the neighborhood. It was surrounded by a number of large cypress trees and a well-trimmed lawn. There were other buildings farther back on the lot but they were largely obscured by smaller trees and hedges. It was a rich man's house—fancy but not really special.

As they got out of the car, Lon quipped, "Here we are. Home sweet home. Grab your gear and I'll show you around." There was another keypad at the front door. They entered the house and Lon led Alen upstairs. "Drop your gear in the first room on the right. I'm across the hall. Let's grab a beer and talk."

The two men walked back downstairs and went to the kitchen. Grabbing two Heinekens from the large refrigerator, Lon walked through a glass door into an enclosed courtyard. They sat at a small table and took sips from their beers.

Alen spoke first. "Okay, I'm impressed. Private jet. Beautiful mansion. You're obviously well-funded but I'm not interested in working for some Russian oligarch who is one pissed-off dictator away from twenty years in a Siberian labor camp."

Lon's face was suddenly serious. "This is not about business, this is about justice and doing what we can to protect Western civilization, even if Western civilization can't always figure out how to do that for itself."

"So, you're talking Islamic terrorism."

"Islamic terrorism, narcoterrorism, political terrorism . . . hell, even eco-terrorism if it comes to that. Our mission is to stop any person or group that is actively engaged in the willful slaughter of innocent people to further their agendas—regardless of ideology. It doesn't matter who they are or who they are targeting."

Alen mulled over what Lon had said for several seconds before responding. "That sounds good, but how does it work?"

"As I mentioned in Belgrade, there is a very informal targeting group representing most of the major intel organizations. It's so informal it technically doesn't exist. They meet periodically, usually in Europe on the fringes of some defense or economic summit. They provide their lists of the worst players. Any target has to appear on at least half of the lists. That is to ensure that no one country can use us as a way to get rid of political or regional military rivals. There is nothing to stop them from going after those people on their own, of course—God knows the Israelis do—but we will not be involved. We also reserve the right to step away if we have concerns over the motives of the group, but we haven't had to do that yet. We do not work for them or answer to them."

"But who pays for all this?"

"Well, our benefactor fronts everything."

"The Texan you mentioned, right? What's his motivation—other than being from Texas?"

Lon didn't smile at Alen's little joke. "His wife was on board American Airlines Flight 77 when it was hijacked by Al-Qaeda and crashed into the Pentagon."

"Oh shit! I didn't mean anything . . ."

Lon smiled, "Don't worry about it. No way you could have known. He is some kind of computer genius, PhD from MIT and all that shit. He started his own computer company back in the 1980s, big data specialists of some kind. He had just sold it for like $3.5 billion in late 2000. He and his wife were going use the money to support charities and invest in small start-ups. She was on her way from DC to Los Angeles to visit her parents when 9/11 happened."

"Well that explains the 'why' but not the 'how.' How did he go from rich computer geek to anti-terror mastermind?"

Lon continued, "In the aftermath of 9/11, the CIA found itself short of discreet transportation options. They reached out to corporate America to borrow private jets to fly people in and out of Central Asia."

"Really? What happened to Air America?"

Lon smiled, "Air America is long gone, my friend. Anyway, approaching the boss was actually a mistake. His wife was an author and used her maiden name. No one immediately connected the dots and realized his wife had died on 9/11. Anyway, he was more than happy to help and offered to do whatever he could. One thing led to another and his role, albeit an unofficial one, increased over time. He was a friend of the president, had a Top Secret security clearance from his company's work on USG contracts, and he was motivated."

Alen found all this a little incredible "Okay, but how do you go from giving someone a ride on an airplane to heading up a terrorist elimination squad—for lack of a better description?"

"Actually, it was his idea. When some of the pansy asses in DC started talking about putting all the assholes in Guantanamo Bay on trial, the boss went ballistic. The idea that KSM, the guy responsible for killing his wife and over 3,000 other people, would get all the rights and privileges as some American kid who boosted a car for a joyride pissed him off. The way to prevent that from happening in the future was to eliminate these assholes from the get-go. I gotta say, his was not an isolated opinion. There were plenty of others who felt the same way—me included."

Alen added, "And me too."

"Anyway, an infrastructure was put in place. The boss was willing to accept the risks and use his money and reputation for cover."

"Does he pay for all this?"

Lon explained, "Not exactly; at least not all of it. He fronts it but the organization ultimately gets money from the various countries who provide the targets. The boss owns a bunch of companies, several of which have classified defense contracts. The money is funneled back in through black contracts the bean counters don't have access to. It works pretty well but governments being governments, they are usually slow to pay. Fortunately for us, he doesn't have a cash flow problem. Hell, he's worth more now than when he sold his company."

"Well, it sounds like a sweet setup."

Lon asked, "So, can I count you as the newest member of the team?"

Alen reached out to shake Lon's hand, "Hell yes. I've got nothing better to do. Where do I sign?"

Lon laughed, "Nowhere. No contracts. No nondisclosure agreements. No paper trail. This a handshake business arrangement. If we didn't trust you, you wouldn't be here in the first place. We know you'll keep your mouth shut. That room upstairs is yours. You can stay as much or as little as you want. Me and a couple of the guys pretty much live here full-time. A couple others keep apartments back home. It's entirely up to you. You can come and go as you please, but we need to be able to find you quickly. Shit can hit the fan pretty fast sometimes. Now let's go meet some of the other team members."

Lon led Alen back into the house. Behind a door next to the kitchen there was a set of stairs leading down to a basement. The basement was cavernous and had a bigger footprint than the house above it. There were several finished rooms set up like offices and a larger unfinished storage area with shelf after shelf of unidentified equipment in black Pelican cases. In the first office an older man stood leaning over a younger man who was working on a computer. Lon interrupted them. "Hey guys, I want to introduce you to Alen Markovic from Belgrade." The older man turned around. He had a patch over his left eye with a large scar that started at his scalp above and continued down to his jawline. He was in his sixties and while his face was time-ravaged, his body was still lean and strong. Lon introduced him. "Alen Markovic, I would like to introduce Juan 'Gunny' Medina. He's kind of like our dad around here."

Gunny stuck out his hand to shake Alen's. "Fuck you, Lon. If I was your dad, I'd have my boot up your ass every damn day. Howdy, Markovic."

Shaking his hand, Alen looked at Gunny quizzically. "You're familiar. Have we met before?"

Gunny smiled. "Yeah, a couple of times. Good memory. The first time was in Kosovo. You almost caught me and my team snatching a Qods Force asshole outside Bijeljina in 2006. I was also involved in that Romanian exercise where you and Lon reconnected."

"Okay, now I remember. So, you're the one who got that Iranian prick. We'd been after him for weeks. Every time we'd get close, he'd slip across the goddamn border."

Gunny smiled. "Yeah, well borders were never much of a deterrent for me. I'm glad you joined us. I was worried you'd never leave the Special Brigade."

Lon added, "Gunny is known as 'Mad Dog' to some so if you hear them cussing about him, you'll know why. He is our scout leader, if you will. He runs the shop, makes sure we have what we need, and can reach back for intel when we need it. He was a Marine but then went over to the CIA. He worked in Special Activities Division for years. He's been everywhere and done everything."

Gunny chimed in, "That makes me invaluable."

Lon shot back, "That makes you fuckin' old."

"I can still kick your skinny ass."

Lon ignored him. "Other guy is Oberfeldwebel Hans Koenig; late of the Budeswehr."

Arel reached out to shake his hand. "German?"

Hans smiled. "Don't be surprised. We are a very international group."

Lon continued, "Hans was a Fallschirjäger in their Special Operations Division. While everyone here has jumped plenty of times, Hans is our de facto jump master. He has more HAHO jumps than any other member of the team."

Alen queried, "HAHO. That's High-Altitude High-Opening, right? I haven't done one of those."

Lon smiled. "Hans will fix that. In addition to parachuting, Hans also speaks seven languages. . . ."

Hans interjected, "Eight."

"Sorry, eight languages and he's pretty damn good with computers."

Alen was impressed. "A Renaissance man? Do you paint too?"

Hans replied, "Well, actually . . ."

Lon broke in, "All right, smartass. He and Gunny are doing forensics on some data we recovered during a recent op. What have you guys found?"

"We just got into it. Still on the first computer. The usual shit—emails to his bros, jihadi videos, and, of course, lots and lots of porn. The usual nasty crap. Someone needs to get these guys a subscription to *Playboy*; something with some class and chicks that don't look like hairy dudes. A lot of the emails we'd already seen, thanks to the malware we loaded. We'll run data forensics with that new software the boss brought us to find hidden data and steganography and then start on the second one."

Lon said, "Great. If you need any help . . ."

Hans shot back, "From you? I'd get more help from Gunny."

Turning to Alen, Lon whispered, "Don't listen to him. He's a dick."

"I heard that!"

"Not like I wouldn't tell you to your face. Where's everyone else?"

Gunny replied, "I think they're all on weapons except Nigel. You may want the new guy to give them a hand since he's the expert."

Alen gaped at Lon quizzically. "*I'm* the expert? I thought you guys had access to all the newest toys?"

"We do, but we use what the mission calls for. On this last one, we used nothing but vintage Soviet-era stuff. If they do any forensics, we want it to support the narrative."

"The narrative?"

"In this case, the narrative is that the guy was suspected of being an Israeli collaborator and killed by his own people. And his people tend to use vintage Soviet stuff so we used vintage Soviet stuff. You're here because of your experience, skills, and dedication but the fact that you are an expert on Russian, Soviet, and old Eastern Bloc weapons makes you extra valuable to the team."

Alen chuckled. "I guess that's the only advantage of having worked for a country that couldn't afford the new stuff. What the hell, any way I can help. Where's the weapons bay?"

"That's our next stop but first let me finish showing you around."

Leaving Gunny and Hans to their work, they walked past two other empty offices to a large, well-equipped gymnasium. There were weight machines, free weights, dumbbells, treadmills, rowing machines, and just about every other kind of fitness equipment. About a third of the room was covered with thick gymnastics mats for martial arts. There was also a regulation boxing ring and speed bags and heavy bags along the wall.

Alen said, "Impressive. Great facilities."

"The best money can buy. Through there are showers, hot tub, and sauna. None of us are as young as we used to be so all this helps keep us in shape or, in my case, to recover. There is also a library of sorts across the hall. Good if you need some quiet time."

They continued on to the end of the hall where a large metal door blocked their way. Access was controlled by a keypad. Lon punched in his code, and there was a loud "clack" as electromagnetic bolts retracted. "We'll get you on the system when we get back. You'll have full access to everything."

Alen was surprised. "Full access? Without vetting?"

Lon smiled. "What makes you think we haven't been vetting you since you resigned your commission? Hell, before. We've been following your career for a while. Gunny's had your name on his wish list since this thing started. We were just waiting for you to wise up and resign. Fuckin' took ya long enough."

Lon pulled on the heavy steel door and it slowly opened to reveal a long, dimly lit tunnel that extended far into the darkness. Unlike the house, which was modern and clean, the tunnel was dank and very old. It clearly predated the house by decades. Had it not been made of crudely poured concrete and still had rails embedded in the floor from some archaic narrow-gauge train, Alen might have believed it was hewn from the rock by ancient Crusaders to hide the Holy Grail. Inside the tunnel was an electric cart with a small truck bed on the back.

"What the fuck is this?"

Lon explained, "We are near the back of the property which abuts the UN buffer zone separating the Greek and Turkish parts of the island. We are only about five hundred meters from the end of the runway for the Nicosia International Airport and about a thousand meters from the old maintenance facilities. When the Turks invaded Cyprus in 1974, the airport was cut off by fighting. It was a prize to be denied to either side and was incorporated in the UN buffer zone. It has been abandoned ever since except for the UN peacekeepers, who use the opposite end as their headquarters, but they never come down here. These tunnels were built by the Brits during World War Two, when the airport was an RAF base. They connected camouflaged underground weapon bunkers to the flight line. They expected the Nazis to attack the island and wanted to make sure their magazines were protected from air attack. The tunnels were put in place to move ordnance without being seen or having surface roads reveal the locations of the bunkers. They were abandoned after the war and the bunkers destroyed. This whole neighborhood used to be one big weapons dump. The tunnel wasn't destroyed, just buried. We bought this property because it sat directly above the old tunnel. It connects to a subbasement under the maintenance building; also built by the Brits. It has a bombproof ceiling—reinforced concrete two meters thick. That makes it soundproof too; perfect for our purposes. We use the subbasement for our weapons bay and firing range. Come on, I'll show you."

Alen and Lon got in the cart and sped off down the tunnel. After a few minutes, they arrived at the other end where another cart was parked. In front of them was another heavy steel door just like the first. Lon keyed in his code and they entered. The room inside was big and well lit, but smelled musty. It was an odd mixture of dust, mildew, gun oil, and burnt gunpowder. The walls were obviously old and crudely poured concrete like the tunnel but they were clean and freshly painted. To the right were rack upon rack of every imaginable man-portable weapons system. There were US, German, Russian, Chinese, British, French, Brazilian, Belgian,

Austrian, and Swiss pistols, submachine guns, and assault rifles. There were also RPGs and Alen even discerned Pelican cases for Javelin anti-tank missiles stacked in the back. In the center of the room were several stainless-steel worktables each with a set of tools, cloths, cleaning kits, and solvents in the middle. From his left came the muffled "pop, pop, pop" of what was clearly a gun range. Two of the tables were occupied by men in the middle of cleaning weapons.

Lon led Alen toward the first table. The man at the table glanced up and smiled. He had earbuds on, and when he removed them, Alen heard the faint pounding of rock music. The man was almost as tall as Alen, probably six-four. He was in his late thirties or early forties but the muscles bulging under the tight brown T-shirt betrayed a body that was lean and brawny. The man reached out to shake Alen's hand, "You must be the new guy. Welcome to the jungle. You ready to rock and roll?"

Before Alen replied, Lon said, "This is John Kernan, our token SEAL. He was a Master Chief with Blue Squadron before we stole him away. He and Nigel are our resident experts on maritime ops, ship takedowns, and that kind of shit. You'll meet Nigel in a bit. He's off checking on the sub."

Alen was surprised. "You have a submarine?"

Kernan answered, "Actually it's a diver delivery vessel (DDV) but it goes underwater so these guys call it a sub. It has limited range so we have a converted commercial salvage tug with a well deck that we use to transport it."

"Jesus, you have a goddamn navy!"

Lon laughed, "Yeah, pretty much." As he said this, the second man who was cleaning guns had walked over.

"Hello, you must be Markovic. These rude bastards forgot to introduce me, I'm Magne Berge." He leaned in and whispered loudly, "I'm the handsome one. They're all jealous of me." He was a tall, attractive blond man. He was not as big as the others but his body lithe and lean. He looked more like an Olympic swimmer than a soldier.

Lon interjected, "We just hadn't got to you yet, ya dumb shit." Putting his hand on Berge's shoulder he said, "Magne here is our winter and mountain warfare guy. If it's cold, we defer to him. He was an instructor at the Norwegian Winter Warfare Training School and before that he was a champion biathlete. He thinks he our best sniper but I can take him."

Berge snorted indignantly, "In your dreams, cowboy."

Kernan added, "His name is kinda hard to pronounce so you can just call him Maggie."

Berge shot him a dirty look. "Fuck you, *Juanita*."

Kernan shrugged. "I'm okay with Juanita. Helps me get in touch with my feminine side."

Lon interrupted, "All right you two, knock it off. We don't want Markovic thinking we're a bunch of fourth graders. Speaking of feminine side, where is Rabin?"

Kernan motioned toward the doorway to his right. "Where else? On the range."

As he said this, Sarah Rabin walked through the door. She was a wearing a black baseball hat, dark ballistic shooting glasses, and a state-of-the-art noise-canceling hearing protection headset. She walked toward the four men, removing her hat, glasses, and hearing protection gear and placing them on the first table she came to. Alen was stunned, she was gorgeous. Sarah was almost six feet tall and built like a dancer; even her walk was sexy as hell. Her dark brown hair, dark eyes, and olive skin made her extremely difficult to place ethnically. She might have been Italian, Greek, Spanish, Arab, or Persian; he just couldn't tell. Lon whispered to Alen, "Close your mouth, you're starting to drool."

Lon's comment snapped Alen back to reality. As she approached, he stuck out his hand and said, "Hello, I'm Alen Markovic."

She shook his hand. He was surprised by her strong grip. "Yeah, I know who you are. We've been expecting you. I'm Sarah Rabin."

Alen couldn't get over how stunning she was. She was wearing black yoga pants, black running shoes, and a sports bra that left little to the imagination. Her body was lean and muscular. Her midriff was bare revealing her sharply defined abdominal muscles. Her breasts weren't large but gave her just the right amount of curves. *She looks like she stepped out of a Victoria's Secret catalog.* Trying not to stare, Alen asked, "What's your specialty?"

"I kill people," she replied coldly.

Lon expanded on her comment. "Sarah has an unusual sense of humor. You'll get used to it. She was with Israel's Mista'avrim counterterrorist unit and worked extensively with Mossad before joining our team. She is our resident expert on tradecraft, cover, and intelligence gathering."

Alen asked, "Intelligence gathering?"

Sarah added flatly, "I make people talk."

Lon continued, "Anyway, Sarah is also our expert on hand-to-hand combat, edged weapons, and infiltration."

Alen smiled, "Hand-to-hand? Uh, yeah. I see."

John, the Navy SEAL, picked up on Alen's skepticism and cautioned him. "Uh, you don't want to go there, brother. I'm still hurting from the last ass whooping she gave me."

Alen peered at Sarah and then the big SEAL. Sarah just stood there emotionless. She'd heard it a thousand times before. Alen glared at John incredulously and then pointed to Sarah. "Really?"

"Really." John had a very serious expression on his face.

Alen shrugged. "Well, okay then. Maybe I'll have to challenge her sometime."

Exasperated, Sarah just sighed, "Stupid misogynists. You only learn through pain."

Lon interceded. "Okay, everyone. Let's head back to the house. Nigel should be back soon and I want to see what Gunny and Hans have found on those hard drives from the other night. Plus, the boss is coming in today. He wants to meet the new guy. So, wrap this up and meet me in the kitchen for a beer."

Lon and Alen drove the cart back to the house. Gunny and Hans were still crouched over the computer in the office where they had left them. They walked up the stairs to the kitchen. There was a man there with his head deep in the refrigerator complaining loudly in a thick Scottish accent. "When are we going to get some real bloody beer? All we have is Dutch and German crap. If we can't get a decent Scottish beer like Tennent's or Fraoch's, can we at least get some Guinness or Smithwicks?"

Lon snapped, "I swear, Nigel, all you do is bitch! You're the only guy I know who complains about free beer. Shut up and meet Markovic. Alen, this is Nigel Finch."

The man straightened up. He was a little over six feet tall but a large man. He weighed at least 240 pounds with a broad chest and thick legs like a rugby player. He stuck his hand out. "So, you're the new bloke Lon and Mad Dog were wanting to bring on? Welcome back to the fight."

Alen shot back, "I never left the fight."

Nigel leaned in and smiled, "You never got to fight like we do. You're in for a pleasant surprise."

Lon explained, "Nigel was a chief petty officer with the British Special Boat Squadron. He and John are of our maritime counterterrorism specialists."

Nigel bellowed, "Posh! I am our *only* maritime expert. That little pissant John only comes along to hold my jock strap."

From down the stairs, John's voice rang out, "I heard that!"

Lon just shook his head. "These two are constantly measuring dicks to see whose is the smallest. Nigel, what's the status of the DDV?"

Getting serious, Nigel responded, "The boat is fine. Her batteries are fully charged and the fuel cell is 100 percent. I powered her down, but she is good to go whenever we need her. As for Mother Goose, she's functional but her engines will need servicing. She's going to need an overhaul next year. She's showing her age."

Alen asked, "Mother Goose?"

"She's the converted salvage tug. She's been around the block a few times, but she's solid. Finch tends to worry."

Nigel shrugged, "Fine by me but if you've ever been in rough seas and had your main engines go down . . . I'm just sayin'."

Lon grabbed a couple of beers and the three men walked outside to sit down in the warmth of the Cypriot sun. Alen asked cautiously, "So, about Sarah? What's her story? Is she . . . seeing anyone?" Nigel just chuckled but said nothing.

Lon smiled, "You don't want to go there. It'll end poorly—for you."

Alen smirked, "I think I can handle one skinny woman."

Now Nigel laughed so hard, beer came out of his nose. Recomposing himself, he said, "Mate, you may want to pump the brakes a bit while you still have a foot to do it with. That skinny little woman has killed more men than cancer." Lon just smiled knowingly and nodded.

Alen choked a bit and said meekly, "Yeah. I should really get to know everyone first. Don't want to step on any toes."

Nigel glared at him in mocking seriousness. "Yes, by all means, certainly the prudent way to go."

* * *

A len retired to his room to unpack and just take it all in. He was surprised to find the dresser and closet in his room were already stocked with casual and tactical clothing—and in his size. *I guess me saying yes wasn't exactly a surprise.* It had been an unbelievable couple of days. He went from being an unemployed ex-soldier in Belgrade with limited prospects—at least legal ones—to being the newest member of what was the most effective counterterrorist operational unit on the planet. The fact that he was now very well paid and living in Cyprus in what could only be described as a mansion was gravy. As he lay on his bed, he heard a knock at the door. It was Gunny. "Hey, Markovic, you vertical?"

Alen got up an answered the door. "Yeah. What's up?"

"Come with me. I need to get you on the security system. Also, there are some forms you need to fill out."

"Forms? Lon said this was a 'handshake' arrangement."

Gunny snorted. "Maybe so, but you want to get paid and have health insurance, don't you? There is also a private retirement investment account and life insurance that needs to be taken care of. It'll take a few minutes but not too long."

They walked downstairs to a paneled study. There were two desks in the room. One was large with an expensive leather office chair behind it. The other was nice but not as fancy. It had a more practical black chair with a mesh back and adjustable in just about every way imaginable. This was meant to be used and not just for show. Pointing the big desk, Gunny said, "That's the boss's; not that he really uses it much." Motioning to a chair in front of the other desk he said, "Sit over here and we'll get started." Gunny issued him a proximity card and Alen picked an eight-digit security code that he could recall but wasn't obvious. Next Gunny took scans of Alen's face from several different angles for the facial recognition software. Alen then started on the forms while Gunny updated the databases and prepared a new photo ID card for Alen. The forms were straightforward but then Alen paused on the last one.

"I got a question. On the life insurance. What if I don't have any next of kin? My parents are dead, I have no kids, and I refuse to leave a penny to my bitch of an ex-wife."

"No brothers or sisters?"

"I have a sister, but I haven't spoken to her in years."

"Cousins? Close friends? Hell, kid, I don't care. Leave it to the Pope for all I care."

"I could leave it to my sister, I guess. Do I have to do this now? Can it wait?"

Sensing a deep-seated loneliness in the big Serb, Gunny said softly, "Sure, kid. We can put a pin in it." Gunny now realized why Alen had agreed to sign on so quickly. He really had nothing else. He was searching for a family. Any reservations Gunny had about the Serb's true motives disappeared.

As Alen finished filling out his last form, Nigel stuck his head in and slapped on the door to get their attention. "Hey guys, the boss is here. Meeting in the conference room in five."

Gunny collected the paperwork and handed Alen his new photo ID. "This is your cover for status. If anyone asks what you're doing on Cyprus, you work for Praetorian Security Services. It's part of a real security company with real customers around the world. Our group is buried inside it. It provides us with cover for travel, logistics, and even weapons. Very few people in the company know about us and fewer know what we really do."

Alen asked, "Those who know we exist but not what we do; what do they think we do?"

Gunny replied, "VIP work—private hostage rescue, specialized protection of facilities in particularly dangerous areas; that kind of thing."

"Sort of like Blackwater?"

"Sort of, but nothing long term and definitely lower profile. It better covers our operational profile."

Alen stared at his new photo card and chuckled.

"What's so funny?"

"Praetorian Security Services. The initials kinda spell 'piss.'"

Gunny grumbled, "Jesus, what are you? Twelve? You're going to fit in with these ass clowns."

* * *

The team filed into the conference room and each took a seat at the big table. At the far end of the table sat a distinguished older man, maybe sixty years old, with Gunny to his immediate left and Lon to his right. He was handsome and distinguished with short, graying dark hair. He appeared to be about the same size as Gunny, about five-foot ten and solidly built. He had a rugged appearance, almost like a cowboy, but much more refined. He had an inviting smile as he chatted with Gunny and Lon, but the lines on his face betrayed years of stress.

The others sat wherever, but being new, Alen chose the far end of the table just in case there was some informal pecking order. When everyone was seated, the man at the head of the table spoke. "Good afternoon, folks. I'm happy everyone is here and in one piece. I want to congratulate you all for an excellent job, especially John and Magne who were the ones in the barrel on this one." Alen picked out a mild but distinct Texas drawl in the man's voice.

Turning to Alen, he said, "I see we have a new face at the table. You must be Alen Markovic." Alen nodded. "We're happy you joined us. I know Gunny has been waiting impatiently for you do retire from the Special Brigade. He's been wanting your skills for some time. I know Gunny tends to be tight-lipped and probably hasn't even given you my name yet, am I right?"

Alen responded nervously, "Uh, yes sir. I mean, no sir, he hasn't."

The man stood up, walked over to Alen and stuck out his hand. "I'm Rusty Wyatt Travis. Welcome to our team."

Alen stood up and shook his hand, "Thank you, Mr. Travis. I appreciate the opportunity."

"Nonsense, you're helping *us* out. And none of that 'Mr. Travis' crap. You can call me Rusty or R.W., everyone else does. I'm just a kid from D'Hanis, Texas, who got lucky."

"Yes, sir, Mr. Tra . . . , uh Rusty."

"That's better." Travis returned to his seat. "Okay, Gunny gave me the rundown on the operation the other night. It went about as well as we hoped. Any issues at all?"

Hans spoke, "Yeah, on the drone, specifically the batteries. It worked fine but we were pretty much at its max range carrying two men with equipment.

I want to upgrade the batteries or possibly consider that new high-output hydrogen fuel cell that the Japanese are developing. If it can replace the batteries completely, we'll get much better payload and range. At the very least, we might incorporate a smaller version to provide some on-demand power or a partial recharge of the batteries when the drone is on the ground like on the last op."

Travis mulled this over. "Okay, look into it and see if it'll work. My concern with the fuel cell is that it may not provide the instantaneous peak power like the batteries. If it can, go for it. How about the DDV? How did it perform?"

Nigel answered, "It was perfect. No issues there at all."

Travis added, "I'm still concerned about its speed. I want you guys to be able to get the hell out of Dodge in a hurry if you need to. One of my companies is working on a supercavitating DDV for the Pentagon but they are taking forever to make a decision, of course. We have two two-third-scale prototypes that were clocked at sixty knots during testing. One will fit within Mother Goose's well deck. I'm going to try shaking one of those loose for us."

Nigel smiled. "Well that should solve it."

"Any other technical issues?" No one spoke up. "All right then. I read the mission report. A perfect op in my book. What has been the response from Hamas so far?"

Sarah Rabin responded. "The chatter I've picked up has all been positive. I checked with my contact within Mossad and he said Hamas is very confused. They found the iPhone we planted and Hamas is convinced that Al-Rafah was working for Israel." Turning to Kernan she added, "Using his thumbprint for the 'Touch ID' biometric to unlock the phone was a nice touch. It really sold it." Continuing, she said, "They can't figure out who took him out, though. The leadership assumes it was their internal security apparatus, but they are denying it. The leadership thinks their counterintelligence guys did it but won't admit it because it wasn't sanctioned. Now everyone is looking over their shoulders. They've canceled every operation he was working on; they assume Mossad and Shin Bet already know all about them. So, from that perspective, the operation was a complete success."

Travis sensed that wasn't the whole story. "Why do I sense a 'but' coming?"

Gunny opened up his laptop computer. "It's about the intel we gathered. We mirrored the hard drive on Al-Rafah's computer. We removed our malware and dumped all his data. Some was encrypted but that new software you provided made short work of that. Nothing really remarkable, and the couple of things that were new have already been nixed by Hamas, who is convinced everything Al-Rafah touched has been compromised. The problem is the other computer."

Travis asked, "The one Kernan found in the armoire?"

"Yes, sir. Having Al-Rafah's finger helped us open it, but all the contents were encrypted."

Lon asked, "Do you still need the finger or can we get it out of the refrigerator?"

Hans answered, "No, I disabled that security feature. You can toss it."

"Thank God. That thing grosses me out."

Hans continued, "We haven't decrypted it all just yet. It uses much better algorithms than Hamas uses."

"Are you saying it wasn't Hamas?"

"No, sir. It doesn't appear so. Whomever Al-Rafah was communicating with on that one is more sophisticated. It smacks of Al-Qaeda to me but the Al-Qaeda from the bad old days before the United States essentially decapitated them."

Travis was a bit concerned. "Hamas always gave lip service to Al-Qaeda but never really cooperated on the ground; at least in a significant way, right?"

Sarah responded, "That's right, sir. They parroted AQ's anti-Israel rhetoric but stopped short of any real cooperation. Hamas didn't want to undermine the support they were getting from leftist elements in Europe or moderate Arabs. If they aligned with Al-Qaeda formally, the Saudis would withdraw their financial support, Israel would withhold transit fees, and Egypt would tighten the border controls. Hamas would starve. Even they're not *that* stupid."

Travis continued, "Okay, so this smacks of Al-Qaeda or someone very much like them but historically there has been no real operational link between AQ and Hamas. So, what is this? Is this a sea change in Hamas's policy or is there another player in the mix? If so, who? And what were they doing talking with Al-Rafah? We know he was much more radical than most of Hamas, but was he radical enough to risk throwing all of Hamas and the Gaza Strip under the bus?"

Sarah said, "I think he was, sir. That's exactly why we targeted him. His hatred of Israel and Jews in general is more than a battle over dirt. If Hamas were given all of Israel and the Jews evacuated completely, he would still call for their complete destruction. He sees them as heretics and blasphemers. He wants us all dead."

This was the first time she referred to the Israelis as "us." *This one struck a nerve.*

Travis declared, "Then it's good we killed the guy. But let's figure out what the hell he was up to before he kicked the oxygen habit. Gunny, get back to work on that data. If you need more help, let me know. I'll see you get it."

Gunny replied, "Thank you, sir. Hans is confident he can break into it, but we'll let you know."

Hans spoke up. "Sir, we have a couple of possible names. They didn't encrypt the titles of a couple of emails. It's something we can at least get started with. They are fairly old but might be useful."

"What names?"

Checking a notebook in front of him, Koenig read off a couple of names. "We have two Western names: Wachner and Ostergaard. We have a few in Arabic. Alkawbra which was Al-Rafah's nom de guerre."

Lon joked, "Well, I guess we can scratch him off the list."

Hans smiled. "I agree. However, there are a couple more. One is Abu Almawt. That is almost certainly another nom de guerre. It means 'Father of Death.'"

Travis quipped, "He sounds like a charmer. How come they never have a nickname like Buddy or Champ? Just once I'd like to run into a terrorist called Buddy. I'm sorry, go ahead."

Hans continued, "There is also a mention of 'Shams Sawda.' It means 'Black Sun.' Nothing on it in the databases. If it's a group, they're new. There is also the words *bariun*, *birutin*, and *mutwi* but I have no context for them."

Travis asked, "What do they mean?"

Hans replied, "Bariun is a small sea bird. A nom de guerre; possibly a woman? Birutin means 'protein.' And mutwi means 'bent.'"

Sarah interjected, "Mutwi can also mean 'folded.'" Everyone stared at her oddly. "What can I say? I was undercover as a hotel maid when I eliminated that Hizballah commander from the Bekkah Valley a couple years ago."

Travis said, "Well, we don't have enough information to get excited about it just yet. Let's see what we can dig up on the names and check those other words against terms used in the usual extremist traffic. If we can't come up with anything, we can pass it on to our official brethren but if there is anything to this, I'd prefer to handle it in-house. Anyone have anything else to discuss?" No one said a word. "Okay then. Fellow Praetorians, I suggest we go get a drink and properly welcome our newest member."

CHAPTER TWO
BLACK SUN

D r. Khalid ibn Mahfous Al-Maadi sat impatiently at his desk at Cairo University Faculty of Medicine. Also known as Kasr Al Ainy, the medical school was arguably the best in the Arab world, and Al-Maadi was one of its best professors. He was waiting for a message from a colleague and it was long overdue. Normally an extremely cool character, Dr. Al-Maadi was nervous, and he finally gave in to his apprehension. He grabbed his sweater, slung it over his shoulder, and walked quickly out of his office. As he breezed past Miriam, his rather plump secretary, he said, "I'm going out for a meeting. I'll be back in an hour or so."

She checked her calendar. "There is nothing scheduled."

"It's personal business," he said without slowing down.

She hated when he did that. He had a habit of randomly adjusting his schedule without consulting her. It had led to more than one embarrassing situation when the university president or a Ministry of Agriculture official called and she couldn't find him. It had gotten worse in the past few months, and she suspected he was having an affair with a married woman or was somehow involved with the government. During President Mubarak's reign, university doctors were often pressed into service to deal with the former leader's myriad health issues. But this new president—or dictator, as many claimed—was pretty healthy. She hadn't heard of any issues with him but then, as a secretary, she probably wouldn't.

Al-Maadi walked quickly down the corridor but rather than heading to the front toward the fountain, he slipped out the back across Cairo University Hospital Road and into the Clinical Pathology building. That wasn't his destination but if anyone spotted him, he could easily explain it. He walked on through the Al-Manial Hospital and into Umm Kulthum Park along the river. He walked south along the Nile until he came to Cairo University Bridge, then crossed the river and into the Giza Zoological Garden. It was a nice spring day and the area was crammed with tourists and groups of schoolchildren queued up to enter the zoo. Along the river behind him were the embassies of Saudi Arabia, Austria, and the United Arab Emirates as well as banks, restaurants, and other businesses. As he surveyed the area, everyone had a cell phone. This was the perfect place.

Al-Maadi reached into his pocket and removed a cheap burner phone, albeit one with a full keyboard. He turned it on and waited for it to register on the cellular system. He accessed the internet, typed in an email address and password. No new messages. *Damn it!* He typed a quick text message. "Where are you? Dinner is almost ready and we will need you to set the table. Please advise your status. AA." He hit send and after getting confirmation that the text was delivered, he powered down the phone and removed its battery before walking over to TGI Friday's for lunch. *Where in the hell is he?*

After lunch, Al-Maadi returned to his office. He picked up a rose from a street vendor on the way back and gave it to Miriam. "I'm sorry I was short with you earlier. I've been preoccupied with the budget discussions."

Miriam thanked him and put the flower in a bud vase in the window. She appreciated the gesture. Although she was married and several years older than him, she was a little bit smitten with the handsome young professor and had to admit, if only to herself, that she liked his attention.

Khalid returned to his office and hung up his sweater. He logged onto his computer and checked the internet. There was nothing on the major news sites, but he dug deeper. Finally, there it was. An anonymous blogger from Gaza claiming that Hamas security had killed a senior paramilitary suspected of being an Israeli spy. There was a description of the scene and even a photograph of the building where the alleged assassination took place. Khalid recognized the building as Al-Rasul Mohamad Hospital. The man must have been his friend Mohammad Al-Rafah, aka Alkawbra.

Well, that explains the silence. But an Israeli spy? Al-Maadi didn't believe that. It made no sense. The fact that he was still breathing was compelling evidence to the contrary. If Al-Rafah worked for the Israelis, then he would certainly have told them about Al-Maadi. And if they knew about Al-Maadi and what he was planning, they would have killed him first. He was integral to the plan whereas Al-Rafah, while technically its originator, was now more of a cog in its execution. If they were aware of it, they never would have allowed it to get this far. The Israelis wouldn't risk alerting Al-Maadi and driving him underground or forcing him to move up his timetable. But what happened? Khalid ran everything through in his mind but just couldn't get back to Al-Rafah being an Israeli informant. It was much more likely he was assassinated by the Israelis. God knows, he had been on their hit list for years. They probably took him out and staged the scene to make it look like another internal Hamas power struggle. A more likely possibility was a jealous husband or disrespected brother or father. Al-Rafah's sexual appetites were well known but he was too senior to confront directly, hence the need for subterfuge and confusion.

Whatever the reason, Al-Rafah was dead and Al-Maadi was not. He would lay low for while—just in case—but he was determined to go ahead with his plan. That afternoon he tossed his burner phone in the Nile. His next order of business would be to replace Al-Rafah, and that would be a tall order.

* * *

Back in Cyprus, Hans Koenig was still working tirelessly on the encrypted data from the second laptop recovered in the Gaza operation. His frustration was growing and he was about to accept Rusty Travis's offer to help. He'd try a little longer before bothering the boss. As he worked, Sarah walked in. "Do you need any help with that?"

Hans only glanced at her before returning to the computer screen. "Uh, I might but I think this is a one-person job. I'm trying to break their encryption and most of it is waiting for the computer to do its thing. I could use some help trying to figure out a correlation with those open-text words we found yesterday."

Sarah sat down at the computer next to him and turned it on. "Let me see what I can do. This has that advanced search program Travis gave us, right?"

"Wise Owl? Yeah, it's on all of them. It's the little owl icon on the bottom left."

"Okay, I see it. I'm going to start with the Western names. See if there are any identifiable correlations. What were those names again?"

"Uh, Ostergaard and Wachner."

Sarah copied the names from Han's notebook onto a Post-it Note. "Wachner is a Jewish name. Unlikely he's an AQ affiliate. And Ostergaard is what? German?"

Hans responded, "Very funny, Sarah. I know you're thinking Nazis but don't go there. Ostergaard is actually Danish. The double "aa" is the clue. It's actually spelled with a 'slash O.'" It means "east farm." Use Option-Shift-O to get the 'Ø' for your search."

Sarah typed it in and got hundreds of hits. She then typed in Wachner and got hundreds more. "No first names for these guys?"

"Nope."

"Damn. This could take a while."

Hans asked, "What about the other words? You can add them to the query."

Sarah asked, "In English, Arabic, Hebrew, Yiddish, or Danish?"

Hans chuckled, "I see your point. Well, since most of the internet is in English, I would start there."

Sarah let out a heavy sigh. "Okay, what were those other words again?"

Hans checked his notes. "They were *birutin* and *mutwi*. *Birutin* means 'protein' and *mutwi* means 'bent.'"

"Or folded," she added.

"Yes, or folded. I didn't mean to insult your inner chambermaid."

"Laundry wench," she corrected. Sarah wrote them down and then asked, "There was another one, right?"

"Yeah, *bariun*. It's a small bird. I assume it's a nom de guerre of some kind."

Sarah asked, "I'm not familiar with that word. What's the bird called in English?"

"Good question, let me check." Hans pulled up Google translate and typed in the word in Arabic. As he did this, Alen Markovic entered the room.

Seeing Sarah and Hans at the computers, he commented, "Ah, computer shit. Not my strong suit. I wouldn't be of much help. Can I get anyone a cup of coffee or tea? Anything?" He was hoping for any excuse to talk to Sarah. He hadn't said two words to her since their initial introduction.

Without looking up, Sarah replied, "No, thank you."

Hans just shook his head. Ignoring Alen, Hans said, "Okay Sarah, *bariun* is Arabic for prion, also known as a whalebird. A small petrel found in the Southern Ocean. That's not much help."

Sarah was exasperated. "Okay, so we have protein, bent—or folded, and prion. Combine that with a common Danish name and we have jack shit— or a body-building bird watcher who's into origami."

Alen interjected, "Uh, I don't mean to butt in but there's another possibility."

Sarah glared at him with a combination of incredulity and derision as if to say, '*Go away ya big oaf.*' "Oh yeah? And what might that be?"

Alen explained, "A prion is also a protein that can cause neurodegener- ative diseases. Specifically, it can cause bovine spongiform encephalopathy or BSE; commonly known as mad cow disease or Creutzfeldt-Jakob disease in humans. Both are incurable brain diseases." Hans and Sarah stared at him in stunned silence. He continued, "Actually prions are misfolded pro- teins with the ability to transmit their misfolded shapes onto normal vari- ants of the same protein. That might explain the use of the words protein and bent."

Sarah turned to look at him. "Are you for real?"

Hans did a quick Wikipedia search on the word "prion" and proclaimed, "Uh, Sarah, he's right. Look at this."

Sarah read the first paragraph of the web page. "Holy shit, Alen, how did you pull that out of your big ol' ass?"

He smiled at her and said, "Big and handsome doesn't automatically mean stupid."

She smirked, "I never said handsome."

He grinned. "Just an oversight on your part, I'm sure. Anyway, both my parents were doctors. My father was a neurosurgeon, and my mother was a microbiologist. I was expected to follow in their footsteps like my sister did but I dropped out of university after my second year to join the army. Pissed them off something fierce, needless to say. I used to proofread their technical papers for spelling and grammar. I guess I picked up some knowledge by osmosis."

Sarah motioned to the chair next to her. "Sit down. You can help me while Hans works on the decryption."

"My pleasure. Maybe I can buy you a drink after?"

"Maybe. We'll see how this goes first."

* * *

The Royal Jordanian Airlines flight from Cairo to Amman was only an hour and twenty minutes long and Dr. Khalid Al-Maadi arrived at Queen Alia International Airport at 10:20 a.m. If all went according to plan, he wouldn't even have to spend the night. Al-Maadi had been to Amman before, of course; many times, in fact. Most recently he was a guest lecturer at the Hashemite University Faculty of Medicine. Other times he had traveled to the West Bank to advise the Palestinian Authority on public health issues. Just last year, he was working in a hospital in Ramallah during his summer break. It was there that he encountered one of his former students, a young Palestinian doctor named Abullah Al-Yasuf. It was Al-Yasuf who he hoped to find again.

Clearing customs was quick. He was a respected doctor who still had a valid VIP visa in his passport from his trip to Hashemite University as an invited guest of the government. Rather than heading east toward the university, he hired a car and headed west along Highway 437 toward the Allenby Bridge and the Palestinian Territories. It had been less than a year since his last visit, so his travel permits, required by both the Israelis and Jordanians, were still valid. It irked him that as an Arab, he had to ask permission from the Israelis to treat Arab patients in an Arab land. As he crossed the bridge, he thought that if all went as planned, he'd never need their permission again.

About an hour after crossing into the West Bank, Khalid's taxi pulled up in front of the Ramallah Hospital. Upon entering the hospital, he walked directly to the chief administrator's office. The secretary actually recollected him from his visit the year before, which made things much easier. He apologized for not calling in advance or requesting a formal appointment with the chief administrator but explained he was seeking out a former student, Dr. Al-Yasuf, who he wanted to use for an epidemiological study in conjunction with the World Health Organization. She explained that Dr. Al-Yasuf was not on duty but she was only too eager to help and provided him with Al-Yasuf's personal cell phone number and address.

Back on the street, Khalid's taxi was still there, but he walked around the corner to hail a different cab. He didn't want any one person to know all the details of his trip. He suspected that most, if not all cabbies, were working for the PA police, or the Israelis, or both. He had the taxi drop him off at the Nijmeh Mall, which was a few blocks from Al-Yasuf's address and he walked the rest of the way.

Abdullah's apartment was a third-floor walk-up in what passed for a middle-class neighborhood in Ramallah. The road was narrow with various shops and professional offices on the street level and apartments above. Khalid nervously glanced behind him as he entered the building. He double-checked the address the secretary had scribbled down for him before walking up the dimly lit stairs to the third floor. The air was filled with scents and sounds. A small dog barking, a baby crying, and Arabic rock music coming from one of the apartments. The air smelled of tobacco, sweat, and food. Most of the apartment doors and windows were open to allow what breeze there was. The smells from the various meals being cooked wafted into the hallway with overlapping aromas of pungent spices. At the end of the hall, he found Abdullah's apartment. The door was ajar. There were voices from a television or radio inside. He knocked on the door but there was no answer. After a few moments, he knocked again and shouted, "Hello. I'm looking for Dr. Al-Yusef. Is this the right apartment?" There was stirring from inside and then a young man dressed in loose slacks and a T-shirt came to the door.

"Dr. Al-Yusef?"

The young man rubbed his eyes. He had just woken up even though it was afternoon. His hair was a mess, and he hadn't shaved in a couple days. "I'm Al-Yusef, but I don't see patients in my home. If you need help, go to the hospital or the clinic."

"Oh, no. You misunderstand. I'm not a patient. I'm Dr. Khalid Al-Maadi, from Cairo University. Your old professor."

It took a couple of seconds before Al-Maadi's words registered, then Al-Yusef's eyes opened wide. "Dr. Al-Maadi! Oh my God! I am so sorry. I didn't recognize you! Please come in."

Al-Maadi laughed, "Have I aged that much? It has been less than a year."

"Oh, no sir. I just wasn't expecting you. Was I? I mean, did we have an appointment? If we did, I am so sorry. I have been working killer hours lately—twenty-four-hour shifts."

"No need to apologize. I remember what it was like being a resident. I should be apologizing to you. I should have called first. It was rude for me to have just dropped by unannounced."

Abdullah led him into the apartment. It was a bit messy, like a bachelor lived there. It was nice though—a large living room with a flat-screen TV, a sizeable kitchen, two bedrooms, a bathroom, and a large patio off the kitchen. "Can I get you something to drink? Tea? Water?"

"Water would be nice, thank you."

Handing him a bottle of water from the refrigerator, Abdullah asked, "So to what do I owe this honor? Are you working in Ramallah again?

"No, not on this trip. There is something I wanted to discuss with you. Something very important and very sensitive. I must have your assurance that it will remain absolutely private. If the authorities or the Israelis were to catch wind of it. . . ."

With mention of the Israelis, Abdullah's mood instantly changed. "Fuck the Israelis." He immediately caught himself, "I'm sorry, sir. I apologize for my outburst."

"No apologies necessary. Your sentiments echo my own. How is your family doing?" Al-Maadi knew this was a sore spot for Abdullah. He purposely wanted to rip the scab off that old wound to assess his young colleague's current attitude.

"Not so good. My father died since you were here last. Heart attack."

"Oh, I am so sorry to hear that. I know he had suffered a lot since . . . well, you know."

"You refer to the fucking Israeli dogs stealing our land and making us destitute?" Abdullah's family had been prosperous farmers in Yasuf with olive groves, oil presses, and a small olive oil bottling facility. Their land was confiscated by the Israelis in 1978 and later became part of the Kfar Tapuach settlement. The settlers claimed that an older brother had sold the land to a Jewish broker but Abdullah's father always disputed that. The uncle was killed by Abdullah's father during an ensuing argument. The murdered uncle's family were labeled collaborators and had to move to Tunisia. Some people questioned at the time how they afforded that and rumors were rampant that maybe the older brother did sell his land to the settlers. His father subsequently spent ten years in an Israeli prison for manslaughter. By the time he was released, he was a broken man who did little beside smoke and curse the Israelis. Abdullah had four older brothers, two of whom died during the First Intifada before Abdullah was even born. Another died in 2000 during the Second Intifada. His only surviving brother was crippled by an Israeli rubber bullet during a street protest and lived with their mother, supported in large part by Abdullah. His family's bitterness and hatred was the canvas on which his own life was painted.

"Yes. It is about the Israelis that I wish to talk to you."

"The Israelis?"

"How would you like to take revenge for your father and your family?"

"You know I would, but how? They have no plans to leave this land, and so long as the Americans are backing them, no one will force them out."

Al-Maadi smiled, reached for the TV remote and turned up the volume. Speaking low, he said, "I have found a way."

Abdullah laughed, "Right. Dr. Al-Maadi, you are a brilliant man, but you are no military mastermind. Nasser, Arafat, Sadat, Hussein, the Assads—all have failed. And they had armies. What do you have?"

Al-Maadi smiled and said, "We have Black Sun, and more importantly, we have science. "

"Black Sun?"

"It is the successor to my cousin's legacy. I have put together a group of like-minded Arab patriots to continue the fight. My cousin and Osama, as brilliant as they were, focused on the wrong objectives and used the wrong people. I do not care about the House of Saud. They will go the way of the dinosaurs, and it will be their own people who get rid of them. I do not care so much about the Americans either. They only want to protect their precious oil supplies."

"You don't care about the Americans?"

"If we make our struggle about them and oil, we will not win. Too many Arabs are in love with American dollars and the rest of the world is just as dependent on that oil as the Americans. If their supply is threatened by us or the Iranians, they will band together to protect it. Not out of any loyalty but economic necessity. The oil-rich countries—like Kuwait and Saudi Arabia—will join with the infidels to protect their oil just like when Saddam invaded Kuwait. They don't care about Palestine and would certainly never fight for it. They throw you a few coins every once in a while, to make sure you remain a thorn in the Israelis' side, but that is it. If you really want to unite the Arab world again, we must do it by destroying Israel. No Arab state will come to their defense. With no oil to protect, the Europeans, Indians, and Chinese may complain, but they will not lift a finger. They have large Muslim minorities. They are not willing to die to defend the Jews and risk riots at home."

"But what of the Americans? We cannot defeat the Israelis militarily so long as the Americans are backing them."

"We will not defeat them militarily; we will beat them biologically. We have what we need already. The only missing piece is you."

Dr. Al-Yasuf looked at Al-Maadi sternly. "Then you shall have me."

* * *

Hans and Sarah had been frustrated by the encryption on Al-Rafah's second computer. They finally had to admit they were at the limits of their skill and asked Travis for help. Rusty, Sarah, and Hans took a copy of the hard drive and boarded the Bombardier 8000 for a flight to the United States. Lon Oden joined them at the last minute. He wanted to take advantage of the break in the action to visit his mother in Del Rio, Texas.

They landed at Bush Intercontinental Airport outside Houston, where they went through customs. Lon bid farewell to his colleagues and left in search of a flight to San Antonio. Travis, Hans, and Sarah got back on the jet for the short eighty-mile flight to Easterwood Airport in College Station, Texas.

Hans gazed out the window of the jet and marveled at the endless expanse of rolling pastures, cornfields, and forests that covered the landscape. Though he had been to Texas before, he was always taken aback by the size of the state. Rusty was at the back of the cabin on the phone talking to someone on the ground. Hans turned to Sarah and said, "Do you realize that Texas, this one state, is twice the size of Germany?"

She laughed. "That makes it what? Thirty times the size of Israel?"

"Yes, I suppose it would." Peering out the window as they flew over the Texas A&M campus, Hans shouted, "Wow! Look at that arena!"

Rusty had moved up and buckled into his seat. "That's the football stadium. It seats over 100,000 people."

Sarah just shook her head, "That's a quarter of the population of Tel Aviv. In one stadium."

The jet touched down at Easterwood Airport and taxied to a private hangar. They got off the plane and walked directly to a waiting Chevy Suburban. They drove around the eastern edge of the campus and then northeast to a nondescript industrial park. They parked in front of a sprawling one-story building. As they entered the lobby, it had a very academic air about it; low ceilings, institutional carpeting, beige walls with rather generic artwork depicting scenes of ranch and farm life. Waiting for them in the lobby was a middle-aged black man with graying hair and glasses. He wore jeans, cowboy boots, and a plaid shirt. The only thing missing was a Stetson cowboy hat.

He greeted Travis warmly. "Rusty, great to see you again! How ya been?"

"I've been good, Tom. And you? How's Maria and your boys?"

"She's doing good. The cancer is in remission thanks to you and MD Anderson. Thomas Jr. got promoted. He's a captain now. Currently on deployment in Afghanistan but should be home for Christmas. Marcus is a senior at A&M. In the Corps of Cadets, of course. He reports to Officer Training School at Maxwell Air Force Base in August. So, who are your friends?"

"Tom, this is Hans and Sarah. They are working with me on a security project that one of my companies is involved in. Guys, this is Dr. Tom Williams, the smartest computer geek I know, and I know some smart ones."

Dr. Williams shook their hands in turn while protesting, "Yeah, in case you haven't figured it out yet, Rusty is full of shit. Well, what can I help you folks with?"

Hans pulled a hard drive out of his satchel but then hesitated. Rusty reassured him, "Believe me, we can trust Tom to be discreet."

Sensing Hans's apprehension, Dr. Williams interjected, "Let's discuss this in private." He led them down a long hallway. Hans whispered to Rusty, "How'd you get hooked up with these guys?"

"Tom and I went to school together."

"I thought you went to MIT?"

"I did. Tom and I got our undergrad and master's degrees here at A&M. I went to MIT for my PhD and he ended up at Stanford for his. He worked in Silicon Valley and did quite well. He came back to A&M to teach. He also works here doing advanced computer forensics and cybersecurity work. Mostly for the government and defense contractors."

"So, this isn't part of the university. Then who owns it?"

"Why, I do, of course. Why do ya think we came here?"

Dr. Williams led them past his office and into a large laboratory space just beyond. The door had both a cypher lock and an electronic spin dial combination lock like a bank vault. Above it was a sign-in sheet logging every entry and a red magnetic sign that said OPEN. Above the door, Sarah noted a camera. "Here we are." He punched in a code and opened the door. Inside there were two young men working on computers. "Could you give us the room, please?" The two men locked their terminals and exited without a word.

The room was cold and Sarah was chilled by the frigid air blasting from the vent above her. The room was crammed with whirring computer equipment. There were several terminals in cubicles along one wall connected to servers, and other equipment. Along the entire back wall were three banks of equipment racks that Hans estimated must have contained at least sixty top-of-the-line IBM Power System servers. Dr. Williams offered Sarah a fleece hoodie. "Here ya go, ma'am. It can get cold in here." She took the hoodie and thanked him. "Okay, let's see what you have for me."

As Hans handed over the backup drive, Travis explained. "This was obtained from a not-so-nice guy in the sandbox. It has higher-level encryption than usual and we're have a bitch of a time breaking in. I figured you could help."

Tom put on a pair of glasses, studied the drive, and found the appropriate plug to connect it to an unnetworked computer at the end of the room. "Just need to check it for malware, viruses, worms, and the like. This should only take a minute." As the machine scanned the drive, he said, "I got one kid in the service and another about to go in. If there is anything I can do for you guys, I'll do it."

Once the computer indicated there were no viruses, he connected the drive to one of the networked terminals. Hans asked, "What is the capability of this setup?"

Tom peered at him over his glasses. "Uh, that's classified. Let's just say it's sneaking up on a petaflop. It's not going to compete with the big boys at the National Labs but it is plenty for what we're doing."

Sarah asked, "I'm sorry, but what's a petaflop?"

Rusty answered, "That is a quadrillion floating-point operations per second. That's a thousand trillion. If you counted one bean per second, it would take you over 31 million years to count a quadrillion beans."

Sarah was impressed. "Wow! In a second? That's pretty fast."

Tom squinted at his screen. "Okay, this encryption is pretty strong." He smirked, "But not nearly strong enough. Give me a couple of minutes." His fingers danced over the keyboard setting up the Linux program and setting the parameters. He double-checked his settings and then hit Enter. "This may take a couple of minutes. Anyone need a cup of coffee or a bathroom break?"

No one took him up on his offer and opted to wait patiently instead. While Rusty and Tom discussed the prospects for the upcoming Aggies football season, Hans and Sarah chatted quietly. Sarah commented, "So Rusty owns this too? Why am I not surprised?"

Hans replied, "Well, he has a PhD from MIT in computer engineering; this would be right up his alley. I must say, this equipment is way above my level. I doubt I could even turn this thing on. This is beyond impressive. There are entire countries that couldn't come up with what you see in this room right now."

After a couple more minutes, the terminal beeped, indicating it was done. Dr. Williams turned in his chair. "Well, that was fast." He rolled in his chair over to the terminal. He typed a few commands and up popped a list of contents. "Okay, let's see what we have. The operating system was Linux. That's kind of surprising for these clowns. They tend to be Windows guys. There are a bunch of emails and SMS messages. All in Arabic so I'll leave those to you. Let's see what else we have." He scrolled down the list. "Okay, there are several documents here. One named 'Shams Sawda,' whatever the hell that is." He opened the document and quickly closed it. "Yeah, the title used our letters but the text looks like Arabic again. This one is just named 'tajriba' and the others are copies of published academic papers. One is in English. I can't read the other."

Hans looked over his shoulder, "That's Danish. And *tajriba* means 'experiment' in Arabic."

Tom shrugged, "The papers are not really worth the encryption since they're published. Any high school kid could get them from Google. Well, anyway, it's decrypted. I leave to you guys to figure out what it all means."

He disconnected the hard drive and handed it back to Hans. Turning to Rusty, Tom asked, "How long you in town for? Maria would love to have you over for dinner. I'm smoking a brisket as we speak."

Rusty turned to his colleagues. Sarah just shrugged while Hans said, "I'm hungry but what is this 'brisket' thing?"

Rusty laughed. "Buddy, you're in for a treat. Tom smokes the best brisket in ten counties. We'll get a hotel and pick up some beer and wine."

"Hotel? Nonsense. You're staying with us. We got room. Marcus is living in his own apartment off campus. Can't be a senior and live with your parents. What's the point of having a five-bedroom house if you can't fill it every once in a while?"

"All right, if you're sure it wouldn't be a burden."

"None at all. Maria lives for this shit. Why don't ya swing by around five, and we'll have a couple of cold ones. You take my Suburban to the airport to get your luggage. You can buy some beer at HEB on the way back. And none of that cheap shit you used to buy back in college. You're rich. You need to act like it."

* * *

That night Hans and Sarah were introduced to Texas hospitality. Tom's wife, Maria, was a pretty Latina from the Rio Grande Valley. They had met in college and married shortly after graduation. Her hair was quite short but was growing back now that she was finished with her chemotherapy. They had a beautiful two-story house on a ranch just outside of town. It was stylishly decorated and included a large pool, stables, and a horse jumping arena—a testament to Tom's own private-sector success. On the fireplace mantel were proudly displayed photos of their two sons. Thomas Jr. was in his army dress greens and the younger son, Marcus, in his Corps of Cadets uniform.

When Marcus found out Uncle Rusty was in town, he came home for dinner. While he liked Rusty and found Hans fascinating, he was clearly enamored with Sarah and spent most of the evening talking to her. Tom's smoked brisket lived up to the hype, and both Hans and Sarah were impressed. After dinner and several beers, they retired for the night.

The next morning, Maria had breakfast waiting for them. As Rusty finished his coffee, Hans pulled him aside. "Hey, boss. I looked over some of that data last night on my laptop. It appears to be medical stuff, but biology is not my strong suit."

Sarah had entered the room and overheard the last comment. "You know, Alen knows a lot about that stuff. Maybe he can make sense of it?"

Rusty scratched his chin. "Well then, maybe we should be heading back?"

Sarah asked, "What about Lon? He's visiting his family out in the middle of nowhere."

Rusty replied, "He'll have to fly back commercial."

Hans interjected, "We may want to hold off on that. One of the papers was written by some guy at Cedars-Sinai Medical Center in Los Angeles. His name is Michael Wachner. I found his LinkedIn profile. Sarah was right; he's Jewish. Born in the Bronx and raised in Ohio. Undergrad from Ohio State. Med school at Harvard. Postgrad work on genetics at Northwestern. Has done research in Israel. Actually, he volunteered to do a year in the IDF after med school so I doubt he's a terrorist. I suggest we go talk to him as long as we're on this side of the Atlantic. I can do a deeper dive once we're airborne."

Rusty nodded. "Good call. Hans, find out if this Wachner guy is in town. If he is, make an appointment for this afternoon. Tell them we're potential donors. Sarah, get ahold of Lon and tell him what's going on. We won't need him in California but tell him if he wants a ride home, he needs to get his butt to Houston. I'll call the pilots and tell them to file a flight plan for L.A. Everyone good with that?" Sarah and Hans nodded. "All right, let's pack it up."

As Rusty finished, Tom and Marcus entered the kitchen. Marcus stared at Sarah like a lovesick puppy. She smiled but otherwise ignored him. Tom said, "Rusty, sorry, but we can't join you for breakfast. I have to teach a class this morning and this young man needs a ride to drill practice."

"No problem. Maria has already taken care of us. We need to hit the road too. Got to go to the Left Coast for a meeting. I want to thank you and Maria for your hospitality. The next one is at my place."

Hans added, "And thanks for your help on that other thing. I never could have done it."

Tom smiled. "Don't sell yourself short. I just had the advantage of having a supercomputer."

* * *

They landed at Santa Monica Municipal Airport at a little after 11 a.m. The flight was two and a half hours but they gained two hours traveling east to west, so they arrived less than an hour after they took off. Rusty had a hired car waiting for them at the airport and they headed straight for Cedars-Sinai Medical Center. The hospital complex spread across several city blocks on Beverly Boulevard in West Hollywood. It was one of the leading research hospitals in California and many of Hollywood's elite were counted among its patients.

Travis had a 1:00 p.m. appointment with Wachner. It was not easy to arrange, but when he mentioned that he was considering a sizeable donation, the doors magically opened. The three of them made an unusual group. Travis played the role of a brash Texan wearing snakeskin cowboy boots with his three-thousand-dollar suit. Hans passed for his bodyguard, a mysterious European man dressed all in black. And Sarah, well, she had movie star beauty with an exotic femme fatale aura; sex and danger in one beautiful package. Wachner wouldn't know what hit him.

They walked to his office and upon arrival were ushered in by his secretary. His office was like a typical academic's—nice furniture buried under piles and piles of papers, textbooks, and scientific journals Wachner would insist he planned to read "someday" when he had the time. He didn't know what to make of Travis, was intimidated by Hans, and intrigued by Sarah.

Hans moved a stack of papers to close the door behind them, which unnerved Wachner even more. Composing himself, he asked, "So, Mr. Travis. I understand you're interested in my research." What he wanted to ask was "How much are you willing to put up?" Researchers were constantly seeking funds through government grants, charities, or private benefactors. He was no different.

"Well, yes and no. I don't even know what kind of research you do."

"You're not interested in medical research?"

"Not really. I was in computers, myself. Now I'm primarily an investor."

Wachner was dejected. *Another hedge fund guy looking for exploitable insight on a topic he couldn't possibly fathom.* "I'm sorry, Mr. Travis, but I don't get involved in hedge funds or any other investing that might open me up to accusations of insider trading or conflict of interest."

"Good. Because we don't give a rat's ass about any of that shit. I had my people check you out while we were on our way here. You seem like a squared-away guy. Family is Hungarian. You lost your grandparents and other family in the Holocaust. After medical school you did a stint in the Israeli Defense Forces even though, being American-born, you had no legal obligation to do so. Respected genetic researcher. Lots of well-received scientific publications. In 2014 you spent a year on sabbatical during which you volunteered at the Medical School for International Health at Ben Gurion University."

"Okay, so you've read my bio; so what? What's this all about?"

Putting her Israeli accent on full display, Sarah spoke. "Can we trust you to keep what we are about to tell you in the strictest confidence?

Wachner was surprised. "You're Israelis?"

"I am. They're not. Mr. Travis is American—which I think is fairly obvious. The quiet guy to my left is actually German, but the good kind." Hans had to smile at that one. "Our company has a contract to do computer forensics on media recovered by law enforcement. We're here to ascertain why one of your publications showed up on a dead terrorist's laptop computer. Does any of your work have weapons applications?"

Now Wachner was shocked and instantly on the defensive. "A dead terrorist had one of my papers? Weapons applications? No, not at all! I research Tay-Sachs disease, for crying out loud!"

Travis interjected. "I've heard of it but what is it exactly?"

Wachner explained, "Its a genetic disorder passed down from parent to child."

"Like hemophilia?"

"Well, sort of. Instead of clotting factor, the victims lack an enzyme that helps break down gangliosides in the body."

Travis interrupted, "Ganglio . . . what?"

Frustrated, Wachner explained, "Gangliosides. They're chemicals in the body that modulate cell signal transduction. The details aren't important. Without the enzyme, the gangliosides build up to toxic levels in the child's brain and damage nerve cells. It starts with a loss of muscle control and leads to blindness, paralysis, and death. My point is that Tay-Sachs is caused by a genetic defect. It is not something that could be weaponized. I think you're barking up the wrong tree."

Sarah chimed in, "However, Tay-Sachs is unique to Jews. If it was weaponized, it would be devastating."

Wachner replied. "That's not correct; well, not completely. Yes, Tay Sachs affects Jews disproportionately. However, it also affects other ethnic groups—French Canadians of southeastern Quebec and other smaller groups like the Cajuns in southern Louisiana. No one knows exactly why it affects these groups and not others. And it only affects Ashkenazi Jews."

Travis looked confused so Sarah explained. "Ashkenazi. European Jews."

Wachner continued, "Right. As opposed to Sephardic Jews who come from Spain and Portugal, or Mizrahi Jews who come from the Middle East. But it doesn't affect all Ashkenazi; just that minority who carry the mutated gene. This disease can't be induced in a person. It's not an infection; it's caused by a genetic mutation in the HEXA gene on chromosome 15. It can't be weaponized."

Hans spoke for the first time. "If a disease can be cured, it can also be caused."

Wachner composed himself. "I'm working on a cure for this disease. We are trying to develop a gene therapy technique that will repair the damaged gene to keep it from being passed on. We are using a gene editing technique called CRISPR to engineer replacement DNA to repair it, but we are years, probably decades away; assuming we will do it at all. It's very complicated. You have to come up with a repair that is not a virus. There is no way some terrorist in a cave solved this problem and then reversed it to cause the disease. Even if they did, you'd have to get all the Jews in the world to line up and undergo gene therapy. I don't think they'd do it."

Travis took a breath. This wasn't what he expected. "All right, Doc. Let's say you're right, and none of your research has any biological weapons application. That doesn't explain why a terrorist was interested in your work."

Wachner was exasperated. "How the hell should I know? I don't even know what paper he was reading."

Hans opened a small notebook and read, "The paper in question is 'Identification of Specific Genetic Marker Unique to Ashkenazim and Sephardic Populations,' published in the Spring 2016 issue of *IGS Quarterly*, which I assume is the International Genetics Society, right?"

Wachner started laughing. "That's the International Genealogical Society. That's family tree stuff; you know, people trying to find out if they're related to a dead president or have some long-lost siblings somewhere. I think this has been a big waste of everyone's time. I published that on a lark. We accidently found a genetic sequence—with no mutations—that identifies Ashkenazi and Sephardic Jews. I was trying to sell it to 23andMe or Ancestry.com so they could add it to their standard genetic testing and make it more accurate. It's of no real consequence but I figured I might make a buck on it, ya know?"

Sarah pondered this for a moment and then said, "So this is found in all Ashkenazi and Sephardic Jews?"

Wachner was still laughing. "Yeah, so what?"

"If you can develop a test to identify that exact sequence, what's to stop someone from developing something that would attack that exact sequence? Maybe something that would destroy the DNA or cause an infection?"

Wachner's laughing slowed. "Well, technically yes, if you found a virus that had specific receptors for that particular sequence. But the odds of finding it are a billion to one."

Travis now asked. "What if you didn't need to find it? What if you made it? Engineered it if you will. Like your Tay Sachs gene therapy fix. Except if you're trying to cause disease instead of cure it, you really don't care about accidently creating a virus in the process. In fact, that might be advantageous, right?"

Wachner wasn't laughing anymore. "Well, technically, I guess so. You'd need a great deal of expertise. Not what I would expect from Al-Qaeda or ISIS. Maybe a state player like Iran, but even then, it wouldn't be easy. Any nation deploying such a weapon could also expect a full retaliation by Israel. The Arabs can lose all the wars they want; Israeli cannot afford to lose even one."

Travis told Hans, "Tell him the titles of the other papers."

Hans went back to his notebook. "From the same computer we have 'Development of Viral Vectors for Targeted Gene Therapy in Mice,' published in 2017 in *Virology Today*, 'Engineered Viruses for Suppression of Tick-Borne Encephalitis,' published last year in *Parasites and Vectors*, and 'Adhesion of Prions in Virus Protein Coatings to Advance Bovine Spongiform Encephalopathy Research,' which was published two months ago in a Chinese neuroscience journal whose name I can't pronounce."

Wachner sat in silence. The wheels were turning in his brain. After a few moments, he said, "Okay, this would be next to impossible to do, but theoretically, you might design a virus that attaches to the host DNA at a very specific chromosome location and either infect the cell to replicate the virus or release a dangerous protein like a prion."

Sarah asked, "Or both?"

"Well, technically, yeah. I mean, it would be extremely difficult to engineer and then you'd have to grow the virus. Not an easy task, even if it can reproduce. Then you would have to find a way to infect people with it. It's not like they're going to line up for it like a flu shot." He paused. "Oh, shit. If they used a flu virus or even an adulterated vaccine as the basis for the vector . . ."

Hans completed his sentence. "Then it would be self-replicating and potentially airborne."

"Potentially, yes. If someone is trying to do this, we need to inform Homeland Security, the CDC, and WHO immediately!"

Travis tried to calm him down. "That's why we're here. We need to fig-ure out what we are dealing with. This is all conjecture at this point. There is no evidence to suggest this is actually going on. And like you said, it would be next to impossible."

"You guys work with them, right?"

Sarah answered, "Yes, them and many other international partners as well. This is what we do."

Wachner took a breath. "Well, regardless of how plausible any of this is, I think your answer may lie with the people who wrote those other papers."

Travis said, "That's our next stop. Please, I must ask you to keep this conversation to yourself."

He nodded. Sarah put her hand on his shoulder. "He is serious. You cannot tell anyone about this; not your boss, not your wife, not your rabbi. Do you understand?"

"Yes, I understand. But what do I tell my department head? He thinks I'm meeting with a potential donor."

Travis replied, "You were." He handed Wachner a $100,000 cashier's check made out to Cedars-Sinai Medical Center. "And you were very con-vincing too."

Travis, Hans, and Sarah walked out of the office and to the elevator. Once in the elevator, Travis said, "I think Wachner was right, we need to talk to the people who wrote those other papers. Who are they?"

Hans answered, "All the same guy. Dr. Andreas Ostergaard."

CHAPTER THREE
THE CONVERT

Travis, Hans, and Sarah were forced to spend the night in Los Angeles so their pilots got the FAA-required rest period. Travis needed the sleep anyway; jet lag always affected him more than the others. Hans used the time to start the analysis of the decrypted hard drive and Sarah hit the hotel gym and sauna before heading to Rodeo Drive for some shopping. They left early the next morning and landed in Houston to refuel and collect Lon before taking off again for Cyprus.

Lon piled onto the plane with two large bags. Travis asked, "How was your mom?" He was a little closer to Lon because of their shared Texas roots. He treated him more like a little brother than an employee.

"She was fine. Complained that I didn't visit enough, of course. Typical mom stuff. Her arthritis is still bothering her, but the doc prescribed some new drug that seems to be helping. I brought back goodies."

Hans perked up. "Really? What?"

Lon pulled a large string of dried chilis out of one of the bags. "Real Mexican red chilis. I also have some fresh green chilis, corn tortillas, flour tortillas, enchilada sauce, pinto beans, and lard. When we get back, I'm going to cook everyone a real authentic Mexican dinner like my abuela always did. You're going to love it!"

Sarah chuckled. "You know Hans doesn't like spicy foods."

"Aw, bullshit. He's going to love this stuff."

Hans groaned. "Did you buy any antacids?

Ignoring his comment, Lon asked, "So what happened in L.A.?" The others filled him in on what they'd learned and then they all settled in for the long trip to Cyprus.

* * *

Nigel and Gunny were waiting for them at the Larnaca airport with two Range Rovers to drive them back to Lakatamia. Magne was there as they walked through the front door of the villa and Travis asked, "Where's everyone else?"

Magne replied, "Alen is in the armory going over some of the AKs and John ran into town to pick up some groceries. He should be back soon."

"Okay, when he gets back, let's all meet in the conference room and we'll fill everyone in. I'm going to drop my stuff upstairs. Lon brought some local food back from Texas." He pulled the Norwegian aside and whispered, "He plans on cooking dinner tonight. Make sure he doesn't make it too hot. Gunny called me a pussy but it damn near killed me last time, and I grew up on that stuff."

Magne smiled, "Will do, boss."

John Kernan returned to the villa about twenty minutes later. After putting away the supplies, they all met in the conference room. With Gunny at his side, Travis started the meeting. "Okay, as you all know, we went stateside to get that damn hard drive decrypted and Williams came through for us. There are several Arabic language documents we are going to need to translate so we'll need to get on that right away. Sarah will be point on that. No offense, Hans, but her Arabic is better than yours, and I need you to read those Danish docs." Hans nodded. "Now some of this stuff appears to be very technical; biomedical stuff. That is not my strong suit. Who can lead the charge on that?" Sarah raised her hand but Rusty waved her off. "No, you'll be too busy with the Arabic stuff."

She interjected, "No, not me. I was going to suggest Alen. He understands that stuff more than anyone else, as far as I can tell."

Travis glared at Alen with mild surprise. "Son, do you think you can manage it?"

Alen replied, "I'm no expert, but I'll give it a shot."

"Well, all right then. I guess ya learn something new every day. Dr. Williams included some of the source code of the encryption software they're using so I'm going to take a gander and see if I can figure out where it came from. Let's get to work. The rest of you help out where ya can. Arabic speakers go with Sarah."

Magne said, "I speak Danish too. I could help Hans with the documents."

Rusty had another idea. "No, you and Nigel see what you can learn about this Ostergaard guy. He's a big unknown right now."

* * *

The translation of the Arabic documents went quickly but they were also disconcerting. The document titled "Shams Sawda" or "Black Sun" was essentially a manifesto. Black Sun was described as a successor organization to Al Qaeda and ISIS but one determined to be more brutal and ruthless while also being more low-key and technically adept. It was not interested in headlines or public attacks like those on 9/11 or car bombs that killed lots of people in some market or mosque. They were PR stunts that didn't help achieve their objective, which was to unite the Arab world through the elimination of Israel as a Jewish state. They planned to do this using biological weapons and demographics. The brainstorming they did with Dr. Wachner in Los Angeles was ominously prophetic. Black Sun planned to develop a biological weapon that would kill most of the Jews in Israel while leaving the Arab minority unharmed.

The next day, Travis called a meeting of the team to discuss what they had learned. In the conference room, Sarah had a translation of the Black Sun manifesto on the large flat panel display which dominated the wall behind Rusty's chair. "Okay, this is the translation of the 'Shams Sawda' document we got from the hard drive. I ran this by the other Arab speakers on the team and they agree this translation is accurate. There is a lot of flowery language and mention of people or things by code names, so we can't be 100 percent certain, but I think it's a faithful interpretation." Pointing to the screen she said, "As you can see here, they discuss destroying the Jews. That is nothing new, of course, but they specifically say 'Ashkenazim and Sephardim' instead of Jews in general. This is worrisome given that Dr. Wachner discovered a genetic marker unique to the Ashkenazim and Sephardim." She scrolled down to the next page. "Here they go into a little more detail. They say this new weapon is airborne and highly contagious."

Alen asked, "How is it supposed to work?"

Sarah scrolled down farther. "According to this, it causes '*marad junun albaqar*,' or mad cow disease."

Alen choked. "Jesus Christ! Does it say how they plan to do this? Or if they've had any success to date?"

Sarah stated coldly, "No. But if they are successful in their bid to kill all the Ashkenazi and Sephardic Jews in Israel, that would be well over four million people—more than half the Jewish population. We are talking about murder on a scale not seen since Hitler."

Alen asked, "Who are the other Jews? Those not affected?"

"The other major group are the Mizrahi, the Edot Ha Mizrach, Communities of the East. They are Jews from the Middle East. Wachner said they don't carry the marker."

Alen continued, "How common is intermarriage between the Ashkenazi and Sephardic Jews and these Mizrahi Jews or even local Arab populations?"

Sarah replied, "With Arabs, not very common. With the Mizrahi, very common. Why?"

"Well, anyone who is a product of this kind of intermarriage might also be affected. You don't have to have blue eyes to carry the blue-eyed gene."

John had been silent but finally spoke up. "Does anyone else see the military and economic implications of this? If you kill off most of the Jews, the economy would be destroyed and the IDF would be decimated. They'd be open to attack from any Arab nation that got there with an army."

Gunny commented, "They wouldn't need to. Israel is a democracy. If you kill that many Jews, the Arab minority becomes the majority. It would become a de facto Arab state almost overnight."

Rusty interjected, "Guys, this goes way beyond Israel. If they develop this thing and use it, it ain't going to just stop at the border. It'll spread around the world and kill millions more. Given the late Mr. Al-Rafah's documented hatred of all Jews everywhere, I suspect that's exactly what he intended. We need to find out who else is involved and how far down this road they've actually gotten. What do we have on this Ostergaard, the Danish guy?"

Magne answered. "Well, we came up with quite a bit. Andreas Ostergaard is a genetic virologist at the University of Copenhagen. He received both his bachelor's and master's degrees at Copenhagen. He got his PhD at Uppsala University in Sweden. Has done postdoctoral work in France, Germany, and Turkey. Collaborative research on virology with colleagues at Cairo University and Johns Hopkins. He is considered a very intelligent and innovative researcher but has a reputation among some as stubborn and difficult to work with."

Rusty asked, "Any extremist connections?"

"Not directly, no. But then I wouldn't expect that on his bio. There's the work in Cairo but, on paper at least, there's nothing out of the ordinary there."

Alen asked, "What kind of work was that?"

Magne checked his notes. "Uh, they were working on a livestock disease."

"Bovine spongiform encephalopathy? BSE? Mad cow disease? Anything like that?"

Magne replied, "No. It was some sheep disease, scrapie—whatever that is."

Alen slowly shook his head. "Jesus, that's another prion disease. It's similar to Creutzfeldt-Jakob and mad cow disease. It's all related."

Rusty stared at the Serb with an expression of pleasant surprise. He whispered to Gunny, "I'd say you picked a good addition to the team with Markovic."

Gunny shrugged, "I didn't know he was smart, I just thought he could shoot."

Turning to Magne, Rusty said, "You said no *direct* extremist connections thereby implying there might be some *indirect* ones."

Magne smiled, "Well, yes—I think so." Magne tapped a few buttons on his laptop and several documents appeared on the screen. "Nigel and I accessed international visa and customs records. As you can see, in the last several years he has only traveled outside the Schengen countries few times—a few trips to Cairo; one to Ibiza, Spain; one to Jordan; and two to China. The Cairo trips make sense given his research project at the University of Cairo, and Ibiza looked to be a vacation. The Chinese trips correspond to scientific conferences, but the Jordanian trip was unexplained."

"We pulled up his Facebook page but there was nothing there other than talk about his current work in Copenhagen; no personal information at all—I mean zero. He's been on Facebook for several years but his page content was all relatively new; nothing more than a year or so old; like it's been scrubbed. People will do this to hide embarrassing shit from their youth so we dug deeper. Nigel found archived Facebook pages including Ostergaard's. When he was in Egypt, he apparently traveled to Gaza a couple of times on some kind of humanitarian thing. It wasn't clear what it was but there were pictures of him working in a hospital or clinic. He also had photos of himself at locations I recognized as being on the West Bank—Church of the Nativity and whatnot. With help from Hans, we dug out the time stamp on the photos and they corresponded to his travel to Jordan. The most interesting thing though, were several pictures of him with a pretty Arab girl." He hit another button and several photos popped up on the screen. "She is identified only as 'Jazmin' but there was this one picture of Ostergaard, Jazmin, and an older Arab man. The time stamp says 6 April 2014. That corresponds to one of his Cairo trips."

As the photograph expanded to fill the screen, Sarah sat up in her chair. "The older man, he looks very familiar."

Nigel smiled. "He was familiar to me too, so I ran him through Wise Owl's facial recognition software. It came back with a 95 percent match for Ahmed Al-Doghmush; the former number two man to Army of Islam leader Mohammad Dormosh. I think the girl is his daughter. Anyway, a few weeks later there is another photo of a smiling Andreas and Jazmin labeled only 'mutazawij.'"

Sarah translated: "Married."

Rusty squirmed in his chair. "You think our Danish doctor was married to the daughter of an Army of Islam leader? That's a stretch. You got something other than one photo? I mean, to folks in Gaza this is like getting your picture taken with Michael Jordon or Tom Brady."

Nigel continued, "Yes, sir. Magne and Hans were skeptical too until we saw the last photo posted on the archived page." He hit another button on his computer and the large monitor screen turned black. "This."

Rusty asked, "What the hell is that supposed to be? It's just a blank screen."

"Actually, it's not. Too much data for a blank screen. It turns out it's a Microsoft Word document; black words on a black background." He ran the cursor over the middle of the screen and the outline of a text box appeared. He highlighted the box, moved the cursor to the top of the screen and clicked on the font color button. When he did, the words "My Love Waits for Me in Heaven with God—August 9, 2014" popped out. "I think this was a memorial to Jazmin."

"What happened to her?"

"Well, sir, August 9, 2014, was during Operation Strong Cliff; the Israeli military operation against Hamas. This was the day Ahmed Al-Doghmush was killed in an Israeli drone strike."

Sarah chimed in. "I remember that. They blew up his car but didn't know his family was riding with him. His wife and daughter, if my memory serves."

Lon now spoke up. "You think Andreas Ostergaard was married to Al-Doghmush's daughter and that the Israelis killed her?"

Nigel answered, "Not intentionally, but yes."

An intensity flashed over Rusty's face. "Yeah, someone killing your wife tends to piss you off." And awkward silence fell over the room momentarily. The group couldn't help but make the connection with his wife and 9/11. Rusty took a deep breath and said, "I guess it all depends on how you react. Okay, moving on. What's next?"

Nigel said, "One last thing. We also found several links to Islamic sites, Islamic sayings, an audio file of the call to prayer, and a photo of a prayer rug. I think Dr. Ostergaard converted. Not sure if it was before or after Jazmin was killed, but I think he definitely converted."

Rusty asked, "And there is nothing on his current Facebook page that mentions Jazmin, Allah, Islam, Gaza, being married, or nothing?"

"No, sir. Not a word. Like I said, it's like it has been scrubbed."

"Damn good work, guys. Let's take a break and reconvene later. We need to hear about the texts and emails." The idea of having something in common with a potential terrorist was a little unsettling and he needed to refocus. "But right now, I need a drink."

* * *

The next session was equally disturbing. Hans started with the translations of the Danish language technical documents. They were all just executive summaries and not the entire papers. However, each pertained to what Wachner had said someone would need to figure out before coming up with a designer biological weapon. Alen explained, "Ten years earlier, any of this would have been a mere fantasy. But with the advent of CRISPR technology, it's possible so long as the people involved had the right technical expertise and enough time. Dr. Ostergaard has the expertise and, if he's dirty, he's had over five years to work on it."

The emails and texts were a bit disappointing. They contained little detail and no real actionable intelligence. There were no true names, just code names or simply initials. While most were in Arabic, others included some English and Anglicized spellings of Arabic words.

Rusty asked Sarah, "What do you make of all this?"

"I don't think all the people talking here are native Arabic speakers. If they were, it would all just be in Arabic. Some of this stuff is phonetic which is indicative of someone who has a familiarity with spoken Arabic but not written fluency. The title of papers by Wachner and Ostergaard are always in English but that may simply be to ensure they're talking about the same document, avoiding something getting lost in translation, if you will. There are a couple of different dialects here. Take the person who signed his emails 'AA', who I assume is this Abu Almawt guy. His Arabic is very classical, educated. He writes in the Arabic equivalent of the Queen's English. I would bet he's Egyptian or a formally educated person at the very least. Al-Rafah I assume is the guy who signed his with AK. He's used the nom de guerre Alkawbra—the Cobra—since forever. He was either too stupid or too vain to change it. His reflects a less-educated, street version of Arabic with lots of slang."

"Not that it matters anymore now," John added with a smirk before exchanging high fives with Magne.

Sarah shot him a dirty look for interrupting her. "If you boys are finished playing with yourselves? That leaves us with two more distinctive writing styles. The person who signed his or her correspondence as AT is from the Maghreb, based on the linguistic style, but I can't tell if that's Morocco, Tunisia, Algeria, or Libya. They also appear educated based on the use of technical terms, maybe a doctor or some sort of technician, but definitely educated. The last one was confusing to me and may be an amalgam of two people. One is definitely Arab and fairly well educated. The writing style reflects a Levantine dialect or education; probably Lebanese but might also be Northern Syria or even Israeli Arab. That person signs their correspondence AF or sometimes KKAF. The other person using that same address is definitely not Arab. He uses mostly anglicized Arabic or English and signs his correspondence KK. I don't know what the initials stand for, maybe a true name or maybe a nom de guerre."

Rusty asked, "Can you say if one of these people is Ostergaard?"

"No, sir."

"Well, what about the email addresses? What do they tell us?"

Hans answered, "Not much. They use a variety of free email services from around the world. The email addresses appear to be randomly generated—all twelve characters long with letters, numbers, and special characters. I ran them through Wise Owl but there were no identifiable patterns or possible matches anywhere. When sending texts, they're using anonymizers to disguise the point of origin. I pulled metadata from some which indicated they originated in Iceland, France, Turkey, Japan, Egypt, Jordan, India, and Saudi Arabia. I don't buy it, though. I think they're running their emails through different servers and VPNs to disguise their locations. Most are in mainland Europe and the Middle East, probably to avoid NSA and GCHQ. I tracked a couple back to European university networks but I think that's simply because they tend to have more open portals to exploit. If I could get into an SMS stream while they're texting I might be able track them down, but all the messages we've seen were single texts sent out with no immediate responses; no conversations. Whoever these people are, they're pretty damn good. They aren't exactly hiding, but they're the proverbial needle in the haystack. It's like saying, 'Okay, I know he's at the Super Bowl,' but by the time you get there, the game's over."

Rusty sat back in his chair and put his feet up on the conference table. "Well, shit. For now, we've hit a dead end. I think our only real option is to talk to Ostergaard."

Nigel asked, "Since he appears to be up to his eyeballs in this shit, why don't we . . . well, you know, do what we do?"

"I understand your sentiment but you're missing a couple of things—we don't know if he is actually up to his eyeballs in this shit and we don't know what this shit actually is. Let's assume for the sake of argument that the man is a Muslim convert. So what? Last time I checked there were damn near two billion Muslims on this planet, almost all of whom are just regular folks. The fact that his papers showed up on Al-Rafah's hard drive doesn't necessarily mean anything either. Wachner's paper did too. I don't think he's a terrorist. From what Hans tells me, half the porn stars in Europe were also on Al-Rafah's computers. You going after them too?"

Nigel was contrite. "Yeah, I see your point." He then smiled. "But if you need someone to interview those porn stars, John and I volunteer." John eagerly raised his hand and nodded vigorously.

Sarah snorted, "You guys are such pigs."

John shot back, "Oh, like if Brad Pitt was on that hard drive you wouldn't be willing to chat him up?"

"No." She smiled sheepishly and added, "Now, if it was Ryan Reynolds. . . ."

Rusty got up and said, "Okay kids, I think we should plan on talking to this guy."

Nigel volunteered, "I'll do it!"

"You're too eager. I think it should be Sarah; this is her area of expertise. But I don't want you going alone. Take one of the boys with you."

She nodded and said, "Hans or Magne in case he pretends he doesn't speak English."

"Take Magne. I have something I need Hans to do here."

"You got it, boss. We'll leave in the morning."

* * *

Magne and Sarah flew to Copenhagen on their St. Kitts and Nevis passports. Their cover for being in Denmark was simple: they were two of the beautiful people on vacation. Anyone who saw them together would believe it. Tall, blonde, and athletic, Magne was also an extremely handsome man. And Sarah? She was simply stunning and dressed like she just stepped off a runway in Milan or Paris.

Their task was to find Andreas Ostergaard and figure out what his story was. Nigel and Magne had found a lot of damning evidence but it was circumstantial at best. At this point it wasn't clear if he was a modern version of Josef Mengele, a dupe, or an innocent bystander. Nigel was convinced he was the former but Magne was more skeptical.

They had found out where he lived from Danish tax records. He owned a two-bedroom apartment not far from the University of Copenhagen, but since it was in the middle of a workday they assessed their best bet would be to catch him at his office on campus. The University of Copenhagen was a very old institution with several campuses scattered throughout the city. Ostergaard worked within the Faculty of Health and Medical Sciences in the cavernous Panum Institute Building on Blegdamsvej across from Amorparken. They'd found his office number in the university's directory. Sarah and Magne walked into the building like they belonged there, and while they turned some heads, no one questioned them.

The building was large and it took them some time to find the right wing. As they walked down a long corridor, Magne pointed to a sign on the wall and translated, "The Novo Nordisk Center for Protein Research."

Sarah commented, "Proteins? As in prions? I'd say we're in the right place." They continued down the hall until they came to Ostergaard's office. Peeking in, they found an empty desk in the outer office. Beyond it was an open door leading to an inner office. There sat a pale, thin, dark-haired man eating a sandwich. It had to be Ostergaard. Sarah stepped back and said to Magne, "Why don't we let me try this alone."

Magne was taken aback. "Why? Don't you think I can handle this?"

"No, of course not. That's not the problem."

"Then what is?"

"While you're handsome and charming, you also look like a goddamn Viking whereas I can pass as an Arab. If he's a convert or even just a sympathizer, I think he'd be less likely to open up to a prototypical Nordic demigod than an Arab woman."

Magne ignored her flattery but couldn't argue with her logic. "You mean a beautiful and sexy Arab woman." She just smiled and shrugged in tacit agreement. "Okay, you have a point. It's not like you really need me for protection. God help him if he were foolish enough to attack you. So, what am I supposed to do in the meantime?"

"Wait here until we know that he speaks English, Arabic, or German. If he does, then go check out his apartment. See what you can find out. If he's here, then we know he's not there. We found nothing indicating he had a roommate or a girlfriend. Even if we're wrong, I'm sure you can charm your way out of it." This time it was Magne's turn to smile in tacit agreement with her.

"You mean with my Nordic demigod charm?" he said sarcastically. "Okay. Call me if you need anything. I won't be far. Otherwise, we'll meet back at the hotel."

Sarah took a moment to compose herself before tentatively entering the office. She meekly knocked on the door to the inner office and, donning a Lebanese accent, said, "Excuse me? I think I may be lost."

Andreas Ostergaard peered up and his expression said it all; he was stunned to see a tall exotic woman standing in his office. Andreas asked in English, "Uh, can I help you?" Out in the hall, Magne smiled to himself, turned, and walked back down the corridor. *That poor guy will never know what hit him.*

Sarah smiled and asked, "Uh, yes. Are you Dr. Ostergaard?"

"Why, yes. I'm Andreas Ostergaard." He got up and walked around his desk and said nervously, "Please have a seat. How can I help you?" He probably lived in his office. He was pale to the point of looking sickly. He wore a wrinkled white button-down shirt over wrinkled black pants. His hair was greasy and unkempt.

"You're too kind." Sarah extended her hand and he shook it. *Not a fundamentalist anyway.* She scanned the office. There was a computer on the credenza behind him but the screen saver was on, so she couldn't see what he'd been working on. The shelves on either side of the computer were filled with textbooks and journals. There was a long table along the wall on the left and a window to the right. The table was completely filled with stacks of papers, folders, and notebooks. Above it was a large bulletin board with photos of splotch-covered petri dishes, fuzzy electron microscope images of viruses, and drawings of other microbes. Most of the notations were in Danish but a couple were in English: *Influenza A subtype H1N1 (1918)* and *Influenza A subtype H5N1 (bird).* On the opposite wall next to the window was a large whiteboard covered with indecipherable scribblings.

"So, Miss. . . ."

"Al-Kouri. Meena Al-Kouri. I'm Mohammad's cousin, the one he told you was coming. He did contact you, right?"

Andreas was obviously confused. "I'm sorry, Mohammad? Mohammad who? Al-Kouri?"

"No. silly. Mohammad Al-Qatani, you and he worked together in Cairo. You wrote a paper together on some animal disease. He did call you to say I was coming, didn't he?"

"Uh, no. He didn't. Haven't spoken to anyone in Cairo for some time."

Feigning surprise and embarrassment, Sarah cried, "Oh my, he really didn't call you?" Andreas shook his head. "Oh, how embarrassing. I'm so sorry to barge in on you like this. I thought you were expecting me! I guess I should have called, but I didn't have your number. When I told Mohammad I was coming to Copenhagen, he insisted I ring you up and said he would call to let you know. He spoke very highly of you. In fact, I think he idolizes you a little bit. Anyway, he said I should seek you out, so here I am. I hope it's not an inconvenient time."

Andreas was still reeling and trying to process what was going on. He didn't remember anyone named Al-Qatani but then a swarm of Egyptian graduate students had helped with that project. He hadn't bothered to learn all their names but there had to be at least one Mohammad in the bunch. *There was that one kid who was always hanging around. Was that him?* Standard operating procedure in academia was, for anyone from the graduate student who cleaned the glassware to the head of the department, to try to get their name attached to as many academic papers as possible. Most contributed little to the actual work, but Andreas tended to include them. Being a young researcher himself, he was especially sympathetic to the grad students' need to "publish or perish." Andreas didn't want to appear rude so he just went with it. "Uh, yeah. I think I remember your cousin but it was several years ago. How is he doing?"

"Oh, he's fine. He graduated and is working in Saudi Arabia. He hates it there, but they pay well."

"When was this, did you say?"

"Sometime around 2013 or 2014, I think." Sarah had done her research. If he checked his old papers, he would find an "M. Al-Qatani" way down on the list of coauthors.

Ostergaard sat on the corner of his desk, trying to act nonchalant, and asked, "So, are you interested in virology or protein expression?"

"Oh, goodness no. To be honest, Mohammad's research didn't interest me at all. I can't even begin to understand it. I'm here to study political science. I'm at the City Campus but was out here so I looked you up. If I didn't at least once, Mohammad would be angry with me. He's like a brother to me so I can't disappoint him." She glanced around the office and out his window. "Not much of a view." Pretending to peruse the books in the credenza behind him, Sarah leaned over him so he could peek down her blouse. "That's a lot of books. Have you read them all?"

Seeing her black bra under her shirt, he gulped audibly. "Uh, yes I have. I even wrote one of them."

He was now trying to impress her. "So, what do you do for fun?"

"I'm sorry, what?"

"Fun," she repeated. "You know what fun is, don't you?" She was being mildly flirtatious to see how he'd respond. "I don't know anyone or any of the nightspots yet. Are there any clubs you'd recommend?"

His mood changed quickly, becoming more formal. "I'm afraid we don't go out much and we don't drink alcohol."

"We?"

"Yes, my wife and I."

Sarah was surprised, genuinely this time. "I'm sorry. Mohammad never said anything about a wife. I didn't mean to be so forward. I thought you were . . . you know, available."

Ignoring her last comment, Ostergaard said, "We married later. Mohammad wouldn't have known about her."

"Well, maybe I could meet her. A woman new to a city needs a girl-friend. What's your wife's name?"

Ostergaard replied, "Nura." *Looking like that, I don't think you'll have a problem meeting people.* "She's my secretary. She stepped out for lunch just before you arrived. I'm surprised you didn't run into her."

A bit of panic flashed over Sarah. *If his wife went home for lunch, she might run into Magne!* In a playfully scolding manner, she said, "You don't take lunch with your wife? Shame on you!"

Ostergaard replied, "I do. She's picking up some soup from the cafeteria downstairs."

Sarah felt better now. "So, Nura? Is that a common name in Denmark?"

"No. She's not from here. We met overseas."

"I didn't think so. Nura is an Arabic name. Did you meet during your trip to Cairo?"

Ostergaard replied cautiously, "Something like that."

Pretending to be a bit flighty, Sarah continued, "Well, I know there are lots of handsome Danish men here. Maybe Nura can teach me how find a rich, smart husband like you."

"Perhaps." He smiled. *Arab women all seem to want European men. I would gladly move to the Middle East if I could have her as a second wife.*

"If you don't mind me asking, how did your family accept your wife? I assume they are Christians and she a Muslim. I mean, was that a problem? I don't know what my father would say if I wanted to marry a Christian."

"Well, my parents passed away some time ago and I converted to Islam, so it wasn't a problem for Nura's family."

"Well, good for you. No issues then." As she said this, the outer office door opened and a surprised Nura entered. She was a thin and plain young Arab woman, maybe in her early to mid-twenties. She wore a black hijab and ankle-length black dress. She was maybe five feet two inches tall. At almost six feet, the glamorous Sarah towered over her. When it came to women, Ostergaard had definitely taken a step down from Jazmin, the pretty girl in the Facebook photos. At the same time, there was an odd familiarity about Nura she couldn't place.

Nura walked into her husband's office carrying two small brown paper bags and two cups of soup. Glaring at Sarah and then him, she asked meekly, "Excuse me, my husband? Who is this?"

Before Andreas answered, Sarah stuck her hand out and said, "Hi, I'm Meena Al-Kouri. Your husband worked with my cousin in Egypt. I was asked to ring him up when I got to Copenhagen. You must be Nura. Dr. Ostergaard was just talking about you."

Seeing the glamorous woman alone with her husband, jealously welled up in Nura and she had trouble tamping it back down. "Then you should know it is not proper for a Muslim woman to be alone with a man who is not a close family member."

Sarah took a step back. "I know and I apologize, but we are not in the Middle East, we are in Europe, and 'when in Rome' as they say."

"I don't say that. A good Muslim stays true to the one faith regardless of where they are. Andreas and I live in Denmark but we don't drink alcohol and we don't eat pork. What is *haram* is always *haram*. That is what the Koran teaches." Nura was uncomfortable.

"Of course, you're right. I meant no disrespect. Before coming here, I was not even aware that Dr. Ostergaard was married, let alone to a Muslim woman. I was also unaware he had converted. Again, my sincere apologies."

Nura responded calmly, "It would appear your cousin didn't know my husband was well as he thought."

In a mildly scolding tone, Andreas interjected, "Now, now, Nura. That was a long time ago. Before you and I ever met. And I have only just met Miss Al-Kouri a few moments ago. I'm sure she meant no disrespect."

Turning to her husband, Nura said, "I just think of those Cairo elitists. They profess to be Muslims but they long to live like the Europeans and dress like whores." Turning to Sarah she added, "Not that I am comparing you to them. I am sure your intentions are honorable and just."

Sarah knew that was exactly was Nura was doing, and she was starting to get mad at this little halfling of a woman. Knowing it would not help her mission, she took a breath to calm down. "Nura, I think you and I have gotten off on the wrong foot. Had I known your husband was a Muslim and married, of course I would have called on you first. As for my outfit, yes, I like nice clothes. I'd bet you do too. I wear the hijab at home in Beirut but I dress like this in Europe so as not to draw attention to myself. The Europeans tend to judge us much more than others. Jews can wear their skullcaps, but we get harassed for wearing a simple hijab."

Nura was not totally convinced but calmed down. "I apologize for my outburst. I did not intend to embarrass you or my husband. Living under the constant scrutiny of the infidels has made me a bit on edge." As she said this, Nura studied Sarah's face and looked her up and down. "So, you are from Beirut? I thought I picked up an accent."

Sarah smiled and asked, "Are you from Beirut? I assumed you were from Cairo. Your accent is so . . . classical."

Nura gave a hint of a smile. "No, I'm Palestinian, but I was educated in Beirut. What part of the city are you from?" The question was more than just small talk; she was probing for information.

Sarah was cautious now. She didn't want to make a slip and undermine her cover. "I grew up in Raz Beirut. My family is in shipping. What part of the city are you from?"

"Shatila."

Sarah paused to digest what she had learned. Shatila was a Palestinian refugee camp and the site of an infamous 1982 massacre where the Phalange, a local militia aligned with Israel, killed hundreds of Palestinian refugees. "Where did you go to university?"

Nura replied, "Beirut Arab University. And you?"

"I studied Political Science at Université Libanaise. What was your field of study? Biology like your husband?"

"No, computer engineering." Nura instantly regretted saying this. She was providing too much information but she wanted Sarah to know she wasn't just some uneducated housewife; that they were on the same level.

Sarah sensed Nura's jealousy but needed to win her over. "How impressive! I could never do something like that. I just don't have that kind of intelligence. Your family must be extremely proud of you. I was never taken seriously, not even by my own family."

Nura recomposed herself and dialed back her aggression a bit. "But you are so beautiful. That certainly helps open doors."

Sarah smiled at her and said, "Maybe, but with most men, they only want to open the bedroom door. You are lucky to have a husband who respects you. You will have brains and respect long after my looks fade. Besides, you are much prettier than you give yourself credit for." Nura actually smiled at this.

"Husband, may I speak to you in private for a moment?"

Andreas nodded. Leaving Sarah in the office, they walked out to Nura's desk and closed the door behind them. There was a muffled conversation so Sarah couldn't discern what they were saying. She took out her cell phone and quickly took pictures of the whiteboard, bulletin board, contents of the bookshelves, and as many of the papers on the adjoining table as possible before the door opened again. Ostergaard came in alone and Sarah assumed she was about to get the bum's rush. Andreas said, "I'm sorry, but my wife and I have a lot of work to do this afternoon so I'm afraid we must excuse ourselves." *Here it comes.* "Nura wanted me to ask if you are available to come to our home tonight for dinner at 6 p.m. so we can show you the appropriate hospitality?"

Sarah was genuinely surprised and it took her a moment to answer. "Uh, yes. That would be lovely! I would like your opinions on the city, your recommendations on a mosque, shopping, and the like. Can I bring anything tonight?"

Andreas smiled, "No. Just yourself." He handed Sarah a slip of paper. "Here is the address. We will see you then."

* * *

While Sarah talked to Ostergaard, Magne made his way to his apartment. It was located in an older residential block west of the university. It was an unremarkable building but close to his office. The building was home to young families and college students, and had no real security. He walked up to the second floor and found Ostergaard's door. He pulled out his cell phone and pretended to be talking to someone as the lady from next door walked by. She gave Magne a suspicious glare but grinned like a schoolgirl when he smiled at her. She stopped after a few feet, turned, and said, "The Ostergaards are at work if that's who you're looking for." *Ostergaards? Plural?*

Magne put his phone away. "Yes, I just found that out. Thank you. Andreas isn't answering his phone either. I'll just leave him a note." He started rummaging around in his satchel for a pad of paper and pen. She continued on her way and turned to go down the stairs but took one last look as he began scribbling on the pad. As she disappeared from view, Magne put the pad back in his satchel and removed a lockpick set from his jacket pocket. He examined the lock and then removed two picks. Within seconds, he was in. He cautiously shut the door behind him. The apartment was quiet; no sign of its occupants.

He began walking through the apartment searching for anything unusual. This was not a bachelor pad. It was neat and tidy. The furniture and knick-knacks were indicative of a female presence. He checked out the kitchen. There were a wide range of utensils and the pantry was full of staples: rice, flour, sugar, cooking oil, pasta. There were also fresh vegetables hanging in wire baskets and a bowl of eggs on the counter. Whoever lived here cooked. He checked the refrigerator and cabinets—no beer, no wine, no alcohol of any kind.

Magne walked into the master bedroom. There was an armoire in the corner full of women's clothing—a wool winter coat, boots, a few dark dresses, simple shoes, and scarves—all black or dark colors. The small closet held simple men's clothing—a couple of cheap suits, some boring shirts, and cheap, double knit slacks. There were no paintings or artwork on the walls except two pieces of framed calligraphy. Magne knew Arabic and could read them. The first read, "There is no God but Allah." But the second read, "We swear by the Quran and Sunnah, and we will not compromise with any infidel." *Cheery group. Maybe Nigel was right about this guy after all.*

On the nightstand was a photo of Ostergaard and an Arabic woman. He peered closer and determined it was not a picture of the girl, Jazmin, they'd seen on Ostergaard's old Facebook page. Though there were some similarities, this one was plainer and much more serious. She was smiling, but it was forced. There was a dresser opposite the bed. The drawers contained men's and women's underwear, socks, and other clothing. Buried under the man's socks he found a couple of photographs of Andreas in happier times. The first was of him and the pretty Arab girl, Jazmin. It was a printout of one of the pictures on his old Facebook page. Both were smiling broadly and appeared very much like a couple in love. The second photo was of Ostergaard with a huge Great Dane dog. In the photo he was much younger and he was beaming as the dog licked his face. A favorite pet? Certainly not a current one—no dog dish, no dog food in the kitchen, no dog bed. *Don't Muslims see dogs as impure? He sure seemed to love this one. Did he get rid of it to be in line with his new religion? Or to appease a new, more pious wife?*

The second bedroom was made up as a guest room but had a laptop computer on a small desk in one corner. The computer appeared to be a top-of-the-line Acer. Connected to it with cables were a printer/scanner and a backup hard drive. The back of the printer had been altered and its wireless connection disabled. The computer wasn't connected to anything else—no fiber optic or Ethernet cables coming from the wall, no external mouse, not even a power cord—except for one device. Behind the computer was a very short USB cable connected to a mobile cellular hotspot. He tapped the computer keyboard but nothing happened. It wasn't asleep, it was off. He turned on the computer and waited for it to boot up. When the screen came on, a dialogue box popped up: "Enter Password" *Damn.* He wouldn't try to log in. Anyone who went to this much trouble to isolate the machine probably had security software that alerted the owner to any unauthorized access attempts. He went through the desk drawers but there was nothing besides a couple of pencils and some printer paper. Next to the desk was a small black shredder. He glanced inside the bin but it was empty. The residue was tiny. This was a high-end shredder and any documents destroyed wouldn't be recoverable.

He checked the living room one more time and the bathroom, but other than a couple of prayer rugs in the small coat closet, he found nothing out of the ordinary. There was a small patio off the living room but a quick glance revealed only a couple of chairs, a small glass table, and a shisha pipe. He took out his cell phone and recorded video as he walked through the apartment one last time. He took separate photos of the laptop and all the related equipment making sure to get a close-up of the cellular hot spot and all its identifying information. He slipped back out into the deserted hallway. Using his picks, he locked the dead bolt and left.

* * *

On the way back to the hotel, Magne stopped off and picked up some beer. He didn't expect to be working again that night. He walked up to the front desk and asked, "Do you have a package for room 1217?"

The man behind the counter checked his computer and said, "Yes, I do. Can I see an ID, please?" Magne showed him his passport and the man briefly disappeared in the back before returning with a small but heavy DHL box. Magne gave the man a five-euro tip and proceeded to the elevators.

Once back in their suite, Magne ripped open the box and dumped out its primary contents: a Sig Sauer P226 9 mm pistol with a threaded barrel. He reached deeper into the box and pulled out a matching SRD9 suppressor wrapped in a cloth, a yellow envelope containing three 10-round magazines loaded with hollow points, and a small tactical knife in a soft plastic sheath. Sarah walked in from the bedroom and upon seeing the gun quipped, "I see your boyfriend Nigel sent you a present."

"Don't worry, he thought of you too." He tossed the sheathed knife over his shoulder toward the sound of her voice and she instinctively snatched it from the air.

She snapped, "Asshole!"

"Just testing your reflexes." He turned to her. She was only partially dressed. She was barefoot and wearing the same skirt from that morning, but from the waist up, she was only wearing a thin black bra. "Jesus, Sarah. Put some damn clothes on, will ya." He didn't mind seeing her that way, of course, but it was distracting and he was trying to remain professional.

"I didn't know you were here. I'm sorry if you're offended by the human form but I'm steaming my blouse in the shower. I'm going to need it again and it was wrinkled."

"You are? For what?"

She smiled. "Ostergaard and his wife have invited me to dinner tonight. Hospitality extended to the cousin of an old friend."

"What?"

"I convinced him I was the cousin of a former fellow researcher. I just pulled a name off one of his old research papers. He fell for it. It turns out he's married—to an Arab girl. His wife, Nura, works as his secretary. She interrupted us in his office. I think she was pissed at first but warmed to me eventually."

Magne flipped through the photos on his phone until he came to the picture of Ostergaard and the dour Arab girl. "Was this her?"

Sarah stared at the photo. "Yes, that's her. I take it you got into their apartment then. Anything of interest?"

"Not really. A couple of prayer rugs and framed sayings from the Koran. I'd say either he's a convert or she's twice as devout as the average girl."

"He is. He told me. She's Palestinian from Shatila. She has a degree in computer science. She seems pretty sharp. Must suck being stuck as his secretary. She was submissive, like a good little Arab wife, but I sensed there is more to her than meets the eye."

"Well you know what they say, an Arab woman walks two paces behind her husband so he can have a running start inside the door when his wife goes to kick his ass." Magne showed her some more photos from inside the apartment. "Look what I found in his sock drawer."

She exclaimed, "Wow, that's a big fucking dog." Peering at the next, she said, "Is that . . . Jazmin?"

"Yeah. That same photo was on his old Facebook page."

Sarah asked rhetorically, "Why would she let her husband keep a photo of his ex-wife in his sock drawer?"

Magne laughed. "You're the girl. I thought you could tell me. If she's that submissive, she may not be in a position to challenge him."

"I can't believe she doesn't know about it. She struck me as the jealous type."

Magne pointed out, "Well, it was *you*. Most women would be jealous."

Sarah smirked at him. "I'm serious, Magne. You should have met this chick. If that photo is there, I suspect it's because she said it was okay. He tried to come off as large and in charge. I suspect in actuality he's a complete mouse."

"Well, maybe you can find out tonight. What time is dinner?"

"Six. I need to get moving."

Magne shot back, "You mean *we* need to get moving. I'm not letting you go alone."

"You're not invited. I'll be fine without you."

"I'm going anyway. I'll wait nearby, in case anything happens."

He was determined and it wasn't worth the fight. It's not like she could complain to Travis or the other guys. They'd only side with Magne. They were always so protective of her. "Suit yourself."

* * *

Sarah arrived exactly at six o'clock and knocked on the door. She had actually arrived a few minutes early to recon the building—no controlled access, halls were narrow with no hidden recesses or alcoves for cover. She also determined which windows belonged to the Ostergaards' apartment. She took notice of the small balcony with larger windows to either side. She glanced at the peephole on the door and it got darker. Someone was looking at her. Then the door opened. It was Nura, and she was actually smiling. Since she was inside her home, she had taken off her hijab and let her hair flow over her shoulders. She was wearing the same long black skirt but had changed to a white blouse. She had also applied a little makeup—an understated shade of lipstick and some eyeliner. She was actually cute. "Hi, Meena. Please, come in."

Sarah entered the apartment and handed Nura a bakery box. "I know you said not to bring anything but my mother would be ashamed if I showed up empty-handed. It's baklava. I am assured it's the best in town but I have yet to meet a European who can cook like an Arab."

Andreas walked up to greet her. "Hello, Meena. Ooh, is that baklava? I love Turkish pastry."

He started to grab the box but Nura playfully slapped his hand. "After dinner. And it's not Turkish, its Lebanese."

Sarah glanced around the apartment. It was just like Magne's video. "I forgot to ask if you have any children?"

Nura responded, "No. Allah has not chosen to bless us with offspring yet but someday soon, I hope. We are not having anything fancy. Roast lamb, baba ghanouj, Lebanese bread, and salad. Is that okay?"

"It sounds lovely—like home. I love your apartment. It's so cozy and inviting. Is there somewhere I can set my purse?"

Nura responded, "Of course, allow me. Please have a seat." She took Sarah's purse and hung it on a hook in the entryway closet while Andreas showed her to the table. Shouting from the living room, Nura added, "I hope you don't mind eating this soon. It gets dark here so early this time of the year that 8 o'clock feels like midnight."

Sarah sat at the table across from Andreas and adjusted her seat. "I don't mind at all. It all smells so good. I can't wait to taste it." She glanced at Andreas and caught a wide-eyed expression of surprise on his face before all went black.

When Sarah woke up, her head felt like she had been hit with a brick. She felt a small trickle of blood on the back of her neck but when she tried to touch it, she discovered that both her hands had been tied to the arms of the chair with neckties. In addition, electrical wire was wrapped around her torso, securing her firmly to the back of the chair. She was groggy, but her head was starting to clear. She heard muffled talking. She made out Andreas's panicked voice rambling on. "Why did you do that? Are you out of your mind? I was only talking to her, I swear. I never met her before today. You're going to get us arrested, or worse!" Clearly it was Nura who had hit her in the back of the head.

Nura's voice came from the next room. "You spineless idiot! She is not who she says she is. That whore bats her eyes at you and you fall groveling at her feet. You are so weak. You have compromised us and our work, you silly ass."

Andreas tried to defend himself. "I did nothing of the sort. She just showed up at my office. You know. You were there."

Nura's voice now had an air of authority to it; she was scolding her husband like a child. "Do you really think she's the cousin of some Egyptian graduate student? Moron! She played you for the fool you are."

"You don't know that. You are freaking out and overreacting, like you do about everything."

"Just watch her."

Sarah finally opened her eyes. Andreas stood across from her in the kitchen pacing nervously back and forth across the small room. When she stirred, he shouted, "She's waking up!"

Nura walked into the room carrying Sarah's purse. She pulled out Sarah's wallet. "Look at this, Andreas! No identification. No credit cards. But she has a hotel room key. I thought she lived here, Andreas. She's a student, right? No student ID." She threw the wallet on the table and then dumped out the rest of the purse's contents and with it the knife. She picked it up and unsheathed it. Running her finger over the blade, she said, "Sharp," before jamming it into the surface of the table in front of Sarah. "How do you explain that, Andreas?"

Sarah moaned and said, "Self-protection. What do you think I have it for?"

"To kill us, you bitch!" Nura shot back.

Sarah grimaced, "Nura, if I was going to kill you, why wouldn't I just shoot you with a gun? Or stab you as soon as you opened the door? Andreas, please talk some sense to your wife. I don't think she is well."

With that, Nura slapped her hard across the face. "Shut up, whore."

Andreas was starting to panic again. "Oh my God. What are we going to do? We're going to get caught."

Sarah asked, "Get caught for what? Me? This?" She stared him in the eye and said, "Let me go and I won't tell anyone. I promise."

He was only half listening and mumbling incoherently to himself. Nura shouted, "Get ahold of yourself. I can handle this. Remember why we're doing all this."

Nura was clearly in charge and Sarah needed to change the dynamic. Turning to Andreas she said, "You're doing this for Jazmin, aren't you? Who could blame you? She was the love of your life. When she died, you had to settle . . . for Nura." That drew another vicious slap from Nura but Sarah continued. "Jazmin was a sweet person. Do you really think she would want you to do this?"

Nura punched her in the gut. "Don't you ever talk about my sister."

"Sister? Well that explains it. He felt some obligation to you and your family. Why else would he marry you? Jazmin at least had fun. Was she fun, Andreas? More fun than this little mouse?"

Nura was about to punch her again. "What did you say? What did you call me?"

Sarah spit blood from her split lip on Nura's white blouse. "A little mouse." She expected another punch or slap and was surprised when it didn't come.

Nura left the room and Andreas sat down in the chair directly across from Sarah. He was staring blindly into space. He was almost catatonic. Sarah was struggling against her bindings when Nura returned with a cell phone in one hand and a small pistol in the other. She was preoccupied and glared at Sarah with a mix of hatred and fear. She dialed the phone and after a few seconds someone answered. "Hello, it's me. I know, I know I am never to call you on this line but call me back on a safe phone. Immediately!"

They waited in silence for the phone to ring. After a few minutes, Andreas had recomposed himself and asked Nura, "Who do you think she is? Danish police?"

"No," she said confidently, "she's Israeli." Andreas's eyes got wide and Sarah just snorted indignantly as if to say "bullshit." Nura continued, "You see, my husband, she doesn't remember me but I remember her. It was in Gaza, many years ago. Before you met Jazmin. I was very young, but I never forgot her face. She was just so damn pretty. I just couldn't quite recall from where. Then she called me 'mouse.' She worked at a café near our house. I used to go there with my parents and Jazmin. I never forgot the beautiful waitress who called me 'little mouse' and asked why she would be working in Gaza? I told her she should be in the movies or in a Paris fashion show. Do you remember me now?" Sarah ignored her questions.

Andreas was shocked. "You mean she's Mossad?"

"Maybe. But I think she is Mista'avrim, their special counterterrorism unit. They're trained to look, talk, and act like Arabs so they can infiltrate us. They are the ones who killed my father and your wife. They are the ones who killed Jazmin." Andreas stared at Sarah with wide eyes. He couldn't believe what he was hearing.

Sarah shrugged. "Well, technically I didn't kill your sister. The Israeli Air Force did. For what it's worth, your father was supposed to be traveling alone."

Nura was about to hit her again when the phone rang. She answered. The conversation was one-sided and in Arabic but Sarah got what was going on. "I know, I know. I'm sorry but we have a situation here. I have an Israeli Mista'avrim agent tied to a chair in my kitchen. . . . How do I know? Because I met her before in Gaza. Before my father was killed. . . . Of course, I'm sure, she's admitted as much. . . . I don't know how much she knows but she hasn't said or asked about anything remotely related to the plan."

Sarah shouted out, "You mean your plan to kill half the Jews in Israel? That plan? Yeah, we don't know anything about it at all."

Nura was angry and scared. The voice on the phone was telling her what to do and she didn't really want to do it. Finally, after a minute she said, "Yes, sir. I understand. We need to cauterize the wound. I will do what must be done."

Nura picked up the gun. She turned to Andreas with tears in her eyes. "I'm sorry but our mission is more important than any one person's life." The gunshot reverberated loudly in the small apartment. Across the table, Andreas clutched his throat as blood spurted through his fingers. The expression on his face told Sarah that he was as surprised as she was; well, maybe a little more.

Nura turned to Sarah, and asked, "What do you know about what we are doing and who told you?" As she said this, there were two dull 'thwacks' as silenced rounds blasted through the lock plate on the front door. Nura instinctively turned in the direction of the noise just as Magne Berge came crashing through the door. She raised her pistol and fired wildly in his direction. Immediately, Sarah pivoted in her chair, leaned back and kicked Nura in the small of the back, causing her to lurch forward while Sarah fell over backward and against the wall. Nura immediately ran for the bedroom and slammed the door behind her. Magne heard her locking it and then a loud thump. He immediately charged the door. It flexed but didn't open. She had blocked it with the armoire.

Magne turned his attention to Sarah but she was already free from her restraints. "Weren't you tied up?"

"I was, but I loosened them a while ago. I would've taken them off sooner, but I was hoping they'd say something useful."

"Did they?"

Sarah got up and moved toward the bedroom. "Not yet. We were interrupted." Immediately there was a crash of breaking glass. Magne and Sarah together tried to force the door only to be met by two bullets blasting through from the inside and narrowly missing their heads. Sarah ran to the balcony just in time to see Nura land on the roof a black Mercedes that was parked below her bedroom window. She ran across the narrow street and jumped in a green Opel parked on the other side.

She started the car but before speeding away, she glared up at Sarah shouted in Arabic, "Fuck you, bitch."

Exasperated, Sarah came back in. "She's gone. The fucking bitch is gone. How's Ostergaard?"

Magne was kneeling over Andreas applying pressure to his bleeding neck with a dish towel. "Not good. He's bleeding out. I don't think he's going to make it."

Police sirens wailed in the distance. "We don't have much time."

Magne looked Andreas in the eyes. "You're dying. You don't want to be remembered this way. Tell us who else is involved in this." Andreas smiled at him with bloody teeth. "Jesus Christ, man. Your own fucking wife just shot you! No real need for loyalty here."

Andreas started to talk. Magne put his ear to the dying man's mouth. "I'll be with my Jazmin soon."

Sarah peered at Andreas just as the life left his eyes. "He's gone, and the police are on their way. We need to leave."

"Okay. I'm grabbing the laptop from the other bedroom."

Sarah replied, "Right. Nura was on a cell phone just before you broke in. I need it." Magne ran to the bedroom and Sarah looked around the kitchen until she found the phone on the floor under her overturned chair. The screen was cracked but it was otherwise in one piece. She put it, her wallet, the knife, and the other contents back in her purse.

Magne returned with the laptop. He handed her the backup hard drive. "Here. Put this in your purse." As she did, he said, "The neighbors are starting to get nosy. I don't think the hallway is our best option."

She shrugged. "Balcony?"

"Balcony." They went out on the balcony. He put the Sig Sauer in his belt and stuffed the laptop down the front of his pants. He climbed over the railing and dropped down on the top of an Audi parked below. Its car alarm immediately started blaring. Sarah jumped down after him and he helped her off the car. That's when he spotted the blood on the back of her neck. As they walked casually into the dark he asked, "How's your head?"

Gently feeling the gash in her scalp, she replied, "I gotta tell ya, it's been better. I think that bitch hit me with a frying pan. I mean, how clichéd is that?"

Checking her scalp, Magne said, "I think you need stitches."

"Well, I plan to check the minibar for a suture kit as soon as we get back."

CHAPTER FOUR
THE FNGS

Immediately after fleeing her apartment, Nura drove west in her green Opel before circling back east toward the Panum Institute on the University of Copenhagen's North Campus. There was something there that was vital for her to retrieve. If she didn't, everything she had worked for during the last five years would've been wasted. She didn't know what was going on back at her apartment but was sure the police were there already. This is Copenhagen, not Gaza; gunshots do not go unreported. She also had to assume that Meena—or whatever her real name was—and the big blond man who had burst through her door got away clean. She also assumed they were both Israeli and well-trained. She needed to leave fast lest they find her again.

She parked the Opel in a car park near the Rigshopitalet across the park from the Panum Institute. She found a spot between two large vans and backed in so her dirty front license plate was hidden in the shadow of the other vehicles. She opened the trunk of the car and removed a black backpack. She stripped off her dress and blouse and replaced them with tight-fitting jeans and a red T-shirt that she removed from a suitcase in the trunk. The T-shirt was low cut and accentuated her modest cleavage. She then donned a gray baseball cap and pulled it low to obscure her face while letting her hair flow over her shoulders. Just another young Danish coed. Nura checked the area for security and then headed southwest across the park. At the Institute, she avoided the main entrance off Blegdamsvej on the southeast side of the building. It was always manned by security guards. Instead, she walked down the ramp into the underground car park. Swiping her university badge, she entered the building and took the stairs up to the Center for Protein Research on the tenth floor.

She was out of breath after walking up ten flights of stairs, but she wanted to avoid any late-working coworkers and the security cameras that were in every elevator. There were other cameras in the stairwell, of course, but she kept her face down to avoid being seen. She expected the police to check the logs and discover that she entered the building, but they wouldn't find out where she went once inside. She always dressed very conservatively and wore a hijab at work, so by the time they grasped that the pretty young girl in the tight jeans, revealing T-shirt, and baseball cap was her, she'd be long gone.

She peeked through the narrow window on the stairwell door before entering the empty hallway. She walked quickly down the corridor to her and Andreas's office. The dim light coming through the window gave her enough to see. She opened the middle drawer of his desk and took his key-card and set of keys for the lab. As a secretary, she didn't have access to the labs, but he did—or had. He used the same password for everything: *Rufus*, the name of that damned Great Dane he had when they married. She'd made him get rid of the dog immediately. She said it was because in Islam dogs were considered "unclean" but in truth she just hated the brute and didn't want to take care of it. She exited the office and continued down the hall. When she came to the laboratory, she paused. She put her ear to the door; it was quiet inside. Using Andreas's key card and password, she entered. The lab was deserted and dark save for a handful of lights that stayed on all the time for safety reasons. This was plenty for her purposes.

It took her a few minutes to locate the right freezer. There were several in the room and though Andreas had showed it to her once, she didn't rec-ollect which one it was. She read the sign-in sheets on the freezer doors until she found her husband's name. *Got it!* The Eppendorf CryoCube freezer didn't appear that much different than a large home refrigerator, except this one came with a lock, had a fancy control panel, and cost over $20,000. She used his keys to unlock it, and a fog of super-chilled −80° Celsius air rolled out when she opened it. She didn't really know what she was searching for. Inside the freezer were racks containing brown cardboard sample boxes.

Some contained slides while others contained tissue samples or vials of frozen liquid. There had to be a hundred boxes, and they were identified only by a lot number or other coded information scribbled on the end. She started to panic. *How am I going to find it?* She took a deep breath. She had time; no one knew she was there. Starting in the upper right-hand corner, she began methodically reading the ends of the sample boxes searching for a clue. Most were marked with some sort of logging system—two letters followed by a four-digit number—and all were out of order. Others included the name of the primary researcher or the name of a city and a date. For a bunch of brilliant scientists, the freezer was an unorganized mess. At the very bottom of the second column she found it: "Osterg. RUFUS." *That goddamn dog again.*

If Nura touched anything inside the freezer, the extreme cold would burn her skin. She glanced around and found a pair of fancy oven mitts. She put them on, carefully removed the sample box, and put it on a nearby table. She gently opened it to inspect its contents. Inside were two vials labeled only BS1 and BS2. She recognized them immediately; they contained the modified influenza viruses that she and Andreas had been working five years to develop and grow. She breathed a sigh of relief. *We're not done yet.*

In the corner of the lab was a smaller chest freezer labeled *"Tøris"*—dry ice. She rummaged around in the cabinets until she found two small insulated foam shipping kits. She carefully placed each vial in its own small polystyrene inner box and gently packed them with paper towels to ensure they didn't move before taping the boxes shut. She placed each inside their insulated outer boxes and packed dry ice around them. This should ensure the samples stayed frozen for at least four days. She taped the two boxes shut and squeezed them into her backpack. She wiped down everything she touched for fingerprints. She'd never been fingerprinted before but expected the police would pull her fingerprints from her apartment, and she didn't want to make it too easy for them. Just as she started to leave, the door to the lab opened.

She ducked behind a fume hood just as the lights came on. There were footsteps but not voices. That probably meant the person was alone. She took a quick glimpse around the edge of the fume hood. At the workstation directly across from the door was a small, young Chinese woman. Nura recognized her as one of the graduate students at the center but didn't recall her name. There was no way to get out of the lab without being seen. She spotted a small fire extinguisher inside the fume hood. She quietly reached around and lifted it off its hook. It was maybe thirty centimeters long and six centimeters in diameter but fairly heavy. She carried it in her right hand and low to her side. She slid the backpack over her left shoulder as she stepped out into the open. "Oh, hi. I didn't think anyone was working tonight."

The Chinese girl turned with a gasp. "Oh, you startled me! I didn't think anyone was here since the lights were off." She squinted a bit as she stared at Nura, obviously trying to identify her. "Uh, who are you? I don't recognize you. What are you doing in the lab?"

Nura approached her keeping the fire extinguisher behind her leg. "I just needed to pick up something."

As she neared the Chinese girl asked, "Mrs. Ostergaard? Is that you? I didn't recognize you dressed . . . like that. And your hair!"

"Yes, it's me." She laughed. "I guess everyone thinks I dress formally all the time, but I don't. Andreas is working at home tonight and needed something from the lab. I offered to come down and pick it up for him. What are you doing here, Miss . . .?

"Chen, Michelle Chen. I'm working late too. I work with your husband's group but under Dr. Navarra. I don't mean to be difficult, but as clerical staff, you're not authorized to be in the lab unescorted. That's just institute policy."

Nura continued to walk toward her, "Yes. Ordinarily, you're right, but Andreas cleared it with the security office and I've got to check out with them when I leave. Can you check to make sure I grabbed the right notebook?" She started to slide the backpack off her shoulder and as Chen turned to look at it, Nura smashed her in the head with the fire extinguisher. Chen crashed to the floor, stunned. Nura dropped her backpack and, with all her might, hit Chen in the head two more times, crushing her skull with a sickening crack. Adrenaline had taken over. Her heart was racing and she was breathing hard, almost to the point of hyperventilating. She took a step back and gaped as Michelle Chen's body twitched involuntarily in its death throes. Nura took slow, deep breaths through her nose to help calm herself down. She had just killed her second person of the night. She had no regrets; Chen was just another infidel. She picked up her backpack to keep it from being enveloped in the expanding pool of blood oozing from Chen's lifeless body before putting the fire extinguisher back on its hook. She checked Chen's pockets and found a set of car keys. Stepping around Chen, she turned off the lights and left the lab. She locked the door behind her and calmly walked out the way she'd come in. In the Institute's underground garage, she pushed the "lock" button on Chen's keyless remote and a car chirped to her right. It was a small black Ford Fiesta that was a few years old and a little beat up. It was perfect. She'd be long gone before anyone found Chen's body and certainly before they figured out her car was missing.

Nura drove Chen's car back to the hospital and parked two spaces down from her Opel. In the trunk of the Opel were two small cheap suitcases full of clothes for her and Andreas and a black nylon bag tucked behind the spare tire. The latter was their bug-out bag. She dumped it out and took inventory. There was a purse, a large envelope, a cell phone and charger, a small notebook, and a Beretta Pico .380 pistol. The purse contained makeup, a hairbrush, tissues, loose change, a roll of mints, and a couple of sanitary pads. In the envelope were two stolen Belgian passports with Nura and Andreas's pictures in them, as well as two wallets. The woman's wallet had over three thousand euro in cash and a fake international driver's license in the name of Lila Renard, the same name on the passport. She took the money from the Andreas's wallet before tossing it and his passport back in the envelope. She put the gun, wallet, passport, and cell phone in the purse. The charger, notebook, and Andreas's money went in her suitcase. Everything else she left in the Opel. She locked the doors before tossing the keys down a storm drain. She had everything she needed to go on the run. She got in Chen's car and drove south and then west to Odense. Though it was quicker to drive through Lubeck, she wanted to avoid the ferry and its security. When Chen's body was found by the janitor at 6 a.m. the next morning, Nura—aka Lila Renard—was already in Germany.

* * *

S arah and Magne went back to the hotel to clean up. Upon closer inspection, the laceration on the back of her head was long but not too deep. No need for stitches. While she took a long hot shower to wash the matted blood out of her hair, Magne was in their suite's small kitchen rinsing the blood out of her clothes. As he took off his own dark brown leather jacket, he observed it had a considerable amount of blood splashed on it. He hadn't even noticed in the dark night. It wasn't his; it was from Andreas. Magne had apparently been on the receiving end of arterial spray from Andreas's neck wound as he applied pressure with the dish towel in his vain attempt to save him. Nura had hit his carotid artery when she shot him. *I guess that explains why he bled out so fast.* Magne used a whole bottle of hotel shampoo and most of the paper towels in the kitchen before he was satisfied. He hung up Sarah's shirt to dry and wiped down his leather coat with the last paper towels before stuffing them in a plastic bag with the others. He then took the suppressor off the Sig Sauer, wiped both down for prints, and put them in the bag with the bloody paper towels. As he finished, Sarah came out of the bathroom wearing a hotel robe. She had a sizeable knot on her head but at least it had quit bleeding. She spent the rest of the evening with an ice pack on her head and a drink in her hand.

Lifting the vodka rocks to her lips, she took a long pull on the drink. "Darling, I don't think the minibar supply is going to last. Can you call down for a bottle of vodka—Grey Goose if they have it—and a bottle of ibuprofen?"

Handing her another small bottle from the minibar, Magne said, "I'll go out. I need to get rid of the bloody paper towels and the gun anyway. Are there any bloody towels in your bathroom?"

"Just a washcloth. I hate dumping the gun. What a waste."

"Yeah, I know, but I put two in the lock plate. When they recover those slugs, I don't want to be holding a gun with matching ballistics. Just like I don't want to leave any of your blood in this hotel room that they might match to what's in the apartment."

"I know, it's just that Sigs are really good guns."

That night, Magne dumped the plastic bag in a commercial dumpster downtown before dropping the gun and suppressor from a bridge into the canal. Sarah drank most of the vodka before falling asleep. He relaxed and drank the beers he had bought that afternoon.

The next morning, Magne let her sleep in and once she stirred, he ordered them both breakfast from room service. Part of it was for show.

He wanted to reinforce their cover story of being a wealthy couple on holiday for the hotel staff in the event they were questioned. Sarah was much better but still had a raging headache. They flew out later in the afternoon. They were confident there was nothing to link them directly to Ostergaard's murder. The hallway had been dark when Magne encountered the neighbor. Sarah had slipped in clean. While there were cameras in the corridors of the Panum Institute, Sarah and Magne made a habit to never face them directly. There were none in Ostergaard's office.

Before leaving, Magne wanted to read what was being reported on the local news. The young professor being shot definitely made the news but the reporter implied it was a case of domestic violence. She mentioned police were searching for his wife and their car was missing. A neighbor had seen Nura flee the scene and was only too eager to point out that the wife was "one of those Arabs." Magne was confident no one was on to them; at least not yet. It would take the police some time to figure out that the bullet that killed Andreas and those in the door came from different guns. Magne collected the computer and backup drive from the apartment, along with Nura's cell phone, and sent them to Cyprus via DHL so they would have absolutely no incriminating materials on them.

Rusty had the jet so they flew commercial; still first class, of course, but commercial nonetheless. To cover their tracks, they booked tickets on the train to Hamburg under the same aliases they'd used at the hotel. They actually got on the train and had their tickets scanned by the conductor before getting off again. If anyone checked, they had gone to Germany. They then took a hired car across the Øresund Strait to Malmö, Sweden, and flew back to Cyprus from there.

* * *

Nura arrived in Hamburg, Germany, early in the morning. The overnight drive from Copenhagen had taken less than five hours. There had been some traffic on the E20 leaving Copenhagen but the E45 south of Kolding was deserted except for the truckers. While the adrenaline rush certainly helped her survive the night, she was now experiencing the inevitable crash that follows. She needed rest but didn't risk finding a hotel while driving a stolen car. The little Ford was running on fumes so she stopped in the small town of Christiansfeld for gas. She was also hungry; her encounter with Meena had ruined dinner and she hadn't eaten since lunch. After filling up and grabbing a bag of chips, she found a place to park on a quiet street and went to sleep. A barking dog woke her up just as the sun was starting to rise. She got out of the car to stretch. Her back hurt and her knees were sore from jumping out of the window. She glanced down at her shirt. It had several brownish splotches—Michelle Chen's blood. *I sure hope the gas station clerk didn't pick up on that.* She went to the trunk and changed into a clean shirt before moving on.

Once in Hamburg, she found a DHL office and waited in her car for it to open at 8 a.m. When it did, she went inside with her backpack. She took out the two boxes containing the vials of virus. She addressed them and paid to have them sent by overnight priority delivery. The clerk read the addresses and commented. "Tunis and Cairo. That's far away. What are you sending in such a rush?"

The man was just making small talk. Donning a French accent, Nura said, "Bull semen. For breeding. We sell the semen from our European cattle to the Arabs so they can breed better livestock."

The man chuckled. "Well, you don't hear that every day. Do you want insurance?"

"Yes. Five hundred euros on each." She didn't really want it but it looked better that she did.

"That much, huh? I'd imagine the bulls would be happy to provide replacements if they're lost."

Nura laughed. "I bet they would." She paid the man, thanked him, and left. As she walked out, she muttered under her breath, "Infidel pig."

She drove Chen's car to a parking garage near the Hauptbahnhof train station where she wiped it down for fingerprints and took off its license plates which she dumped in the nearest trash can. With luggage in tow, she walked to the station and into the women's restroom. She found the first vacant stall and changed her clothes. She put on tennis shoes, capri pants, and a tank top with a long-sleeve shirt over it. She also took off her bra so that her nipples were partially visible through her shirt. At the sink she brushed her teeth and put on deodorant. She produced a makeup kit from her luggage and expertly applied mascara, eyeliner, foundation, and lip gloss. Once she was done, plain Nura had been transformed into sexy Lila Renard, a Belgian girl on holiday. The transformation was nothing short of remarkable. Anyone searching for Nura wouldn't suspect Lila in a hundred years. She put her hair in a ponytail, packed up her luggage, donned a big pair of sunglasses, and caught the first train heading west.

Nura took full advantage of the Schengen Agreement and traveled from Denmark to France without anyone taking more than a cursory glance at her passport. She traveled first to Brussels. If anyone asked, she was a Belgian citizen going home. She arrived in Brussels in the late afternoon and once there booked a seat on the overnight train to Marseille. It had been less than forty-eight hours since her ill-fated meeting with Meena in Copenhagen. In that time, she had killed her husband; been in a shoot-out with a couple of Mossad agents; broken into a laboratory where she killed another person; stolen a car; transformed herself from a pious Muslim woman into a slutty Belgian tart; and traveled halfway across Europe on a stolen passport. She'd been a busy girl. Now she was in southern France about to depart for Algiers.

She opted not to push her luck by flying. Her passport was real but it was still stolen. It would hold up to a cursory inspection but the photo on the computers wouldn't match the one in her passport. Security on the ferry, especially the Algérie Ferries line, would be less rigorous. She booked a cabin on the El-Djazair II which wouldn't leave for another day. In the meantime, she found a hotel, took a long hot bath, ordered room service, and got some desperately needed sleep.

The trip from Marseille to Algiers took over twenty hours. The seas were a bit rough, and the motion of the ship made Nura nauseous. She was a desert girl, after all. Though Gaza was on the Mediterranean, she had never been on a boat before. After a few hours, her stomach settled down, and she began to appreciate being on the ocean with its fresh salty air. She had smelled that in Copenhagen, of course, but the Mediterranean smelled like home; or at least it did in her mind. What would the beaches in Haifa be like once they got rid of the Jews?

She got little sleep on the ferry. Maybe it was the ocean. Maybe it was the idea of being trapped in a steel box if something happened to the vessel.

Whatever the reason, she was happy when they pulled into port in Algiers. She changed her clothes and dressed more conservatively. She didn't wear a hijab since, officially, she was still a Belgian tourist. The city was vibrant and exciting. It wasn't as clean and sterile as those in Europe but along with its dust and smog came a more human quality; a sense that it was inhabited by people rather than robots. As much as she wished to take in the sights, she was on a mission and had to move on.

Despite being in a Muslim country, Nura couldn't risk flying, not this close to her objective. Even if she checked her bag, she risked someone discovering her Beretta. So, what should have been a four-hour flight would have to be a fifteen-hour ordeal. Since this final leg would be grueling, she splurged on a hotel for the night. Finally feeling safe, she got the best sleep she'd had in months. She also gorged herself on the local cuisine, enjoying Arab food cooked by real Arabs. While it wasn't the Levantine food she grew up on, it was still better than the tasteless pap that passed as Arab food in Denmark. The next day she packed her bag and bought a bus ticket for Annaba, Algeria. The nine-hour trip on the crowded bus played havoc on her back. She had gotten used to a cushy European existence. There was no bus service from Annaba to Ghardimaou, Tunisia, so she had to hire a car. There were plenty of options but her aching back made her opt for the old man in the comfortable Mercedes. She paid him in advance, which he appreciated, and he chatted with her for the whole two hours. As they approached the border, Nura asked nervously, "I forgot to get a Tunisian visa when I was in Algiers. Is that going to be a problem?"

The old man laughed. "No, of course not. You can get one here if you like but save your money. These guys know me. Just give me a couple of euros." She handed him the money. She was afraid that the guards might stop them and search the car. What would happen if they ran her passport on a computer? What if they found the gun in her luggage? All her worrying was for naught. The old driver was a regular on this route, and the Tunisian border guards took his money and just waved him through. When he dropped her at the train station she gave him an extra twenty euros, which was more than twice the cost of the eight-hour bus trip. He thanked her profusely for her generosity, but she considered it money well spent. She bought a ticket and waited for the train to Tunis. In four hours, she'd be ready to start the next phase of their operation to free Palestine from the Jews.

* * *

Cyprus was sunny and warm compared to Copenhagen. It was good to be home. Sarah and Magne had arrived late the night before so their friends let them sleep. There had been a good deal of concern over Sarah's injury, but before going to bed she assured them she was fine. The next morning, the DHL package with the computer and cell phone arrived and Hans got to work on it immediately. Magne hadn't slept at all on the plane. He stayed awake to monitor Sarah for any sign of concussion. Despite being thoroughly exhausted, he still woke up early out of habit. He briefed the others on what happened in Copenhagen and how close Sarah had come to getting killed. While they chastised him for letting her go in alone, they also agreed that there probably was no other choice given the situation.

Sarah finally got up around 10:00 a.m. Before she even got her first cup of coffee, John Kernan cornered her. He had been a corpsman in the SEALs and he insisted on examining her. She protested but gave in when all her other colleagues sided with John. They were very protective of her. John examined her wound, applied antibiotic, and put on a clean dressing. He also checked her blood pressure, pulse, and pupil reactions. A cognitive test indicated signs of a concussion but it was mild. She would be good as new in a couple of days.

They retired to the conference room for an after-action debrief. In Rusty's absence, Gunny Medina led the meeting. Talking to Sarah, he said, "Maggie has filled us in on his part of the op. Since you had all the personal contact with these two *pendejos*, why don't you give us the highlights?"

"Yeah, it was certainly not what I expected." Sarah spent the next forty-five minutes detailing her interactions with Andreas and Nura. She was very methodical and provided as much detail as she could. Even the most insignificant details could provide valuable insight. She provided her personal assessments of the couple as well. Her opinion of Nura changed completely after their run-in at the apartment; the mouse turned out to be the cat. When all was said and done, the team agreed that they'd dodged a bullet in Copenhagen.

Gunny asked, "What have we learned from the other electronics we recovered?"

Hans had been working on the computer and backup drive since they'd arrived. "I'm sorry to say, whoever was using these computers was good; too good for me. I don't want to have to keep running back to Dr. Williams every time we snatch electronics."

Gunny replied, "Yeah, we're working on that. Rusty thinks he has a solution. You guys were selected for the Praetorians for your special ops backgrounds, not your computer skills. It's nice that you're as good as you are, but it's not realistic to expect you to moonlight as computer geeks." He chuckled, "That's Rusty's job if anyone's."

Gunny was right but Hans still felt like he'd let down the team. "I know, but still." He sighed. "Well, we made some headway on the cell phone."

Gunny smiled. "Great! What did you find out?"

"Well, from what Sarah said, we know Nura talked to someone just before she capped her husband."

Sarah interjected, "Yes, there were two calls. Whoever it was, on the first call he scolded her for calling him on that phone. He called her back, apparently on a different phone—I'm guessing a burner. This is when he told her to kill Andreas. She said something about 'cauterizing the wound' before she shot him."

Gunny asked, "How long between the two calls?"

"Several minutes." She added with a smirk, "We had a bit of a conversation. She actually remembered me from back when I was gathering intel on her father."

Alen asked, "You were involved in that?"

Sarah just smiled.

Gunny got them back on point. "We can talk history later. Back to the phone."

Hans continued, "Both of those last two calls came from phones with no subscriber information. The second one was new. It had only registered a couple calls in the last couple of weeks. We pinged it through the international cellular system but it didn't register this morning. It's either turned off or destroyed. My money is on destroyed. Last time it registered it was on Vodafone Egypt's network in Cairo just before the call to Nura. It went off, permanently, shortly after. It was on a cell tower in Giza. It's a very busy tourist area, lots of transient users and few police cameras, so no chance to get any kind of correlation between the phone and surveillance footage."

Gunny said, "That's all good but I'm more interested in the first one."

Hans nodded. "The other has no registered user either, but it has more of a call history. It is also a Vodafone Egypt burner. Vodaphone has to share all call record data with the Egyptian Ministry of Communications and Information Technology, which we hacked. The phone has been active for over a year and, while it hasn't been used a lot, it has been used consistently with almost all calls within Egypt. It hasn't registered on the system since that night."

Sarah asked, "What about Nura's phone?"

"Also a burner. No contacts and the call log was empty."

Gunny groused, "Well shit."

Hans grinned and continued, "She had cleared her call log but not the SIM card. I pulled the SIM and found one number—another Cairo number she had called a few times. I checked it out. It's another burner. It has been active for a few years and has received calls from all over the Middle East—Jordan, Gaza, Saudi, UAE, the West Bank, Libya, Pakistan, Malaysia, and more. On average, two to three incoming calls a week but no outgoing calls—at all. It may be an electronic "dead letter box." Here's the kicker: it's still on. I pinged it this morning. It's still on and available—in Cairo."

Gunny snorted. "I guess all roads lead to Cairo on this one. Ostergaard did research there. He traveled there before going to Gaza. And now Nura was communicating with at least three telephones in Cairo. One is still around, but we have no clue who owns it."

"Nope. It's also a burner, so why didn't he trash it too? From Sarah, we know she violated some sort of security protocol. They should have dumped it and every phone they had ever used to avoid link analysis, but it's still on. Why?"

Nigel chimed in. "Nura bailed as soon as Magne busted in. She left her phone and computer behind. If she ended the call before, maybe the guy on the other end didn't realize it had all gone sideways. Maybe she has no other way of contacting him. If he is the head guy, maybe this is the only way other members of this Black Sun group can reach him. He may *have* to keep it on until he can get them details of a new comms plan."

"Well, all that makes sense but it's still conjecture," Gunny mused. "What else do we know about this phone? Which towers does it ping off of?"

Hans opened his laptop and tapped a couple of keys. A map of Cairo appeared on the large monitor at the end of the room. "Okay, this is Cairo." He tapped another couple of keys and a bunch of push pin icons started populating the map. They were all over the city but most were clustered in the middle of the city on both sides of the Nile. He zoomed in and tapped a key and a box appeared over the area. "Approximately 80% of the calls were received in this area. Notice anything odd?" The pins were thick but there was a noticeable blank spot.

Lon spoke. "Yeah, there's a big empty spot on the east bank of the Nile across from that green area. No calls there. What is that?"

Hans smiled, "Yeah, I saw that too. That's the University of Cairo. None of the calls were received on campus; all were in the surrounding neighborhoods. We see calls in parks, commercial areas, residential neighborhoods, and business centers but nothing within the university."

John queried, "Is it a closed campus? You know, restricted access? Students and professors only?"

Sarah answered, "No. I have been there many times. It's open to the public. You know what this must mean, right?"

Gunny responded, "Yeah, our bad guy probably works on campus. He's practicing good comsec by not turning his phone on while he's on campus but he was so meticulous, it became obvious when you looked."

Sarah commented, "That's indicative of someone who is highly intelligent and disciplined but lacks actual operational experience."

"I agree completely," Hans added. "Someone told him exactly what to do and he's doing it but he doesn't understand that by trying to avoid a pattern, he inadvertently created one."

Gunny grinned. "That's damn fine work, Hans. Now we just have to find this motherfucker. I assume it's a big university."

"Yeah, according to its website, about a quarter of a million students and over twelve thousand staff."

Gunny's grin disappeared. "Jesus Tapdancing Christ! That's huge! Well, we've gone from 7.7 billion on the planet to less than three hundred thousand in Egypt. I guess that's something."

Alen interjected, "I think we're better off than that. Given the level of expertise we are talking about here, we can disregard the undergraduate population and probably master's students too. You can also nix anyone not in the sciences. No sociologist or historian is going to develop this. Focus on faculty, postdocs, and doctoral students—in that order. I would consider the hard sciences first: medicine, microbiology, pharmacology, genetics, and veterinary sciences."

John laughed. "Veterinarians. Really? Doggie doctors?"

"Absolutely. With the notable exception of smallpox, practically all biological weapons are zoonotic diseases. Those are animal diseases that happen to affect people too—anthrax, bubonic plague, Ebola, tularemia, Lassa fever, Marburg hemorrhagic fever, glanders, and in this case, bovine spongiform encephalopathy or Mad Cow. Don't forget, Ostergaard was researching scrapie. That's a sheep disease."

John replied, "Well, okay, Dr. Markovic. I was not aware of that. I stand corrected."

Gunny took a deep breath. "Okay, folks, I think we have enough to keep us busy until Rusty gets back tomorrow."

Hans asked, "What about the laptop?"

Lon added, "For what it's worth, this thing is getting bigger by the minute. As much as I hate to deal with official intel guys, I think we need to share this with some of our clients."

Sarah agreed. "Mossad and Shin Bet need to know what might be coming."

Gunny smiled. "Like I said, Rusty gets back tomorrow. He'll take care of it; all of it. He always does."

* * *

Upon arrival in Tunis, Nura checked into a modest hotel in the tourist section. As she was traveling in the guise of a European, she didn't attract the judgmental stares that a lone Arab woman would have. As soon as she reached her room, she plugged in her cell phone and took a bath to wash away the road grime of the last twenty hours. Once out of the shower, she took out the small notebook and found the phone number encoded in a phony address on the third page. She called the number but no one answered. She didn't expect them to. She left a brief message and then lay on the bed to get some rest. About an hour later, the phone rang.

"Yes?"

A male voice on the other end of the line asked tentatively, "Is this my Danish cousin?"

"This is his wife. "

"Where is he?"

"He couldn't make the trip. He had to go to a funeral."

"I'm sorry to hear that."

"Don't be. Did the package arrive?"

"Yes, yesterday. All is good. We need to meet. Today at 3:00 p.m. I'll text you the address. Double-check it with my telephone number."

Nura replied, "I understand." The line went dead. A few seconds later the phone chirped, indicating it had received a text. The message read "1718 Al Qadr Blvd." Per their communication plan, she was to take the house number and subtract from it, using false subtraction, the last four digits of his telephone number to get the real address. False subtraction was simply subtraction without carrying any digits. The house number was 1718; minus the last four of the phone number, 2024, yielded 9794. She was to meet him at 9794 Al Qadr Blvd.

The house at 9794 Al Qadr was a nondescript mud brick structure at the end of a street in the poor section of town. Beyond it was an empty field with a few grazing goats. The house immediately adjacent to it was empty. The black soot around the windows indicated it had recently burned but its brick shell was otherwise intact. Nura had a taxi drop her a couple streets over and she walked the rest of the way. She knocked on the door and after a few moments, it opened. In front of her stood a portly man in his late forties or early fifties. He wore a dirty white thobe and a traditional white keffiyeh on his head. She said in Arabic, "I am Alfaar, a daughter of the Black Sun. Are you the new guy?"

He checked if anyone was on the street and then ushered her in. "Yes, I am Al Thaelab. Abu Almawt contacted me and said he needed someone to replace Kalib Kabir on short notice. What happened to him?"

"He's dead," she responded coldly.

"I can see you're all broken up over it. But what happened?"

"We ran into a bit of a problem. A couple of Mossad agents found him. I don't know how they figured it out but they did."

"Must have been from Alkawbra. He's dead." She was surprised, so he elaborated. "I assumed you knew. He was killed several days ago in his apartment in Gaza. Some said it was over a woman. Others said he was killed by Fatah for being an Israeli spy."

"Nonsense! Al-Rafah was no spy. He would die before he helped the Jews."

"Well, maybe he did. Abu Almawt doesn't believe he was a traitor either. If the Jews knew about our plan, they would've gone after Abu Almawt first or you and Kalib Kabir; may he rest with Allah. He assessed the woman thing was also plausible, though. Alkawbra always had that . . . weakness."

"That's true," she said, "but it doesn't explain how they found out about us. I think the Israelis killed him and made it look like he was a traitor to discredit him. Maybe he was sloppy and left them clues, but he didn't talk."

"So, Mossad, eh? What happened?"

"A woman came to my husband's office pretending to be an Arab. She said she was the cousin of someone my husband worked with in Egypt and the fool believed her. I was suspicious, so, playing the good little Muslim wife, I invited her to our house for dinner. Her story didn't make sense, and I found a knife in her purse, so I knocked her out and tied her up. I was in the middle of questioning her when she called me a little mouse—*alfaar*. That's when I recognized her from Gaza, a long time ago. She worked in a café near our house and used to call me that when we came in. In truth she was Mista'avrim and was gathering information on my father. She set him up; she's responsible for my family's death."

"Alfaar? Is that where you got your nom de guerre? From a Mista'avrim spy?"

"I guess I did. The nickname just stuck with me. Anyway, as soon as I found out who she really was, I called Abu Almawt. He told me to 'cauterize the wound' and get out, so I shot Kalib Kabir and was about to kill the Israeli bitch when her comrade interrupted my plans. I barely got out with my life."

Al Thaelab said, "Well, at least you saved the virus. Too bad about Kalib Kabir. He worked so long on that virus to never see it used. Where did he get his nom de guerre anyway?"

"Kalib Kabir? Big dog? He used to have this stupid Great Dane. He loved that beast more than me. I think he picked that name just to irritate me." *Always with that goddamn dog.* "His death was not so tragic. If he had been captured, he would have talked. He was weak. I also don't think he was capable of doing what we need to do next."

"Still, he was your husband," Al Thaelab said sadly. *I'm glad I'm not married to her!*

Ignoring his comment, Nura asked, "Where do we stand on the next phase?"

"All is ready across the border. I found an old Mizrahi Jew near Sfax. We have already grabbed him. He lived alone on a small farm so no one will miss him anytime soon. We also picked up two Arabs who are . . . disposable."

"How so?" she asked.

"They're heroin addicts. They live on the streets. No one cares about them. That's okay, isn't it? Them being addicts won't affect the test, right?"

Nura replied, "I don't think so. You're the doctor; don't you know?"

"I am a doctor, yes, but I have no expertise in these diseases."

"You'll do fine. Andreas briefed me on the protocols. Who else?"

"There is a Romanian prostitute. I bought her from her pimp. I told him she was for soldiers in Zawara. He didn't care so long as he got paid."

Nura mulled all this over. "Okay, they should do. So, all we need now are the Jews, right?"

"Yes. We have already identified two candidates. They're both French Jews and on holiday. They're camping on the beach instead of staying at a resort—to save money."

"That's good. It's less likely anyone will miss them right away. Where are they?"

"They are on Plage Essaguia Djerba. It's a resort area south of Sfax. It's about seven hours from here but less than two hours from the border. It's about as good a location as we could have hoped for."

"How did you find them?"

Al Thaelab explained, "They stayed at a hostel in Tunis when they first arrived. The clerk identified them to us. He chatted them up and they told him their plans. I sent my cousin to find them. He found them near the beach. They're camping in a bright yellow backpacking tent but they change locations every night to avoid security. They put their stuff in a beach locker during the day and eat at the local restaurants."

"That will make them hard to find."

Al Thaelab grinned. "They go to the same bar every night, where they drink cheap wine and hit on girls. That's where we'll find them."

Nura smiled menacingly, "So they like to hit on girls, eh? Maybe tomorrow night they'll get lucky?"

* * *

Rusty's jet landed in Larnaca first thing in the morning after an overnight flight from the United States. Gunny was there to pick him up along with another passenger. Gunny called ahead and the rest of the Praetorians were waiting in the conference room when they arrived. The group was surprised when a young Asian man walked into the room behind Rusty and the murmuring started immediately. Ignoring them, Rusty stopped at the small table by the door to grab a cup of coffee from the urn Lon had set out. The Asian guy got a cup too. Rusty took his seat at the head of the table and Gunny sat in his usual spot to his right. The young Asian man appeared a little uncomfortable and just sat in a chair along the back wall. Gunny said to him, "No, take a seat at the table. There's plenty of room." He sheepishly slid over to a chair at the far end of the conference table, away from the others.

Rusty took a sip of his coffee and said, "God I need this." Placing it on the table, he continued. "Good morning everyone." They all responded in unison. Motioning to the Asian man he said, "Okay, as you can tell, we have a guest." As if on cue, everyone swiveled in their chairs to face the new guy, who gulped nervously. "He ain't no guest; he's our newest team member. I'd like to introduce Chang. He's our new computer guy."

Hans spoke first. "Any reason we didn't know about this ahead of time? I mean, we are a team, right?"

Travis replied, "I remember someone saying we needed help in that department." He added sarcastically, "Gunny, you remember that too, don't you? I'm not losing it, am I?"

Gunny responded in mock seriousness. "I do recall that. Maybe we're both losing it?"

Hans smiled awkwardly. "That's not what I meant. It's just that we usually have input when we add new people, that's all. I mean, we don't know anything about him, you know, his qualifications . . . or background?"

Rusty understood exactly where Hans was going and figured he wasn't alone. He had a little fun at everyone's expense. "Oh, background, right. Mr. Chang Yu Li is from Shanghai. He's in the People's Liberation Army where he is one of their leading hackers and cybersecurity experts. He also speaks Mandarin which might be useful in the future. They've loaned him to us for a while. He has to go back in a couple of weeks but, if this works out, we might get him full-time."

The room was silent. Everyone stared, stunned and stone-faced, at Rusty. The Asian guy was trying to suppress a chuckle. Finally, Rusty and Gunny burst out laughing. Rusty roared, "We're just fucking with ya! Gunny thought this would be a hoot. You should see your faces!"

Hans was visibly relieved and the others, getting over their shock, groaned. An exasperated John said, "You guys are such assholes!"

Lon asked, "Okay, who the hell is this guy, really?"

Still laughing Rusty said, "Well, he *is* our new computer guru and his name *is* Chang but its Steven Chang and he's from Indiana or somewhere."

Chang smiled and said, "I'm actually from Cleveland and you can call me Steve."

Rusty continued, "Steve was recommended by Dr. Williams. Steve graduated from the Air Force Academy and then got his master's in computer science at A&M under Tom. He's been working at NSA for what? The last six years?"

Chang interjected, "Seven."

Rusty added, "His time was up and I convinced him to come with us instead of re-upping." He smiled and added, "I made him an offer he couldn't refuse."

Lon turned to Chang and asked, "What was that?"

Chang replied, "He told me he would pay me a boatload of money and I'd get to kill terrorists. It was a no-brainer. NSA's bureaucracy can just suck the fun out of life."

Alen asked, "Married? Kids?"

"No and no. Completely unencumbered. Gunny said I could live here full-time, and I plan to do just that."

Nigel chimed in, "Uh, not to be Debbie Downer, but where is he going to live? I think we're full."

Rusty replied, "We're putting bunkbeds in Alen's room since you two are the FNGs."

Alen asked, "Uh, what's FNGs?"

Magne answered, "It's an Americanism. It means Fucking New Guys."

Rusty laughed again. "I'm still fucking with ya. He's going to take Gunny's room and Gunny is going to move into the guesthouse. He deserves some privacy at his age."

Gunny shot back, "Besides, you assholes snore at night and fart during the day."

Alen was relieved. Sarah asked Steve, "So you're from Ohio. How long has your family lived there?" She wanted to get a sense of his connections to China. He was used to it.

"My family moved to Ohio from California. My family immigrated in the '40s." He paused for effect. "The 1840s. My great-great-great-grandfather immigrated to the United States from Canton before the Civil War. He was a fisherman in San Francisco Bay and then worked in the gold fields for a while. During World War Two, my grandfather couldn't get a job in California because everyone thought he was Japanese, so he moved to Ohio to work in the steel mills."

Lon said, "So, your family has been in America . . ."

Steve finished his statement. "For over 170 years. A lot longer than most other Americans."

Hans stood up to go shake his hand, "Well, Dr. Williams is the smartest man I know. If he recommends you, that's good enough for me. Welcome to the Praetorians." The rest of the group got up to shake his hand in turn.

Steve said, "Well, I'm happy to be here. Mr. Travis said you had a laptop that needed breaking into? I want to start earning my pay, so where do I set up shop?"

Hans replied, "Well, I can show you where the computers are, but I doubt they'll be up to your standards. We can get you whatever you need; just come up with a list."

"No worries. I brought my own. Dr. Williams hooked me up with three IBM Power System servers that he tricked out himself. I'm going to network them through my Alienware Area-51 Threadripper gaming computer. Dr.

Williams also recommended we get a Silverdraft Demon MP Extreme workstation for any video work. The specs he suggested require a custom build. It's going to run about $60K but Mr. Travis is paying extra to expedite it, so we should have it next week."

"Wow, that's some serious firepower!"

"Nothing but the best. Go big or go home. The stuff is out in the Range Rover. Can you give me a hand getting it in? By the way, how's the power here? Stable?"

Leading Steve out to the front door, Hans answered, "Yeah, it's pretty good but we have uninterrupted power supplies, backup generators, and line conditioners, just in case."

Steve and Hans went to work setting up the new computer network in the basement while Lon brought in Steve's luggage and helped Gunny move his stuff out to the guesthouse. Hans was a great special ops guy but he was a computer nerd at heart. He peppered Steve with questions as they hooked up the computer equipment and ran it through its paces to make sure it was configured properly.

Meanwhile, down the hall, Sarah and Alen were working out in the gym. Sarah was working on the heavy bag while he was using the free weights. After about twenty minutes, Alen stopped to watch her work out. He was impressed both by her hand-to-hand techniques and how she looked in just yoga pants and a sports bra. After a few minutes, she stopped and asked, "Do you want to spar or are you just here to gawk?"

Alen smiled. "I guess gawk. I'd spar with you, but since you took that shot to the head . . ."

Sarah snorted, "I'm fine. John gave me a clean bill of health. Don't be a pussy."

Alen laughed. "I'm sorry, I don't hit girls."

"What makes you think I'd let you hit me? Come on. We can wear headgear and gloves if it makes you feel any better. Or are you afraid to get your ass kicked in front of the guys?"

Alen turned as Nigel, Magne, Lon, and John entered the gym. Referring to her last comment, John said, "Don't fall for it. It's a trap."

Alen was in a spot now. Based on everyone's comments, he was leery about sparring with Sarah, but he didn't want to appear weak in front of his teammates. He was in a lose/lose situation. Either he beats up a girl, in which case he's a bully, or he gets beaten up by a girl, in which case he's a pussy. Sarah kept goading him. "Oh, come on, I won't hurt you too bad. I'm sure a big, strong guy like you can handle a skinny little girl like me." He just shook his head. She added, "So, tell me Alen, did your parents have any male children?"

The other guys let out a loud groan. John shouted, "Burn! You can't let that stand, dude. We'll have to revoke your man card."

Nigel piled on. "Hey, laddie. If you're not going to use your testicles, can I borrow them?"

Finally, Alen had had enough. "Okay, girlie, you want to spar; we'll spar but I won't be responsible for the outcome."

As he and Sarah walked over to get headgear and open-hand gloves, Magne said, "I can't believe he fell for that. I'm going to get Hans; he'll get a kick out of this."

Sarah and Alen moved to the middle of the mat just as Magne returned with Hans and Steve in tow. John whispered to Steve, "Watch and learn, young man, watch and learn."

Sarah yelled, "Somebody call it!"

John shouted, "Go!"

Alen put his hands up but with open palms; no clenched fists. Sarah started walking toward him, her fists clenched in front of her like a boxer. She took a couple of probing jabs which he deflected easily. Talking to Steve, John said, "Okay, she's digging the hole." Alen sent a couple of jabs back. The first missed completely but the second glanced off her headgear with a light pop. "Now she's covering it with sticks." Sarah approached again. She tried a light kick which glanced harmlessly off Alen's hip as he turned. John smiled and said, "Now she's covering it with grass and leaves." As Alen came at Sarah with an overhand right, she ducked under and to her left. She planted her left foot and spun like a ballerina, except instead of a pirouette, it was a spinning heel kick that hit Alen in the back of the head and sent him reeling. John laughed. "And he stepped right in it."

Steve was impressed. "Wow. She's good."

"She's not done yet."

Alen recovered quickly and turned to face his opponent. He was both surprised and embarrassed. "Okay, girlie. If that's how you want to play it."

He charged at her. Instead of ducking this time, she gave him a hard jab that bloodied his nose and then pushed him aside as he rushed past. *Where the hell did that come from?* He was surprised by her power; she hit harder than most of the men he'd fought. He threw a wild punch that somehow connected with the side of her face.

John sighed. "That wasn't smart. Rookie mistake."

Sarah reached up to touch her cheek where he'd hit her and then just smiled. She charged at Alen. When she feigned a punch to his face, he instinctively raised his guard only for her to thrust kick him in the solar plexus and knock the wind out of him.

Steven winced but John said, "Oh, she's still not done."

Sarah grabbed the back of Alen's head with both hands and slammed it down onto her upward moving knee. As his head flew up and he staggered back, another spinning leg kick caught him on the side of the head and he went down for good. "Okay, now she's done."

As the big Serb hit the mat with a thud, the guys let out a roar. Sarah stood over him as he got his bearings. She offered him a hand up and said, "Not bad, but you never really had a chance." Reluctantly, he took her hand and let her pull him up. Turning to the other guys, she asked, "Anyone else want to take a shot at the title?"

All the guys begged off. Lon commented, "No fuckin' way. I done died on that hill."

They started to disburse when Steve Chang meekly said, "I'll give it a shot."

John grabbed him and pulled him back. "Uh, dude, did you not see what just happened? Alen is twice your size and she just handed him his balls."

"I know. It's just that, you know, I play a lot of video games. I've seen all the moves. It can't be that hard. It's not like she's big or anything."

The other guys started laughing. Nigel said, "Hey mate, you may want to let John save you from yourself."

Steve replied, "No, if I'm going to be part of this team, I need to do what you guys do, right?"

Lon shot back, "Getting our asses kicked is not what we do; at least not on purpose. This ain't no video game, computer boy. She'll hurt you, in real life."

"No, I think it's important that I try," Steve said naively. Sarah just shook her head as he bent over to take off his shoes and socks. He was wearing jeans and a polo shirt.

Magne said to John. "He's going to die. And on his first day too."

Nigel added, "Someone better tell the boss to start looking for another computer guy."

Hans shouted to Sarah. "Don't kill him. I need him to break into that hard drive."

Sarah gave Hans a thumbs-up as she tossed Steve Alen's now-discarded headgear. Steve tossed it aside. "No thanks. It's uncomfortable. Whenever you're ready."

They walked out into the center of the mat. Steve just stood there with his hands at his sides. Sarah shook her head in disgust and approached him. She threw a quick right jab but as she did, Steve rotated his hips counterclockwise while leaning slightly back causing her punch to pass just millimeters from his nose. As her gloved fist retracted, he pivoted back into his original stance. His hands never left his sides. Surprised, Sarah threw a sharp left jab at Steve's chin. Again, he just rotated his hips, clockwise this time, and her punch passed harmlessly past his face. She immediately threw a right cross at Steve's nose but in a flash, his right hand shot up from his side, grabbed her right wrist and pushed her fist away. As he did this, he pulled her toward him, pivoted on his left foot, bent over, and threw her over his right shoulder. She now lay flat on her back on the mat. Still holding onto her right wrist, he put his right foot on her throat and pulled on her arm causing her to choke. He immediately released her and stepped away. "Are you okay? I didn't mean to hurt you."

Sarah was more shocked than hurt. The other men in the room were suddenly completely quiet. *What just happened? Steve is a computer geek! He weighs maybe 170 pounds on a good day. How the hell did this happen?* Steve offered Sarah his hand and helped her to her feet. She quipped, "What video games do you play?"

Steve just smiled.

Rusty had been standing in the doorway and witnessed the whole event. "Oh, did I forget to mention that Steve was Air Force Pararescue before he went to NSA? He also happens to be the military jujitsu champion in his weight class."

Sarah was genuinely pissed. "So, you brought in a ringer to make us look bad."

Rusty corrected her. "You mean to make *you* look bad. Sorry, honey, you did that all by yourself. You extended the challenge, he just accepted it. You assumed he was a pushover. Always assume your opponent is capable. You've gotten spoiled beating up on these other lazy bums."

Lon protested, "Hey, I resemble that remark!"

Sarah was contrite. "Yeah, you're right. I should've learned that after that bitch clocked me in the head. Still, it was a dirty trick."

Rusty replied, "Steve here is a computer expert, but you know me; I don't hire pussies. Williams filled me in on his background. One of the reasons I picked him was I figured we will use him operationally if we ever need an extra body."

Steve added, "And I would really appreciate the opportunity sometime. You know, put my training to work."

Gunny snorted. "We'll see. In the meantime, just figure out what the hell is on that goddamn hard drive."

Steve shot back, "Yes, Gunnery Sergeant, I'm on it."

"The rest of you can soothe your bruised egos with some cold ones."

CHAPTER FIVE
LAB RATS

After her meeting with Al Thaelab, Nura went over what she'd need for the next phase of the plan. She did a mental inventory of her things and determined she needed to go shopping on her way back to the hotel. She headed toward the *suq*, the local market. There she bought a red bikini. Normally one wouldn't find such things in an Arab market but this one catered to tourists. She also bought a loose swimsuit cover-up, some thin linen pants, a pair of sandals, and a big beach bag. Next, she went to a drugstore, where she bought a razor, some shaving soap, makeup, and hair dye. Back at her hotel, she dyed her hair a light brown and shaved her legs and armpits. She turned her attention to the makeup and applied mascara, a light purple eye shadow, and foundation to lighten her skin just a little. She then tried on the bikini. The top was actually quite flattering and gave her some cleavage despite her modest breasts. She looked in the mirror to apply some lipstick and was surprised by her transformation—she was actually quite pretty; sexy even. The linen pants were thin enough to allow a faint outline of her red bikini bottoms. As she put on the cover-up over her bikini top and tied the two shirt tails together in the middle to expose just enough of her flat stomach. *I could easily pass for a European slut.* As she admired herself in the mirror, she thought about how her life might have been different if she'd been born in France or Italy instead of Gaza. *Too late to worry about that now.*

The next morning, Nura waited impatiently for her phone to ring but finally Al Thaelab called. He would pick her up in twenty minutes. She gathered her beach bag. In it she had her purse, one of the hotel towels, and a bottle of cheap Italian red wine she'd bought in the grocery next door. She wrapped the Beretta in a T-shirt and placed it in the bottom of the beach bag. She headed down to the lobby to check out and wait for Al Thaelab.

When he arrived, he strode right past her. She walked up behind him and tapped him on the shoulder. He initially didn't recognize her but when he did, shock came over his face. "Alfaar?" he said under his breath. "Is that you?"

She smiled. "What do you think?"

He was still stunned. "You look amazing. But . . ."

She finished his question, "Why? If you're going to go fishing, you must have the proper bait. Do you think I will get their attention dressed like this?"

He smiled. "You could get any man's attention dressed like that."

Her face turned serious now. "Good, let's go. Where is your cousin?"

"He's in the car."

As they walked out of the hotel she asked, "What's your real name? Just in case we are stopped and questioned."

"Omar. Omar Trabelsi. What's yours? I mean what's on your passport?"

"Lila Renard. From Belgium. How did you pick Al Thaelab—the fox—as your nom de guerre? Did you hunt foxes or do you just think you're particularly clever?"

"None of that," he laughed. "I grew up admiring German General Erwin Rommel. His nickname was the Desert Fox. My father never liked the British, so we had a picture of Rommel in our house growing up. Not nearly as interesting as your story."

Parked around the corner from the hotel was an old Citroën sedan. Trabelsi put her suitcase in the trunk and motioned for her to get in. Nura slid in the passenger seat. In the back was a young Arab man about her age. Trabelsi said, "This is my cousin, Saad. He can identify the two Jews for you." Saad was very surprised by the pretty, young European-looking girl in the car. "Saad, this is Alfaar, but in public you must call her Lila. Do you understand?"

"Yes, sir. I'm just surprised that she's so. . . ."

Trabelsi chuckled. "Me too. Do you think they will approach her dressed like this?" Saad just nodded vigorously.

The drive to Plage Essaguia Djerba took almost eight hours with traffic. They arrived in the area at about 7 p.m. Djerba was an island and the only way on or off it was a single causeway on the southern tip of the island. Nura was not particularly happy about this. If things went bad, it represented a perfect choke point for the police but things were in motion and it was too late to worry about that now. Plage Essaguia was located at the extreme eastern tip of the island. The area catered exclusively to tourists and the rich who had expensive villas in the area.

Saad guided his cousin to a stretch of beach just north of Club Med La Fidele. This section of the beach was still mostly undeveloped. West of the beach was an area of low dunes dabbled with scrub brush and short trees. Nura saw a number of tents pitched among the trees. Saad said, "Okay, this is where they've been camping. They pack their stuff up every morning because the local police harass the campers during the day but leave them alone at night, so long as they aren't too loud or drinking too much."

Nura asked, "Where do they eat at night?

"It changes all the time. Sometimes they go to restaurants, sometimes they eat from street vendors."

"There's no pattern?" she asked.

"No. But they always go drinking at Café Lagone, a small café/bar just up the road. It has cheap drinks and caters to young European tourists."

"Show me," she demanded. Trabelsi followed Saad's directions and they drove north before turning east on a dirt road parallel to the beach. A few hundred meters ahead were the lights of the café. Nura and Saad got out of the car. She asked Trabelsi, "Did you get the pills I asked for?" He handed her a small plastic bag with four oblong green pills in it. It was Rohypnol, more commonly known as roofies. "Stay close. I'll call you when I need you."

Turning to Saad, Trabelsi said, "Do whatever she says. Do you understand me?"

"Yes, sir." He didn't question Trabelsi; it was clear Nura was in charge.

Nura and Saad walked up to the café. The sun was going down and a number of people were sitting outside drinking wine. She asked, "Do you see them?"

"No, not yet. I'm going to go inside. I need to use the toilet."

She went in the restaurant a few moments behind him and took a seat at an empty table. The waiter came over and she ordered a bottle of Perrier. She studied the room. There were a number of young people there but mostly couples. No one who fit the descriptions Saad had provided. In a few minutes, Saad came out of the bathroom. He was subtly trying to get her attention. When they made eye contact, he gestured with his head toward the door. She turned as two young men in their early twenties walked in. They were unkempt. Their clothes were wrinkled and a little stained. Their hair was neatly cut, but both were sporting scruffy beards indicating they hadn't shaved for a few days. One was ordinary. He was soft, almost pudgy, with little definition to his legs, chest, or arms. He had dirty black hair and his formerly pasty skin was now rosy from a combination of sunburn and wind rash. He reminded her of a younger version of Andreas. The other boy was actually quite attractive, or would have been if he took a shower and shaved his scruff. He had dark brown hair but had more of an olive complexion that had a glow from the sun. He was wearing floral board shorts that exposed his muscled legs. His arms were not big but they were toned. He also had a swagger about him. He definitely was the one who attracted the ladies; his friend was not. *What do the Americans call it? A wingman?*

Nura drank down her water and approached the bar; walking directly in front of the two young men. In French, she asked, "A glass of white wine, please?"

The bartender poured her a glass of wine and she asked, "How much." He said it was five dinars—about 1.5 euros. She tossed a ten-dinar bill on the bar and said, "Keep it." As she turned to go back to her table, she made eye contact with the two men and smiled.

They ordered glasses of wine and sat down at the table next to Nura's. The handsome man turned around in his chair and said to Nura, "Hello. You speak French. Where are you from?"

She turned and said, "Brussels. I see you speak French too. Where are you from?"

He smiled, "Oh, us? We're from Paris. We're just down here for a couple of weeks. We are getting ready to start medical school soon."

Nura didn't know if this was bullshit or not, but didn't care either. "Ooh, doctors! That's impressive!"

"What are you doing here? From the looks of you, I'd guess a fashion magazine photo shoot?"

Nura fluttered her eyelashes, "Not hardly. You flatter me. Is that a line?"

"Oh, no, an observation. Just look around. You're definitely the prettiest girl in the café. Hell, you're the prettiest girl I've seen in, well, I don't know how long! Let me buy you another drink. What's your name?"

"Lila. Lila Renard. What's yours?"

The handsome man said, "I'm Michael. Michael Aaronovich. And this is my friend, Abel Chelouche. So, can I buy you a glass of wine?"

Nura chugged her wine and giggled insipidly, "Sure. That would be nice. But the next round is on me, okay?"

Michael practically sprinted to the bar to get another wine for Nura. After he left, she asked Abel, "Are you guys really going to be doctors?"

Abel smirked. "No. We're both studying finance. Michael's father, my uncle, runs an import/export company in Paris. We'll end up working for him when we finish college."

"That's okay. My family is in banking in Belgium, so I get it. Aaronovich sounds Russian. Are you oligarchs or something?"

Abel laughed. "No. We're Jews." He added cautiously, "Does that bother you?"

Nura smiled, "Not at all. I'm part Jewish on my mother's side, or so I've been told."

Michael came back with a drink for Nura. "So where are you staying?"

"I'm at Club Med. Where are you guys?"

Michael replied, "We're camping on the beach. We wanted an adventure."

Nura giggled, "That sounds so exciting. I'd love to do that."

Michael moved in closer and put his arm around Nura. "You want to check out our camp? We're just down the beach a bit; not far from your hotel."

Nura ran her finger down from his chin to his chest and then let her hand rest on his thigh. "That sounds fun. I have a bottle of wine in my bag. We can stop at your tent for another drink and then walk down to my cabana. I have a sauna. You should check it out."

"Great. Let's just steal a couple of glasses."

Nura gazed at him seductively. "You're so bad."

The three of them got up and headed for the door. On her way out, she glanced at Saad and nodded. He got up and followed. As they walked down the beach, Abel stayed a few paces back. Michael put his arm around Nura's waist and then let it slip down on her ass. When she didn't protest, he pulled her tight and kissed her.

About halfway to Club Med, Michael led her away from the beach and into the low trees beyond. Just ahead in the dark she barely made out a small yellow backpacking tent—she smiled. Nura and Michael sat together on a beach towel while Abel sat on a rock not far away. Nura removed the bottle of wine from her bag. "Do you have a corkscrew?"

Michael replied, "Yes, in the tent. One second." While he crawled in the tent, Nura shoved two wineglasses in the sand to hold them up. The third she tossed aside. Abel was across from her but it was dark and he couldn't see much. Using her big beach bag as a screen, she stealthily removed the pills from the baggie and dropped two in each glass. Michael returned with a corkscrew and quickly opened the bottle. Nura poured two glasses of wine and handed one to each of the young men. Michael asked, "Aren't you having one?"

She pouted. "Only two glasses. I must have dropped the other on the beach. I'll just drink from the bottle." After saying this, she pretended to take a big swig of wine straight from the bottle.

Michael took a sip of his wine but Abel just sat there. He was a fifth wheel. Michael asked, "Hey, Lila, you want to see the inside of the tent?"

"Sure!" She crawled in. He chugged his wine and crawled in after her. He immediately started kissing her and grabbing her breasts. Nura subtly deflected his hands but not enough to discourage him. More heavy kissing followed until Michael became bleary-eyed. A few seconds later, he was passed out. Nura crawled out of the tent alone. Abel, who was now sitting on the beach towel, gawked at her quizzically. She said with mock sadness, "Your cousin passed out. And I wasn't done partying yet. I guess that just leaves you and me?"

There was genuine terror in Abel's eyes. No girl ever came on to him— ever. He didn't know what to do. His wine was still untouched. He stammered, "Uh, I . . . um . . . I'm not really the partying type."

Nura crawled over and sat on him, straddling his legs with hers and putting her breasts at his eye level. She handed him his glass of wine and said, "You just need to loosen up a little."

He took the wine but didn't drink it. Nura took off her cover-up and took a deep breath so her breasts would heave toward his face. He was still paralyzed with fear. She then reached behind her neck, untied her bikini top and let it drop, exposing her breasts. She grabbed the back of his head and pushed his face into her small, round breasts. "You're too tense. You need to drink up." That was all the encouragement he needed. He chugged the wine and started nuzzling her nipples. She let him kiss her, even though it disgusted her. She kept telling herself, *he's no different than Andreas.* After a few minutes, the drugs took effect, and he passed out. She immediately got off him and put her bikini top back on. She walked toward the beach and called out softly, "Saad? Are you there?"

A few seconds later, Saad appeared. He had been hiding in the trees nearby. He had witnessed a lot of what happened; he was shocked, embarrassed, and aroused—all at the same time. Nura was standing in front of him wearing just a bikini. As she picked up her cover-up and put it on, she said, "Call your cousin. Tell him where we are and to bring the car."

It took them about twenty minutes to get the two young men in the trunk of the old Citroën. Two hours later they were at the Tunisia/Libya border crossing at Ra's Ajdir along the Mediterranean coast. Trabelsi handed the senior border guard a wad of dinars, and with that, they were in Libya.

* * *

Steve Chang made quick work of the laptop computer and hard drive Sarah and Magne recovered from the Ostergaard's apartment. His powerful computers coupled with Dr. Williams's software cracked the encryption in about an hour. Hans was impressed but had to rib Steve a little anyway. "Ya know, Dr. Williams cracked the other computer in just a few minutes."

Chang replied defensively, "Well, yeah. I'm sure he did. If I had a few hundred more teraflops at my disposal. . . ."

"Sure, I get it. Just sayin'." He chuckled, "A word of advice: you'd better grow a thick skin around these guys. They can be brutal." Glancing at the computer screen, Hans asked, "So, what's there?"

Steve opened a couple of the files. "These are really technical."

Hans asked, "Aren't you the technical expert?"

"No, these are microbiology technical, not computer technical. Do we have anyone who understands this stuff?"

"Yeah, Alen gets it."

Steve was taken aback. "You mean that big gorilla Sarah beat down yesterday?"

Hans laughed, "Yeah. Surprised us too. Turns out he was studying microbiology when he quit university to join the Serbian Army. Both his parents were doctors or professors. I'll get him down here."

A few minutes later, Hans returned with Alen in tow. Alen sat down next to Steve and said, "Nice job with the chick yesterday."

Steve smiled, "I got lucky. She assumed I was just another computer nerd and was overconfident."

Alen replied humbly, "Well, she sure handed me my ass."

Steve reassured him, "That's because she was expecting you to be good whereas I was a complete surprise. I'm sure she'd kick my ass in a rematch—not that I plan on giving her one. I have no problem taking the win and walking away."

Alen nodded. "Good plan. So, what do we have here?"

"Some very technical bio-shit that I won't pretend to understand. I sent it to the other workstation so you can read it. I still have more files to go through on this one."

Alen rolled his chair to the adjacent computer screen, opened a file, and started reading while Steve continued his analysis. After about twenty minutes, Alen rolled his chair back away from the computer screen. "Oh fuck."

Hans and Steve stared at him. Hans asked, "What is it?"

Alen was ashen which began to frighten them. "We need to talk to the boss. Now!"

Gunny called an emergency meeting in the conference room. Everyone was already there when Rusty finally walked in wearing a robe. His hair was wet. Gunny had pulled him out of the shower. "This had better be good."

Hans said, "Steve cracked the hard drive and found a couple of bio papers. Alen has read them and it's pretty serious."

Rusty turned to Alen. The big Serb cleared his throat. He had never formally addressed the group before. "Uh, like Hans said, I read the papers, and it's bad. The first paper indicates that Ostergaard was successful in developing some sort of bioweapon based on Wachner's paper. He identified the marker for those two types of Jews. Sorry, I don't remember what you call them. Anyway, he engineered a receptor specific to the DNA sequence of the marker. He attached that receptor to two different strains of influenza viruses. All viruses have protein coatings, and his receptor segment does too. Now, here's the really clever part. The protein coatings for these receptors are actually prions, the ones that cause mad cow disease and Creutzfeldt-Jakob. They are released when the receptor attaches to the host DNA at the marker site but only then. If you don't have that marker, the virus acts like a regular flu virus. You get sick but your body's immune system reacts and clears the virus. Now, here's the scary part."

Rusty interrupted, "You mean that wasn't the scary part?"

"No. Ostergaard incorporated the receptor into the virus RNA itself, so when the virus replicates inside the host cell, the subsequent generations of the virus also include this prion-coated receptor. So, if you're one of the targeted groups, when the subsequent generations of virus go on to infect other cells, they release more and more prions. The virus titers—that's their concentrations—grow geometrically until the body's immune system kicks in. But by that time, enough prions have been released to cause a very rapid onset of Creutzfeldt-Jakob."

Sarah asked, "What if you are not an Ashkenazim or Sephardim?"

Alen replied, "You get the flu but not Creutzfeldt-Jakob. However, you are still shedding virus every time you sneeze or cough, so you're spreading the virus to more and more people—everyone essentially becomes Typhoid Mary."

Rusty asked, "What about this flu? It's not fatal on its own, right?"

Alen responded, "Not in most cases, no. Most people catch it and get over it. They quit being infectious after a few days. But there is another clever thing this asshole did. He incorporated it in two different strains of flu. The first was H1N1. That's the Spanish flu. He chose it because it is especially virulent."

Rusty commented, "I've heard of that. My grandfather talked about how it wiped out entire families when he was a kid."

Alen continued, "Yeah, no shit. It hit in 1918 at the end of World War One. The outbreak spread all over the world and lasted for almost three years. It infected over 500 million people and killed somewhere between fifty and a hundred million people. That was three to five percent of the world's population at the time."

Magne spoke up. "You said two strains. What's the other?"

"He also used H5N1, Asian Avian Influenza—fucking bird flu. It is highly pathogenic and like the name suggests, it primarily infects birds."

Magne quipped, "Why use that, then?"

Alen gaped at him in disbelief. "Why? Because birds fuckin' fly. If it gets into the migratory bird population, it'll spread all over the world. Even if you can somehow contain the Spanish flu version, the other version will be shitting on your shoulder in the park. Like I said, this evil asshole was clever."

Rusty asked, "Okay, this all sounds scary but also complicated. That's what he *wanted* to do, but did he?"

Alen took a deep breath. "I think he did. In his notes he claims he grew the modified virus strains in his lab. He even has PCR results to confirm that subsequent generations still contain the prion-coated receptor."

Lon asked, "What's PCR?"

Alen explained, "That stands for polymerase chain reaction. It's common in molecular biology. It allows you to make copies of specific DNA or RNA segments for testing. He actually attached the results to his notes. Now, growing viruses is much harder than growing bacteria. It would be difficult for him to grow very much in his lab without other people noticing. Researchers usually use microgram quantities. If he was going to weaponize it, he would need more. However, he's been growing a little bit at a time for over a year, so there's no telling how much he accumulated."

Magne spoke up. "Okay, something makes sense now. I have been monitoring the Copenhagen police log and media to see if there was any mention of Sarah or me. The night Ostergaard was killed, there was another murder in the Panum Institute where he worked. A Chinese researcher in the Center for Protein Research was killed in the same lab Ostergaard used. I saw it in the news but didn't think anything of it because nothing was reported stolen—other than her car. But if he was growing this virus and storing it in the lab, it's not like it would appear on an inventory."

Sarah got on her iPad and started surfing the net. After couple of minutes she said, "Okay, the police in Copenhagen reported that Ostergaard's car, the green Opel, was found abandoned in the parking lot of the

Rigshopitalet—that's just across the park from the Panum Institute. There were clothes and a fake ID found in the trunk—but just one set, in a man's name. The Chinese researcher's car was located in Hamburg yesterday— near the train station. That's just too much of a coincidence. I'll bet my paycheck it was Nura. She was getting the virus before blowing town."

Magne added, "According to the story on the researcher's murder, the police were searching for a suspect—a small dark-haired woman in her twenties wearing jeans, a red shirt, and baseball cap. Could be her."

Rusty took charge. "Okay, let's work from the premise that these two are connected. If it was this Nura woman, then she's gone and with the virus. It's a long shot but let's look at people leaving out of Hamburg within forty-eight hours of Ostergaard getting capped."

Steve interjected, "That's got to be thousands of people."

"Start with single female travelers. I bet they were both planning to bug out, but after she shot hubby, that changed. Did it say anything else about the fake ID?"

Magne pulled up the article and scanned it. "Uh yeah, a Belgian passport."

Rusty mused, "If you're planning to skip town with your wife, you'd be traveling as a couple. If hubby is traveling on a Belgian passport, it would make sense that the wife is too. Add that to the list of things to search for. Do we have access to the German rail ticketing system?"

Steve smiled. "If we don't, we will soon."

Rusty said, "Let's get on it. Commandeer whoever you need to help you on this."

Alen spoke up. "Uh, boss. I wasn't finished; there's more."

"Good God, what else?"

"They are planning to test the virus for efficacy. Human tests."

Rusty gulped. "They're going to test this shit on people? When? Where?"

"I don't know. I was hoping there would be more intel on the rest of the hard drive. I think we have to tell more people about this. We can't handle this alone. Countries need to know."

Rusty replied, "I'm well aware. I have a meeting scheduled with the targeting committee next week but I'm going to call and move it up."

Alen asked, "Move it up to when?"

"Now!"

* * *

After Nura, Omar Trabelsi, and his cousin, Saad, crossed the Libyan border, they continued driving east on the Libyan Coastal Highway until they reached the city of Zawara. There they refueled the Citroën and turned south on Jadu Road into the desert. The country was still in the middle of a civil war, and the area around Zawara was controlled by the Tripoli government, at least for the time being anyway. Farther south and east, forces for the opposition had made some strategic gains, including taking over Al-Watyah Airbase, from which they launched occasional air raids on the capital. Black Sun took advantage of this chaos and distraction to set up their own temporary facility in the empty desert between the two forces. Neither side was willing to risk direct conflict over an empty stretch of worthless sand, so Black Sun was left alone.

About fifty kilometers south of Zawara, Omar turned west onto a dirt track just north of the Al-Watyah road. He continued west for about ten kilometers and then turned south into the empty desert. It was still dark out, but Nura could see by the light of the moon. The landscape around them was devoid of any sign of civilization. After about ten minutes, she asked, "Where are we going?"

Omar smiled. "A secret place. We will be safe there."

"I think I'll need more than that."

The Citroën started to slow and came to a stop. "We're here." Omar got out of the car and started walking to his left. Nura peered through the moonlight. There was nothing except a small hill a few meters ahead of him. She got out and followed. As they approached the hill, she made out an arched concrete structure about three meters tall protruding from the hill. Omar clicked on a small flashlight and walked back into the black space. Nura could see it was a short tunnel that after about five meters ended at a large steel door. Omar opened the door, reached in, and turned on a light. The hill was actually an earth-covered bunker. Omar yelled to someone inside, and a few minutes later two young Arab men came running out. Omar said, "Saad needs your assistance."

"Yes, sir," one of them responded as they trotted over to the car.

Nura asked, "What is this place?"

Omar replied, "This is an old medical bunker. It was for Gaddafi. He was always afraid the West would invade. He planned to evacuate to Al-Watyah Airbase but it was always a target, so this facility was built in case he needed medical assistance. It was near the base but not so close as to be accidently bombed by the West. Little did he know that the fatal attack would come from within."

"How did you know about it?"

Omar grinned. "I was one of his doctors."

He led her down the short corridor to a small empty room. Across from them was another steel door and next to it a window with thick bulletproof glass like one would see at a bank's drive-through teller. "This was where you entered. There were armed guards behind the glass. Obviously, not anymore." He opened the door and walked back farther. "There was an operating theater, examination rooms, a couple of offices, a dispensary, supply rooms, and guard quarters. Gaddafi had a private suite in the back."

The place was trashed. Nura asked, "What happened here?"

"As with everything else, when Gaddafi fell, it was looted. Troops from the airbase came and took everything. That is to our advantage. Everyone who knows about this place also knows there is nothing left to steal." He gave her a tour of the bunker. "The two drug addicts are down the hall on the right. We have them chained to the wall. The prostitute and the old Jewish farmer are on the left. Gaddafi's old suite has been reserved for the Jews. My men and I will sleep in the old dispensary. We have made up a space for you in one of the offices. It is the only one that has a door that still closes. We have bottled drinking water and electricity but no shower or toilet, I'm afraid."

Nura said, "This will be fine. I grew up in Gaza. There were many times when the Israelis were attacking us that we had to live in our basements like animals."

Omar continued, "Besides myself and Saad, we only have the two men— Ivan and Abdul. They can be trusted."

Nura replied, "Have them go into town to get enough supplies to last at least two weeks. Once they get back, no one is to leave again until we are done. But don't tell them that now. I want no leaks. No one talks to anyone until we have finished."

"I understand."

The two Jewish students were starting to come around so they were brought in quickly, and when they woke up, they found themselves chained to a heavy pipe protruding from the wall of the room that would be their cell. Nura inspected the other prisoners. The two drug addicts were curled up on the floor in the fetal position. One of them was lying in his own filth. Nura asked, "What's wrong with him? Is he sick?"

Abdul replied, "He is going through withdrawal. They both are. They haven't had any heroin since we took them four days ago. They feel like shit but they won't die. The prostitute is in the same condition. The pimp sold her because she was a junkie. She was so bad she could no longer work the streets. She won't die either but she wishes she would. I have some khat I can give them. It will help with the pain."

Nura said coldly, "Why bother? They will die soon enough."

Trabelsi was a little surprised how heartless she was. "It will help us manage them easier. Remember, there are six of them and only five of us."

Nura just snorted, "Suit yourselves. What about the old Jew?"

Abdul said, "He has been asking why he's here but he hasn't been too much trouble. He's too old to do anything anyway."

"You'll need to keep your eye on these two young Jews. They're healthy and smart."

Abdul nodded. "Understood."

Nura asked, "When do we get started?"

"Soon."

* * *

Rusty had never called a meeting of the so-called Targeting Committee before; they always contacted him. Because this was so unusual, he got a quick response—especially when he mentioned biological weapons (BW). The meeting took place in Rome on the fringes of some NATO meeting. The non-NATO members of the committee, like the Israelis, found some other excuse to travel. The meeting was held in a private villa north of the city.

Rusty came prepared with copies of translations of Ostergaard's papers in English, French, and German, which included a short assessment from

Alen. Rusty also had a summary of what they had recovered from Al-Rafah's and Ostergaard's computers, as well as Hans's and Steve's cell phone data. He gave the members time to read over the information and digest it. The Israeli representative brought along a BW expert from the IDF who was asked to wait outside. When the expert was given the chance to read the papers and Alen's assessment, he turned white as a sheet.

Rusty opened the meeting. "Gentlemen, as you can see the Praetorians have stumbled across a credible threat to use biological weapons against the State of Israel. While that is certainly bad enough, if my man's assessment is correct, it will extend well beyond that country's borders."

The Israeli representative spoke. "My expert agrees 100 percent. This thing has the potential to kill upward of 14 million people across the world. This is not just an Israeli problem. He tells me there is a good possibility that it might affect people with even small amounts of Jewish blood. Anyone who carries the marker would likely be affected."

The French representative said, "That's over half a million French citizens alone. I think we all agree on the seriousness of this threat."

Rusty continued, "We have prepared data packages with everything we know for each of you to take back with you. We need everyone—and I mean everyone—to go after these people with whatever resources you have."

The German representative asked, "What are the Praetorians doing?"

Rusty replied, "All we can. We are trying to determine where Nura Ostergaard went. We believe she has the virus or at least knows where it is. We are also trying to positively identify the other people who we know from the emails are involved. Unfortunately, they are all using aliases, none of which—besides the late Mr. Alkawbra—show up in any of the counterterrorism databases. This is a totally new group or old players using new tradecraft. They have very good comsec and use strong encryption. They are not talking unless they have to and they are not worried about taking credit or releasing propaganda videos. We would be interested in what anyone else can do to ID them. "

The American representative said, "We'll scour our databases and let you know what we find. Right now, your people are in as good a position as anyone to intercede. I mean, your people are the only ones who have actually seen this Nura Ostergaard."

"Actually, she is Nura Al-Doghmush. She is the daughter of Ahmed Al-Doghmush from the Army of Islam."

The Israeli said, "But he's been dead for what? Five? Six years now?"

"Yes. And we think that was the match that lit the fuse on this firecracker. Ostergaard's first wife was Jazmin Al-Doghmush. She was killed in the same drone strike that killed her parents."

The Israeli reacted defensively, "He was a mass murderer. Any one of you . . ."

Rusty cut him off. "No one is blaming you guys. It could have just as easily been any of us who capped the guy. I certainly wouldn't have hesitated to pull the trigger. The thing now is that we need to find Nura Ostergaard and this Abu Almawt guy before they can release the virus. We think we have at least a little time. They were planning a test and we have no indication it's been completed. In addition, we assess they don't have enough virus to guarantee a successful deployment, but to be honest, we don't even know how they plan to use this thing. We need to make sure they don't have the opportunity to make more of this shit. My guy tells me viruses are much harder to grow than bacteria. If they want to grow it on a large scale, it probably won't be in a university lab. They're going to need an industrial facility; like a commercial vaccine production line or something. There can't be too many of those out there, right?"

The Israeli commented, "A lot of countries have those."

"Well then, we need to start reaching out. Make sure they're aware of what's going on in their own factories. If anyone doesn't want to cooperate, let them know that they will be held personally responsible if this crap is traced back to them in any way. Between all the countries represented here, we can pressure anyone on this planet. If anyone has a better idea, I'm all ears." No one said anything. "In the meantime, I suggest we all work together to find these guys."

The French rep asked, "And then what?"

Rusty raised his voice, "You fucking kill them, that's what."

"We have a huge Muslim minority. I'm not sure my country . . ."

Rusty was disgusted. "For Christ's sake, man. You guys sank a Greenpeace boat over a nuke test and you're worried about this? Okay, if you find 'em, let me know and we'll do the rest. You won't even have to know how, when, or nothing."

The American addressed the group. "I think Mr. Travis is right. We need to put on a full-court press—telecommunications, satellite imagery, HUMINT, SIGINT, MASINT, everything. This goes way beyond violating some antinuke demonstrator's civil rights. We're talking about people who want to eradicate an entire ethnicity. No disrespect to my German colleague, but this could make Hitler look like a jaywalker." Turning to Rusty, he said, "I can speak for my government. As far as we're concerned, it's open season on these guys—take them out, anytime, anyplace. You'll get no push back from us even if you kill them in Times Square on New Year's Eve."

The Israeli said, "We concur. We'll do the same. I pledge that we will share any information we develop but, when it comes down to it, we cannot let these people succeed—no matter what the cost." The others nodded in agreement.

Rusty said, "Well, I'm going to consider that a consensus. I gotta go. You know how to reach us."

* * *

D r. Khalid ibn Mahfous Al-Maadi—aka Abu Almawt—sat in his office at Cairo University staring at the small box on his desk. It had arrived from Hamburg via courier a few days earlier. As soon as it arrived, he refilled it with dry ice and locked it in a heavy metal cabinet in a closet next to his office. This is where he kept valuable laboratory items like gold foils and expensive reagents that disappear if they were left in the labs. He had the only key to the cabinet so he wasn't worried about the package being discovered by anyone. To safeguard this most precious of treasures, he just needed to make sure it stayed cold until he was ready to use it. He really didn't want to put it in one of the lab's Ultra Low Temperature (ULT) freezers but in the longer term he wouldn't have a choice. It had taken the better part of five years to develop and grow the viruses. Now that they were so close to deploying them, he didn't want them destroyed for want of a little dry ice. He would repackage the box and label it "foot-and-mouth virus" and put it in the most restricted freezer in the lab. Foot-and-mouth disease (FMD) is a painful cattle disease but can also affect humans, so no one would open it on a lark. He also put his name on the box so the grad students who did have access would disturb the box at their own professional peril.

With that one simple problem solved, Al-Maadi now moved on to the myriad of others he needed to solve before he completed his scheme. They had to test the virus to make sure it worked as advertised. At least that task was out of his hands. He had to figure out how to take a small laboratory sample and grow enough virus to launch a country-wide attack without anyone knowing—including those actually growing the virus. He then needed to figure out how to deploy the virus to ensure the maximum number of people were infected before the Israelis, and the world, understood what was going on. Finally, he had to secure sufficient funding to pay for all of the above. He definitely had his work cut out for him.

Al-Maadi repackaged the virus, labeled it FMD, and buried it deep in a ULT freezer in the virus lab. When he returned to his office, he was surprised to encounter two men in suits in his office nosing through his shelves. "Excuse me, may I help you?"

One of the men turned around and asked, "Are you Dr. Khalid Al-Maadi?" The other man glanced up briefly but continued pouring through the shelves.

"Yes, I am." He repeated with a more authoritarian tone, "May I help you? Who are you and what are you doing in my office?"

The man reached into his jacket pocket and removed some credentials. "I am Asim Nader, from El Mukhabarat. My colleague is Sergeant Darwish."

Al-Maadi's blood ran cold. Mukhabarat, more formally known as the General Intelligence Directorate, was Egypt's domestic and international intelligence service and primary counterterrorism organization. "Oh, I'm sorry. Did we have an appointment?"

Nader replied with a smile, "No, we thought it might be better to come unannounced. If not, we find people tend to disappear before we can show up."

They tend to disappear afterward too. Al-Maadi asked, "So, what can I help you with? Uh, does Sergeant Darwish have to do that?"

"He's just doing his job, doctor. We need to ask you some questions about a former colleague of yours."

"Colleague? I hope it's not serious."

Nader replied, "I am afraid so. It's about a Dr. Andreas Ostergaard. He is, or was, a young Danish researcher who worked in your lab for a time. Do you remember him?"

Al-Maadi feigned shock. "Was? Are you implying that he is . . . dead?"

"Not implying—stating. Dr. Ostergaard was murdered a few nights ago in Copenhagen. Do you remember him or not?" Nader's tone was one of impatience and irritation.

"Oh, yes. I remember Andreas, of course I do. He was a brilliant scientist. I'm sad to hear that he has died."

"Not died, he was murdered," Nader stressed.

"Why would anyone murder him? Do they know who did it?"

Ignoring his questions, Nader asked, "Dr. Al-Maadi, what was Ostergaard working on while he was here?"

Al-Maadi answered, "He was here doing research on animal diseases. Viruses to be more specific. Uh, his work had to do with rapid diagnostics if I recall. It was several years ago. He was working on foot-and-mouth, parvo, and others."

Nader checked his notes. "Do you recall if he was working on scrapie, influenza or . . . bovine spongi . . ."

Al-Maadi interrupted, "Bovine spongiform encephalopathy. It's a mouthful; we just call it BSE. No, we don't do research on that disease here. It's not endemic to Egypt. We do work on scrapie, however; it's a similar disease but affects sheep. As for influenza, we do work on that as it can devastate our poultry industry. I don't recall if he was working on those viruses specifically but I can check if you would like." He wanted to appear as cooperative as possible. Everything they were asking was a matter of record anyway.

Nader commented, "From our initial investigation, it would appear that you and Dr. Ostergaard were close. I mean you worked together, you conducted research together, and you traveled together—to the Gaza Strip, Jordan, and the West Bank."

Nader was trying to bait him. "Uh, actually, I only traveled with him to the Gaza Strip. I think he said he had traveled to Jordan and Palestine—and so have I—but we didn't go together."

"What was your business in Gaza?"

"We were there on a humanitarian trip organized by the medical faculty. Dr. Ostergaard and myself, in addition to being virologists, are medical doctors. We and other doctors were providing medical assistance in Gazan hospitals. Several of us do it every year or so. And before you ask, I traveled to Jordan to lecture at the Hashemite University at the invitation of the Jordanian government. I traveled to Palestine at the request of our Ministry of Health to provide advice to their health care system."

Nader already knew all of this, of course. He then got to the real reason for his visit. "Do you know if Dr. Ostergaard had any extremist connections or leanings?"

"Extremists? You must be joking. Andreas? No way."

Nader said coldly, "Does it look like I'm joking?" He didn't expect an answer. "The Danish authorities have evidence to suggest that Dr. Ostergaard had converted to Islam and was assisting extremist elements."

Al-Maadi replied, "Extremists? Here? In Egypt?"

"That's what we're trying to determine."

Al-Maadi replied, "Well, this is news to me. When he was here, Andreas was a Christian—Catholic or Lutheran, I think. I don't believe he was active, though. He had only a passing interest in Islam. I think he asked one of the graduate students to take him to the Mohammad Ali Mosque. In hindsight, I guess it could have been more than just a tourist thing, but extremist connections? No, I can't believe that."

Nader smirked. "Don't be so surprised. Anyone can have extremist connections—even you, Dr. Al-Maadi."

Khalid knew what was coming. "I assume you're referring to some of my distant family members."

"Not so distant, Dr. Al-Maadi."

"Okay, we both know what you're talking about. Yes, my father's aunt was Ayman al-Zawahiri's mother. That makes him my cousin, and he is allegedly the so-called emir of Al Qaeda."

Nader was flabbergasted. "Allegedly? Seriously?"

Al-Maadi stammered, "No. I mean . . . it's just that no one in my family has talked to him in years. I'm not even sure if he's alive. It's not fair to judge our entire family by the behavior of one misguided member. Do I also need to point out that my great grandfather was the president of Cairo University, the founder of King Saud University, and a former ambassador to Pakistan? And his brother was Azzam Pasha, the founding secretary general of the Arab League?"

Nader was irritated Al-Maadi was throwing his pedigree in his face. "Yes, I am aware your family is quite distinguished. When was the last time you spoke to your cousin?"

"Zawahiri? When I was a child. I think I was five or six. I barely remember him at all."

"Yet you followed in his footsteps and became a doctor."

Al-Maadi replied angrily, "There are lots of doctors in my family, including my father. Ayman was but one. I have no time for his extremist nonsense. He has disgraced our family like Bin Laden disgraced his. Why do you think I use the name Al-Maadi? My father insisted that I needed to distance myself from Ayman to be taken seriously as a scientist."

Nader didn't expect Al-Maadi to get mad, and it put him back on his heels. "Dr. Al-Maadi, I meant no disrespect, but you must understand that we have to investigate every possibility."

Composing himself, Khalid said, "I'm sorry. It's just that we have to put up with these questions all the time, and it gets extremely frustrating."

Nader asked, "When was the last time you communicated with Ostergaard?"

"Oh my, I don't know. I may have received an email from him a year or so ago, but I really can't remember."

"Email? On your personal or university account?"

"University. I like to keep my family and work communications separate."

Nader said, "I will need the password to your university account."

Without hesitation, Al-Maadi said, "Of course. I have nothing to hide." He scribbled down the username and password and handed it to Nader. "I routinely delete unimportant emails to keep the clutter manageable, but they're backed up on the mainframe so the IT guys can get them for you if they're not in my inbox or archive. So, what is it Ostergaard is accused of doing?"

"I'm not totally sure. Apparently, he was working on some sort of chemical or biological weapon to use against Israel or the Europeans. Our government is very concerned that if any attack were somehow traced back to

Egypt, it would be devastating to the tourism industry. It would be worse than the Luxor Massacre in 1997."

"So, who killed Ostergaard? Was it the police?"

Nader replied, "They said his wife killed him. He was married to a Palestinian woman it turns out. Personally, I blame the Israelis. They just blamed the woman because she was Arab."

Al-Maadi checked at his watch and said, "Well, if there is nothing else, I'm afraid I have a class to teach. If I can help you with anything else, please don't hesitate to call. We are all proud and patriotic Egyptians, after all."

"Thank you, doctor. I don't think I'll need to talk to you anytime soon. I have several other interviews to conduct. Where is Dr. Hamdi's office?"

"Take a right when you leave. He is the second door on your left."

"Thank you." Nader smiled. "Don't tell him I'm coming."

Al-Maadi gave a slight nod. "Of course not."

"Oh, one last thing. According to your secretary, you have a trip coming up to Malaysia. What is that about?"

"That's for the Ministry of Agriculture. We are developing a new vaccine for foot-and-mouth disease and we're trying to identify a manufacturer."

Nader nodded. "A noble cause."

Al-Maadi smiled, "Oh, it is. Very noble."

* * *

Nura woke up in the dingy office in the inky blackness of the underground bunker. It took her a few seconds to get her bearings. She was lying on an ancient, musty Russian military cot. The wooden frame was rough and snagged the sleeve of her shirt as she reached to the floor to fumble for the flashlight that she'd left there the night before. Finally, she located it and snapped it on. The room was dusty and dank; cluttered with boxes of canned goods, cases of drinking water, flats of soda, and a small refrigerator. In the corner was her little black suitcase, the same one that had made the trip from Copenhagen to France to Algeria and Tunisia and finally to the deserts of Libya. She swung her legs over to the floor, stood up, and stretched. Her back was sore. All those hours in buses and cars, and then the uncomfortable cot had taken their toll. *Damn I miss my bed back home.*

She shuffled over toward the door and snapped on the light. A single bulb dangling from a bare wire lit the room. When the place was looted, the thieves stole even the light fixtures and wall outlets. *How did they see what they were doing? Who would even buy a used 1970s era military light fixture anyway? I guess if it can be stolen, someone will endeavor to steal it.* It was only then that she began to appreciate all the work that Omar and his men must have put in to make this place functional. She was still wearing her beach cover-up and thin linen pants from the beach in Tunisia. She changed into something more appropriate and functional.

When Nura emerged from her room, she was wearing a pair of jeans, a long sleeve khaki colored shirt, the gray ball cap, and tennis shoes. She wasn't worried about a hijab or an abaya; this was work and she needed to be practical. She walked down the dim corridor toward the exit. She peeked in the little guard room off the first alcove; Saad was sitting on a wooden box snoring heavily. *Great security, guys.*

She walked down the last hallway and outside through the heavy steel bunker door. The desert sun was blinding and it took a couple of minutes for her eyes to adjust. Omar was standing just inside the entrance smoking a cigarette. Beyond him she made out the outline of the Citroën under some old camouflage netting. She eased up next to him and asked, "Do you have another one of those?"

Startled, he turned to her with a jerk. "Oh, good morning! I'm glad you're alive. You slept like you were dead." He handed her a cigarette.

"What time is it?"

After he lit her cigarette, he said, "After 10:00 a.m."

"Really? I was in bed for over eleven hours! Why did you let me sleep so long?"

"You were exhausted." He joked, "As your doctor, it was my recommendation that you sleep until your body told you to wake up."

"Well, I'm awake now. How are our test subjects?"

Omar took a long drag on his cigarette and then ground it out in the sand. "The prostitute had a fever, but it broke last night. She reacted well to the naltrexone. The two Arab junkies are taking longer. Their addiction was worse, but I expect they will catch up to her by this afternoon."

Nura asked, "What is nal . . . ?"

"Naltrexone. It is naloxone hydrochloride. It's used for rapid opioid detoxification."

Nura was surprised and a little angry. "We should have started the test by now. Why are we wasting our time trying to cure these junkies?"

Omar took a deep breath. "For us to get accurate information, we need test subjects who are at least in somewhat similar physical health. The girl and the two junkies have been feverish and trembling ever since we got them. It is because they are detoxing, not because they are really sick. If we want to know if our virus is infecting them and, more importantly, when, then we have to be in a position to know that any fever is because of the virus and not because of the DTs."

Nura understood but she didn't like the delay. "Okay, you're the doctor. I defer to you, but when can we start?"

"I expect all will be ready this afternoon."

"How are the other subjects?"

"The old man is scared and confused but otherwise healthy. The two Jewish boys are a bigger problem. They are refusing to eat until they know what's going on. In addition, they have been trying to escape from their chains. The pretty one almost did. Fortunately, I brought some handcuffs, so he is secure, but he is extremely annoying. They are demanding to know where they are, why they were taken, and what happened to the poor Belgian girl who was with them."

Nura smiled sarcastically. "Oh. How sweet. I guess we'll have to tell them something. Certainly not the truth. We need them to be at least minimally cooperative—eating, drinking, sleeping."

Omar said, "Yes, we do. What are you going to tell them?"

"I don't know just yet. First I need to use the toilet and get some food."

Omar pointed off in the distance. "Past the car is the privy. Just follow the wire and noise of the generator and look for the tarp. I'll have some food for you by the time you get back."

There was a heavy electrical cable on the ground that ran toward the car. Nura followed it until she came to a Honda 7000-watt gas-powered generator purring away under a small brown tarp with several jerry cans of gasoline nearby. Behind it was a small square canvas structure built of light wood over a couple of heavier wooden skids. It was about a meter on each side and two meters tall. One side was open and the other three were canvas. Inside was a small military shovel and a folding camping toilet over a shallow hole. On a piece of wire nailed to a board was a roll of very rough toilet tissue which Nura was certain doubled as sandpaper in a pinch. The smell was horrible and, in an attempt to tamp down the stench, she threw a couple of shovelfuls of dirt over the disgusting contents. Apparently, when the old hole filled up, they simply dug another hole and dragged the latrine over it and repeated the process. As she sat there urinating, all she thought about was how future holes were going to be dug much more often.

After she finished, Nura returned to the bunker. Saad was no longer sleeping in the little anteroom. She walked back to her room and grabbed a bottle of water. She found Omar in the operating theater huddled over a small propane camping stove. He was heating up some sort of stew. When he noticed her, he jumped up and said, "Breakfast is served. I apologize for the fare but we cannot keep eggs. We do have some melons. They should last a few days, at least. After that, it's all canned food, old military rations, or dry food."

Nura scooped some of the stew into a plastic bowl, grabbed a spoon and began eating ravenously. She was starving. It had been almost a full day since she last ate. "Where are the others?"

"Feeding the prisoners. Ivan and Abdul are dealing with the Jews. I won't let anyone go in there alone. They are tricky, those two. We may need to separate them. They don't speak Arabic or Romanian, so they won't be able to plot with the others."

"We'll do that soon enough. It is necessary for the testing protocol anyway. When do we start?"

Omar smiled. "Saad just checked on the two junkies. Their fevers have begun to break. We can start as soon as you have eaten."

"Good. Split up the Jews. Put one with one of the junkies. Move the other in with the whore. Put the old Jew and the other junkie together."

"Understood. I will have it done." Omar got up to pass on Nura's instruction to the others.

As she finished her breakfast, there was shouting down the hall. She made out the French protestations of Michael and Abel. She put down her bowl, took a big swig of water, and walked out. She came to the first room.

Inside was an old man sitting on the floor next to a skinny young Arab man. The young man was gaunt and his eyes were hollow. He was the junkie she had seen lying in his own filth. He was dirty and smelly. When she peered in, the young man looked up but said nothing. The old man protested in Arabic, "I don't know why I'm here but if I have to be in the room with this man, can you at least wash him? I have goats that smell better than him."

Nura smiled. "We'll see what we can do." She moved across the hall to the next room. Inside that room she found the other junkie chained to a pipe. Sitting next to him was Abel Chelouche, the pasty-faced Jewish boy. When he glanced up, a glimmer of hope washed across his face.

"Lila! It's you! You're alive. Are they treating you okay? Do you know where we are or why we're here?"

Nura smirked. "Hello, Abel. Yes, I'm alive, but my name isn't Lila; it's Nura. I'm being treated a lot better than you but thanks for asking." In the corner of the room was the plastic five-gallon bucket that was their toilet. "I was going to complain about my accommodations but I think I'm good."

The realization that she was not a prisoner finally dawned on him. "You're part of this! We're here because of you! What do you want from us? I don't understand."

"Abel, we took you to exchange for some of our comrades in arms who are languishing in French prisons. If the French government cooperates— and we think they will—in a week or two, you will be home in Paris with a great story to tell, and my friends will be breathing free air once again."

Abel stared at her with a mix of confusion and suspicion. "Then what's with the guy in here with me? He's not French. He's Tunisian—I think. He's a druggie too. No one is going to swap anyone for him."

He was smart. Thinking quickly, she said, "You're right. He is simply a bargaining chip. They always ask for the release of a prisoner as an 'act of good faith.' They will want you, of course, but we will give them this loser instead—in exchange for one of our comrades. We will comply with their request so they will have to comply with ours. Our goal is to get as many of our brothers out as we can. You are a Jew who is studying business so you must understand the concept of bargaining. Anyway, we want you to be healthy when we exchange you, so please eat to keep your strength up." She left before he objected further.

Finally, she walked down the hall to where Michael Aaronovich was being held along with the Romanian prostitute. Nura was actually looking forward to this encounter. Before she even said anything, he said, "I thought that was you. I heard your voice and thought, 'No way, that's not poor little Lila!' But here you are—you lying fucking bitch!"

When he said this, Saad, who had been bringing food to the girl, punched Michael in the gut. "Show some respect, you filthy Jew!"

Michael took the punch without flinching and just stared at Nura. She smiled impishly. "Oh, I'm the liar? *Doctor* Aaronovich. Are you mad because you didn't get laid? I have news for you; it was never going to happen. You let your penis think for you and now you're here. I guess your cock just isn't that smart. Since you overheard me talking to Abel, then you know what's going on. Be a good boy, behave, and you should be fine." Motioning to the Romanian girl cowering in the corner she added, "If you're still horny, I understand this girl is a professional. Do you have any money? No? Maybe she will give you one on credit; you know, you can *finance* it."

Nura left the room and found Omar. "Is the serum ready?" He nodded. "Good, let's begin."

* * *

Rusty Travis returned to Cyprus immediately after the meeting with the committee. He had the mandate he wanted but didn't really need. He would have gone after Black Sun no matter what they said. It was a matter of principle. Plus, Sarah made it personal for him. She was representative of all the people Black Sun was targeting. It was like they were going after his family—again.

Once he got back to the villa in Lakatamia, he told everyone about the meeting. Like him, they were proceeding anyway but were pleased that they would not have to go against their own countries in order to do their jobs.

It had been a week since Nura killed her husband and vanished. That was the last information they had. Rusty was hungry for an update and Steve's visit was well timed.

"Hey, boss. You got a sec?"

"Always. You have news?"

"I think so," Steve said tentatively.

"Well, you should share it with the group. Everyone sees everything around here. I don't believe in compartmentation when everybody is putting their asses on the line."

Steve found Rusty's attitude refreshing. At NSA, he was not allowed to discuss his work with the guy in the next cubicle even though they all had the same clearances and were working on different parts of the same puzzle. While he understood the justification for compartmentation, in practice he found it frustrating and counterproductive. "Roger that, sir. I'll muster the troops."

In a few minutes, everyone was gathered in the conference room. Alen smelled of gun oil and burned cordite, which betrayed what he'd been doing. Lon was in the kitchen cooking and still wore an apron and the biting smell of chili peppers. Gunny apparently came directly from the gym as he was wearing sneakers, sweats, and an old special forces T-shirt, and smelled of Bengay. When the last person arrived, Rusty called the meeting to order. "Okay folks, Steve has some info for us on these Black Sun bastards."

Steve was nervous. This was his first time addressing the group like this. "Okay, Hans and I worked the Nura Ostergaard problem. She fell completely off the grid after she shot her husband and jumped out the window last Wednesday. We searched for her assuming she was the one who killed that woman at the Panum Institute and stole her car, which, as you recall, was found near the train station in Hamburg. We started looking for single female travelers who departed within forty-eight hours of Nura's disappearance. We know from hacking into the Copenhagen police computer network that the passport recovered from the trunk of the Ostergaard vehicle was Belgian. It was stolen but not reported stolen."

John asked, "Meaning?"

"Someone paid a Belgian citizen for their passport. It's a pretty common practice. With Schengen, you can travel throughout Europe without a passport. If you aren't planning to travel outside Europe, you don't really need one at all. People will apply for a passport and then sell it through a broker. If it pops up on the grid, like Andreas Ostergaard's just did, and the owner is approached by the authorities, he'll claim it must have been lost or stolen and he didn't even know it was gone. It's hard to prove otherwise so the chances of getting caught are slim. That's exactly what happened here. The registered owner, one Rene Boucher, claims it was stolen. Of course, he never reported it."

Nigel quipped, "Well Ostergaard is dead so we aren't looking for him."

Steve continued, "Rusty said something in that last meeting that stuck with me. If they are—or were—a couple and planning to bug out together, it would make sense that their passports came from the same country. I started searching for single females in their twenties or early thirties traveling on a Belgian passport. There were actually quite a few; more than I expected. If someone has a passport, they probably have used it to travel outside Europe, at least once. If Nura's passport was part of her bugout bag, there is no telling how long she's been sitting on it. And if it's in her bugout bag, then it's not being used. So, we looked at Belgian females, traveling alone, whose passport has either never been used or hasn't in at least a couple years. This really narrowed it down. I found two. One was a seventy-three-year-old grandmother from Bruges. The other was Lila Renard, a twenty-six-year-old waitress from Brussels. Last Thursday, the morning after Nura evaporated, Lila Renard used her passport to buy a one-way ticket to Brussels. That was the first time it was ever scanned anywhere since it was issued three years ago. This would not have been particularly interesting, just a girl going home—except that within twenty minutes of arriving in Brussels, Ms. Renard bought another one-way ticket on the overnight train to Marseilles."

Sarah sat up in her chair. "Now that's interesting."

Steve smiled. "Oh, it gets better. Foreign visitors checking into hotels have to provide their passports, which are then scanned and passed to the local police electronically. I accessed the Marseilles Metro Police database and found that Lila Renard checked into a hotel Friday and spent only one night. I scoured all the rail, airline, and bus ticketing systems and she didn't show up anywhere. If she had an apartment or safehouse in Marseilles, why risk staying in a hotel for a single night? I was beginning to think either she hired a car or someone picked her up. If so, she was in the wind. But then I remembered that old movie, *Papillon*, with Steve McQueen, about a criminal who was sent to Devil's Island. His ship left from Marseilles. So I checked ship manifests. Ferries, actually. And there it was: Lila Renard booked a one-way ticket to Algiers from Algérie Ferries line on the El-Djazair II. It departed Saturday morning, the day after she arrived in Marseilles, and arrived in Algiers on Sunday."

Rusty leaned back in his chair. "Well, holy shit. That's damn fine work, guys."

Hans chimed in, "It doesn't end there. We figured she was avoiding commercial airlines because of the security and that wouldn't change all because she was in Algeria. All international airlines have pretty much the same security procedures. So, we started searching trains and buses. On Monday, the day after arriving in Algiers, Lila Renard took a bus to the town of Annaba on the Med. There is no record of her checking into a hotel, getting on a bus, or hopping a train. She just stopped."

Lon said, "Maybe that was her end point. Maybe her safe haven or even Black Sun's headquarters. We don't know jack shit about these guys."

Hans said, "We thought about that but dug deeper. You remember the Egyptian burner on Nura's cell phone's SIM card, the one that is still around and pinging? It never received a call from Algeria but it did from Libya. There's no train or bus service between eastern Algeria and, well, anywhere. To get to the closest country—Tunisia—you have to take a car to the border. The closest town is Ghardimaou. Once there, you can pick up a train to Tunis—which is exactly what she did. She bought a ticket on the last train. She arrived in Tunis early Wednesday morning. Lila Renard rented a room in a local hotel Wednesday night and checked out Thursday morning. After that, there is nothing—no airline ticket, no bus, no train, nothing. It's possible she is staying with friends or paying cash for a room at some youth hostel or underground local hotel, but that doesn't fit her pattern so far."

Sarah asked, "Do you have any photos? Security camera footage?"

Steve pulled up the official passport information and put it on the monitor. "Here is the passport photo for Lila Renard." It was a picture of a plain girl in her twenties with purple hair and a nose ring.

Sarah said, "That's not Nura."

Steve replied, "That's just the official passport photo." We took surveillance footage from the Marseilles train station when the overnight express arrived and the ferry terminal the day she departed. I used the new Silverdraft Demon MP Extreme video workstation to process the video through the Wise Owl facial recognition software to separate common travelers. I only got one match." He tapped a couple of keys and two photos popped up on the screen. They were of a woman in her twenties with dark hair wearing jeans and a T-shirt.

Sarah peered at the photos and exclaimed, "Well fuck me. That's her! That's Nura!"

Rusty asked, "Are you sure? Are you positive? You're the only one who really saw her."

Sarah hit the table with her fist. "Yes, I'm sure. That's her. She's ditched the hijab and the ankle-length skirt, but that's her. She might be any young Italian or Spanish girl. Is she wearing makeup?"

Steve zoomed in and enhanced the photo. "Uh, yes. I would say she is."

"Well, she's not so pious after all."

Rusty interrupted. "Okay, this is great work, guys. We know she has changed her appearance, she's traveling as Lila Renard, and, as far as we know, she's in Tunisia. How do we find her?"

Steve shrugged, "Beats me. This is as far as I got. I'll keep looking, of course, but if she is heading toward Libya it's going to be tough. They're in the middle of a civil war and they have a very long and sandy border. It wouldn't be difficult to sneak in right now. As for the government in Tripoli, I don't think stopping illegal aliens is a top priority."

Rusty mulled this over. "Given our Cairo phone has been in contact with someone in Libya, let's assume she's headed that way. It's a great spot to hide."

Hans interjected, "Oh, on that Cairo phone, we dug into that too. Since it's on and pinging, we figured to get a rough fix on it by using the cell towers to triangulate. Turned out to be harder than we thought."

"How so?"

"Well, ever since we found it on Nura's phone in Copenhagen, it's been moving almost constantly. The only time it's stationary for more than a few minutes is in the middle of the night. Either our bad guy is the most restless person on the planet or he is using a moving relay to disguise his real location."

Lon asked, "How does that work?"

"You essentially have two cell phones. You call the relay phone and then the relay phone calls the person you want to talk to. If the person you call is being monitored by the police and they trace the call, they'll only get the relay. Likewise, if the cops are monitoring you, they'll only get the relay. These devices aren't really legal but you can get them. The way this thing is constantly moving, my guess is it's in a vehicle like a bus or a taxi. Connect it to the vehicle's electrical system and you don't have to worry about batteries. The odd thing is, it is still staying in Cairo and avoiding the Cairo University campus."

Sarah commented, "It's in a bus. Buses aren't allowed on the central campus of Cairo University; too congested. I'll bet if you check out where it is at night, you'll find a bus depot or storage yard there. If it was in a taxi, it might end up anywhere—the pyramids, Karnak, the airport."

Steve said, "That makes a lot of sense."

Magne asked, "Well, if we can find this relay cell phone, why can't we see who it's calling? I mean, we can do that with any person's phone."

Steve replied, "Yeah, we thought about too but there are no outgoing cellular calls from that phone."

"How is that possible?"

"Internet calling. The relay phone is making its outgoing call via the internet. The cell tower logs it as data, like you're Googling something. It doesn't register as a call at all."

Magne said, "That's smart, but if internet calling is so hard to trace, why not use internet calling for incoming and outgoing calls to the relay? Hell, why even have a relay at all?"

It was a good question and no one had a good answer until Lon chimed in. "Shitty coverage. In parts of west Texas, you don't have LTE or even 3G. Hell, sometimes you're lucky to have fuckin' 1G. You can barely make a phone call, let alone use the internet. The incoming calls to this relay phone are coming from all over the place, right? They have to use voice to make sure the call gets through but since Cairo is a major city with good cell service, the outgoing calls can use the internet."

Steve smiled. "Lon's right. If you're out in the middle of nowhere—like the Libyan desert—simple cellular or landline is the only way to go."

Rusty took a deep breath. "Well, we have new information. Let's see what we can do with it. Also, now that we have more computing power, let's go through the few communications we do have—texts, emails, and the like—and see if the computer can find any relationships or patterns that we missed. Steve, put together the details of Nura's travels so I can pass it to the clients along with her picture. The more people hunting for this little monster, the better. Do you think we can find this relay in Cairo and exploit it?"

Steve replied, "Abso-fucking-lutely."

* * *

Nura ate lunch alone in her room within the bunker. She opened a can of spaghetti that Omar's men had brought in the night before. She didn't bother heating it; she just wanted the sustenance. After finishing the can along with a couple pieces of bread, she sought out Omar. She found him in the operating theater roasting a piece of mutton over a propane stove. Next to it was a bowl of lentils and a chunk of bread. "Would you like some? It's fresh."

"No, thank you. I ate a can of pasta."

He chuckled. "We should eat the meat, bread, and fresh vegetables first. If not, they'll go bad. We're going to be here for a while. There's plenty of time for the tinned food."

"Yes, you're right. Are we ready to begin?"

Omar's smile faded. "As soon as I finish. I have the virus in that refrigerator. We will need to prepare it. It'll need to be diluted with saline solution so we have enough. Kalib Kabir's instructions were very precise."

Nura nodded. "Then we should follow them to the letter. He designed this protocol, so we should not deviate from his instructions."

Omar finished his meal and put away his dishes. He washed his hands in a basin in the corner of the room and dried them with paper towels. He then used a generous amount of hand sanitizer before putting on latex surgical gloves. He nodded at Nura, indicating she should do the same.

Omar removed the polystyrene package from the small refrigerator. He carefully removed the small vial and placed it on a towel that was spread out on the table. The liquid inside had thawed. In a bit of a panic, Nura said, "It has melted! Is it ruined?"

Omar shook his head, "No, I thawed it on purpose. It is still cold enough to preserve the virus. Let's not forget that our subjects are ninety-eight point six degrees, so it must heat up eventually." He opened the large black plastic case on the floor next to him. It was full of medical supplies. He removed a large glass vial full of sterile saline solution. Then he removed five empty ten-milliliter vaccine vials and placed them in a plastic holder on the table. He then took out a hypodermic needle and removed the cap. He inserted the needle into the small vial of virus, turned it upside down, pumped in air from the syringe, and carefully drew out all the liquid containing the virus. He studied the markings on the side of the hypodermic. "We have seven-point-five milliliters of virus. Perfect. Now hand me an empty vial." Nura did and he carefully injected one-point-five milliliters into the vial. "And the next." They repeated the process until all five vials had been implanted with virus. He put the syringe in a small red box to be burned later. He picked out another, larger syringe and with it, drew out eight milliliters of sterile saline and injected it into one of the small vials. He repeated this for each of the five vials. When he finished, he put the large syringe in the red box with the other. He then picked up each small vial and shook it to ensure that the virus solution and the saline were thoroughly mixed. "Okay, we are ready."

Nura removed five hypodermic needles from the case and laid them out on the table. Omar took a syringe, removed the safety cap, filled it from a vial, replaced the safely cap, and placed it on the towel. He repeated the process for each, but when he got to the fifth and last vial, Ivan came into the room. Ivan was a large clumsy man selected for his strength, not his grace. As he walked in, he tripped over a chair and fell into Omar. The vial slipped from his hand, bounced off the table, and shattered on the floor. Omar's eyes got wide as saucers. Nura immediately moved to secure the syringes. One fell on the floor but since it was made of plastic, it didn't break.

Nura shouted, "You stupid oaf! Look what you have done!" Ivan recoiled in fear and just cowered in the nearest corner. "I will deal with you later!" Nura picked up the syringe from the floor and put it back on the table. Omar was paralyzed with fear. He just kept staring at the liquid on the floor where the vial had smashed. *This is a biological weapon, and it splashed on me!* Nura recognized the terror in his eyes and said, "Don't be such a baby. It won't affect you—unless you're a Jew."

Omar replied, "You mean it isn't *supposed* to affect me. Even if you're right, it's still a dangerous strain of influenza that killed millions." Nura reached in the case and pulled out a one-liter bottle of bleach and poured it on the floor where the vial had broken. "There. Satisfied?"

"No! I don't want to catch this influenza!"

Nura gawked at him in disgust. "You are such a woman." Turning to Omar, she said, "Let's get on with it before your men screw it up even more."

Omar asked, "We don't have enough now. Do we take a little from the others to fill a new one?"

"No, Andreas was very precise. We don't inject one of them. There is some redundancy in the protocol. We can skip one of the junkies. You pick which, it doesn't matter. Pull him out and take him outside." Omar nodded and told Ivan to unchain the junkie in the cell with Abel and take him outside.

Nura and Omar took the four remaining syringes and headed down the hall. They grabbed Saad and Abdul in case any of the prisoners were difficult. They first dealt with the old Jewish man and his junkie. They told them the shots were inoculations against leishmania, and they accepted them without further issue. Next, they went in Abel's room. He was hunched in the corner and almost catatonic. Nura asked Omar, "Is he okay?"

Omar whispered, "Yes, physically he is fine, but his mental state is . . . delicate. He goes between agitation and this. It will not affect the test."

Nura walked up to Abel and said, "Hi, Abel. This will all be over soon. We have been talking to the French government and they are negotiating with us. They have insisted, however, that we guarantee your health. Given this area is rife with sand flies and they transmit leishmaniasis, we are going to give you a vaccination for leishmania. We want to make sure you stay healthy. Will you let me do that?"

Abel slowly turned to her. His eyes were empty and blank. She started to reach for his arm but he lashed out, screaming like some sort of wounded animal. He lunged at her but was stopped by his chain. She stepped back and Omar took the syringe from her hand. He yelled at Saad and Abdul, "Restrain him!" The two men grabbed him, pulled his arms behind his back, and forced him to the floor. As Saad sat on his back, Omar took the needle and injected him in his left buttock.

The last room was Michael and the Romanian prostitute. As they entered, Michael was messing with his handcuffs. His wrist was red and bleeding, and the skin along the base of his hand was chafed and torn. He had been trying to work the handcuffs off to no avail. Nura said, "Michael, Michael, Michael. We are negotiating your release but we promised the French to return you in one piece. They are not going to believe that you injured yourself." As she said this, Saad grabbed the prostitute's arm and held her while Omar injected her.

Michael shouted, "What are you doing to her?"

Nura replied, "Just a vaccination."

"You're not putting any of that shit in me."

Nura smiled. "No, of course not. You are plenty healthy. This girl is in a weakened state due to her drug use. She needs it, you do not. We are in negotiations with the French to exchange you for our colleagues but it will take a few days. In the meantime, I suggest you eat to keep your strength up."

"Fuck you, bitch!"

"Have it your way." Nura and Omar returned to the operating theater. When they got there, Nura asked, "How long?"

Omar shrugged, "The influenza? A day, maybe more. As for the other? I have no idea. Like I told you, I have no expertise in these diseases."

Nura said, "Okay. Today is Day Zero. Oh, we have one more thing to take care of. I need to go to my room first, but meet me outside in a few minutes."

Five minutes later, Nura walked out into the bright sunshine of the Libyan afternoon. Omar was already out there waiting for her. Off by the car, Ivan stood with the junkie he had removed from Abel's room. Nura walked up to them, pulled her Beretta .380 from her belt, and shot the junkie in the head. He collapsed on the ground, twitched, and died. Omar came running over. "What did you do that for?"

"It's not like he was going to survive this anyway. Now we have one less prisoner to guard and one less mouth to feed."

Omar protested, "But I needed him! I was going to use him to test whether or not the pathogen is airborne."

Nura replied flatly, "It is."

"But I wanted to separate him from the other prisoners to determine how easy it is to contract the virus when not directly exposed to the infected."

Nura turned to him and said, "You still can. You have all of us for that."

Omar cringed. "I had hoped we might take precautions . . ."

Nura laughed. "Like they would help? We're sleeping in an underground bunker with no ventilation next to six, uh five, people exposed to a biological weapon. You think a cloth mask is going to save you?"

She was right but he wouldn't let it go. "But what if Kalib Kabir was wrong? What if it affects more than just the Jews?"

She replied with a shrug, "Then we're all dead." Just as she said this, she turned and shot Ivan in the chest. As he collapsed to his knees, she shot him again in the head. Omar stood there in stunned silence. Putting her gun back in her belt she said, "He was incompetent. This was your fault for selecting him. Now get Saad to clean this mess up."

* * *

The prisoners started to show symptoms the next afternoon—except Michael. Abel and the prostitute were first. They became feverish and developed a cough. Abel complained of a headache and the prostitute started vomiting. The surviving junkie was next. He had a fever, sore throat, and diarrhea. The old man followed right behind him with diarrhea and a bad cough. On day two, Michael began showing the initial signs of infection. He was the healthiest of the test subjects but by day four he was suffering from a high fever, cough, sore throat, and body aches. This continued for three days. All except Abel ended up requiring IV fluids to keep them from dehydrating to the point of death.

At Omar's insistence, the terrorists wore surgical masks in an attempt to avoid contracting the disease. This worked for Nura and Omar but Saad and Abdul, who were tasked with emptying the buckets the prisoners used as toilets, started showing symptoms on day five.

Omar was concerned. After all, Saad was his cousin and he didn't want to have to explain to his aunt that he had killed her grandson. Nura tried to reassure him, "Saad is young. He will fight through this. It is the very old and very young who most often die from the flu. But at least this confirms its transmissibility." He did not share her optimism. With Saad and Abdul sick too, all the work of caring for the prisoners fell to Nura and Omar. He wanted to bring in another person or two but Nura refused. They had to stick to the plan.

Finally, on day seven, the inoculated prisoners started to recover. Abel's fever broke and his cough was gone but he grew ever more listless and his appetite wasn't returning. Michael was a day or so behind him but he too wasn't eating and was suffering from exhaustion. The three other prisoners grew stronger each day, and when Saad and Abdul were sufficiently recovered to resume their duties, Omar had them put Abel and Michael in the same room and put the prostitute in a room by herself. By day nine, Abel was catatonic, but this time it wasn't due to fear. Michael was trying to talk but couldn't put together a coherent sentence. As he struggled to find words, he became frustrated. Nura took this as a sign that at least some of his higher brain functions were working; he was aware that his body and brain were failing but he was unable to do anything about it. On the morning of day ten, Abel was in a coma. He died later that afternoon. Michael started the day sitting in the corner rocking back and forth babbling incoherently. By evening, he had slipped into a coma and died sometime in the night.

Upon finding Michael dead, Nura approached Omar and said, "The last Jew is dead. I think we can consider this a successful conclusion to our test. We need to let Abu Almawt know the good news."

Omar cautioned her. "Don't be too hasty. We need to confirm the results."

"What do you mean? The Jews are dead. The old Mizrahi Jew, the European girl, and the Arab junkie—along with Saad and Abdul—are all alive, just like Andreas predicted."

"Yes, Kalib Kabir predicted who would die and who would live, but that does not mean it was his prion disease that killed them. People die from influenza every day."

Nura protested, "But the symptoms were exactly as he predicted!"

Omar nodded. "Yes, they were. But that might also be the result of encephalitis or some other complication. I need to perform necropsies to be sure. I need to examine their brains and compare them to the brain of one of the others."

"Very well, then do it."

Omar had a heavy steel table brought into the room where Michael and Abel's bodies lay on the floor. It was to be his makeshift autopsy table. He then ran an extension cord down the corridor to the room to plug in his electric autopsy bone saw. Saad and Abdul lifted Abel's body onto the table, put a bucket under the low corner to catch the blood, and left. They knew what was coming and didn't want to see it. Omar took a scalpel, made an incision around the top of Abel's head, and peeled off his scalp, revealing the skull below. With the saw, he cut the cranium all the way around his head and, using a small screwdriver, pried off the top of his skull. Omar cut away all the blood vessels and started rolling the brain from the brainpan. He reached under to cut the brainstem, lifted the brain out of the cranium, and placed it in a large, shallow plastic bowl. He sliced the brain in half laterally and examined the two halves. The interior of the brain was gray and hollow. When he finished, he called Saad and Abdul back in to put Abel's body in the corner and put Michael's body up on the table. As they left, Omar started to repeat the process.

As he was cutting back the scalp, Nura walked into the room. She wasn't bothered in the least by the sight of the dead bodies or the brain in a bowl. "How's it going? Do you have your confirmation yet?"

Exasperated, Omar said, "It's not that simple." Motioning to the bowl, he said, "That's the brain of the Jew who was inoculated. I'm about to remove the brain of the one who caught it via airborne transmission, but I still need to compare them to otherwise healthy brains. So, if you'll excuse me . . ."

Nura studied the brain in the bowl. "Healthy brains, huh? Okay." She walked out.

A few minutes later, there were gunshots. Omar dropped his scalpel and ran toward the entrance of the bunker. Outside, Saad and Abdul were cowering behind the old Citroën. On the ground were the bodies of the old Mizrahi Jew, the prostitute, and the remaining junkie. All had been shot in the chest. Nura was kneeling over the junkie with a machete hacking on his neck. Blood sprayed over her face and clothes. After three hard chops, the junkie's head rolled from his body. Omar shouted, "What the hell are you doing?"

"Speeding up the autopsy process. I'm getting you your healthy brains."

He was appalled by the scene of this pretty young girl hacking the heads off corpses. "Oh my God! This is barbaric!"

"Don't be ridiculous. We were going to kill them anyway, and you were going to cut out their brains anyway. I'm just saving Saad and Abdul the trouble of carrying their corpses inside. This is much more efficient, don't you think?" Omar was speechless. She moved over to the next corpse. She swung the machete, and there was a disgusting "shwack" as it sliced into the neck of the dead Romanian prostitute. "Now, finish your work so I can tell Abu Almawt the good news. And please tell your cousin and his friend I have no plans to kill them so they can quit cowering." Wiping blood from her eyes she added, "They can dispose of the bodies while I get cleaned up."

CHAPTER SIX
THE BEST-LAID PLANS OF MICE AND MEN

Since Steve Chang was new to the Praetorians, Gunny assigned Hans Koenig as the lead on the trip to Cairo to find and exploit the Black Sun telecommunications relay. Steve was part of the team, of course, since he had the most technical expertise, but Hans had operational control. They had no idea what they might run into once there so Gunny insisted they bring Nigel Finch and John Kernan for security. For his part, Rusty Travis stayed out of it. He was upper management. He certainly had a good deal of technical expertise, a very good understanding of their targets, and a lot of common sense, but he understood his limitations. Once they decided on an objective, he left it to the team to plan and execute the operation. His job was to make sure they had whatever they needed to accomplish it. Even if he had some concerns that some of them occasionally were a little too gung-ho for their own good, he had full faith that Gunny would temper their enthusiasm when necessary. Even if they didn't agree with Gunny, none of them would dare question his authority.

The four men flew to Cairo on a commercial flight; using a $50 million private jet might be a little too high profile. Rusty, being a billionaire, could certainly get away with it, but not a bunch of ex-military types. They packed their electronic gear in Pelican cases and shipped it on the plane. Their cover story was they were with a private security firm doing a system upgrade for a wealthy Egyptian businessman.

They checked into a hotel closer to the industrial areas west of downtown and away from the popular tourist destinations. Upon arrival, Steve and Hans checked their gear to make sure it had arrived in one piece. John and Nigel went about their own work. John left to rent a vehicle. He settled on a black, South Korean-made SsangYong Actyon SUV. It wasn't as roomy as he would have liked but it'd blend in better with local traffic and didn't shout "foreigner" like a big GMC or Mercedes would. Nigel took care of the weapons. He had some retired SBS buddies who worked security in the Ras Qattara oil fields west of Cairo. He'd reached out to them and told them he was on his way. One of them met him at a café a couple of kilometers from their hotel. He told Nigel where to pick up some reliable small arms—no questions asked. Armed with cash and his friend's name for bona fides, he came back with two Beretta 9 mm pistols and a box of ammunition. Back at the hotel he stripped and cleaned the weapons. They were old but functional. This was purely precautionary anyway. If all went as planned, they wouldn't actually be interacting with anyone. John went out and returned with McDonald's hamburgers and a six-pack of Sakara beer. Once they all ate, they went over their plan for the night.

Hans laid it out. "Okay, our first task is to find the incoming cell phone for the relay. We have the number, thanks to Nura Ostergaard, but now we need to physically find it. Almost all modern cell phones have GPS, so when you call 911 or its equivalent, your location is automatically provided to the operator. Unfortunately, these clever bastards either used an older non-GPS phone or they disabled it. Either way, we're going to have to go old school and use tower triangulation. It's going to be moving and there's a lot of clutter in this city so the signal will be bouncing all over the place. It may take a while. Steve, any suggestions?"

Steve thought about it for moment and added. "I suggest we fire up the equipment here first to make sure our target is on and active. Once we have it, we wait."

"Wait? For what?"

"For it to stop. If it's in a bus or truck and the vehicle goes to ground at night, it'll be easier to locate—you know, stationary target versus moving one. Even if we can't isolate the specific vehicle, we'll at least know what we're searching for. If we geolocate it right now on Ramsis Street or out by the airport on the M67, which one of the thousands of trucks, buses, or cars is the one we want? If we track it to a taxi company, a bus station, or a truck terminal, we'll at least know what kind of vehicle it is. Then in the morning, we can set up nearby to see when it leaves."

John said, "Not to rain on your parade, but if it's a bus terminal like Sarah suggested, there might be fifty buses leaving at the same time."

Steve replied, "That's true, but at least we'll know what general direction it goes. In the United States, the same buses and drivers tend to work the same routes. If they do that here—and I'm hoping to God they do—then we can narrow it down more each day. It may take a few days to zero in on the right one but we'll get it."

Nigel asked, "And if it isn't in a bus?"

Hans answered, "Well, if it's in a taxi or delivery truck, then we're screwed and this will take longer. I hope you all brought plenty of clean undies."

Nigel quipped, "I just turn 'em inside out. You get twice as many days out of them that way."

John grimaced in disgust. "You are a nasty, nasty man."

Nigel shot back, "Oh, like you never wore the same shorts for weeks on end."

"Well, sure—in combat. Not when there was a goddamn laundry downstairs. Do us all a favor and wash them. I don't want to be sitting in a van with you smelling like ass."

Hans interjected, "Okay guys. I like Steve's plan, but I want to modify it a bit. My concern is that if the relay is hardwired into the vehicle's electrical system, it may power down when the vehicle is turned off. I want to pick it up on the road close to the end of the night and follow it back home. Grab a couple hours of sleep. The buses don't stop running until 0100 hours and they start again at 0530, so we're in for some long nights."

While the rest of the guys took a nap, Steve went to work triangulating on the relay. He was too keyed up to sleep. This was his first operation for the Praetorians and he was nervous. What he didn't tell his teammates was that this was his first real operation, period. He'd traveled to US military bases around the world when he was in the Air Force and a couple of times with

NSA, but that didn't count. This was a real operation in a potentially hostile environment against an opponent that wouldn't hesitate to kill them if they were discovered. There was little room for error.

The men woke up around 2300 hours. Steve had been monitoring the movements of the relay for several hours. When Hans finally got up, he asked, "Where are we?"

Steve replied, "The relay has been on the move pretty much since we got here. It's over in Giza at the moment." Hans leaned over and peered at the screen of the laptop computer. There was an electronic map of Cairo with a series of red dots indicating the locations where the bus had been during the past two hours."

Hans asked, "How's the system working? What's the refresh rate?"

"Depends on where the target is. Out in Giza it's fairly open; relatively little clutter. I can get a good position every thirty seconds to a minute. The closer to downtown, the worse it gets due to backscatter from the buildings. It's following a set route, so I am hoping it's a bus; that would make our life easier, at least I think so."

Hans replied, "Well, maybe. A city bus yard may have security."

"Yeah, but probably somebody's fat uncle Omar. You know government workers."

Hans cautioned him, "Don't make assumptions. We're all former government workers too. I wouldn't want to run into any of us in the middle of the night, would you?"

Sufficiently humbled, Steve concurred. "Yeah, I guess you have a point there. Well, regardless of what it is and where it is and who's guarding it, we need to get at it."

"You got that right."

After getting some strong Arab coffee from the café next to the hotel, the men piled into the SUV. If anyone asked, they were prepared to explain they worked at night when the client's offices were closed—but no one asked. Cairo was a modern city with over twenty million inhabitants. People there were on the move twenty-four seven. John got behind the wheel of the Actyon with Nigel riding shotgun. Both men were armed and ready to confront any threat. Steve and Hans got in the back seat. Steve fired up the cellular intercept equipment and the laptop computer. The equipment connected to the local cell system through a maintenance channel reserved for radio frequency engineers in the field. Steve used it to connect to the internal network. As he typed in the telephone number of the relay's cell phone and hit enter, John asked, "Where to, guys?"

Hans looked at the screen and after a minute replied, "Okay, got it. Drive north."

The black SUV cruised along the dark Cairo streets. They weren't trying to intercept whatever vehicle was hosting the parasitic relay, they just wanted to stay close. It would've been difficult to intercept anyway. The streets were still very busy despite the late hour, so there were plenty of "suspect" vehicles.

Nigel was bored so he asked, "I'm probably going to regret this, but how exactly does this triangulation work?"

Steve replied, "Okay, cellular triangulation takes advantage of the fact that a cell phone, like the one in the relay, is constantly searching for a cell tower. It repeatedly sends out a 'handshake' that tells the network 'here I am!' All the networks talk to each other. This has to happen so that when someone calls your phone, the network knows not only what country you're in, but exactly which cell tower to route the call through. That's usually the primary tower, the closest tower with the strongest signal. As the phone moves, like we're doing now, the closest tower changes and the phone's location has to be updated on the network. If your cell phone is sitting on your kitchen counter at home that tower doesn't change, but when you're moving it has to update its location thousands of times a day. Knowing the identity of this primary tower gives one point of reference: coverage area of the tower, which could be a city block or several square miles. Because there are usually three antennas pointing in different directions, we can also get a rough bearing from the tower to the target."

Steven continued, "But a cell phone also identifies a secondary tower in case the primary tower is too busy to handle a call. This information is also passed to the network: 'Tower A is closest, but if it's busy, I can use tower B.' This now gives two points of reference—two tower coverage areas that overlap in a limited area. Like an old Venn diagram from school."

Steve took a breath. "There is still one more factor at play—cell phone output power. As a cell phone gets closer to its primary tower, it doesn't need a lot of power to reach it so it dials back its power to save battery life. As it gets farther way, it ramps up power just enough to make sure it can reach the tower and a call can go through. This minimum required power information is also sent to the network for both the primary and secondary towers, providing two more data points—essentially the phone's distance from the two towers. Put these all together and the network can locate a cell phone to within a very small area. The only problem is that the signals tend to bounce off buildings in built-up areas. This degrades the location accuracy and slows the update time. That's what we're dealing with here. By the time the system zeroes in on the target's location, the target has already moved on."

Nigel groaned and John laughed, "Aren't you happy you asked?"

Hans said to John, "Okay, keep heading north. The signal is moving northeast on Salah Salem Street toward the airbase. Just hang in that area. Don't go north of Merryland Park unless I say so."

John chirped, "Roger that. Continuing north."

They followed the signal loosely until 0045 hours. Hans checked his watch. "If it's a bus, it should be going home soon. Service ends in fifteen minutes." About five minutes later he took a deep satisfying breath. "Okay, boys and girls, our target has turned around and is heading back south. Someone is going home early. I'd say it's a bus. Let's see where he goes."

They followed the signal as it continued southwest and finally stopped. "Okay, target is stationary."

John asked, "Where?"

Hans replied, "Give me a minute. I want to make sure the signal stabilizes." After two or three minutes, he said, "Okay, we have a firm location: Ahmed Helmy Bus Station just north of Ramsis Railway Station."

Nigel yawned and said, "Well, I guess Sarah was right. Now can we go back to the hotel?"

Hans said, "Sure, but we need to be back out on the street by 0430. Fortunately, this place isn't so far from our hotel. Let's go home, grab a few Z's, and go back out. Everyone meet in the lobby at 0415 just to be safe. And Nigel, change your shorts."

John was up at 0400 hours. He was groggy given he'd only had a couple of hours of sleep, but it was nothing he hadn't experienced in Afghanistan, Iraq, Syria, and any number of other crappy places around the world. The hotel room came with a small coffee maker, and John's first task was to make a strong cup before he did anything else. This morning's work wouldn't be hard or dangerous but he did need to be awake for it.

He hit the lobby fifteen minutes later. Steve and Hans were already there waiting for him. "Where's Nigel?" The others just shrugged.

From behind him came the Scotsman's booming voice. "Right behind you, ya bloody woman!"

Hans asked, "Did you change your shorts?"

"No need, it's been less than twenty-four hours. Tomorrow, I promise."

They walked out to the parking lot and piled into the black SUV. Traffic was light at that hour and they made good time. They parked in front of the Allah Mahaba grocery across the street from the Ahmed Helmy Bus Station. Steve fired up the computer, logged into the cell company's server, and pinged the cell phone number associated with the relay. There was nothing.

"The relay isn't registering. Could be a problem."

Hans remained calm. "Too early to worry. If the bus is shut down, it may be too. I'm more worried about this neighborhood; it's a fucking nightmare. We have the railroad tracks to the south and Nafka Al Sabtia Street to the west. We have a road that goes under the train tracks and another that goes over. Then there are all these damn minibuses. There must be a thousand of them. We still don't know if the relay is in one of them or a full-size city bus. If and when it moves, it's going to be a bitch to figure out which one it's in. To make matters worse, all these damn apartment blocks are making the signal bounce all over the place. By the time we get a fix, the damn thing might be gone."

Steve smiled, "No worries. We'll get there." They all sat quietly for the next several minutes until the computer chimed. "We're up!"

Hans checked the screen. A red dot had just appeared on the map right in the center of the bus station. They stared at the dot for several more minutes until it started to move. Hans checked at his watch. "Okay, we have movement at 0450. Why so early?"

From the front seat, John said, "You don't know shit about buses, do you. The route doesn't start at the bus yard, it starts somewhere out there at one end of the route or the other. He's headed for his start point."

Nigel was in the passenger seat with a pair of binoculars. He was fixed on the front of the bus station. "Okay. I've got four, no five, buses moving toward Emtedad Ahmed Helimi."

Hans asked, "Are they going east or west?"

Nigel shot back, "How the fuck should I know? None of these assholes use turn signals. Okay, they're moving. I have two going east and the other three are coming west right toward us." He put down the binoculars and pointed them out to John. "There. That's them."

John nodded. "Roger. I see them. There are also about ten of those fucking minibuses pulling out with them."

Nigel said to Hans. "We got two buses going north and one going south. Which way, boss man?"

Hans said, "Go with the numbers, go north. But get me the number on the southbound bus if you can."

"Roger that." As John pulled out into traffic, Nigel picked up his binoculars and scanned south. "Okay, southbound is 1459, that's one-four-five-niner."

Hans scribbled it down on pad of paper. "Okay, got it."

They continued north following the two buses and about four minibuses for several minutes on Shobra Street. As they approached the Rod El-Farag Metro Station, Hans asked, "Steve, we need an update on our target."

"Give me a second. This backscatter is a killer." After about thirty seconds he said, "Shit. It just updated. Our target is heading south; repeat, bogey is southbound. He's approaching the 6th October bridge over the Nile. We picked the wrong horse. Damn it. I guess we can regroup and try again tomorrow."

John said, "Fuck that shit. It's a goddamn bus." John turned left in front of opposing traffic just past the Shoubra Engineering school onto Dnshwai Street and cut into the neighborhood. He had no clue where he was going and was operating purely on dead reckoning. He took another left on Saeam Al Daher past the Nasser Girls' School and another hard left onto Al Yazgi Street and then a right to go south on Shobra. He gunned the engine of the Actyon SUV and sped after his quarry.

Nigel was laughing heartily. "Jesus Christ, John. Now you're driving!"

Hans yelled, "Goddamn it, John. Was all that really necessary?" Steve just tried to keep the computer in his lap from flying across the SUV's cabin.

John shot back, "Just tell me where it is. I'll get us there. If I can't catch a fucking bus . . ."

John drove aggressively—like an Egyptian. He worked his way south and west while Steve gave him regular updates on the target's location. Traffic was getting progressively heavier as they approached the Nile. After about twenty minutes they were over the 6th October Bridge speeding toward Giza.

Steve called out, "Whoa, whoa, whoa! He went south on Nile Street along the canal!"

John snapped, "Too late, already past it. I'll need quicker updates, my man."

Steve shot back, "You get 'em as I get 'em. Okay, keep heading west and then go south on Wazaret Al Zeraha. This road ends there. Stay in the left lane and take the ramp down, then stay south. We should catch up to him by the zoo." John followed Steve's directions and Nigel acted as his navigator to make sure they were on track. After a few minutes the green expanse of the Orman Botanical Gardens opened in front of them.

John slowed down. "Decision time. Right or left?"

Hans replied, "Uh, go left and then circle the park until we get a fix on him."

"Roger that."

Steve peered at the computer screen, willing it to give him the information he needed. Finally, it did. "Okay, he's stationary. Opposite end of the park. He's at the west end, by the university. Take a right and another right on Nahdet Masr and he'll be directly ahead of you—about five hundred meters."

"Roger that." As John made the turn west on Nahdet Masr, Nigel picked up his binoculars. He scanned the area ahead of them but had trouble seeing around a delivery truck. Then he spotted it.

"Okay, I have a bus stopped on the other side of the cross street. He's stopped in a circular turnaround on the other side of that big fancy pillar over there."

Hans asked, "Any of those minibuses around?"

Nigel panned right and left. "Nope. Just one bus, some private cars, and a couple of taxis."

"What's the bus doing?"

"Nothing, just sitting there."

John interjected, "I'm pulling over up here on the right. I think I can hang here for a few minutes. If I have to roll by him, it might be hard to reacquire."

Hans concurred. "Good thinking. We can keep eyes on him from here. Nigel, can you make out the bus number?"

Nigel peered through the binoculars. "I'm blocked by a truck. Hold on a second. Uh, okay, I have 1459. That's our baby."

Steve interjected, "Just got another update. The relay is not moving and according to this is about one hundred meters west of our location."

John asked, "How accurate is that reading?"

"Should be pretty accurate. I would like to get a couple more just to be safe."

They sat parked on the side of the street for another five minutes. It was almost 0530. Nigel sat up. "Okay, we have activity. The driver opened his door and is taking on passengers. Our boy is right on time."

Steve asked, "What are the chances that this bus driver is a member of Black Sun? I mean he could have the relay in his lunch box or something and he plugs it in the cigarette lighter when he gets in. That would explain why it goes off at night. He unplugs it to take it home."

Hans answered. "Not likely. The relay stays active from 0500 to 0100. That's a hell of a long day for one bus driver. My bet is that it's buried somewhere in the wiring system. Probably not in the passenger section; too big of a risk that someone finds it or spills a Coke on it or something. No, if you have offline access to the bus, you have the time to bury it deep. That is not to say there isn't someone in the bus yard or maintenance facility who is Black Sun. Someone had to put it in there. All conjecture at this point. We need firm confirmation that this bus is our bogey."

A minute later, the bus pulled out, crossed Cairo University Road, and drove east on Nahdet Masr past the team on the opposite side of the road. Steve chimed in, "Target eastbound on Nahdet Masr. I'd say that's our bogey."

Hans agreed but wanted to make sure. "You're probably right, but let's follow him a little bit longer to confirm."

John replied, "You're the boss. Not like I had a date anyway." After following municipal bus number 1459 for two more hours, Hans was satisfied, and they returned to their hotel to plan the night's activities.

The team mustered at 0100 in Hans's hotel room. They wanted to give all the buses and their drivers ample time to return to the bus yard and go home. The area was difficult. It was wide open and had little cover. The area was surrounded by apartment buildings, restaurants, pharmacies, and other businesses. Most of them would be closed, but in a city as big as Cairo, even at 0200 you expect to run into someone. They hid in plain sight.

The buses were built by Mercedes so their cover would be as a team of Mercedes engineers upgrading the bus's electronics. Steve created some work orders on Mercedes letterhead as well as some official-looking company IDs that he laminated at a local print shop. They went out and purchased matching gray coveralls, and John even found some embroidered Mercedes logos at a small shop specializing in exotic car paraphernalia. Hans had the advantage of actually being German and also speaking Arabic. He would be in charge while Steve would pretend to be a Chinese technician. Nigel and John would be mechanics and just stay quiet. At 0200 hours on the dot Hans and the guys strode into the bus yard. Hans directed the others to fan out and find bus 1459 while he stood in the middle of parking area looking rather imperious. Within minutes, a tired security guard walked up to him and began interrogating him in Arabic.

He wiped some food off his chin as he approached. With his hand on his nightstick as an implied warning, the security guard bellowed, "Hey! You there. What do you think you're doing here?"

Hans turned to face him, "Ah, there you are. Where have you been? We were looking for you."

The guard was confused. "You were looking for me? What for?"

"We are here to service one of the buses. We're from Mercedes."

Pointing to the logo on Han's coveralls, the guard retorted, "No shit. But what are you doing here? No one told me anyone was going to be here tonight. And why in the middle of the night? It seems very suspicious to me."

Hans produced the phony work order and gave it to the man. It was in German, of course, and the guard couldn't read it. He did recognize the Mercedes logo and the City of Cairo crest on the top of the paper. "We're here now because we can't exactly work on a bus while it's in service, now can we? Believe me, we'd rather do this during the day, but the city transportation authority doesn't want to take the bus offline, even for a day. This is just an upgrade, not a safety recall, so they want to make sure all the buses stay in service."

The guard scratched his scruffy chin. "I guess that makes sense. I should call my supervisor about this."

Hans glanced at his watch. "Well, it's after 2:00 a.m. already. If you're going to call him and wake him up, you'd better do it now. We have five buses to work on tonight."

The guard did not relish the idea of waking up his boss in the middle of the night. He studied the work order again and then handed it back to Hans. "Okay, but how long is this going to take?"

"Not sure, but if all goes well, not very long at all." As he said this, Nigel whistled from across the yard and pointed. "Well, it seems my colleague found the vehicle in question. If you'll excuse me, I have work to do. I have allocated twenty-three minutes for this work and I need to stay on schedule." He turned on his heel and left.

The guard watched him leave and muttered to himself, "Fucking Germans." He walked back to his office and his dinner.

Hans quickly walked over to where Nigel was standing. Steve and John were walking over too. Nigel said, "Back here. It's hemmed in between two or three other buses. That should give us some screening."

Steve walked up to the bus. He opened the briefcase he was carrying and removed a small radio frequency detector. As soon as he turned it on, the detector started chirping. He turned down the volume and set the frequency to match the command channel for the cell phone. "We need to fire up this bus to power up the relay."

John said, "I'm on it." He climbed in the bus and in a few seconds, it rumbled to life. He jumped out and said, "All yours."

Steve was impressed. "Did they teach you that in the SEALs?"

"No, auto shop. The keys were on the visor." John and Nigel took positions a few meters away to provide security. Steve got on the bus and waited for the relay to boot up. It took only a minute or so. It immediately began searching for the nearest cell tower. Steve turned on a cell tower spoofer and the phone connected to it. Then, pretending to be the cellular network command channel, he told the phone to increase its transmit power to its maximum—four watts. He then started walking around the bus with his RF detector and quickly found the device. It was under the dashboard of the bus attached to the wiring harness using zip ties. It was a relatively small device—about seven inches by four inches and about an inch and a half thick. There were two wires coming out of the box; one was spliced into one of the wires in the harness and the other was screwed into the metal frame for a ground.

Hans watched as Steve gingerly cut the zip ties and pulled the relay out while leaving it connected. "Well, that didn't take long. Good job, Steve."

"Thanks, boss. Now I need to see what we're dealing with." He removed the four small screws that held the back plate on the box. He opened it up and peered inside. He was surprised at how simple it was. It was just two old Samsung Galaxy smartphones wired together. "Okay, this thing is pretty much unaltered. That means the relay is being accomplished via software."

"You mean an app?"

"Yeah, pretty much. I think they're using internet calling. The incoming call comes on one phone which automatically answers and sends the audio to the other phone which then sends it back out via an internet phone service like Skype or Cloudphone. All I have to do is get the login and password for the app. These old phones are easy to crack. Should only take a minute." He connected the phones to his laptop computer one at a time. Within a few minutes he had downloaded all the login information for both phones and any apps running on them. He confirmed they worked by logging on to each phone in turn and accessing the call logs and apps. Satisfied, he put them back in the plastic case and, using new zip ties, reattached them to the wiring harness under the dash. "Okay, we're done. Let's blow this popsicle stand."

Hans gaped at him in disbelief. "That's it? How are we supposed to listen in?"

Steve grinned. "From the comfort of our own home with a beer in hand. I have all the login data, phone EMEIs, SIM card numbers, and everything. I can clone this entire relay so that we can listen to every call and collect every phone number from Cyprus or anywhere else. In the meantime, I'm going to tell the internet calling app to make every call a conference call with this computer and save them as .wav audio files."

Hans smiled. "Damn, I love technology."

* * *

D r. Omar Trabelsi continued the grisly task of slicing open the brains of the test subjects Nura had shot and then decapitated. Trabelsi was not really squeamish but the sight of this slight, attractive girl hacking people's heads off with a machete was more than a little shocking. Seeing her dress and act like a young European woman made him forget that she was a cold-blooded killer—a fact she reminded him of repeatedly. He was from Derna, a city east of Tripoli, with the reputation of being the most fundamentalist city in all of Libya. He deserted Gaddafi's army toward the end of the war and joined the ISIL fighters who took control of Derna after Gaddafi's death. He stayed there even after ISIL was ousted by the Shura Council of Mujahideen in 2015. Doctors were in such short supply that even a former ISIL-affiliated doctor was wanted. This was especially true during the ensuing two-year-long siege of the city by forces loyal to General Haftar. Trabelsi escaped by sea to Egypt just before it fell. In Egypt he reconnected with some of his old extremist colleagues. This is when he learned about Black Sun and its young, educated leader—Dr. Khalid ibn Mafous Al-Maadi.

For each brain he dissected, Trabelsi took measurements of the brain's weight and dimensions. He also took photographs of their interior structures. Nura didn't care. To her, it was an unnecessary waste of time. She just wanted to know that the virus killed the Jews. But in his own mind, Omar was still a scientist and he felt obligated to collect data for posterity. Unbeknownst to Nura, he had also been taking blood samples from the test subjects. He meticulously collected and logged their blood before exposure, during the infection, and after their immune systems had cleared the virus. He was particularly interested in those samples collected when the virus titers in their blood were at their maximum. The virus could be easily isolated from this blood or the blood itself used to infect other people. This was a weapon, and he wasn't willing to just toss it aside. What if something happened to Al-Maadi's virus and it was accidently destroyed? His blood samples would be the only way to salvage the plan. He was planning ahead for his own power, his own legacy. When Black Sun united the Arab world, someone would have to run Libya. It might as well be him.

As he was finishing with the last brain, Nura walked into his makeshift laboratory. "When will you be done? You've been at this for hours."

Trabelsi stripped off his surgical gloves. "I have just finished with the last one."

"And?"

He smiled. "Well, there was some trauma due to the decapitations, but I can state unequivocally that the virus worked. The two young Jews showed clear signs of Creutzfeldt-Jakob disease. The onset was very rapid and impressive. In the course of a few days, their brains had deteriorated to the level of someone who had suffered from the disease for years."

She smiled. "So, it's ready to deploy?"

"I should say so, yes. Do you want me to call Abu Almawt and let him know?"

Nura knew Trabelsi was a sycophant and just wanted to ingratiate himself with Al-Maadi to her detriment. "No, you need to clean up here. I'll tell him."

Trabelsi grumbled, "Yes, by all means. You do it."

"You need to dispose of the bodies. Have Saad burn them. I want no trace for anyone to find. Then burn out this bunker. Every trace must be gone, do you understand?"

"Yes, but we don't have enough petrol. I'll send Saad to Zawara. Now that the tests have been completed, it should be all right." Trabelsi was lying. There was plenty of petrol. In fact, there were three other bunkers of similar size in the immediate area that he didn't tell Nura about. It was in one of these bunkers where he was storing his blood samples. It hadn't been looted and was still connected to the power grid.

Nura mulled this over and then said, "Okay. That's fine, but do it after I leave. I don't want anyone slipping up and leading government forces here before I can leave. It is imperative that I get to Abu Almawt." *Go ahead and get yourselves killed. We don't need you anymore. But do it after I'm gone.*

This was hyperbole on Nura's part. While she had secured the virus and made sure the samples got to him and Abu Almawt, her role was essentially over and she was no longer vital to the success of their mission. If she disappeared completely, it wouldn't affect the deployment of the virus. He considered just killing her. She'd been a pain in his ass ever since he'd met her. It irritated him to no end to have to take orders from her. She was little more than a girl while he was a doctor, had been a colonel in the Libyan Army, and an active member of ISIL while she was still flirting with boys in junior high school. However, Abu Almawt was very fond of her and he couldn't afford to anger him. Abu Almawt was the head of Shams Sawda; their plan and, indeed Black Sun itself, could not succeed without him.

"Of course. I understand completely. I'll have Saad take you to Zawara. We have arranged to get you to Egypt on a fishing boat so you can avoid all the skirmishing between the Libyan National Army and Haftar's forces. Once you are safely at sea, he can return with the petrol, and we will finish here."

"Good." Nura left and went to her room. She retrieved her cell phone and powered it on. She walked out of the bunker. The signal was weak. She scrambled up the steep side of the dirt-covered bunker to the top, where she got two bars; it'd have to suffice. She dialed the number and waited. It always took a couple of minutes for the call to go through, but that was a cheap price to pay for security. North of downtown Cairo, the old Samsung cell phone in municipal bus 1459 came alive. It received the call and sent the audio through the short 3.5 mm cable to the other phone, which accessed an internet telephone app and called Khalid Al-Maadi's burner.

He answered, "Yes?"

"It's me, Alfaar. Kalib Kabir's recipe worked as planned. The soup was a total success."

"That's excellent news! I'll now make sure the caterer prepares enough for the whole wedding party."

"When are the nuptials?"

"I'm not sure, exactly. We need to make sure the bride is ready, but soon. Are you coming home?"

"Yes, it will be a couple of days though. Traffic is terrible here."

"I understand. I may not be here when you arrive. I have to meet with the, uh, caterers."

Tears welled up in Nura's eyes. "I miss you, my love."

"And I miss you. When you get here, go to the apartment. We will be together soon. I have to go now. Travel safe."

"I will." With that she ended the call. She wiped the tears from her eyes and stumbled back down off the bunker. Seeing Saad, she said, "We're leaving. Be ready to go in ten minutes."

Saad stammered, "Uh, I need to ask my cousin. It's his car, I mean."

"Tell him what you like but Abu Almawt put me in charge here—not Al Thaelab."

Saad ran in to let his cousin know what was happening. Nura gathered her meager belongings, got in the old Citroën, and waited.

"Cousin, that woman ordered me to drive her in your car."

Trabelsi sighed. "I know, she's leaving, and the sooner we're rid of her, the better. Take her to the coast and put her on that damn boat. Then gather the rest of the men and return here. If she asks, you are getting fuel to burn everything. Do you understand?"

Saad nodded, "Yes, cousin. I will get rid of her. Then we can make plans to secure this area for our own people."

Trabelsi corrected him, "Not just this area—the whole country."

Saad grinned, "No wonder you are Al Thaelab, the Fox. You are so clever. Did you tell her that bullshit story about Rommel?"

Trabelsi laughed, "Of course! Never tell a potential enemy the truth unless you absolutely have to."

* * *

In Cairo, the team slept in. It had been a long night and the hours they were working on this trip had played havoc with their circadian sleep patterns. While they all forced their bodies to adjust when they were younger, with the exceptions of Steve and Sarah, most of them were now over forty, and their bodies were beginning to push back. Steve got up at 9:00 a.m. and checked the computer. He was shocked that a phone call had come in to the relay. He pulled up the app and found the .wav audio file. He clicked on it and it played, but the conversation was in Arabic. He threw on a pair of pants and a T-shirt before running across the hall to pound on Hans's door. It took a few minutes but a bleary-eyed Hans answered the door wearing boxer shorts and a white undershirt. "What the hell, man? This has better be good."

"There was a call."

Hans immediately woke up. "When?"

"About half an hour ago. I just saw it when I woke up." Going off on a geek tangent, Steve said, "I guess I should have set up some sort of alert

function, maybe a chime or a flashing screen. Maybe some combination of
. . ."

Hans cut him off. "Focus, computer boy. What was the call about?"

"Oh, sorry. Yeah, I'm not sure. It's in Arabic and mine isn't that great.
You need to listen to it."

Hans grabbed his room key and rushed over. Steve cued up the .wav file
for him, and when Hans sat down he hit play. Hans listened intently to the
short conversation and then played it twice more. "Go wake up the other
guys. I'm calling Gunny. I think this is big."

Steve was a little confused, "What did you hear? All I got out of it was
something about soup, a caterer, and a wedding, but my Arabic isn't great."

Hans glanced at him and said, "Your Arabic is better than you think. In
old school Al Qaeda code, 'marriage' was always a reference to a terrorist
attack. They are talking about the attack. Do we know where the call came
from?"

Steve's fingers danced across the keyboard as he accessed the Vodafone
database for North Africa. "Okay, the call came in from cell tower in western
Libya, south of a town called Zawara. That's an area of weak coverage. That
tower has a southern footprint of many square miles. The call came in on
the antenna with bearing of two hundred degrees—so south-southwest. The
transmit power of the phone was pretty much maxed out, so it wasn't close.
That puts it in the middle of the Sahara Desert."

Hans asked, "Any GPS info?"

"No. None came through. I think it was disabled. These fuckers are smart."

"Okay. We need to get the hell out of here. Go rouse John and Nigel. Tell
them to pack. You pack your shit too." Hans ran back to his room, grabbed
his phone, activated the Signal app, and called Gunny. Signal wasn't perfect, but it provided end-to-end encryption and would prevent the Egyptians
from listening in. When Gunny answered, Hans said, "Hey, it's me. We were
successful last night and it's already paying off. We got a call this morning. A woman calling a man talking about a wedding. She identified herself
as Alfaar and said Kalib Kabir's soup recipe was a total success. I think it's
about the weapon."

Gunny snorted but was quiet for a second. "Alfaar and Kalib Kabir. That
is 'mouse' and 'big dog,' right? AF and KK from Al-Rafah's messages?"

"Oh shit! I didn't even think of that."

Gunny continued, "Didn't Sarah say she used to call Nura 'little mouse' when she was working in Gaza?"

Hans added, "And Magne found pictures of Ostergaard with a Great Dane—big dog, which in Arabic is . . ."

"Kalib Kabir. You guys need to get back here pronto. I think we need to go to Libya."

"We have a flight out this afternoon but I'll try to move up the flights."

"Bullshit. I'm sending the jet. It's only a thirty-minute flight. You get the guys to the airport, executive terminal at Cairo International. I'll get the plane in the air and then call Rusty."

Hans answered, "Yes, Gunny. Not to rain on your parade, but we don't have GPS on the call. We have a distance and heading from a cell tower in western Libya but it's rough, real rough."

Gunny grumbled, "Send what you have. We'll pull up imagery and see if anything pops out. I'm going to assume we can find them and put Alen, Lon, Magne, and Sarah on pre-op planning. Get your asses back here. We have bad guys to kill—assuming we can find the bastards."

* * *

Saad drove Nura north to Zawara. He took her to the docks and put her on the sixty-foot trawler Trabelsi had paid to smuggle her to Alexandria. As Nura took her things belowdecks, Saad pulled the captain aside. He pushed a wad of euros into the man's hand and said, "My cousin asks you to make sure you stay far out to sea for several days to avoid any patrols . . . and cell towers."

The crusty old seaman smiled. "Not a problem. That's where all the best fishing is anyway—especially to the west."

After seeing the boat cast off and clear the breakwater on its way into the Mediterranean Sea, Saad called his cousin. "She's gone, Al Thaelab."

"Good. Gather the men and come back. We have work to do."

"Yes, sir."

Immediately after hanging up on Saad, Omar Trabelsi called Al-Maadi. The phone rang, there was a long pause, and then it connected. "Yes?

"Abu Almawt, it's me, Al Thaelab. I just wanted to give you an update. Alfaar is on her way to you now. It will be a few days before she arrives."

"Good, thank you for that. Is there anything else?"

"Yes. Since you and I are both professionals, I wanted to tell you that I have collected blood samples from the . . . lab rats. I took blood samples when titers were at their maximum."

Al-Maadi was surprised. "You did? That was not part of the protocol set out by Kalib Kabir; may he rest with Allah. Did Alfaar tell you to do that?"

"No. I did it on my own initiative."

Al-Maadi asked, "Why?"

"We might need a backup supply of virus just in case."

"In case of what?" he said angrily.

Trabelsi was now nervous but continued, "In case something happened to your sample. If it was damaged in transit. If the courier company's plane crashed. I know Alfaar insisted on sticking to the protocol but it does not make any allowance for the unknown. Bad things happen. Your uncle knew that. That is why they used four planes, not one."

There was silence on the other end of the phone and then finally Al-Maadi said, "That was very good thinking. We must always have redundancies. Kalib Kabir's untimely death made us alter our plans. Do you have these samples with you?"

"Yes, sir. I can preserve them and ship them to you, if you so desire."

"I do. Send them to the same place Alfaar sent the last material. You have the address?"

"I do. I will send them."

"Mark them as . . . bovine blood samples that need to remain refrigerated. I have to leave town but I will tell my secretary to expect them. Again, that was good thinking. I'm surprised Alfaar did not think of that."

Trabelsi added with a note of condescension, "Well, she is smart, but she is not a medical professional."

* * *

John, Nigel, Hans, and Steve packed up their gear and headed for the Cairo International Airport. The Bombardier 8000 would be landing soon and they still had to go through customs. Nigel put the two Beretta 9 mm pistols in a box and passed them to one of his old SBS buddies; no point in wasting them. It took them a little while to go through security but since they were traveling at the executive aviation terminal, they were treated with a little more deference than the average traveler.

The jet taxied out and, after getting clearance from the tower, rolled down the runway before lifting gracefully into the clear desert sky. The trip to Cairo had been mercifully short. They had been lucky and good— the best combination. For John, Nigel, and Hans, any lingering doubts about Steve's usefulness to the team had been erased. He proved to be very smart and very efficient. His work started yielding positive results almost immediately.

Cruising at nine hundred kilometers per hour, the trip to Larnaca was short—about thirty minutes. They would spend almost as much time on the ground waiting to take off and taxiing to their hangar as they would in the air. As soon as he got onboard, Steve connected his laptop to the jet's WiFi; about five minutes later, his laptop dinged. There was another call. It was being recorded, of course, but he wanted to hear it live. He shouted at Hans, "We got another incoming!"

He turned up the computer's internal speakers to maximum. Hans quickly slid into the seat next to him. John and Nigel came over too and listened from over their shoulders. The call was from Trabelsi to Al-Maadi, but of course they didn't know that yet. While the audio played, Steve opened up another window and started typing furiously. Nigel asked, "What are you doing?"

"Trying to get a lock on his location. I can't find the guy on the end of the internet call but I can zero in on the guy calling from a cell phone." The four men sat huddled around the computer straining to listen to the conversation. Hans had the best Arabic language skills but everyone else had enough to at least get the gist. The call lasted under two minutes.

Hans commented, "Well, that was interesting. They collected blood samples. That means they have even more virus. Was the call long enough to get a fix on them?"

Steve smiled. People have visions of tracing phone calls like in the movies where the police have to keep the bad guy talking so they can trace the call. "Yeah, I got him. This one is not so clever. His phone is GPS enabled and he didn't disable it. He's at 32°34'57.69" N, 11°49'34.43" E. He pulled up a satellite map and plotted the location—the western Libyan desert. "This is where he is right now."

Hans asked, "How does that compare to where the woman called from this morning?"

"We don't have an exact location on her, of course, just a tower and general bearing." He overlaid the cell tower's coverage footprint on the same map. There were three different colored cones emanating from a dot in the desert south of Zawara, Libya. "Her call came from the pink cone. As you can see, they overlap. I would bet the calls came from the same location."

Nigel pointed out, "But in the call, this Al Thaelab guy said she was gone."

Steve replied, "Well, she could be. She called over an hour ago. Her phone has been off the grid since. I'll bet this guy is still at the location where they conducted their tests. Just as important, from the conversation, the blood samples are still there too."

Hans patted him on the shoulder, "Great work, rookie. Send that information back to the villa. I want Sarah to listen to this. If there is any nuance we missed, she'll hear it. Also, they'll probably do it anyway, but ask them to pull any and all imagery for that area. Let's see what's down there. I doubt they were doing this in a tent in the desert."

Steve said, "Roger that. I've already sent this morning's .wav files back to Cyprus, but I'll pass along the new info right now. Oh, and this guy, Al Thaelab, the Fox? He ain't so sly."

"What do you mean?"

Steve smiled. "His phone is still on. It's still registering with the network. The girl from this morning? She shut hers down immediately after the call. She may not be a 'medical professional' but she has better comsec than this arrogant prick."

Hans added, "Well, let's just hope he doesn't wise up before we can get to him."

* * *

K halid Al-Maadi's mind was racing. He had a lot going on right now. According to both Nura and Trabelsi, the test of the virus went exactly as expected. Now he needed to grow enough of the virus to weaponize it. He couldn't do this himself, of course. He had to find a facility to do it for him and without that facility even knowing what they were doing. That was not going to be easy, but he had a plan.

Dr. Al-Maadi first contacted MalayVax in Kuala Lumpur a couple of years earlier to discuss the production of veterinary vaccines for Egypt. Acting on behalf of the Ministry of Agriculture, he had even traveled to Malaysia on a couple of occasions to inspect MalayVax's production facilities. MalayVax was new to the vaccine industry. It was started by Dr. Mentari Tuk with a sizable investment from the state. While it was a modern and technologically advanced facility, it was struggling to compete against cheaper Chinese rivals and customers in developed nations who still viewed Malaysia as some backward, developing country. Tuk had been aggressively marketing his company's services to poorer Middle Eastern and African nations who, while interested, didn't always have the money to pay. Egypt was the most populous country in the Arab World and Tuk was eager to win their business, so he always treated Al-Maadi with deference. Getting an appointment for this new "project" would not be a problem.

* * *

A s soon as the jet rolled to a stop, the men tumbled out. Magne and Lon were waiting for them with a couple of Land Rovers. As they sped back to Lakatamia, Hans and Steve filled them in on what had transpired. Lon said, "Rusty is going to want to hear this."

The Land Rovers cruised into the compound, and they were greeted by Gunny and Sarah. They dropped their luggage just inside the front door and headed straight for the conference room, where Rusty was already pouring coffee for everyone. Lon motioned to Steve that he should sit next to Rusty opposite Gunny Medina. Once everyone got seated, they started. They briefly covered the effort to find the bus and gain access; they focused primarily on the two calls. Steve had forwarded the .wav files and the geographic coordinates of the second call to the villa from the plane.

Sarah said, "I listened to both audio files. I am about 95 percent certain the woman in the first call was Nura. As for the second, this Al Thaelab character, he is not Palestinian, Lebanese, or even Egyptian. His dialect is definitely from the Maghreb—North African. From the inflections in his voice, I'd say he is a Berber or at least is from a Berber area. I would guess he grew up speaking Berber and learned Arabic later. Voice analysis of the two calls indicates Nura and this Berber guy called the same person, this Abu Almawt. He sounds Egyptian. He speaks classical Arabic. Definitely educated."

Hans asked, "What did you find out about the site in the desert?"

Gunny answered. "Well, it's pretty much in bumfuck Libya. It's about thirteen klicks northwest of Al-Watyah Airbase. Its forty-five klicks from the Med but the coastal area is populated; lots of farms and villages. To complicate matters, the Tripoli government controls that part of the coast—at least this week. Haftar's forces control the airbase and areas to the south and east. They've used the base to launch air attacks on Tripoli but to no real effect. The location is in a kind of no-man's-land between the two forces. It's empty desert and not really worth fighting for, so neither side is willing to risk resources. From that perspective, it's a good location for these Black Sun assholes: close to Tunisia and the coast but in a hole in the desert no one is paying attention to."

John asked, "Have we identified a camp or village or anything?"

Gunny smiled. "Nothing shows up on the regular commercial imagery, so I made a call and got unofficial access to some higher-resolution stuff from Defense Mapping Agency but it's pretty dated. It was from an old targeting package from when we were enforcing the "no-fly" zone a few years ago. It turns out that our terrorist buddies were broadcasting directly above some old VIP bunkers. It was a bugout location for the old leadership. They'd fly into Al-Watyah Airbase but be at a safe distance in case the JDAMs started falling. Radar imaging from the time confirmed four underground bunkers. We don't know their current status but this is definitely where they were calling from."

Nigel asked, "Any idea on numbers of hostiles?"

"None. We'll need to get eyes on. I don't want to risk anyone right now so maybe we can put up a long-range drone if we can get close enough."

Rusty spoke up for the first time. "This begs the question. How do we get at these assholes?"

Gunny sighed, "Yeah, that's a problem. If it was anywhere else, I'd say we drop in and drive out but this is an active war zone. Not at the site itself but all around it. I don't want to have to fight our way out through two different armies."

Lon asked, "How about from the west? How far is this place from Tunisia?"

Magne responded, "Already checking that. The closest point is about twenty-four klicks. The route in from the west is pretty clear; a lot of empty nothing. Tunisian highway C203 runs north/south about ten klicks west of the border. The desert is flat—we could actually drive there cross-country if we needed to. I would suggest flying—quick in, quick out."

Gunny interjected, "What would we need?"

Magne replied, "Two light helos or one medium lift. We stage in the open desert west of the border. Like I said, quick in and quick out. Any helo would have plenty of range. If there were a problem with weather or the birds, we exfil over land. The only question would be how do we get in-country with a team of heavily armed men and a helicopter."

Rusty asked Magne, "What is the distance from the terrorist camp to your proposed staging area?"

"About forty klicks."

"How about from your staging area to the coast?"

"About fifty-five klicks."

Rusty scribbled some figures on a piece of paper. "What type of helo do you need?"

"Well, if we go with one, a Bell 412 or an AS365 would do it."

"What is their range?"

Lon answered, "The Bell is officially just under a thousand kilometers but less with a load."

John added, "The Coast Guard uses the AS365. It has a range of a little over eight hundred kilometers. Why?"

Rusty said, "Well, you guys are the experts, but if we launch from just outside Tunisian territorial waters, we can fly to the staging area and the camp, and then fly back on one tank of gas with plenty to spare. By my calculations, we're talking about 220 kilometers—round trip. Hell, we could do it two or three times without refueling."

Lon asked, "How would we get the helo out in the middle of the Med? We'd have to clear Mother Goose's fantail of any possible obstructions. That would take time. Plus, she is a good ship but she ain't exactly a speed demon. It's what, two thousand kilometers away? By the time we get on station, they might be gone."

Rusty smiled. "I know. I was going to suggest *Cynthia*."

Gunny grinned. "Hey, that'd work. She already has a helo deck, and she's fast as hell."

Steve whispered to Sarah, "Who is Cynthia?"

She replied, "His yacht. He named her after his late wife. She was killed on 9/11."

Steve was surprised. "I didn't know about that! Holy shit!"

Sarah added, "Why do you think he does all this?"

Unaware of their side conversation, Rusty continued, "She's sitting in Malta right now. Can we lease a helo to do this on short notice?"

Gunny replied, "I think so. We'll find one in Sicily. There are some there that are used to service offshore oil rigs."

Magne added, "There are Libyan offshore fields just north of Zawara. If we flew in squawking like an oil rig service flight, I doubt anyone would pay attention. We drop down low and fly along the border under radar. We wouldn't need to stage in Tunisia at all. We could fly in direct from the *Cynthia*."

Gunny overruled him. "No. That's a single point of failure. If there's a problem with weather, the *Cynthia*, or anything else, the team is stranded. If we stage in Tunisia, we're only forty klicks away and we'll drive in and pick you up if we have to." Rusty nodded in agreement. "Okay, Magne, you and Lon start planning transportation. I need you to ID a staging area away from prying eyes, and detailed vehicular and air routes into and out of the target area. Also, I want all-terrain vehicles for backup. I want them on hand and at the staging area ahead of time. Range Rovers, Jeeps, or Unimogs if you can find some. Steve, I want you to monitor the comms. If this Fox guy calls anyone or goes off the air, I want to know. Hans, I want you to find out frequencies, procedures, call signs, and anything else associated with these offshore service companies. The rest of you get on assault planning and weapons. I'm going to get on the horn and line up a helo."

Lon asked, "Uh, not to be a downer, but who's going to fly the thing?"

Gunny said, "Gil will do it."

Lon shot back, "Gil? The Bombardier pilot? That Gil?"

"Yep."

"Does he even know what . . .? I mean can he even . . .?"

Gunny grinned. "He's fully briefed. Just because he doesn't run his mouth like you guys doesn't mean he's ignorant of what's going on."

John asked, "Is he even qualified on helos?"

Gunny shrugged. "I think so. He was when he was a Marine flying Cobra Gunships during Desert Storm."

John was surprised. He assumed Gil was just some commercial pilot. He joked, "Well, yeah, sure. Anyone can fly a Cobra but it isn't a Bell 412."

"Well, the Huey he flew to infiltrate my recon team behind enemy lines at night about ten feet off the deck was pretty damn close."

John answered sheepishly, "Yeah, I'd say he's qualified."

Lon asked, "Why did they tap a Cobra pilot to fly a Huey?"

"Because he was the best damn pilot in the entire division."

Rusty interjected to get everyone back on track. "Which is why we hired him in the first place. Now, Gunny, what do I need to do?"

"Call your captain and have him fuel *Cynthia* and get her moving toward Sicily." Gunny pointed to Sarah, "I need to talk to you alone. Rusty, will you stay a minute too?"

The meeting broke up and everyone went off to attack their assigned duties. Sarah stayed behind. She sat down next to Gunny and Rusty and asked, "What's this about?"

Gunny said, "You're not going on this one."

"What?! Are you fucking kidding me?" She turned to Rusty to plead her case, "You know I'm as good an operator as any of these guys. If this is because I'm a woman, that's bullshit."

Rusty was taken aback. He didn't know what Gunny was going to say. "Uh, I don't know what to tell you. This is a surprise to me too." He looked at Gunny for help. Sarah was about to kill someone.

Gunny tried to calm her down. "This has nothing to do with you being a woman, it has to do with you being a Jew."

"What?!" she exploded, "I can't believe that you, of all people, are an anti-Semitic asshole. Are you fucking kidding me?"

Gunny backtracked, "No, you misunderstood . . . let me explain. Just give me a second." He took a deep breath. "You know I have the deepest respect for you and I don't give a shit if you're Jewish, Christian, or Buddhist. This thing, this bioweapon they've developed; it only kills Jews, and you're a Jew. You heard what that guy said, he has contaminated blood on-site. We are going to destroy it but if there is an accident, if he releases it, spills it, or it gets hit by a round—someone might be exposed. If Lon or Alen are exposed, they get the flu. We quarantine them and they get over it. If you get exposed, you die one of the most horrible deaths I can imagine."

Sarah pleaded, "I know the risks. I know what this shit is and what it can do. That's why I *have* to go on this mission."

Rusty chimed in. "Sarah, I have to agree with Gunny on this one. You're too valuable to risk on this kind of thing. I have full faith that you know how to keep yourself from getting shot, but this shit, this bioweapon; it's not something your skills will protect you from."

She continued to rage, "It's my life. I'll risk it if I want to."

Gunny interrupted, "Do I need to raise this with the team? Put it to a vote? You know how that'll go."

Sarah took a deep breath. She was losing the battle. "Okay, you're the boss. I will do as you say because I follow orders, but if and when we corner Nura and this Abu Almawt fucker, I *will* be in on the kill. Do you understand?"

Gunny smiled. "I understand. No one deserves to off these assholes more than you."

* * *

Al-Maadi contacted Dr. Tuk at MalayVax and requested a meeting. Tuk was more than eager to comply. Tuk had a business trip to South Africa already planned so they set the meeting for the next week. At the appointed time, Al-Maadi retrieved the Black Sun virus sample from the laboratory freezer and put it in a dry ice transportation box. He plastered an official Ministry of Agriculture seal on the box, labeled it "veterinary vaccine culture," grabbed his suitcase, and drove to the airport. He boarded Egypt Air Flight 910 for Dubai on his way to Kuala Lumpur.

The flight was almost twenty hours long after the layover in Dubai. The dry ice in the shipping container would keep the virus safely frozen for four days, but he was still nervous. Al-Maadi was completely wrung out when he finally arrived in Kuala Lumpur just after midnight. Despite his exhaustion, he was unable to sleep on the plane. After going through customs, he went straight to his hotel to get some desperately needed sleep.

He woke up the next morning at 10 o'clock. He stumbled into the bathroom to shower and shave. He stared at himself in the mirror and was shocked by what he saw. The vibrant and handsome young doctor suddenly was an old man. He hadn't shaved in a couple of days, and the gray in his beard glistened in the harsh lights of the bathroom vanity. The smattering of gray hair on his temples that made him distinguished had thickened and spread almost overnight. His eyes were puffy and bloodshot. The crow's-feet at the corners of his eyes were deeper and more pronounced. *I just need a shower.*

The hot water from the shower poured over his body. He made it as hot as he could stand. It soothed his aching muscles while the steam filled his lungs. After about twenty minutes in the shower, he felt like a new man. He shaved and put on his suit. Staring in the mirror, he once again was greeted by the dashing, heroic man he always envisioned himself to be—the savior of the Muslim world. He called Dr. Tuk's office to confirm his appointment and ordered some food from room service. This was an extravagance he wasn't really used to, but he was unwilling to leave his precious virus unattended. Finally, it was time. He called down to the concierge and ordered a car to take him to MalayVax.

MalayVax was located in a shiny new building in an industrial park north of the Patronas Towers. The building was long and low, and clad entirely in blue glass. It was like a semiconductor factory or any other high-tech company. This one just happened to make vaccines. Dr. Al-Maadi stepped out of the car and instructed the driver to wait for him. He walked into the lobby and announced himself to the receptionist.

"Good afternoon. I am Dr. Khalid Al-Maadi from Cairo University. I am here to see Dr. Tuk."

The receptionist smiled at him and said, "Yes, Dr. Al-Maadi, Dr. Tuk is expecting you. If you will just have a seat, his secretary with be right out to escort you." In a few minutes, a very pretty Chinese woman came out and led him back.

"It is nice to see you again, Dr. Al-Maadi."

He replied, "It is nice to see you again too, Ms. Zhou. Have you been well?"

"Yes, thank you." She ushered him to an overstuffed leather chair in the foyer outside the office. "It'll just be a minute. Can I get you some tea or a coffee, perhaps?" He politely declined and sat down.

Five minutes later, the door to Dr. Tuk's office opened. Two men in suits walked out, and Dr. Tuk followed after them, saying, "I want an update on those orders by Monday." Turning to Al-Maadi, Tuk smiled broadly and said, "Khalid, it is so good to see you again! What can we do for the Ministry of Agriculture today?"

Al-Maadi lifted up the cryopack and said, "We are finally ready for production."

"Great! Come in and we can go over the details." Tuk was the product of an ethnic Malay father and Indian mother. He had smooth, dark skin, and his features were an odd mix of Indian and East Asian. He was about five feet six inches tall and shaved his head so it was difficult to determine his age, but Al-Maadi estimated he was about forty-five years old. Al-Maadi took a seat on a leather couch while Tuk sat in an adjacent chair. Al-Maadi put the package on the coffee table. Tuk motioned to it and asked, "Is that the . . .?"

"The vaccine strain. Yes, it's the FMD virus we've been working on. We finally perfected it. It's a live virus but fully attenuated. It will not cause disease in the inoculated livestock but it will trigger an immune response. We have tested it for safety in other animals and humans. I sent you the results via email. That said, since it is a live virus, you still need to take the standard precautions. If someone with a compromised immune system were exposed . . ."

"Of course. I understand completely. I did receive the documents you sent but I just got back from Durbin last night and haven't had time to review them myself. I forwarded them to our laboratory safety department for review. If there are any questions, they'll reach out to you, but I am sure everything will be fine. What kind of a production run were you anticipating?" This is what Tuk really wanted to know—how many doses did Al-Maadi want to buy.

Al-Maadi nodded. "Of course. We need pricing for one, five, and ten million doses, as well as delivery schedules for each. The Ministry is trying to determine if they should phase in the purchase over multiple years or make one large purchase and maintain a stockpile. Your opinions on this would be most useful. We will need data from MalayVax on preferred storage conditions, expected shelf life, preparation times, and so on—all the usual information—so they can make a decision. This would be for the initial order, of course."

Tuk's eyes lit up at the prospect of a ten-million dose order. An initial order? That implied follow-on orders and even more sales down the road. "Of course. We will provide whatever your Ministry needs. Uh, we will also need to discuss payment. I don't want to appear callous, but I have a board of directors to answer to and their first question is always 'how will they pay?' You understand."

"Of course. I understand completely. As for payment, it will be coming from the Saudis. The impetus for this project is really them. They buy so much of our livestock. They cannot afford an outbreak in their feedlots. Can you imagine what would happen if there was no meat available—during the Haj? It would be a huge embarrassment for them." Al-Maadi knew Tuk was a Muslim and that this would resonate with him.

For his part, Tuk only focused on the word "Saudis," which meant cash on the barrelhead. There would be no fighting the Egyptian government over payment. He played the "Muslim card" as well. "That makes perfect sense. It is also important that we show the world that Muslim scientists and companies can take care of our own problems without help from the Europeans or Americans."

Al-Maadi continued, "Now, per Ministry of Agriculture rules, we must insist on a test run of the vaccine so it can be tested for efficacy before we commit to a multimillion-dose order."

"Of course. How many doses are you thinking?"

"Not many, maybe five hundred doses. We have a small localized outbreak among some donkeys in the northern Sinai that would provide an excellent test population."

Tuk mulled this over. "Five hundred is more than is normal for something like this. We can do it, of course, but we must have some money to offset the culturing and bottling costs. We can credit that money against any subsequent order but I can't justify to the board spending that kind of money on spec."

Al-Maadi was prepared for this. "Of course. That is very reasonable. A man deserves to get paid for his labor. How much money are we talking about?"

Tuk paused. He had no idea and was pulling a figure out of his ass. "Since it's you and we are friends, I will do it for $250,000. That will establish the strain and speed up production when you place the final order."

Al-Maadi didn't want to seem too eager. "Hmm. That is higher than I expected. I was thinking more like $150,000?"

Tuk smiled. "We appear to have settled on $200,000. The board will question it, but I will smooth things over with them once I tell them there will be a very large order to follow, inshallah."

Al-Maadi nodded. "Agreed. I'm sure your product will be excellent. What is the time frame for delivery of the test batch?"

Tuk shrugged. "Four to six weeks."

"We need it sooner. Can you make it two weeks?"

"That would be difficult." He lied. "We are very busy. That would require changing the laboratory schedule and extra man-hours."

This was clearly a ploy but Al-Maadi didn't argue. "We'll give you an additional twenty thousand."

Tuk reached out to shake his hand. "Okay, five hundred doses for $220,000, two weeks after payment."

Al-Maadi shook his hand and smiled. "Give me the banking instructions and I will have the money wired to MalayVax before I get home."

Tuk beamed. "Fantastic. I will have Ms. Zhou send you the information. Now, how about dinner tonight to celebrate?"

"That would be nice, thank you. I don't fly back until the morning." Pointing to the package on the table. "Is there somewhere I can leave this? My hotel room doesn't come with dry ice."

Tuk laughed. "Of course." He buzzed for Ms. Zhou and she entered the office a few seconds later. Handing her the package, he said, "Get this to

Mr. Mantia in production and tell him to prep it for virus culture immediately." Turning back to Al-Maadi he said, "If you'll wait for me in Ms. Zhou's office, I have a quick telephone call I have to make. It's a personnel issue; you understand."

"Of course, I'll meet you outside."

Ms. Zhou left with Al-Maadi in tow. As soon as Ms. Zhou closed the door behind her, Tuk walked over to his desk and dialed the phone. "Mantia? It's Tuk. My secretary is going to be bringing you a cryopack of virus from Egypt. Despite what she will tell you, do not, repeat *do not*, prep it for culture. Put it in a freezer until I tell you otherwise. I don't want to spend any time or money on this stuff until we get paid."

The next day, Al-Maadi flew back home. During his layover in Dubai, he used one of the public computers to send an email. It was to a nonattributable email account similar to those the Praetorians found on Al-Rafah's laptop computer. The message was simple:

Meeting with supplier a success. Things proceeding as planned. Headed to your location to discuss funding and provide banking instructions.

* * *

Al-Maadi landed in Dubai on his return trip from Malaysia, but instead of continuing on to Cairo, he booked a flight to Jeddah on Gulf Air. It was a three-hour flight, and the waiting was unbearable. He was usually very calm and collected. Traveling didn't bother him. Now, however, he felt his blood pressure inching up. He had been pursuing this objective for years and now that it was practically within his sight, he was losing his grip on it. He had done so much right. He had picked the right man in Andreas Ostergaard; the right combination of genius, emotional pliability, and desire for revenge. He was right to put Nura with him despite the personal cost. She knew when to push and prod Andreas; when to cajole and when to berate. As Jazmin's sister, she was also a constant reminder to Andreas of why he was doing what he was doing. She was obedient enough to follow his orders without question and ruthless enough to do anything he asked. Al-Rafah was the right man to oversee the plan's execution. He was ruthless and knew how to operate against the Israelis. He was also the start of Black Sun's current problems. Why was he killed and who killed him? Did he talk before they killed him? Did he make some critical error that led the Israelis or Americans to Black Sun? These were questions Al-Maadi could not answer. If he was successful, they wouldn't matter anyway; nothing would.

The Airbus 321 landed at King Abdulaziz International Airport in the early afternoon. Al-Maadi passed through customs quickly and proceeded to his hotel. Upon arrival, he went to the hotel's business center and sent a message to his comrade advising of his arrival and then went back to his room to wait. About two hours later, the telephone in his room rang. "Yes?"

"You arrived safe, my brother. I will come to your hotel in an hour. Meet me in the lobby."

Al-Maadi replied, "Yes, I need to . . ." The line went dead. He was a little surprised by this but told himself that he was just practicing good security.

An hour passed. Al-Maadi had been in the lobby for about fifteen minutes. He told himself he should not have gone down so early to avoid raising his profile, but he was going stir-crazy in his room. There were plenty of other people in the lobby, so he didn't stand out. As he scanned the lobby for the hundredth time, a tall, middle-aged Arab man wearing a white thobe and red keffiyeh walked in. Al-Maadi recognized him immediately. He walked over to greet him and the two men kissed each other's cheeks in the traditional Arab manner.

"Do you want to meet in my room?" Al-Maadi asked.

"No, we can finish our business here. The quicker the better." They walked to a small table along a far wall and sat down. "What do you have to report?"

Al-Maadi replied, "I met with the vaccine company in Malaysia. They have the sample and will produce five hundred vials of what they think is an animal vaccine."

The Saudi man queried, "Only five hundred? Will that be enough?"

"Yes. That is what the plan calls for. Actually, it is more than we need. This virus is highly contagious. Our recent test was a complete success, which means it is airborne. All we need to do is infect a couple hundred people. They will act as the vector to ensure it spreads to the rest of the population. With the remaining vaccine, we infect migratory birds to ensure it spreads well beyond Israel."

"Excellent. How much money does the company require?"

Al-Maadi replied, "They need $220,000 US in order to expedite the order."

The Saudi mused, "This is a larger sum than I expected. Did you not bargain with him?"

"I did. He wanted $250,000 and six weeks to produce it. It is well worth the cost."

"Yes, you are right. Do you have the banking instructions?"

"Yes, I do." Al-Maadi passed the Saudi the envelope that Dr. Tuk had given to him with the account numbers.

The Saudi man opened it and scanned the information. "This should suffice. I will need a day or two to make sure the funds come from an account that is not directly connected to my family. We are under constant scrutiny, as you are well aware."

"I do. While Dr. Tuk said he would start working on this immediately, I think he was lying and won't do anything until he receives the payment, so time is of the essence."

"Hmm. I understand." He turned to face Al-Maadi. "So, how is everything else going? I heard about Alkawbra. That was unfortunate but, given his history, not unexpected."

"Everything is going exactly as planned," Al-Maadi lied. "His loss, while unfortunate, will not affect the plan."

The Arab man pushed back his sleeve to reveal a $500,000 Bulgari Magsonic Sonnerie Tourbillon watch. "It is getting late and I have another meeting. I am afraid I cannot extend to you my usual hospitality. I am sure you understand."

"Of course, I do, Sheik. I know your time is valuable. I'll take my leave but remember, the next time we meet, the State of Israel will be no more." As Al-Maadi left, he was seething. The Sheik was complaining about the cost despite having spent more than twice as much for his watch as Black Sun needed to destroy the State of Israel.

* * *

Planning for the Libya raid was frenzied but under control. Everyone had their assignments and went about completing them. Gunny and Rusty flew the jet to Sicily to rent a helicopter. The offshore oil business in Libya was in the doldrums due to low oil prices and the civil war. The helicopter company was only too eager to offer them a short-term lease on a Bell 412 utility helicopter. At first the leasing company insisted that Rusty use one of their pilots but they backed off this demand when Rusty put down a deposit of five million euros in addition to paying the full lease price in advance via a wire transfer. Gil conducted a preflight inspection and, satisfied with the condition of the aircraft, he fired up the twin turbine engines, lifted off, and flew over the Mediterranean to rendezvous with the *Cynthia* anchored offshore. Once the helicopter was on board, they lashed it to the deck and headed south for Libya.

While Lon and Magne were in Tunisia arranging ground transportation, the rest of the team were riding in comfort aboard the *Cynthia*. She was not one of the newer style of superyachts with tall, streamlined superstructures; rather, she was of an earlier style with a lower silhouette and with the passenger section pushed forward to allow for a long fantail—ideal for landing helicopters. Rusty Travis had her custom built for his wife in the style of the *Christina O*, Aristotle Onassis's yacht named for his daughter. Where the *Christina O* was a converted anti-submarine frigate, the *Cynthia* was a modern vessel with a lightweight aluminum superstructure and four MTU 20V 4000 M73 turbocharged marine diesel engines, each generating up to 4,828 horsepower. This combination gave her a top speed of almost thirty knots, making her one of the fastest yachts in the Med. She was under construction on 9/11, and Cynthia Travis never got to see her namesake go to sea. It was only appropriate to use the vessel to go after terrorists like those who killed her.

Lon and Magne located two all-wheel-drive SUVs. They found a seven-year-old Land Rover Defender and a six-year-old Toyota FJ Cruiser. Both were rather old and a little beat but had oversized tires that were ideal for the sandy desert. It would be a tight squeeze, but they could collect everyone in a pinch. They would be short of drivers, however. They were planning on an assault team of six. If something went wrong with the helicopter, they would need two people from the base camp to drive in and collect them.

Sarah volunteered but was overruled. If one of the team was exposed to the bioweapon, they might bring it back and infect her. Gunny and Steve would stay at the base camp, and Sarah would monitor comms with Rusty on board the *Cynthia*.

As a precaution, they used vinyl tape to alter the helicopter's tail number so if seen, it wouldn't be traced back to the company in Malta. In addition, they also changed the registration number on the *Cynthia*'s maritime transponder and temporarily covered her name on the stern. The Bell 412 helicopter they leased had a maximum load of over two thousand kilograms; more than enough to carry six men and their gear. The plan was to fly in from the Med and when they neared the offshore production platforms, turn on their transponder so they would just be another offshore support flight taking off from a platform. Once they approached the coast, they would drop down low and kill the transponder before speeding south. Anyone monitoring them on radar would think they landed. Just before dark the team loaded their gear and piled aboard the helicopter. Though it had been a while, Gunny could fly a Huey, so he slid into the copilot's seat. If something happened to Gil, he could at least land the damn thing. In the back were John, Alen, Steve, Hans, and Nigel. Lon and Magne would be waiting for them in Tunisia. Gil fired up the turbines and spun up the rotor. Sarah and Rusty stood on the deck as over eight thousand pounds of aircraft and men slowly lifted off the fantail of the Cynthia and sped east toward the oil fields.

The helo flew straight and level about two hundred feet off the water. It was getting darker by the minute so Gil had to rely more on his instruments than his eyes. Up ahead they made out the lights of the offshore oil and gas production platforms. Gunny pointed to a large structure to the east and Gil vectored the aircraft in that direction. When they were about five hundred meters from the platform, Gunny switched on the transponder. Gil increased his altitude to a thousand feet and changed his course to 228 degrees, a straight line to Zawara. In about thirty minutes, they could make out the dim lights of the coast. Zawara was not brightly lit, but they could clearly make it out. Gil dropped down to five hundred feet and steered the helicopter slightly west toward what passed as the Zawara airport. He gradually reduced his altitude as he approached the runway. As he reached a hundred feet, Gunny gave him the thumbs-up. Gil killed the interior lights and flipped down his night vision goggles while Gunny turned off the transponder. Gil dropped the nose, turned southwest, and sped toward the Tunisian border.

The forty miles from Zawara and their Tunisia base camp flew by without incident. They were not sure what kind of radar the Tunisians operated but they didn't want to push their luck so when they entered Tunisian airspace, they were only about forty feet off the deck. Ahead of them, Gil and Gunny clearly saw the IR strobes Lon and Magne used to mark the landing zone. They circled around to make sure there were no obstructions and then landed the helo in a cloud of sand and dust.

As the helicopter rotors spun down, the men piled out. John pitched Lon a large duffel bag containing his and Magne's tactical gear. They moved that and the other equipment to the vehicles and put it in the back of the Land Rover. As Lon strapped on his web gear and checked his weapons, he sent Alen and Steve to the west to check for anyone who might have seen or heard the helicopter and wanted to investigate. Gil and Gunny climbed out of the cabin and stretched. Gil said, "Once she's cooled off a bit, I need to check the sand filters. These birds are rigged for offshore work. Not a lot of sand out there. I need to clean them out before we take off, just to be safe. I don't want this thing fouling."

"Good idea. Let me know if you need a hand."

While the rest of the men gathered near the vehicles, Hans and Nigel were carrying a large nylon bag from the helicopter to a clear area about fifty meters away. They unzipped the bag and started assembling the carbon fiber, gas-powered drone packed inside. Steve and Alen returned a few seconds later. "All clear to the east. Had at least fifteen miles of visibility; absolutely nothing moving."

Hans replied, "Great. Get on the downlink for this thing."

"Gotcha." Steve removed a hardened tactical laptop and a portable antenna. He scrambled up on the hood of the Land Rover and attached the magnetic antenna mount to the roof with a "clunk." He attached the antenna, trailed the wire into the cabin of the SUV, and plugged it into the laptop. "Ready to go here." He turned on the laptop and did a quick radio check with the *Cynthia*.

Sarah was on the other end. "Read you loud and clear, Alpha Base."

Steve asked, "Hey, do me a favor and check if this Fox guy's cell phone is still up on the network?"

"Sure, give me a second." There was a long pause and then she came back on. "Yeah, it's still pinging the network and in the same location. This guy is a fucking idiot."

Steve quipped, "Well, not for too much longer."

Behind him the drone was firing up. Nigel gave a thumbs-up/thumbs-down to ask if he was ready. Steve double-checked his computer and gave thumbs-up. Using a handheld controller, Hans powered up the drone and it leapt into the air heading east on a preprogrammed route. Nigel walked over to Steve. "Check the cameras."

"Roger." He tapped a couple of keys and on the screen appeared a greenish picture of the desert as the drone cruised over it. They clearly made out dunes and scrub brush. "Everything is nominal. Enough starlight for the light-enhancing mode." He toggled between light-enhancing and infrared (IR). The scene was little changed until he made out an animal running below him. "IR is good. It will only get better as the night gets cooler. We're good to go."

The little drone covered the twenty-three miles to the terrorist camp in about as many minutes. As it approached, it increased its altitude to prevent people on the ground from picking up the high-pitched whine of its propeller. The little drone started orbiting over the camp, sending its video feed back to the Praetorians. The men all huddled around to watch. They made out seven vehicles parked in a cluster. As the angle of the drone changed, they also picked out the four arched entrances to the different bunkers arrayed in an arc south of the vehicles and facing generally north.

Lon pointed to the vehicles. "The terrain sucks. It's great for tanks but not for us. No mystery why Rommel loved this place. Flat as hell with no cover." Pointing to the screen he said, "Magne, this hill, about three hundred meters to the northwest, it's the only high ground. I want you up there with your sniper rifle. Alen and I will approach from the north. We'll take out any sentries on that side and use the vehicles as a firing position. We'll have the worst of it. The curve of the bunkers' layout means all of them point at us and the bad guys can fire at us without leaving the entrance tunnels. We'll pin them down until you can come from above and frag them."

Lon pointed to the four bunkers. "Let's number them one through four from east to west. John, Hans, and Nigel; you guys approach from south. I want you on top of bunkers one, two, and three. This will give you the high ground and avoid getting stuck in the gap between the bunkers. Take out anyone who exits or tries to run south. There is no sign of a rear exit but that doesn't mean it's not there, so watch your six. Magne, if any bad guys try to escape west of bunker four or you see someone pop out of some spider hole, wax 'em."

The Norwegian smiled. "It would be my pleasure."

"Alen, you'll be in the center with me but you'll also be responsible for secondary containment to the east if anyone slips out from that first bunker. We'll all be converging on the area in front of the bunkers so make sure your IR beacons are on; I don't want us shooting each other by mistake."

John chirped, "Roger that."

Lon continued, "We don't know how many bogeys we have but based on the number of vehicles it might be anywhere from seven to thirty. If they come out and fight, fine. But if they retreat inside, we're going to need to clear them out. I don't want to go door to door with these assholes, so if it comes to that, we use the thermobarics. Any objections to that plan?" Everyone shook their heads. He turned to Gunny, "Any suggestions or changes? You've done this more than any of us."

"No, it's workable. Sound will travel across this open desert so you'll need to drop pretty far out. That little knoll Magne's going to be set up on will provide some sound deflection, so you can get away with dropping him about a mile to the northwest. I'd drop him first so he can get in position and provide overwatch. The range ain't much so he can use his suppressor without significant effect on the ballistics. Then drop the two to the north; at least a mile and a half out. Two would be better. The bunker openings face generally north so if anyone is hanging around or smoking it's most likely to be on that side. That's more ears to hear something coming. The others can be dropped to the south but a little closer in since there are no apparent openings in that direction. That's not to say there won't be a sentry but if there is, Magne can take him out. Once everyone is in position, the groups converge and execute."

Gil was standing in the back. "Northeast, north, then south. I can make that happen. I'll swing out high and wide to keep the noise down. This Bell

412 has four blades instead of the two on the UH-1 so it doesn't have that "thump" of an old Huey. It won't be as loud. Ya know, Gunny, this is a lot like that Safwan ride I gave you guys back in Desert Storm."

Gunny smiled. "It is indeed. I recollect you damn near killed us, too."

"Hey, you said you wanted to go in low. I didn't know camels were so damn tall."

"You sure scared the shit out of those Bedouins."

Lon checked the time. "Okay, it's 2100 hours. I want to hit them no earlier than 0100. Let's retrieve the drone and refuel her. I want her in the air when we hit 'em. Gunny, Steve? That's on you guys. I need you to ID and call out any sentries or bogeys leaving the bunkers. Get it up as early as her loiter time will let you and let's see if we can get a partial head count before these guys bed down for the night."

Steve nodded. "I'm on it."

"Let's do a final weapons check and get some grub before we lift off." Telling them to get some rest was a waste of time. The whole team was keyed up, just like he was.

* * *

Omar Trabelsi walked outside his bunker to have a smoke. He was still in the process of cleaning out the four bunkers to make them a suitable command post for what he believed would be the fundamentalist army that would take over Libya in the near future. Nura had only seen the easternmost of the bunkers, and that was by design. The entrances to the other three had been completely buried by the drifting desert sands, which saved them from the looters. Trabelsi, of course, knew they were there. The bunker on the west side had been partially dug out by Omar's men some weeks ago. Before Nura arrived, they disguised the entrance with camouflage netting augmented with scrub brush and debris. She didn't explore the area. This was where Trabelsi was storing his blood samples. As for the two in the middle, his men had been hard at work since Nura's departure clearing away the sand, opening them up, and making them habitable. They were dusty but otherwise intact. They would serve as barracks for his men.

As he ground out his cigarette, he peered at the collection of trucks and vans parked across from him and then up at the sky. He would need more camouflage netting to hide them from drones or satellites. Maybe convert the first bunker to vehicle storage? That would be hard but might be necessary. Just another thing on his "to do" list. A shooting star streaked across the clear desert sky. A good omen? What he didn't see, or hear, was the small drone circling overhead and looking down at him. It was orbiting about four hundred meters above his head. What little noise from its muffled engine that reached the ground was lost in the gentle desert breeze.

Trabelsi lit another cigarette and took a deep drag from it. As he did, Saad approached him from his right. "Cousin, I want to change the sentries."

"Oh? How so?"

Saad said, "I want to put two of the men to the east. We keep picking up activity in that direction—aircraft flying and some random gunfire. It seems to be coming from the area north of the airbase. I am sure it's just Haftar's men skirmishing with the GNA forces, but I want to be on the safe side. If there is a threat, that's where it's going to come from. I'm not worried about Tunisia invading Libya."

"Okay, but keep men to the north and south in case the GNA or Libyan National Army units use this area to try and flank each other. I don't want any surprises."

"Yes, cousin. I will see to it."

* * *

The Bell 412 helicopter lifted off and headed east into Libya. It would be a short flight. As they approached Magne's dropoff point, Lon's radio squawked. "Alpha One, this is Alpha Base. Do you copy?" It was Gunny.

Lon replied, "Alpha Base, this Alpha One. Good copy. What's up?"

"There is movement at the camp. They're changing the sentries but the guy to the west is not being replaced. They are putting two men to the east. Repeat, two men to the east about two hundred meters from the camp. There is one to the north just past the vehicles and one man on the back slope of bunker number two covering the south. All appeared to be armed with AKs.

No sign of NVGs or any other advanced gear. There are also two men standing outside bunker number four."

"Copy. What are they doing outside four?"

"Nothing. Talking and smoking. One appears to be older and fatter, like Alpha Six."

With that Nigel perked up. "Hey! I'm mature and big boned."

Lon chuckled, "Yeah, right. Weapons on the two?"

Gunny replied, "Old man may have a sidearm but that's it. Younger one has an AK."

Lon asked, "Do we have any kind of head count?"

"Afraid not. The sentries and their relief were out at the same time so with the two smokers, we have at least ten. All are coming and going from bunkers two, three, and four. There is room for plenty more bad guys in there, so you need to be alert."

Gil broke in, "If there are two to the east and no one to the west, I'm going to drop Alpha Three closer to his hilltop. After I drop Alpha One and Two to the north, I'm going to swing back west before dropping the others to avoid the two sentries on the east."

"Alpha Base copies. Good plan."

Lon patted Magne on his shoulder, "You copied that?" Magne nodded. "Get set up ASAP and keep my ass from getting shot. You're on the ground in three minutes."

The helicopter swung about four miles northeast of the camp, dropped down to twenty feet off the ground, and sped southwest. About fifteen hundred meters from the little hill, it hovered and then dropped down to about three feet off the ground. As it did, Magne jumped to the ground with his sniper rifle slung over his shoulder. He also carried a Heckler & Koch MP7A2 submachine gun and a Sig Saur 9 mm pistol. The MP71A2 fired a 4.6 x 30 mm cartridge that was much superior to the standard 9 mm cartridge, and the compact weapon was ideal for close quarters battle, if it came to that. Magne's primary weapon was going to be his Finnish SAKO TRG 42 sniper rifle chambered to fire the .300 Winchester Magnum round. His was fitted with a night vision telescopic sight, a bipod, and a suppressor. As soon as he hit the ground, he moved away from the helicopter and waited for it to lift off and fly north. When it was gone, he unslung his rifle and used its powerful scope to scan the area for any signs of life. Seeing none, he turned his focus to the little hill fifteen hundred meters southeast of him. He studied it for a couple of minutes and then reslung his rifle, pulled down his NVGs, grabbed his MP7, and trotted off toward the hill.

Farther north, the helicopter banked to the east and then dropped low and scooted south just above the desert floor. In a couple of minutes, it was three kilometers north of the camp. Gil broke in on the intercom. "Alpha One, I'm going to drop you here. We're three klicks out, but the wind is coming from the north, and I don't want my rotor noise to blow with the wind."

Lon gave him a thumbs-up.

The helicopter hovered and dropped down until it was just off the sand. Lon and Alen piled out, moved away from the aircraft, and knelt down with their backs to the helicopter to keep the blowing sand out of their eyes as it lifted off. As soon as it cleared the area, both men scanned the desert for any sign of activity. Seeing none, they started off at a trot toward the south.

The helicopter flew north for a mile or so before banking west and south for a few miles and then turned to the east. When it was directly south of the camp it turned north and dropped low, skimming over the desert surface. All the cockpit lights were off, and Gil was flying with NVGs. It was unnerving to the uninitiated, but he had done it countless times before, including when people were shooting at him. This was a cakewalk. He pulled the helicopter into a hover some two thousand meters south of the camp. For the same reason that he dropped Lon farther out, he dropped Nigel, Hans, and John closer. The wind would blow the noise of his rotors away from the camp. With the last of the team safely on the ground, Gil turned the helicopter to the west and flew back to Alpha Base.

The team took its time getting into position. They were in no hurry. The later the hour, the more likely their opponents would be asleep and those on guard duty would be dozing off. Magne was in position first and ensconced himself at the top of the little knoll. He dug out a little depression on the back side of the crest of the hill to provide him with some cover. Only the end of the barrel and scope of his rifle extended on the other side and both were draped with camouflage netting. He immediately started marking his targets. The sentry to the south was partially obscured by the crest of the adjacent bunker, but Magne had a clear view of his head and upper torso. The sentry to the north was much closer but he was in among the vehicles. Unless he moved into the open, he would be a tougher shot. Ironically, he had the best shot at one of the sentries on the far side. The northernmost of the two was almost directly across from him, albeit at over six hundred meters. He was in the open with no cover. It was a no-brainer. The other guy to the east was farther south, and he was obscured completely by bunker number one which was only slightly lower than his little hill. He continued to glass the area like a hunter spotting caribou in his native Norway. The two men who had been seen outside earlier were now gone but there was a cluster of three men outside bunker two. They appeared to be smoking and talking. They had AKs, but their weapons were leaning against a wall. Not an immediate threat. He reported what he observed and settled in to wait for the others to get in position.

About an hour after Magne set up on his hill, the radio squawked. "Alpha Four, Five, and Six in position."

"Alpha One copies. Give us about ten minutes."

The time crawled. The anticipation of action was almost maddening. Finally, the radio squawked again. "Alpha One and Alpha Two in position. Alpha Team confirm, in order."

"Alpha Three, ready."

"Alpha Four, ready."

"Alpha Five, ready."

"Alpha Six, ready."

Lon said, "Okay, it's showtime."

With that, Magne lined up the southern sentry in his sights. The man's head was all he could see, but that was enough. He lined up the man in his crosshairs and pulled the trigger. It took the 190-grain Boat Tail Soft Point bullet about one third of a second to cover the three hundred meters to the terrorist. It hit him in the head just above his right ear with over five thousand joules of energy. It passed through his skull and the resulting shock wave turned his brain to mush before passing out the other side and burying itself in the desert sand beyond. The man never knew what hit him. Magne keyed his mic, "South sentry down." He chambered a fresh round and put the northeast sentry in his crosshairs. This was a tougher shot since the man was over six hundred meters away, and there was a breeze blowing perpendicular to the bullet's path. Magne made a windage adjustment on his scope, lined the man up in his sights, and squeezed the trigger. This time it took two thirds of a second for the bullet to reach its target. The round hit the man in the back of his skull and exited just under his left eye. "Scratch northeast sentry. I don't have a shot on the southeast guy. Alpha Two, he's all yours."

Almost immediately after he said this, to his left Lon's suppressed H&K 416 assault rifle flashed as he sent a burst into the north sentry. One of the rounds passed through the man and shattered the window of one of the trucks parked behind him. This alerted the men standing outside that something was up. The first man reached for his AK-47 only to have Magne's next round explode through his forehead, dropping him like a sack of cement. The other two men instinctively dropped to the ground and crawled back inside the tunnel. They had no idea where the fire was coming from but they understood enough to get the hell out of there.

A few seconds later, one of the terrorists came back with an AK and started shooting blindly out of the tunnel. As luck would have it, this was in the direction of Alen and he was cut by flying glass when the AK's rounds started slamming into the car next to him. He dropped to a knee behind the car. As he did, he saw the other sentry to the east start running toward the bunkers. Ignoring the thunk, thunk, thunk of the AK rounds hitting the car next to him, Alen shouldered his rifle and dropped the running sentry with a three-round burst. He then crawled around to the back of the car, popped up, and put a burst down the entrance of the tunnel from where the fire originated. The two terrorists in the tunnel backed up but then the brave one, the one who had fired at Alen, approached the mouth of the tunnel. He rolled a grenade in Alen's direction, but it was way too short. It exploded with a thunderous boom but had little effect other than blowing out car windows. The terrorist moved toward the entrance with his weapon raised, ready to take another shot. As he pointed his AK in Alen's direction, he edged out just into Magne's visual. Before the terrorist squeezed the trigger, the .300 Win Mag round tore into his neck at the base of his skull. The bullet shattered his spine and almost took his head off. Witnessing this up close, the man's comrade had seen enough and ran to the back of the tunnel and through the steel blast door into the bunker.

Lon ran over to check on Alen. He had some superficial cuts on his face from the flying glass and his ears were ringing from the grenade, but otherwise he was okay. Nigel, Hans, and John quickly worked their way up from the south with each of them running up on top of their assigned bunker. Magne continued to sweep his scope across the entrances of the four bunkers. "Okay, this is overwatch. All sentries are down. We have two other dead Tangos just outside bunker two. Activity at the entrances of bunkers two and three but I have no shot. No visual on bunker four due to my angle. I have what appears to be flashlights at bunker three. Alpha One and Two, take cover. You're the only ones they could possibly hit from that angle. Okay, I have muzzle flashes!"

Lon responded, "Roger that, we see them." As he said this, Alen put a burst of fire into the entrance of bunker two, sending bullets ricocheting off the concrete walls. Lon did the same for bunker three.

John was working his way along the crest of bunker three and said, "Alpha Five going forward on bunker three. Don't shoot me." As he neared the north end, he crawled out on the concrete roof of the tunnel entrance. He had to be careful because the curved structure was slippery, with the sand acting almost like little ball bearings. He inched toward the edge on his stomach. Taking a fragmentation grenade from his web gear, he pulled the pin. "Fire in the hole!" He extended his arm straight out over the edge and tossed the grenade back into the tunnel with a flip of his wrist. He heard men scrambling below him before there was a muffled explosion followed by a hollow reverberation within the tunnel.

Magne quipped, "Well that ruined their night." He moved his scope over to the entrance of bunker two. He had a better angle on this one. He saw a man moving gingerly up along the far wall of the tunnel but then he stepped back just out of view. Magne saw the muzzle flash as the terrorist poured rounds blindly into the cluster of cars where Lon and Alen were hunkered down. Magne waited patiently for the man to move forward enough for him to shoot him. He watched as the AK came slowly into view; he saw the weapon but not the man shooting it. The terrorist was holding it out in front of him while he shot wildly. Magne took a shot and hit the upper gas cylinder of the assault rifle, knocking it from the man's hands. Without thinking the man peeked around the corner to see where the round came from. When he did, Magne put a bullet through his right eye.

The remaining terrorists were beginning to recognize they were outgunned. They retreated to the back of their tunnel and through the blast door. They left the door open just enough to stick out the barrel of a gun and fire off some random shots in the hopes of keeping their unknown attackers at bay. There was still no activity at all from bunker one. Nigel moved up along the crest of bunker one. He keyed his mic and said, "Alpha Two, this is Alpha Six. Can you see the entrance to bunker one?"

Alen moved around the back of the truck that was providing him cover and concealment. "Yeah, no movement. Nothing on thermal either. The front is clear but I can't say what's behind the door at the back."

"Roger that. Alpha Three, I'm going forward. Repeat, friendly going forward on top of one."

Magne replied, "Alpha Three copies."

Nigel said, "Alpha Two, cover me will ya? I'm going to frag it first."

"Alpha Two copies."

Nigel scrambled off the top of bunker one and down the east side. He moved around the entrance using the concrete shell itself to protect him from fire coming from the other bunkers. He pulled the pin from a grenade and flipped it into the tunnel. It went off with a loud pop. He spun around the opening into the tunnel to find it was empty. The door at the end of the tunnel was slightly ajar. He tossed another grenade through the opening and into the room beyond. It exploded but then there was silence; no yelling, no screaming. "I think this one may be empty."

Lon got on and said, "Roger that. Alpha Three, keep an eye on it just in case. Let's clear number two."

Nigel replied, "Copy that. Moving to two."

Lon changed his position to get a better line of fire on the entrance to bunker two. There was still sporadic unaimed fire coming from the tunnel. Nigel exited bunker one and darted across to bunker two. He edged up to the side of the bunker entrance. He took another grenade off his web gear and pulled the pin. He gave Lon a hand signal and Lon fired a burst into the tunnel. As soon as he did, Nigel tossed the grenade in, and it exploded. A scream came from a man in the back of the tunnel and then silence. The tunnel was full of smoke and dust. He squatted down next to the entrance and swung into the opening keeping his body low. He fired a burst at the door and it quickly slammed shut, pushed from the inside. A wounded terrorist groaned in the corner and Nigel put a burst in his chest. He keyed his mic. "The entrance is clear but there are more behind the blast door."

Lon replied, "Copy that. No activity from three either. There has been nothing from four at all."

John got on. "This is Alpha Four. What's the call, Alpha One?"

Lon asked, "Six, how thick is the steel on those blast doors?"

"Quarter inch maybe."

"Okay, since they don't have any windows, use a demo charge to punch a whole and then hit them with the thermobarics."

"Copy that."

"Okay, prepare to do two and three. We know they're full of assholes. We'll check one and four separately in case we might have intel."

John replied. "I'm on it." John slid down off the bunker's east side, slipped off his backpack, and removed a small platter charge. He sidled up to the entrance of bunker two. "How does it look, One?"

Lon had a straight shot down the tunnel. "It's clear. The door is closed."

John eased around the entrance and moved quickly down the tunnel. When he got to the door, he stuck the platter charge on it and trailed out the wire as he backed out. He ducked around the concrete entrance, plugged the wire into his detonator, and hit the switch. There was a low rumble from inside the tunnel. He then placed an XM1060 40 mm thermobaric grenade round into his old M79 grenade launcher. He moved back into the tunnel, stuck the barrel of the M79 through the hole created by the platter charge, rolled back out of the way, and pulled the trigger. There was a muffled "whump" followed by a loud, slow explosion. He retracted his M79 just as the blast came out of the hole in the door. Thermobarics yield a surprisingly slow-moving explosion that, when used in a confined space, burns up all the available oxygen in a matter of seconds. "One down."

John moved over to bunker three and repeated the process. Just to be safe, he also fired one of the grenades through the open door of bunker one. They didn't want to take a round in the back from someone who had been hiding in a closet somewhere.

The only one left now was bunker four. There had been no fire coming from that one during the entire engagement. However, earlier Steve had spotted people out in front of it on the drone feed. Lon wanted intel but he didn't want to lose anyone to get it. He contacted Steve to check on their perimeter. "Alpha Base, this is Alpha One. We are down to one bunker. What's our perimeter look like?"

"Alpha One, this is Alpha Base. We have zero bogeys. No activity for at least eight klicks in any direction. No increase in cellular activity and all emergency radio channels are quiet."

"Roger, thanks."

Lon moved over toward bunker four. John, Nigel, and Hans were kneeling in the area between three and four. "Well, what do you guys think? Breach it or blow it?"

John said, "Blow it and go home."

Nigel said, "I say breach it. There might be some valuable intel in there. Maybe a clue as to who this Abu Almawt fucker is."

Hans chimed in. "I'm with Nigel. There might be good info there and there is still that tainted blood that's unaccounted for. Even if we hit it with a thermobaric, we still need to go in every bunker to make sure that shit is gone. If it's in a safe or freezer, it might easily survive the thermobaric. It doesn't need oxygen to survive. If we find it, we need to burn it."

Lon contemplated this for a minute. "Okay, let's try a breach. If we run into any resistance, we'll blow the place. Fair enough?"

Nigel said, "Sounds good. I want to lead the breach since it was my idea."

Lon clapped him on the shoulder. "I can't argue with that logic."

Lon keyed his mic and said, "Alpha Three, we are going to breach bunker four. Cover our asses. Alpha Two, you cover our six from out here. With my luck, one of the assholes in the other bunkers was holed up in some fortified room or something."

Alen replied, "Alpha Two copies."

Nigel eased down the tunnel to the blast door. He checked the handle but it was locked. He placed a powerful breaching charge over the lock and retreated. Once outside, he hit his detonator and a loud explosion rocked the whole area. As a cloud of dust rolled out of the tunnel, Lon said, "Ya think ya used enough dynamite there, Butch?"

Nigel shot back, "Well, Sundance, when in doubt—overload! I'll bet the goddamn door is open." They walked into the tunnel to find the door mangled and wide open. "Told ya."

Nigel shouldered his H&K and slipped in. The room directly behind the door was trashed. A large chuck of steel had been blown across the room and was embedded in a thick piece of bulletproof glass on the opposite wall. There was a door just to the left of the window. Nigel tried it and found it unlocked. He motioned for the others to follow as he cautiously slipped through. In front of them was a long hallway with several rooms on either side. There was a dim light coming from one of the rooms up ahead but otherwise it was dark.

Nigel was turning to clear the first room on his right when a figure darted out of a room on the left at the far end of the hall ahead of him. It was Saad. He fired a burst from his AK-47 and ducked back into the room. Two rounds slammed into Nigel's left side, sending him crashing into the doorframe. As he collapsed to the floor, another gunshot came from within the room he was about to clear and hit him in the shoulder. Hans and John reacted immediately. John dragged Nigel back and away from the door while Hans put a burst of gunfire toward the door down the hall and another into the room on their right. As John dragged Nigel back down the hall, Lon moved up and trained his rifle on the door to their right. John started to check Nigel's wounds but the big Scot stopped him. "I'm okay. The vest took it. Just knocked the wind out of me."

John snapped, "Bullshit. You're bleeding."

"It's just a scratch. I've had worse wounds in titty bars." John quickly inspected the shoulder wound. Nigel was right, it was bleeding but superficial. "Help me up." John pulled him to his feet while Hans kept his weapon aimed down the hall. Nigel removed a fragmentation grenade from his web gear and pulled the pin. Slipping past Hans, he said, "Excuse me, will ya?" Hans moved back but kept his weapon pointed down the hall. Nigel tossed the grenade into the room to his right. It exploded and dust rained down on them. Nigel pulled his handgun and eased around the corner so that he could clear the room without exposing himself to fire from the uncleared portion. When he finally got all the way around to the far right corner of the room he encountered Trabelsi's lifeless body slumped against the wall with a pistol in his hand. "Clear."

They then moved to the next room on the left and then the next room on the right. Nigel and John took turns clearing the rooms while Hans and Lon kept their weapons trained on the hallway in front of them. Finally, they came to the room that Saad had disappeared into. John lifted a fragmentation grenade off his web gear and pulled the pin. Silently, he used his fingers to count down from three; when he got to one, he tossed the grenade. There was a deafening roar and then silence. John eased around the corner and immediately discovered Saad's bloodied body on the floor behind a large wooden box. He was moaning. John quickly finished clearing the room. Keeping his weapon trained on Saad, he yelled, "Clear." Nigel and Lon cleared the final room while John and Hans dealt with Saad. He was badly wounded and bleeding out.

Hans spoke to him in Arabic. "You are hurt but we can help you. What is this place? What's its purpose?"

Saad smiled through bloody teeth. "This is the headquarters of Libyan Black Sun. Once the Jews are dead and Jerusalem is once again in the righteous hands of the Muslim faith, the people of Libya will unify with the rest of the Arab world and they will recognize us, Black Sun, as the true and deserving leaders of a world Caliphate. My cousin will be in charge of Libya and I will be at his side."

Hans said, "Your cousin? Would that be Al Thaelab by any chance? Tell me where the tainted blood is. The blood from your weapons test; where is it?"

Saad was clearly surprised this infidel was aware of Al Thaelab, their test, and the contaminated blood. "I'll tell you nothing. And as for Al Thaelab, he is a great, great man. He is a doctor and a colonel and a . . ." He coughed and blood ran from the corner of his mouth.

"If your cousin is that dead fat guy up the hall, I think you mean he *was* a doctor and a colonel." Saad's defiance faded. Hans said, "That blood running out of your mouth means your lungs have been punctured and you will die unless we help you. Now, tell me where the blood is." ·

Saad whispered, "Fuck you." He coughed again, his eyes rolled up in their sockets, and he died.

"Well shit. He's fucking gone, and he didn't tell me shit."

Lon entered the room. He had a big grin on his face. "Found it! It was in a refrigerator in the back room. Several vials of blood."

Hans stood up and fired two rounds into Saad's lifeless body. "Fuck me? No, fuck you."

John asked, "What are we going to do with it?"

"Burn it. We're going to burn that shit up."

"With what?"

"Thermite."

Hans chuckled, "Well, that should do the trick."

Lon collected the blood samples, put them in a large metal bucket, and carried them outside. Alen walked over and peered in the bucket. "The blood?"

"Yep, gonna burn it."

Alen asked, "With what?"

"Thermite."

The big Serb shrugged. "Hmm, four thousand degrees should do it. Can I make a suggestion? Put some aluminum and scrap steel over it. The aluminum will burn and the scrap steel will melt and puddle at a couple thousand degrees. Also, open the vials first."

Lon was taken aback, "Open them? Why?"

Alen explained. "If you heat the blood rapidly inside a closed glass container, you might get a steam explosion and blow that shit all over the place."

"Good point. Why don't you do it?"

"My pleasure, boss." While Alen went about destroying the contaminated blood, the rest of the men went through the bunkers. They recovered a laptop computer, Trabelsi's notes, and his cell phone. They counted a total of twenty-three dead terrorists. They took photographs of all the dead to identify them postmortem before piling them inside the bunkers. For Trabelsi and Saad, they also took fingerprints. They called Gunny and asked him to send the helicopter. While they waited for it, the Team set C4 demo charges to seal the entrances of the bunkers. Gil arrived with Gunny and Steve on board as the last charge went off, collapsing the front third of bunker four. The team piled onto the chopper and they flew north toward the Mediterranean Sea. Less than an hour later they were landing safely on the helipad on *Cynthia*'s fantail.

* * *

Al-Maadi finally got home to Cairo. He was exhausted both mentally and physically. The stress of the past few days was taking its toll on him. He just kept reminding himself that they were close to the end. He wanted to go home and rest but went to his office first. He told himself he would take the next day off to recover from his trip. Nura should be there by now and he looked forward to spending time with her. As he walked into his office he was greeted by Miriam, his secretary.

"Good morning, Dr. Al-Maadi. I assume your trip went well?"

"Yes, quite well. Thank you. Malaysia was lovely."

"Oh, speaking of Malaysia, a Dr. Tuk called for you this morning. He said it was important and asked that you call him as soon as you got back."

Al-Maadi sighed. *What now?* "Thank you, Miriam." He walked past her desk and into his office, shutting the door behind him. He sat at his desk in silence for several minutes. There was a pile of mail on his desk along with several pink "while you were out" messages. Dr. Tuk's was on top of the pile. He collected himself, picked up the phone, and dialed Tuk's number.

"Dr. Tuk? This is Khalid Al-Maadi. My secretary said you called. What can I do for you?"

Tuk paused before answering. "I am afraid I have some bad news. We are not going to be able to complete your order."

Al-Maadi was surprised. "Do you mean you will not be able to complete it on time?"

"No, at all."

Al-Maadi was stunned. "What? Why? I mean, why not? I will get you the money; it will just take some time. Our Saudi benefactors have already agreed . . ."

"It's not the money."

"Then what is it?" There was a hint of panic in Al-Maadi's voice as he started to see his plan unravel.

"It's my investors. We are in the process of selling a majority interest in our firm to a German pharmaceutical company. As part of the due diligence, they insisted that all contracts be validated. When I told them of our potential deal for up to ten million doses, they contacted your Ministry of Agriculture to verify it. Apparently, whomever they spoke with was unaware of the project and could not confirm the contract was valid. The Germans were not pleased and accused us of booking false sales in order to pump up our stock value. This is completely false, of course, but in response, my board of directors ordered us to void any contracts that we don't have deposits for. Unfortunately, our agreement falls in that category since we have received no payment to date, so the arrangement has been vacated."

Al-Maadi said, "I understand and that's unfortunate, but the initial funds for our contract are forthcoming, I assure you. It's only been a couple of days! The funds should be arriving any day now. Once they do, you can start work on the vaccine and we will be back on track."

Tuk hemmed and hawed. "It's not that simple, I'm afraid. There is pressure from the Germans and even people within the Malaysian government to cancel our work for you. They are very concerned that your Ministry of Agriculture is apparently unaware of a project that is allegedly being done at their behest. There were also some irregularities with your vaccine strain. Initial assay by my production scientists indicate it may be contaminated. Its profile does not fit similar FMD vaccines."

Al-Maadi pleaded, "It's not contaminated. It doesn't fit your known profiles because it is new. We've been working on it for years. We plan to patent it once the tests are completed. When that happens, people all over the world will be clamoring for it. I was planning on MalayVax to be our exclusive manufacturer." This was a lie, of course, but he wanted to appeal to Tuk's avarice.

"Well, if that is indeed the case then I wish you the best of luck, but I'm afraid MalayVax cannot be your partner on this. I suggest you straighten out this confusion with your Ministry of Agriculture before you approach any other manufacturers as this problem will not just go away."

Al-Maadi's mind was going a hundred miles an hour. "Okay, thank you for the advice. I will call the Ministry immediately. I just need you to return my vaccine culture as soon as possible."

"Uh, yes, about that. There is a matter of the outstanding bill."

"What outstanding bill? You didn't do anything! If it's the shipping cost, I'll gladly give you the university's account information so you can send it by DHL."

"No, it's not that. When you left my office, we had a deal and I put my team to work on your vaccine immediately. We spent a lot of time and money on setting up the chicken egg virus production protocol and even rearranged some lab space. Then there were penalties we paid to other customers whose deliveries were delayed so that you could move to the front of the line."

Al-Maadi was getting angry. Tuk was simply gouging him now. "I never authorized that and you never told me about any such costs."

"What do you think the extra twenty thousand was for?"

Al-Maadi bit his tongue and composed himself. "How much. How much money do you want to release my vaccine?"

"One hundred thousand dollars."

"Are you mad?!"

Tuk responded calmly, "That is what my accountants tell me it will be. I can send you an itemized accounting if you need to review it first?"

"Where am I supposed to get that kind of money?"

"That is not my concern. Business is business. I am afraid we cannot return any of your starter culture until payment has been made. I have a meeting in a few minutes. Call me to let me know what you decide." Before Al-Maadi answered, there was a click as Tuk hung up. Tuk had not been completely truthful with Al-Maadi. What he didn't say was that the Europeans and Americans had put pressure, not only on the German pharmaceutical company interested in buying MalayVax, but on the Malaysian government to halt any and all vaccine production that was not absolutely verified as legitimate. Only Al-Maadi's vaccine fit this description. Tuk being Tuk, however, he used this to squeeze some additional money out of Al-Maadi to line his own pockets—off the books.

Well, this is fucked up. How am I to go back to the Sheik and tell him I need $100,000, for which I will get nothing in return except my own property? At least we still have Al Thaelab's blood samples, right? Al-Maadi walked out to Miriam's desk and asked, "Uh, Miriam. I was expecting a parcel. Some blood samples. They would have come from Libya or maybe Tunisia. Have they arrived?"

"No, Dr. Al-Maadi, they have not, but I'm sure they'll arrive soon."

"Let's hope so."

CHAPTER SEVEN
PLAN B

After the raid, the *Cynthia* sailed back to Sicily. Gil flew the Bell 412 helicopter back to the Sicilian leasing company. Afterward he flew the Bombardier 8000 to Larnaca while the rest of the Praetorians took a well-earned rest aboard Travis's yacht as it motored east toward Cyprus. Steve and Hans got to work on exploiting Trabelsi's laptop computer while Sarah reviewed the photographs of the terrorists killed during the raid. She was both disappointed and relieved that there were no female bodies. Nura was not among the dead. While she wanted Nura dead, she wanted to be the one who killed her. She downloaded the photos of the dead terrorists from the team's cameras onto a laptop. She didn't recognize any of them but then again, many of them were pretty messed up. When they got back to the villa, she would digitally clean them up and run them through their facial recognition software.

She kept focusing on Trabelsi's photo. She assessed that he was the leader; he was the oldest, he had his own bunker, someone was protecting him, and he was the only one with a cell phone. Fortunately, the hand grenade that killed him didn't mangle his face. If he was in any terrorist database, they would identify him. She was happy they recovered his cell phone but the results were a little disappointing. There was the call to the relay in Cairo which they had intercepted. There were also a couple of calls to and from the burner they had identified as Nura's. She found a few other phone numbers in the call log and a couple more on the SIM card that were not erased when he deleted his call log. She would work on these when they got back to identify more Black Sun operatives.

Nigel's shoulder wound wasn't serious. John used his medic kit to clean and irrigate the wound before closing it with staples. He put him on Cefoxitin, the antibiotic he carried in his kit, applied a liberal amount of topical antibiotic, and secured the wound with a battle dressing. Nigel also had a couple of abrasions and serious bruises on his left side where the AK-74 rounds had hit him. He was wearing Level 4 body armor, like everyone else, but the ceramic plates, which provided the bulk of the protection, were on the front and back. The gaps on the sides were only reinforced Kevlar. While they stopped the round's penetration, his ribs still absorbed most of the impact. John offered him painkillers, but Nigel opted for a bottle of Scotch whiskey instead. He stretched out on the deck along with Lon, Magne, Alen, and John to bask in the Mediterranean sun. There would be more fighting ahead, and they wanted to relax. After an hour or so, Sarah joined them. She wore a black bikini, sunglasses, and a big floppy hat. Despite having worked with her for a long time, the guys still stared as she sauntered by. She reclined in a lounge chair while sipping a glass of white wine and reading a book. After a couple of minutes gawking, the guys returned to their conversation. From where he was sitting, Alen was staring right at her. He hoped his mirrored sunglasses hid the fact he was fixated on her. He was a leg man and her long legs stretched out forever. *These Praetorians sure aren't like any military unit I've ever served in before.*

While the rest of the team lounged, Rusty and Gunny walked into the yacht's galley where Steve and Hans had set up their equipment to work on Trabelsi's laptop. Hans asked, "Hey, boss. What are the guys up to?"

Rusty replied, "Relaxing on the deck and catching some rays—something you should be doing too."

Hans replied, "We wanted to get started on the computer exploit."

"You can do that after the sun goes down, can't you?"

Hans laughed. "Not if I start drinking with those guys. What bikini did Sarah bring this time?"

Gunny shot back, "That little black one."

Steve perked up. "Sarah in a bikini? I'd like to see that."

Hans looked at him and smiled. "Yeah, you would but it'd only frustrate you, like being on a diet and working in a donut shop. You're better off down here."

Steve snorted. "Sorry, you ain't that good looking."

Gunny interjected, "Okay, okay. Back to reality. What'd you find?"

Steve said, "Well, this Fox guy wasn't as smart as his cohorts. His security was cursory at best. That Nura chick is a hell of a lot better. We cracked his security quickly; just a simple password. He kept a lot on this thing; too much really. I guess he felt safe out where he was."

Rusty asked, "What's on it?"

"Well," Steve said, "it details their intentions for deploying the bioweapon. They're going to contract with a commercial vaccine manufacturer. The plan is to tell the manufacturer that the virus is an attenuated veterinary vaccine strain and have them grow it, prep it, and bottle it."

Gunny asked, "What's attenuated?"

Hans explained, "We asked Alen about that. He said that's when you take a live virus and weaken it so it can't cause disease, or at least not a bad disease. When you're vaccinated with it, you don't get sick but your body still makes antibodies to it, so if you're exposed to the bad version down the road, you can fight it off. This is how the oral polio vaccine works."

Steve interjected, "Anyway, they're planning to relabel their killer vaccine as flu vaccine and put it into the Israeli health system. When people get a flu shot, they'll actually contract this modified Spanish flu that also gives you rapid-onset Creutzfeldt-Jakob. The infected people will then pass it along to others like the normal flu. Because it's so virulent, it'll spread quickly."

Gunny asked, "What about people who've had a flu shot? Won't they be protected?"

Alen had just walked in. "Not likely." They all turned to him. "Every year, the flu vaccine is different. They try to predict which strains are most likely to hit a population but it's not an exact science. Sometimes they get it right and sometimes they don't. It's usually a combination of different strains, but it's rarely H1N1, the Spanish flu. That one hasn't been circulating in a long time. Even if the vaccine were engineered for H1N1, there is no guarantee it'll work, and there are lots of people who don't get vaccinated at all. Let's not forget, they also have a modified bird flu in this soup."

Rusty asked, "How long does it take to grow the virus and make the vaccine?"

"Most countries start working on their vaccine months in advance. It takes time to manufacture the millions of doses they need. That said, according to Black Sun's plan, they don't need millions of doses; maybe only a few thousand, maybe less but that's just an estimation. That would be quicker to manufacture but you still have to grow the virus. That could take a while, weeks maybe. I honestly don't know. I was a soldier, not a virologist."

Rusty clapped Alen on the back, "Well, you know a lot more about this than we do. As soon as we get back, we'll find out how much time they need. Our clients are already reaching out to all the vaccine manufacturers to shut down any questionable or suspicious production runs. I hope that at least makes the terrorists change their plans, but this will not be over until we find and destroy that vaccine culture, wherever it is."

Alen replied, "Agreed. We need to find it and kill it. Since we destroyed the blood in Libya, that should be all that's left."

Hans added, "According to this guy's medical logs, they burned and buried the bodies of the people they tested this shit on. The vaccine stock should be all that remains. We just need to find it."

Rusty mulled this over for a moment. "I think whoever is on the other end of that Egyptian burner knows exactly where it is and we need to make him tell us."

* * *

Khalid Al-Maadi left work and headed home. It had been a long week, and he was thoroughly exhausted. This plan was to be his legacy. The one spectacular act that would put him in the pantheon of Arab heroes— he would be the Suleiman the Magnificent of his generation. His great-grandfather had started the Arab League. His grandfather was the president of Cairo University and the founder and first rector of King Saud University, the first university in Saudi Arabia. His father was a famous surgeon who had treated kings and presidents. Though he was a doctor and a respected professor, he always believed his parents were somehow disappointed in him, that he had failed to live up to his full potential. By destroying Israel as a Jewish state, he would unite the Arab world and accomplish more than all his distinguished ancestors had combined. Now his plan, the plan he had worked on for the last five years, was in jeopardy, and worse, its fate was out of his hands.

At least he still had Nura. He hadn't seen her in what? Three years? She was on her way to him but he didn't know when she would show up. She was the one part of the plan he regretted. It was he who suggested that she marry Ostergaard and move to Denmark. Al-Maadi recognized that Ostergaard, while brilliant, was also weak. He needed someone to guide him, to cajole him, and, when necessary, threaten and shame him. That person needed to be there for him every day and in every way. The best role for that was of wife and colleague. The best person to do it—the only person to do it—was Nura.

Nura, above all others, was motivated enough to push through any obstacle. She was also a constant reminder of Jazmin, Ostergaard's late wife and his motivation to do something that went against his nature as a doctor and as a human being. Al-Maadi correctly assessed that if Ostergaard's resolve wavered, he'd want to back out. If he tried, he would have to face Nura, someone who had not only lost a sister, but both her parents. No, Nura was definitely the right choice, and she eagerly took on the assignment, but Al-Maadi did not, as a man, relish the prospect of his lover sharing her bed with another man, regardless of the justification.

As Al-Maadi walked up to his apartment door, he saw a small piece of folded paper on the floor opposite the door handle. He always placed the paper between the door and frame just above the middle hinge every morning when he left. It was a simple trick to determine if someone opened the door. Even if an intruder spotted it and tried to put it back, they'd have to put back in the exact same spot to avoid detection. It was still on the floor. Someone had been there—or still was. He quietly placed his key in the lock and slowly opened it. The apartment was unchanged, but he heard something—soft music. He picked up a cricket bat he kept in a closet near the front door and rested it on his shoulder. He quietly crept from room to room until only his bedroom was left. As he walked in, he sighted a small black suitcase on the floor along with some clothes. He continued into the bathroom where he discovered Nura soaking in his tub.

She said, "About time you got home. Is the bat for me?"

Khalid let out an audible sigh. "Oh Christ, it's you. You scared the life out of me."

She was lying in the water up to her chin. Her legs were crossed to get as much of her body under the water as possible. She floated up and her breasts were just visible under the soapy water. He leaned down and gave her a big kiss while letting his left hand slide under the water to caress her breasts and then her thigh. She smiled. "I had to take a bath. Two weeks in the desert with nothing more than a damp cloth. I felt positively filthy. Libyans are such pigs. I can't imagine living like that if you don't have to."

Khalid sat down on the edge of the bathtub and chuckled. "Living in Europe has made you soft."

She reached up and playfully grabbed his crotch. "I hope living in Cairo hasn't made you soft."

Embarrassed, he pulled her hand away. "Living in Europe has made you a bad girl."

"You are my husband. I think it's allowed."

"Well, I'm not technically your husband, at least not as far as the Egyptian government is concerned."

Nura purred, "So you don't want to sleep with your wife?"

Khalid leaned down and kissed her while he slid his fingers inside her. As she squirmed, he whispered, "I never said that." He got up and grabbed her a towel. "What do you want to do for dinner?"

"Fuck my husband; then maybe eat something." He handed her the towel and she stood up. She let him admire her naked body before taking the towel and wrapping it around her.

She let down her hair and started to dry it. Khalid took a step back, stared at her quizzically, and asked, "Did you change your hair?"

"Yes, I dyed it a lighter color. I also shaved my legs and put on makeup." He was a little taken aback. "You got me a passport that said I was Belgian; I needed to look the part."

He smiled and said, "I like it. It's good on you. It makes you more . . . exotic."

She walked over and kissed him. "You want exotic, get me in bed. They have pornography on TV in Copenhagen. I learned some things."

Khalid picked her up and carried her into the bedroom. He placed her on the bed as he started to get undressed. While he was unbuttoning his shirt, she unbuckled his belt and removed it. She then unzipped his pants and pulled them down to his ankles. She pulled down his black underwear exposing his erect penis. She grabbed his cock with her right hand, looked up at him, and smiled. She said, "On second thought, I think I'll eat first."

He grabbed her head with his hands and guided it onto his cock before he moaned and said, "You *have* learned some things." They spent the rest of the night having sex. It had been three years, and they had a lot of time to make up for.

The next morning when he awoke, he found Nura in the kitchen making coffee. She was wearing his robe. He walked up behind her and put his arms around her waist before letting them slide inside the robe and up to cup her breasts. She leaned back and kissed him. "What do you want for breakfast, my love?"

He replied, "I don't normally eat breakfast, but after last night and this morning, I think I need to keep up my strength."

"I checked your refrigerator. I can make basturma and eggs while you run to the bakery for fresh bread. Does that sound good?"

"Perfect. Let me get dressed and I will be back in a minute."

She smiled at him coyly. "After breakfast, we should take a shower together."

He kissed her. "That sounds great."

After breakfast they took a shower and had sex again. Al-Maadi was starting to worry if he'd be able to keep up with her. She was a lot younger than he was and, apparently, insatiable. After they got dressed, he sat her down. "We need to discuss the operation."

Nura got serious. It was as if she had forgotten her entire purpose in the last twenty-four hours and it suddenly came back to her in a rush. "Of course. Where do we stand?"

Al-Maadi explained the situation with MalayVax and the fact they were holding his "vaccine" strain hostage for $100,000. Nura was furious and suggested they travel to Kuala Lumpur and kill Dr. Tuk. Al-Maadi calmed her down and convinced her the best solution was to contact the sheik and ask for more money. If that didn't work, well, he had a Plan B.

"Plan B?" Nura asked. "What Plan B? Andreas made no mention of a Plan B. He was very specific about what was to be done. We completed the test in Libya and it went perfectly—despite that bumbling fool Al Thaelab. The next phase was to manufacture vaccine from the strain sent to you, insert it into the Israeli health care system, and wait until flu season."

Khalid replied, "I know all that. It was my plan. It wasn't Andreas's plan, it was mine. He just came up with the protocols. But we have to be flexible and be ready to address any contingency. If MalayVax does not or cannot make the vaccine, we need to proceed anyway. The altered vaccine was the ideal infection scenario. Hundreds of people will simultaneously be infected, become contagious, and spread the virus to people all over the country. By the time the epidemiologists realize there is a problem and trace it to the vaccine, it will be too late. But there is a really good possibility that won't happen now. I have come up with a workable, if less ideal, scenario for starting the outbreak. I started working on it right after Al-Rafah was killed—just in case he talked."

Nura growled, "Alkawbra would never talk!"

"I couldn't take that chance so I made preparations."

"What are they? What is this Plan B?"

Al-Maadi took a breath. "We use the vaccine virus to infect Arabs who work or, ideally, live in Israel. There are thousands of people who live in the West Bank and work in Israel as laborers, maids, restaurant workers, and even health workers. Think about it. If you put an infected person in a school cafeteria or a hospital or on a crowded bus, they'd infect scores of people—maybe hundreds. If you turn twenty or thirty such people loose in Israel, think of the damage they could cause!"

Nura paused to think about it. The plan had merit. "Okay, that makes sense. How do we find these people?"

Al-Maadi smiled. "I have already done that. I have recruited a young doctor in the West Bank to our cause. His family lost everything to the Israelis. He lost three brothers during the Intifada. He is very motivated. He has many patients who work in Israel. He can give them injections, tell them they are flu shots or antibiotics. They'll never know."

Nura pondered what he said. "This can work. We know the virus is airborne and virulent. We also know it doesn't affect Arabs—beyond the flu."

She walked over and kissed him. "You are a brilliant man, my husband, but we need to get that virus sample from the Malaysian bastard."

"That would be ideal but there is a backup to the backup." She was surprised and confused. He continued, "You may not have liked Al Thaelab, but he has done us a great service. He kept blood samples from the test subjects, when the virus in their blood was at its maximum. We can use these as another source of the virus."

Nura flashed red. "What? That wasn't part of the protocol. Did you tell him to do this? Behind my back?"

Al-Maadi moved to calm her. "No, my love, I didn't tell him to do it. He did it on his own accord, I promise you. He only told me the day you left the camp. I was angry at first too, but Al Thaelab was right; it was too valuable a resource to waste. He was currying favor with me for . . . after. I think he expects to run Libya. Regardless of his motivations, it was good he did this."

"Where are these blood samples?"

"He said he was sending them to me right after you left."

"Then they should be here by now. Do you have them?"

Al-Maadi sheepishly admitted, "No, they haven't come yet."

Nura started to boil. "And I doubt they will. That son of a whore is going to keep them. They are a great weapon and he is ambitious. He will not turn loose of them for nothing."

Al-Maadi stammered, "Uh, I don't think he would . . . would he?"

"Of course he would. I spent two weeks with him in the desert. I know exactly what kind of man he is. He is a liar. If we want those samples, we will have to go and take them from him."

"You want to start a fight with him over this?"

Nura scoffed. "That won't be necessary. The man is a jellyfish. If we show up there, or should I say *you* show up there, he'll turn them over without as much as a cross word. Whether we get the vaccine strain back or not, we need to control those blood samples. They represent power, and all power needs to be in our hands."

Al-Maadi didn't argue with her. "Yes, you are right. I don't relish the idea of traveling to Libya, but I don't see where we have a choice. If he is not in Zawara or Tripoli, do you think you can find his camp again?"

"Yes, I can find it. That's where he will be. It's the home base for his cell. They have four well-hidden underground bunkers there."

"Four? I thought there was only one?"

"That's what he wanted me to think too. There were three others buried in the sand. I found them the first day but pretended not to."

"Why?"

"Knowledge is power. I had it, he didn't. We should leave immediately."

"I can't. My department is hosting a major conference right now. I have to give an important presentation later this week. I am the keynote speaker and will be lecturing to a large theater full of people. If I'm not there, it would be very, very suspicious. We don't need any added scrutiny right now. Besides, it wouldn't hurt to give Al Thaelab's package a few more days to arrive."

Nura nodded. "Yes, you're right. We'll leave afterward. In the meantime, I will try to contact Al Thaelab again. I will take a bus to Giza before I call. If I hear anything, I'll contact you immediately through the relay, so leave your phone on."

* * *

It took the *Cynthia* just under two days to cover the thousand miles from Sicily to Cyprus. Rusty and Gunny made the conscious decision to travel by sea to force some badly needed rest and recuperation upon the team. If they flew back on the jet, they would dive into their work immediately. After combat, the team needed time to wind down. They would be back at it soon enough.

As soon as the group hit the villa, the Praetorians immediately broke up into pairs to start tackling the various tasks. Steve and Hans took Al Thaelab's cell phone to glean what they could from it. Sarah and Lon started uploading the terrorist photos and running them through the Wise Owl program's facial recognition to identify any of the dead and determine their affiliation. Alen and John took the data Steve pulled off the computer and were going through it line by line to find any useful details about Black Sun, Al Thaelab's cell, or the plot. Nigel and Magne assumed weapons detail to inspect and clean all the weapons used on the raid.

Sarah and Lon immediately got positive results. Several of the dead came back as known terrorist affiliates, but Al Thaelab yielded the most information. They collated their results with those of Alen and John to come up with some very interesting conclusions. The next morning, Gunny called a meeting to go over what they had learned. As the team filed into the room, there was a palpable sense of anticipation.

Rusty called the meeting to order and started with Sarah. "Okay, what did you guys find?"

"Well, several of the men killed in the raid came back as known or suspect terrorists." She populated the large monitor with several photos taken during the raid next to photos pulled from various counterterrorism databases across the globe. "We have one who was definitely Al Qaeda. He was a Saudi who was picked up in Afghanistan and released from Gitmo in 2012. Three were Iraqis who graduated from the Abu Ghraib Terrorist Charm School and Prison in Iraq. Two ID'd as ISIL from Syria and one from Afghanistan; either AQ or Taliban. Seven were positively ID'd as being in Derna when ISIL took over in 2014 and they left when ISIL was ousted in 2015. All appear to be foot soldiers or minor players except for this guy." She tapped a couple of keys on her computer and two photos of Al Thaelab appeared on the screen—one was several years old and the other postmortem. "The facial recognition came back with a 99 percent match for Dr. Omar Trabelsi. We're sure he's Al Thaelab—or the Fox—who we intercepted talking to a guy in Cairo about the contaminated blood. He was a medical doctor in the Libyan Army with the rank of colonel. He was one of Gaddafi's personal physicians. Apparently, he has held extremist views for quite some time."

Rusty asked, "What makes you say that?"

Lon answered, "Well, he is from Derna, the most radical city in Libya. He deserted from the Libyan Army just before Gaddafi's overthrow and assassination in 2011. He first fled to Derna and then to Cairo. While in Cairo, he hooked up with the Muslim Brotherhood and was reportedly seeking their assistance in combating more secular Libyan forces in the eastern part of the country. The Muslim Brotherhood took over in Egypt when Mubarak was ousted and all seemed good for him until Morsi was overthrown in July of 2013. He fled Egypt and went back to Derna, where he was active with the Islamic Youth Shura Council. These guys took over the city in October 2014 and pledged allegiance to ISIL and al-Baghdadi. They controlled the city under ISIL's banner until they were booted out in June 2015. Since then, he has been in the wind. Apparently laying low. There were rumors he was back in Cairo, but these were unconfirmed. No one had seen him until we fragged him a few days ago."

Gunny grinned. "That's good work, guys." Turning to Alen and John, he asked, "What did you guys find out?"

John said, "Well, we haven't gone through all of it just yet, there's a lot there, but we have some interesting stuff gleaned from Omar's logs. He was documenting the test of the bioweapon. It's pretty gruesome stuff. Alen can talk about it more than me. They identify the victims only by first name. There were two Arab males who they claim were junkies; a female Romanian prostitute, also a drug addict; an old Mizrahi Jewish man from Tunisia; and two Jewish males named Abel and Michael. One of the dead Tangos turns out to be Omar's cousin—Saad. Saad worked at a hostel in Tunis, the same hostel that was the last known location for two young French Jewish tourists who disappeared a few weeks back. Their names were Michael Aaronovich and Abel Chelouche. They were their fucking guinea pigs."

Rusty asked, "What happened to them? The two boys, I mean?"

Alen answered, "They died. They all died, even the ones who weren't killed by the virus. Abel was injected with the virus and Michael was allowed to contract it through the air. Both ended up with Creutzfeldt-Jakob and died. Apparently, it was very rapid onset. It killed them in days instead of years. The others were executed so Omar could remove their brains and dissect them. These fuckers were pure evil. In my opinion, they died way too quickly. Anyway, according to Omar's notes, the bodies were burned and buried on-site. We didn't see anything that would suggest that, but then it was night and we weren't looking."

Rusty sighed, "Not your fault. You didn't know and you guys had your hands full. It certainly wouldn't have changed anything for those people. Okay, I know there's more to analyze but if ISIL was AQ 2.0, can I safely conclude that this Black Sun could be described as AQ 3.0?"

John said, "Yes, I think that's a safe characterization."

Rusty turned next to Hans. "Okay, the cell phone. What did you find?"

Hans said, "Steve is still working on something and will be up in a minute. As for the phone we recovered, it is definitely the one Al Thaelab used to call Abu Almawt in Cairo. The idiot never cleared his phone log. He also had calls to and from what we ID'd as Nura's phone. These were in Tunis a few days after she fled Denmark. Since he left his phone on all the time, we went back into the Libyan and Tunisian cell networks and found out where it was pinging. When it was in Tunisia, it was pinging off towers up and down the east coast—Tunis, Sousse, Sfax, Djerba, and Ben Gardane. In Libya it was mostly in Tripoli for several weeks before Nura showed up. After that it was either at the camp or in Zawara. We spent more time on Abu Almawt's burner in Cairo. It has been on and off randomly for the last week or so. It is pinging off towers primarily in and around Cairo University's campus just east of the Nile. It has been hard to pinpoint because it's only on sporadically. Steve is still working on it."

Just as he said this, Steve burst into the room. "We got a hit! Just after Hans left." He sat down at the table and opened his laptop computer. "Nura called Abu Almawt via the relay. He didn't answer so she left a voicemail." He played the audio.

It was in Arabic, so Sarah translated. "Okay, she said she called Al Thaelab and got no answer. She said she texted him about the whereabout of the blood samples. Now she's calling him a fat asshole and complaining that they can't trust him. Blah, blah, blah. Says she will see him tonight."

Rusty chimed in, "Tonight? She's in Cairo."

Steve interjected, "She is. I checked the network. She was calling from Giza."

Lon asked, "Why Giza?"

Sarah replied, "It's a busy tourist area. Lots of people, lots of phones. Easy to get lost in the mix. Smart."

Steve commented, "I'd say she doesn't know Al Thaelab is dead. She thinks he's playing them. That's to our advantage. If they think they're dealing with a troublesome comrade, they won't be expecting us. They won't be pushed to move up their timetable or do something rash."

Lon nodded. "Agreed. If we can keep them calm or focused on something else, it gives us an edge."

Rusty said, "We have Al Thaelab's cell phone, right? Can we retrieve the text? Maybe send them one back so they think he is still alive? If they are fighting with him, that will distract them."

Gunny added, "Yeah, we send her a text and then shut the phone off. Just poke the bear a bit. She is a hothead. If we spin her up and get her focused on this Al Thaelab guy, then we might be able to use that time to find her before she even realizes we're hunting for her."

Rusty smiled. "I like it. Can we make it look like the text came from Libya? I mean, from what we've seen, she's the smart one—at least when it comes to phones."

Steve grinned. "Leave that to me. I can spoof where it's coming from. I can make it look like it's coming from the moon if I want to."

Gunny asked, "Have we had any luck on pinpointing this Abu Almawt guy's phone?"

"We're still working on it. He turns it on and off a few times a day. When it comes up, it's been on or near campus, but for the last couple of days it's been off after about five o'clock and doesn't come up again until after 8:00 a.m."

Sarah nodded. "This makes sense." Everyone turned to her as if to ask why. She explained, "Nura. She's in Cairo. I think they're romantically involved. In Denmark, whoever she called she was very deferential to. It was probably Abu Almawt. When she called him from Libya, she called him 'my love.' If they're involved, then she's probably staying with him. If the only person you talk to on your phone is lying next to you in bed, you don't need to have the phone on, now do you?"

Magne said, "Ya know, that makes a lot of sense."

Rusty stated, "Okay, this is what we're going to do. We're going to send a message from Al Thaelab—not to Abu Almawt but to Nura. Make it a bit condescending, to piss her off. Let's get her pointed in that direction. Then we find out where the hell this other phone is. If we can find the phone, we can find its owner. We find its owner and we can stop this nightmare."

A little while later, Sarah and Hans were in the basement working to draft a sufficiently condescending text to Nura. Steve was in the same room using his cell tower spoofer as a mini cell site. He assigned it the same tower number as the Vodafone tower south of Zawara and routed it into Vodafone's

Libyan network. If Nura checked, the message would indicate it originated on the same cell tower that she connected through to call Abu Almawt from the camp. They didn't know if she had that capability but they didn't want to leave anything to chance.

Sarah said, "You know, if this pisses her off enough, she'll probably want to vent to her boyfriend immediately. We need to be up on his phone as soon as we send this."

Steve grinned. "Good thinking. I'm on it." He rolled his chair over to the adjacent workstation but turned back to them and said, "Have I told you guys how much I love this job? I have never had as much fun in my life!"

Once everything was set up, Sarah sent the text. It read:

Received your message. If AA has any questions, he should contact me directly—professional to professional. Not sure how much information that you, as a woman, are allowed to have.

Steve smirked, "If that doesn't get her panties in a twist . . ."

Sarah chuckled, "I think we just pulled the pin on the Nura grenade." They sat back and waited.

* * *

Khalid went to work early in the morning. Nura stayed in the apartment. She was bored and decided to clean up but that didn't take long. She even did a little grocery shopping at the corner market but soon she was going stir-crazy again. Sitting around waiting for others to do something was incredibly frustrating. She went out and checked if Al Thaelab had responded. She picked up her phone, put it in her purse, and headed down to the street. She walked to the street corner and waited for the bus. When it arrived, she got on and moved toward the back. She didn't even check where it was going. It really didn't matter anyway. She was going to use it as a mobile calling platform. After a few minutes, the bus rumbled northeast toward the airport. When she was a mile away from their neighborhood, she turned on her cell phone. It took a few seconds for it to register with the network but when it did, there was a familiar "ping" indicating she had a text message. She recognized the number of Al Thaelab's cell phone. She opened the message and read. It was short but she reread it several times. She did not believe what she was seeing. Rage boiled up inside her and she flushed red. *That arrogant motherfucker!*

At the next stop, Nura practically jumped off the bus. She was near Ain Shams University and stormed into the park adjacent to the large mosque southeast of the university. She found a park bench, sat, and read the text message again. The more times she read it, the madder she got. She had to suppress the urge to scream out loud. She never really liked Al Thaelab, but he had always treated her with at least some respect. Now that she wasn't there to confront him, he let his air of superiority come to the forefront. She had to call Khalid to vent if nothing else. In her rage she didn't dial the relay but called his number directly.

After a couple of rings, he answered. "Are you all right? Why are you calling me directly?"

Nura instantly grasped her mistake. "I'm sorry. I'm so angry right now, I forgot. I'll call back." She hung up and dialed the relay number. Khalid answered after one ring. "This will only take a second. That arrogant fat asshole sent me a text."

Forgetting about her breach in their communications protocol, Khalid asked, "What did he say? Did he send the blood samples? Did he say when they would get here?"

Nura gritted her teeth and said, "He said if you have any questions, you should contact him directly—professional to professional."

Khalid was confused, "What? He didn't answer your questions?"

"No. He said, since I was a woman, he wasn't sure how much information I was *allowed* to have. That fat pig thinks he's better than me. He thinks he is more important than me; probably you too! If he were here, I'd put a bullet in his smug face." Her voice got louder as she said this and the old woman sitting on a nearby bench gave her a very queer look. Nura composed herself and in a whisper said, "We need to address this problem immediately. Do you understand me?"

"Okay, okay. Calm down. I am about to give a lecture and can't exactly walk out on an auditorium full of people. Once I finish here, I will come home and we can leave. Put some things in a bag for us; enough for a couple days. It shouldn't take longer than that to straighten this out."

Nura took a deep breath. She was calmed by the fact that Khalid apparently took this as seriously as she did. "Okay. I will. Come home as soon as you are done."

"I will, I promise. Forward me his text so I can read it."

Nura replied, "I will, right now. I love you."

"I love you too."

Khalid hung up the call as he walked into the auditorium. Just as he was going to turn off the cell phone, the text message chime sounded. He opened the text from Nura and read what Al Thaelab had written. *Omar, you arrogant fool, this is not some little girl you can marginalize.* He walked up to the podium, powered down the phone, and slipped it in his pocket. More than two hundred students filled the room. "Well, I am surprised so many people are interested in zoonotic diseases! Who would have dreamed avian influenza was such a popular topic?"

* * *

Back in Lakatamia, Steve's computer beeped. "We have a call! Nura is calling Abu Almawt directly. Damn it!"

Sarah asked, "Why is that bad?"

Steve replied, "No audio. Oh, wait. She just hung up. What the . . .?"

Hans commented, "Our message from the dead may have been too good. She was so pissed she forgot her own security procedures."

Steve cut him off, "Uh, uh! Another call. Through the relay this time. I'm pulling up the audio." The three of them listened as Nura unloaded on Al Thaelab to Abu Almawt.

Sarah said, "Wow, she is pissed!" They listened in silence to the short conversation. When Nura hung up, they stared at each other in amazement. Sarah quipped, "Well I guess that worked about as well as we could have hoped." She added sarcastically, "And isn't it sweet? They're in love."

Hans shot back, "Okay, okay we get it. You called that one correctly."

Steve interjected, "He's about to give a lecture? Did I hear that right?"

Sarah replied, "Yes. To an auditorium full of people."

Steve got on his computer terminal and started typing furiously. After about twenty seconds he shouted, "Got him! Abu Almawt's burner was pinging off that microcell in the Faculty of Medicine at Cairo University when he got the call."

Hans shrugged. "Okay, we've seen him there before. It's a big place."

Steve grinned. "Yeah, but the text came through on another cell. A pico cell."

"Meaning?"

"Meaning, a pico cell can cover an area as small as large store, a gym or . . ."

Sarah finished his sentence, "An auditorium!"

"Exactly!" Steve started typing furiously. "Okay, I have the cell base station ID number. I just need to find out where it's physically located." The others waited impatiently as Steve dug through Vodaphone Egypt's computer network. "Okay, here's the list and our tower is . . . in Conference Hall B at the Faculty of Medicine, Kasr El Ainy School of Medicine, Cairo University."

Hans mulled this over. "Okay, but there are still a couple hundred people in there—most are likely doctors and any of them could be our guy. And it's not like we have an attendees list or anything."

Sarah smiled. "But our guy said he was lecturing."

Steve smiled back. "Exactly." He pulled up the website for the Medical Faculty and found the dean's email address. "This will take a few minutes."

Sarah asked, "You need anything?"

"A beer would be good."

"Coming up." She got up and headed for the stairs while Hans peered over Steve's shoulder. A few minutes later she returned with a beer and the rest of the Praetorians in tow. "Here ya go, Steve. I also brought your fan club."

Steve was a little intimidated. Hacking was not something one normally did in front of an audience. He took a sip of the beer and went back to work. After about five more minutes, he sat back in his chair admiring his work. "Okay, got it. I hacked the department events calendar. There is a conference on zoonotic diseases going on at the university this week. According to the schedule, right now in Conference Hall B, is a lecture on avian influenza presented by Dr. Khalid ibn Mahfous Al-Maadi."

Rusty had been standing in the back of the group quietly. "Okay, what can we find out about him?"

"On it." Steve's fingers danced across the keyboard. "Okay, Dr. Khalid ibn Mahfous Al-Maadi is forty-one years old. He's a medical doctor specializing in communicable diseases. He also has PhDs in genetics and microbiology from Stanford. This guy is no moron. Here's a picture."

Sarah leaned in. "I don't recognize him. If this is him, he's handsome. I see why Nura is smitten with him."

John said, "Did you just say 'smitten'? Are we in the nineteenth century?"

Sarah shot back, "Some of us have a vocabulary that extends beyond grunts."

Rusty interjected. "What's his background—beyond education. Where's he from? Who's his family?"

Steve said, "Okay, let me see." He read on and then sat back in his chair. "Jesus, this guy is almost Arab royalty!"

"What do you mean?"

Steve pointed at the screen. "According to this, his father and grandfather were both doctors. His great-grandfather was Abdel-Wahhab Azzam, the president of Cairo University, the founder of King Saud University, and a former ambassador to Pakistan. His great uncle was Azzam Pasha, the founding Secretary General of the Arab League. Pasha's daughter, our guy's cousin, was married to a Saudi prince—the real kind—King Faisal's son. Are we sure this is our guy?"

Gunny squeezed to the front. "Al-Maadi. Why is that familiar?"

Sarah offered, "Maadi is a neighborhood in Cairo. So, Al-Maadi means 'from Maadi.' You've been to Cairo, maybe you saw a street sign or something?"

"No. It's more than that. This guy is practically Egyptian royalty and his name means 'from Maadi'? That would be like being a Kennedy but changing your name to 'from Boston.' Something isn't right here."

Steve typed "Maadi" into Google and hit enter. "Well, lots of info. According to this, Maadi is an affluent, leafy suburban district of south Cairo so his name is more like 'from the Hamptons' than 'from Boston.'"

Gunny leaned over and said, "Search 'Maadi' and 'terrorism' and see what you get."

Steve added 'terrorism' to the search bar and hit return. "Okay, Gunny, we have a terrorism fact sheet from the Egyptian Embassy, some travel advice . . ."

Gunny pointed to the screen. "Look at that." The sixth entry down the list was the Wikipedia page for Ayman al-Zawahiri, the leader of al-Qaeda.

"Holy shit!" Everyone crowded around as Steve clicked on the link. "He's from Maadi too. Coincidence?"

Gunny said, "Go to the section on his family."

Steve gulped. "Uh, these are the same people in Al-Maadi's bio. They're fucking related!"

Gunny frowned, "Not a coincidence. Work up a full bio on this guy but I'm going to bet that he's Abu Almawt. Any takers?" Everyone else just shook their heads and said no. "Okay, everyone get ready to deploy to Cairo. As soon as we locate this guy, we snatch him up. Where is he now?"

Steve said, "Not sure. The phone went dark just after he got the text from Nura. It's not back up yet."

"Okay, you stay on this twenty-four seven. Find out where his office is and where he lives. Find out how much money he has in the bank, what credit cards he uses, where he likes to eat, everything—I want to know what brand of fucking toilet paper he wipes his ass with. Everyone else be ready to roll out on zero notice."

* * *

Immediately after his lecture, Dr. Khalid Al-Maadi went home, where Nura was waiting with their bags packed and a taxi waiting. She was outwardly calm but still seething inside. "I booked us two tickets on Air Libya flight 143. It leaves at 1 o'clock; if we hurry, we can just make it." Khalid offered their driver a hefty tip to get them to the airport on time, and they just caught their flight. They were literally the last two people to board the airplane. They arrived in Tripoli at about 3 p.m. Al-Maadi and Nura checked into a hotel as husband and wife, and then set out in search of Trabelsi.

Tripoli was almost surreal. The city hadn't suffered much damage during the civil war, but what damage there was was still apparent. The UN-backed Government of National Accord, the GNA, had been locked in a fight with its own House of Representatives based in Tobruk and didn't have the money or manpower to waste on cosmetic repairs. The two groups were battling for control of the country, and while each had its own list of foreign government supporters, neither had enough men or matériel to defeat the other. Basically, it was a shit show and was fated to drag on indefinitely. This chaos allowed Black Sun to set up a Libyan component with the goal of taking control of the country for themselves.

Nura had never been to Tripoli before and didn't even know where to start, so she deferred to Khalid. Before they left, he sat her down. "Nura, I understand you're mad at Al Thaelab, but you must keep your emotions in check. Once we find him, let me do the talking. We cannot afford to anger him, especially if he still has the blood samples. We must have them or our plan and Black Sun itself will fail. Do you understand?"

"I want to kill the bastard."

Exasperated by her stubbornness, Al-Maadi repeated, "I will do the talking. If you cannot promise me you will control yourself, I will leave you here in the hotel. If, after we retrieve the samples, you still want to kill him, that's fine, but not right now. I no longer trust him anyway. But we must wait until I can identify a suitable replacement. If we kill him too soon, we risk losing his people. Do you understand?"

Nura took a deep breath. "Yes, I understand. I'll be quiet and let you do the talking."

Khalid smiled. "That's my good girl. Omar is old and set in his ways. He is a Berber, and they're much less civilized than Egyptians or Levantines, but Libya is crucial to our plan for North Africa and we cannot risk screwing that up over an insult."

Nura nodded. "Okay. But when it comes time to remove him, I want to be the one who does it."

Khalid reached down and kissed her. "Of course, you can kill him." Shaking his finger at her, he added, "But only when the time is right."

Nura donned more traditional garb including a black hijab before they left the hotel. They hired a taxi and had it drive them to a neighborhood off Sawani Road, north of the airport. Khalid and Nura got out of the taxi about three streets from their destination. Once the taxi cleared the area, they walked the rest of the way to Trabelsi's house.

It was an unremarkable place: a two-story concrete building indistinguishable from the myriad of others in the neighborhood. They scoped out the house for several minutes. It was rapidly getting dark, and Khalid wanted to see if any lights came on. After a short time, a lone light came on in one of the upstairs windows. They didn't see anyone as the curtains were drawn but the shadows that passed behind the drapes indicated that someone or something was in the house. They had no choice but to knock on the door. Khalid knocked, but there was no answer so he knocked louder. He was about to try climbing over the wall into the backyard when the door opened. He was shocked by the small, frail, old woman standing there. She must have been ninety years old. Her wrinkled and weathered face was framed by the black hijab she wore. Her eyes were clouded by cataracts. She was blind.

"Yes, what is it you want?" the old woman asked.

"I'm sorry to disturb you. I am looking for an old colleague of mine and I'm afraid I must have the wrong house. He is a doctor. His name is Omar."

The woman smiled a toothless smile. "My son! Omar is my son. You're in the right place, this is his house. I live here. He takes care of me." Nura started to reconsider her plans to murder Trabelsi. She didn't want to leave an old woman with no means of support.

Al-Maadi said, "Well, my name is Khalid. Your son and I worked together in Egypt a few years ago. He asked me to look him up if I was ever in Tripoli. Is he home by any chance?"

The old woman frowned, "No, he isn't. He hasn't been home for a few weeks now. Have you talked to him recently?"

Khalid answered, "Well, not for several days, I'm afraid. Do you know where he is or when you expect him back?"

"No, I don't. Omar is a very important and very busy man. He's a colonel as well as a doctor, you know. He was Gaddafi's personal physician. I'm sure he is engaged in something very important—something he cannot tell me about. He was going west for some scientific program, but that was two or three weeks ago. He didn't say when he'd be back. He took his cousin Saad with him. Maybe Saad's mother knows. Do you want me to try and call her?"

Nura nudged Khalid and shook her head. He said, "No, that won't be necessary. We have to meet with some other people while we're here. I'm sure they'll know where he is."

"Do you want me to tell him you were here?" the old woman asked.

"No, thank you. I'm sure we'll run into him soon. We're sorry to have disturbed you."

The old woman smiled. "It was no bother at all. I get so few visitors these days. You seem like a very nice couple, but then, Omar always did have good friends."

Khalid and Nura said their goodbyes and departed. As they walked down the street Nura asked, "What do you think that means?"

"Well, the blood samples aren't here. If the woman hasn't seen him in weeks, he must have them secured somewhere else. But where?"

Nura said, "His camp. He must still be at the camp in the desert where we conducted the tests. It's fairly close to Zawara but well-hidden out in the desert. It's close enough to the fighting to discourage casual visitors but far enough away to avoid the GNA and LNA soldiers."

Khalid asked, "Do you think you can find it again if you had to?"

Nura said, "We drove there in the middle of the night, but they drove me out during the day. It's west of Jadu Road, which leads south out of Zawara. Get me to Zawara and I will find the camp."

"That's my girl."

The next morning, they got up and prepared to check out of their hotel. While Nura packed, Khalid went out and rented a car. He had to leave a significant deposit when he told the man he was driving to Zawara, as the Coastal Highway is dangerous, but the man also sold him a pistol for self-protection. He picked up Nura at the hotel, pointed the little rented Fiat west, and drove.

It took about two hours to drive the 120 kilometers to Zawara. They turned south on Jadu Road and had driven for another forty-five minutes when Nura told Khalid to pull over and stop. She got out of the car and studied the area. She walked around to the back of the car and stared north. Khalid asked, "Aren't you looking the wrong way? Or did we miss it?"

"No, we haven't missed it. We were driving north, so I need to see what I saw then. The turnoff will be a couple more kilometers ahead on your right. I'll tell you where to turn."

They got back into the car and continued south. As she predicted, there was a dirt road two kilometers ahead. "Turn here. Drive about eight kilometers and then slow down. There will be a dirt path on your left but I'm not sure exactly how far." The little Fiat bounced over the rough track for eight kilometers. Nura said, "Stop. Let me drive." They switched places and she continued to drive west on the dirt road but peering to the south the entire time. After a couple of minutes, she stopped. "This is it. But there are a lot more vehicle tracks now. More people have been here. He was supposed to abandon this place. Just another lie from a liar. I'm not surprised." She picked up the pistol Khalid had bought in Tripoli and made sure there was a round in the chamber before turning south on the dirt path. Just ahead she made out a number of vehicles parked in the desert. "This is it. This is the place."

She parked the Fiat about twenty meters from the other cars and they got out. They stood outside the car and surveyed the area. Nothing was moving. Khalid said, "They must be in those bunkers you talked about."

Nura scanned the area. "Something isn't right here." Slowly they started walking toward the cluster of cars. Several had their windows blown out. Then they saw the bullet holes. They walked around to the opposite side of the cars. Those on the south side had been peppered with rifle fire and shrapnel from a grenade or RPG explosion. "These vehicles weren't here when I was here. Look at this; there was fighting."

Khalid commented, "A lot of damage but no bodies." They cautiously approached the first bunker.

Nura said, "This is where we conducted the tests." The concrete tunnel leading to the bunker was essentially intact but once she walked back farther, she saw the blast door was damaged and the bunker behind it collapsed. She walked back out and said, "It's been blown up."

"Well, you said it was contaminated. Maybe Trabelsi destroyed it to keep the virus from spreading? I'll bet the bodies of the test subjects are buried inside. He was probably too lazy to burn them."

Nura pointed toward the other bunkers. "No. Look at the others. They are all sunken in behind the entrance tunnels. They weren't like that before." She walked over to the next bunker entrance. "There were explosions and gunfire in here." The walls were scorched and shot up. There was a large brown stain on one of the walls. She ran her fingers over it and some of it flaked off at her touch. "This is blood." She picked off what appeared to be a small rock or shard of pottery stuck to the wall. Showing the small rocklike object to Khalid, she asked, "Do you recognize this?"

"It looks like bone."

She just nodded. She walked on back and peeked through a hole in the damaged blast door. "It's collapsed, just like the other one." They checked out the last two bunkers and found them in a similar condition. She reentered the second bunker and approached the shattered blast door. She brought her face close to the hole made by the platter charge and sniffed. "Come here. Smell this."

Khalid walked back, put his nose to the hole and took a big sniff. He instantly recoiled and retched. "Ugh! That's awful!"

"That's the smell of death. I know it well from the Intifada. When Israel was bombing us, we didn't have time to find all the dead so they rotted where they fell."

Khalid walked out of the tunnel and took a deep breath of fresh air. "What happened here? I mean, certainly they were attacked but was it by the LNA or GNA troops?"

"Neither." As she walked out, Nura pulled a damaged AK from the rubble. The upper gas cylinder had a large hole blown through it. She carried it with her as she walked back over to the cars. She knelt down and picked up a shell casing.

Khalid walked over and asked, "What's that?"

"It's a NATO 5.56 mm shell casing." She handed him the AK. "Trabelsi's people were armed with AKs. Someone shot the upper gas cylinder of this rifle. I don't think that's a lucky shot."

Khalid inspected the damaged weapon. "Well, if it isn't luck, what is it?"

"Skill." She surveyed the area and her eyes fell upon the little hill to the northwest. She pointed to it and said, "From up there, I would bet. That's a great deal of skill."

Khalid scoffed. "Nonsense. It was just a lucky shot. If there are enough bullets flying, you're bound to hit something."

"No, this was from a sniper. The caliber of the bullet that made that hole in the AK was bigger than the 5.56 casings scattered around over here. It was fired from a different type of weapon. You walk up on top of that hill and you will probably find the empty cartridge casings."

She knew what she was talking about and Khalid had no intention of walking hundreds of meters across the desert just to prove her right. "Thanks, but I'll pass." She ignored his comment and started walking

toward the hill. He dropped the ruined Kalashnikov and followed behind
her as she climbed to the top. There was an indentation in the sand from
Magne's sniper position.

"The sniper was here. Judging by these footprints, he came from the west
and exited to the east, toward the bunkers." She hunted for spent casings;
there were none. "Whoever was here picked up his spent cartridges. He was
a professional."

Khalid was out of his element. He turned back toward the bunkers. It
was very far to him. "So, who can shoot men this far away?"

"A military-trained sniper."

"But wouldn't they hear him after the first shot?"

She replied, "Not if he was using a suppressor; and I'd bet he was."

Khalid's eyes traced the path from the hilltop to the bunkers and back.
"Who has such weapons?"

"Well, any military sniper team; probably Western."

"That doesn't narrow it down much. Are you sure it wasn't GNA troops?
They get assistance from NATO countries."

Nura surveyed the surrounding desert. "Okay, we know there was battle
here. Look around the desert. What do you see, or more importantly, what
don't you see?"

Khalid didn't know what he was looking for. "I don't know, what?"

"Tracks."

"What?"

"Tracks. Vehicle tracks, there aren't any. If GNA or LNA soldiers did
this, they would have arrived in trucks or tanks. Even if they came in on foot,
they would have left in a vehicle of some sort. No need for stealth after the
battle is over. But there are no tracks. On the road we drove in on, all the
tracks were those of cars or civilian trucks. No big military trucks, no tanks,
no armored personnel carriers. Whoever did this, they came in from the air."

"You think they parachuted in?"

Nura continued to peer down on the scene of the collapsed bunkers.
"Maybe, but they didn't parachute out. They left in a helicopter."

"Well, the GNA and LNA have helicopters."

"Very few, and why bother if you can just drive up with a superior force?"
She stomped down off the hill and back toward the camp.

Khalid trailed after her and asked, "Well, what difference does it really make? Judging by the smell, people died and are probably entombed in one or all of these bunkers. That doesn't tell me where Trabelsi is or, more importantly, where my blood is."

"Trabelsi is dead."

"How do you know that?"

She pointed to the cars. "That black Citroën over there. It's his. We brought the two Jews here in its trunk. It's also what Saad drove me to Zawara in when I left. If it's here, he's here. If he somehow survived this, he would have at least contacted his mother, don't you think? No, he's dead along with his men. Buried inside these bunkers." Nura walked around the area taking it all in. There was trash strewn about and she came upon the melted metal bucket. She knelt down to examine it closer. "Khalid, come here. Look at this."

He walked over. "What is it?"

"I don't know but something was burned here and it was very, very hot."

"How do you know?"

"Not only was the bucket melted but so was the sand underneath it." She lifted up the bucket; the bottom was completely missing. "On the ground, that's melted steel! This was no petrol fire. This was something much more intense; something military—like thermite or white phosphorus."

Khalid reached down to pick up a couple of small light-blue objects. "Goddamn it!"

"What? What is it?"

He said, "These are shipping caps for collection tubes like the kind you keep blood samples in. They have a rubber membrane that you stick the needle through but you use these caps when you transport them so they don't leak. Without them, the lowered air pressure on an airplane can force some of the blood through the membrane. These caps mean they burned the blood samples. That has to be it. A fire this intense would guarantee the virus is completely destroyed. Whoever did all this knew what they were searching for."

Nura walked over to her left. On the ground were two long parallel indentations in the sand. "These are from helicopter skids." She seethed. "The fucking Israelis. It has to be."

"But how?"

Nura's mind raced. "We have to leave—now!"

"What? Why?"

"Look around, Khalid. This happened days ago. Trabelsi texted me yesterday morning! How did he do that if he was dead?"

"Well, maybe he isn't dead. Maybe he survived or wasn't here when it happened?"

"Then why pretend like it didn't? No, he's dead and whoever killed him has his cell phone and sent that message. They baited me and it worked. That means we've been compromised." Panic spread across her face. "Oh my God! That means the relay is compromised. Oh God, oh God! I need to get to a computer." Thinking back over their telephone conversation, she asked, "Did I mention coming to Libya on the phone this morning?"

Khalid stammered, "Uh, um, I don't . . ."

She yelled at him, "Goddamnit! Did I mention Libya or didn't I?"

"No! No, you didn't. You only said we had to address the issue immediately. You never mentioned Libya."

"Okay, well there is at least that. Neither of our phones have been on since we left Cairo, so they can't track us with them. We need to destroy them immediately. They probably think we're still in Egypt. We can't go back to your apartment. Your phone was connecting to the cell network from there. That won't give them an address but we have to assume they are staking out the area. We need to go to somewhere safe."

Khalid now appreciated the severity of what she was saying. "Okay, I have a place. An apartment the university uses for visiting researchers. It is empty right now. Before we do anything, I need to contact my office."

"Why? They'll be watching the university area for sure."

"Those blood samples were our last hope. Omar was power hungry, but he wasn't stupid and I don't think he would cross me. He didn't have the resources to pull off the attack. He needed me for that. If he kept a set of blood samples, why not keep two? He might send one to me to curry favor and keep another in reserve for his own purposes. If, by some miracle, he sent the sample before he and his cell were wiped out, they might be sitting in a refrigerator in my lab right now."

"No, Khalid, it's too dangerous."

"I can get a new burner and call Mariam, my secretary. She can at least tell me if something came in."

Nura mulled this over. "Okay, that could work. Let's wait until we get back to Cairo. I want to leave here as soon as possible."

They drove back to Tripoli as fast as the little Fiat would carry them. They were most nervous waiting to get on the flight back home. They expected security to pull them out of line at any second but it never happened. When they landed late that evening, they took a taxi to the university apartment. They were exhausted and scared. They crawled into bed and passed out.

The next morning, Khalid Al-Maadi woke with the sun. He was tired, depressed, and more than a little frightened. Everything he had been working for was crashing down around his knees. If the Israelis didn't assassinate him or the Americans didn't scoop him up and send him to some black site somewhere, his own government would probably arrest him. He didn't know which outcome would be the worst. Nura was still sleeping when he dressed and walked down to the local market. He bought some food and a cheap burner phone.

He walked a couple blocks away and ordered a coffee at a small sidewalk café. He checked his watch. It was early, but Miriam might be there so he called. The phone rang twice before she answered. "Good morning, Dr. Al-Maadi's office."

"Miriam, good morning. It's me."

"Oh, good morning, Dr. Al-Maadi. What happened the other day? You went to the conference but never came back."

"Uh, yes. I had to go out of town for a couple of days. I was in Alexandria. I'm sorry, I should have told you. It came up last minute and it slipped my mind."

She replied cheerfully, "That's okay. There was nothing pressing."

He asked cautiously, "Um, did anyone come by while I was gone? Were there any visitors?"

"No. I don't think so. It was pretty quiet. Everyone in the department was at the conference."

Khalid breathed a sigh of relief. Even if the authorities had come by and ordered her to keep it secret, he'd hear it in her voice. She was never good at lying for him; he doubted she'd be good at lying for others. "Did I receive any mail or . . . packages while I was gone?"

"Nothing pressing in the mail. You did receive a package though. It was marked perishable so I gave it to Ahmed to store properly. I never know what to do with that stuff and besides, with all the diseases you all work with, it kind of scares me to handle it. I mean, I know it's properly packaged and all, but still."

Al-Maadi was cautiously excited. "This package; was it from Tunisia or Libya by any chance?"

"No, sir." His heart sank. "It was from Malaysia. It came from MalayVax. It was one of those dry ice shipping containers. That's why I gave it to Ahmed, so he could put it in one of the freezers."

Al-Maadi's heart started racing. "Did it say what it was?"

"Uh, there was a memo attached to it. Let me find it." Khalid heard papers rustle in the background. "Here it is. It's from Dr. Tuk. It says it's your FMD vaccine culture. He says the payment from Saudi Arabia came through and he was returning the culture as promised. He said he was eager to work with you in the future once this 'misunderstanding' is cleared up. What's this all about? I don't recall anything about Saudi money."

Al-Maadi tried to contain his excitement. "Oh, that. It's something for the Ministry of Agriculture. It didn't come through the department. Please don't mention it to anyone. The dean might get angry if he found out I was helping the Ministry without billing them for my time. You know how he is when it comes to the budget."

Miriam laughed. "Yes, sir. I know. I won't mention it. When are you coming to the office?"

"Uh, later today. I have a couple of things I need to take care of first. Personal business. Thank you, Miriam. I'll see you later."

Khalid practically sprinted back to the apartment. Nura was just getting up and was a little angry that he had left her alone. "Where have you been?"

Khalid was beaming. "I have great news!"

"Good, I need some. Did the blood samples show up?"

"No."

Nura scoffed, "I thought not. Trabelsi was a liar and a pig."

"It's better. Dr. Tuk at MalayVax has returned my vaccine culture. The Sheik got him the money."

Nura was unimpressed. "As well he should have, given he didn't produce the vaccine he promised."

"You don't understand. We can proceed with Plan B. The vaccine culture is even better for the plan than the blood would have been. We can infect Arabs in the West Bank and send them into Israel. It may take a little longer for the disease to spread across the whole country but we can start immediately. All I have to do is retrieve the culture from the university lab."

Nura's eyes lit up. "Khalid, you're a genius! Can you get it safely? I mean, whoever killed Trabelsi is probably hunting for us right now."

"My secretary said no one has been by asking about me—no one at all. They may not know yet or they don't know who I am. If not, by the time they figure it out, it'll be too late. We need to move. Our plan is back on track!"

CHAPTER EIGHT
IN THE WIND

Steve Chang was up most of the night gathering information on Dr. Khalid ibn Mahfous Al-Maadi. Rusty had called a team meeting for 0900 hours and he'd be expecting results. Steve didn't want to let down his new boss or his teammates. He finally went to bed at about 0400 hours to grab at least a couple of hours of sleep. Most of the focus would be on him, so he was up early and guzzling coffee in lieu of sleep. He was on his third cup when Sarah walked in for her first.

"Good morning, Steve. You look like shit."

"Gee, thanks. I wish I could say the same. Why is it every time I see you, you look like you just stepped out of a fitness magazine?"

Sarah shrugged. "Hard work and good genetics. I guess. Why do you look like you've aged fifteen years in the last three days?"

"I've been up all night pulling data on this Al-Maadi guy."

Filling her coffee cup, she quipped, "Well that's what you get for being the computer guy. At least no one is shooting at you."

Steve chuckled. "Or hitting you in the head with a frying pan?"

Sarah rubbed the spot on her head where Nura had whacked her. "Yeah, that too."

Gunny walked in with his coffee cup in hand and filled it at the large urn. The old cup sported a faded KGB logo on the side and was stained to the point its original color was unknown. Sarah shook her head. "That thing is filthy. Are you ever going to wash it?"

"Never. That 'filth' is the patina of years and years of great coffee. Washing it would be like scrubbing the green off the roof of the Belvedere Palace. It would be a crime against humanity."

"Whatever. You're going to get tetanus from that thing."

Gunny took a big swig of coffee from his mug. "Mmmm. Now that is some damn good coffee. Conference room in five."

Steve already had put his laptop in the conference room and connected it to the large monitor. It would be his show. He took a seat in the middle of the table while Sarah sat across from him. The rest of the team drifted in. Hans brought in a fresh urn of coffee and Magne had a large platter of pastries. Putting them in the middle of the table, he said, "Fresh, homemade Norwegian kringle pastries. I made them last night."

Steve was starving and immediately grabbed one. Taking a bite, he said, "Damn, this is really, really good! You are a renaissance man."

Magne smiled. "Yeah, I know. Not only am I the most handsome and the best shot, I'm also the best cook."

Lon pretended to cough and said, "Bullshit." Several of the other men followed suit.

Magne chuckled, "You wear your jealously well."

Lon grabbed one of the pastries and took a bite. "This shit is pretty good, but it can't hold a candle to my chili."

John snorted. "Your chili is like eating a candle—a lit one."

Lon sniffed, "You just can't handle spicy food. Tell me, John, how much did you get when you sold your balls?" The other guys snorted but the laughter died down when Rusty Travis walked in.

He sat in his chair and said, "Okay folks, what do we have on this son of a bitch?"

Gunny motioned to Steve who tapped a couple of keys on his computer. A large photo of Al-Maadi popped up on the monitor. "Okay, I started with his financials. Nothing stands out about his bank accounts. He has a balance of a little over 320,000 Egyptian pounds in his account; that's about $20,000. As a full professor, he makes about 85,000 pounds a month or about $5,200 a month. He has other sporadic income from the Ministry of Health, the Ministry of Agriculture, and a couple of private-sector companies that appears to be from consulting gigs. His family is affluent by Egyptian standards and I have to assume he has access to family money that is not readily apparent. He owns an apartment near the university. He paid 2.5 million pounds for it about three years ago and he has a mortgage. Nothing out of the ordinary, really."

Rusty asked, "How does he spend his money?"

Steve continued, "Okay, he has a couple of credit cards. I pulled his statements for the last year. There are the usual charges—restaurants, clothing, and the like—but he also travels a lot."

Sarah asked, "Anything to Copenhagen?"

"No. He has traveled primarily in the Middle East—Jordan, Saudi Arabia, Lebanon—and also Malaysia."

Rusty commented, "Malaysia? When was that?"

"Just after Nura left Libya. A week or so before we hit the compound."

"What did he do there?"

"Well, he only spent two nights. I have the hotel receipt. Stayed near the airport. A hotel car was also charged to his room but no indicator of where it went."

Gunny said, "So that's a dead end."

Steve smiled. "Well, not exactly. I hacked into his university email account. There was no mention of a trip to Malaysia but in his contacts, I found his personal email account. I hacked that too and found that in the weeks before the trip, even before Ostergaard was killed, Al-Maadi had been in email contact with a Dr. Mentari Tuk, the president of MalayVax, a Malaysian vaccine company. They were discussing the production of a new veterinary vaccine for something they refer to as FMD."

Alen chimed in, "That's foot-and-mouth disease. It's a painful cattle disease that causes wasting and weight loss. It's prevalent in Africa and the Middle East."

Steve continued, "Well, they set a meeting for the twelfth to discuss production of a new vaccine that Al-Maadi said he was developing for the Ministry Agriculture. I hacked into the ministry's server and found no mention of a new vaccine, but it could be that I just didn't find it or the details were not on that server. However, I did find their research budget and there was no reference to any new vaccine development program. Anyway Al-Maadi and Tuk appear to have met on the twelfth in Kuala Lumpur."

Rusty mulled this over and then said, "Maybe someone should go talk to this Dr. Tuk?"

Steve interjected, "There's more. On the way back to Cairo, Al-Maadi changed his flight. He flew to Dubai but then booked a separate round trip to Jeddah, Saudi Arabia. It was an overnight trip. Rather than fly from there to Cairo, he flew back to Dubai and then to Cairo. I don't know what he did in Jeddah. There was no mention of it in any of his emails."

Rusty said, "Saudi, huh. That's interesting. Given his family background and their contact with nefarious Saudi characters, it'd be nice to know who he met there."

"Like I said, there's no mention of Jeddah or Saudi Arabia in any of his emails. He may be using a completely different, anonymous account like that Al-Rafah guy in Gaza was using. That would be impossible to trace without knowing the account name."

Hans spoke up. "Let me see what we pulled from Rafah's computer. There might be something there we can use."

Rusty said, "Yeah, get on that. Let's see if we can tie one of those accounts to Al-Maadi. If we can, it would fill in some blanks for us. Do we know where Al-Maadi is right now?"

Steve replied, "No, sir. The last location we had on him was at the university when he was addressing a conference. There has been nothing since. His burner went off and has never come back up. Nura's is MIA as well. I made a couple of Arabic language robocalls to his apartment telephone number but there has been no answer. He could be out of town—if he drove somewhere we wouldn't know it so long as he paid cash for his gas and hotel. He might be staying with family in Cairo, or he's gone to ground."

Lon asked, "Can we access their immigration or border security networks? Maybe he drove to an adjoining country and went through an immigration check or something?"

"I can check but he doesn't own a car, and there is no car rental on his credit cards. Also, no bus, airline, or train ticket purchases. My guess is he is still in Egypt somewhere."

Rusty said, "Gunny, we need people in Egypt to get eyes on his office, apartment, or anywhere else he might be."

Gunny nodded. "I concur. We'll send a pair to Malaysia to interview this Tuk guy. They can pretend to be Russians and say that Al-Maadi stole their vaccine or something. Russians scare the shit out of everyone so he'll talk."

Rusty smiled. "I like it. Alen knows this stuff better than anyone else and can play a Russian." Turning to Alen, he asked, "You up for it, Markovic?"

He answered in Russian, "*Da, konechno*."

"All right, sounds like a plan. Magne speaks Russian. He can go with Alen. Send our best Arabic speakers to Cairo to see if we can track these two assholes down over there."

Gunny smiled. "You got it."

* * *

Alen and Magne were taking the private jet to Kuala Lumpur, but before they left, they drove into Nicosia to do some shopping. If they were going to play the roles of Russian heavies, they needed to dress the part. They bought a couple of expensive silk suits, matching snakeskin shoes, and expensive—if a little gaudy—ties. The shiny suit stretched over Alen's imposing frame made for a very scary image. Anyone would be a fool not to tell him exactly what he wanted to know.

Lon drove Magne and Alen to the airport in Larnaca where the Bombardier 8000 was fueled and waiting. When they got on the jet, Gil was in the cockpit along with another, younger man. They hadn't seen him since the operation in Libya and they had a whole new respect for the man now. They greeted him warmly. Alen shook his hand, "Good morning, Gil. Nice to see your smiling face again."

Gil grinned. "Now that you know I'm just not some hired throttle jockey?"

Magne interjected, "We didn't know how much you were in on." Motioning to the copilot, he added, "Is he, uh . . . in the loop too?"

Glancing over his shoulder, he said, "Who him? Nah. He's pretty much worthless."

A voice came from the cockpit. "I heard that!"

Gil said, "Come forward, I'll introduce you."

Magne and Alen followed Gil toward the cockpit. The co-pilot turned in his seat to look back at the men. Gil said, "Fellas, this is Donny. Donny, this is Magne and Alen. Two of the guys we've been flying around."

Donny smiled at Alen. "I remember you. We picked you up in Belgrade a while back, right?"

Alen said, "Yeah, that's right. What's your story?"

"Some old fart was getting too long-in-the-tooth to fly without a chaperone, so I got tapped to make sure he didn't nod off during the longer flights and kill everyone."

Gil snorted. "Bite me."

Magne asked, "How long have you two known each other?"

Gil said, "Uh, thirty-three years."

Donny shot back, "Thirty-four! Jesus, Dad, you don't even remember how old your own kid is!"

Alen was surprised. "He's your son?"

"Yeah, someone had to give the little shit a job when he got out of the Navy. McDonald's wasn't hiring."

Donny quipped, "I tried Burger King, but I didn't pass the background check. Apparently too many questionable people in my family tree."

Gil led the two men back to the cabin. "We roll out in five. Buckle up. And Donny is fully read in on what you guys do, in general, but he knows not to ask questions. Need to know and all. He was an F/A-18 pilot flying off the *Nimitz*, so he knows the drill. The flight will be around eight hours, so get some rest if you can. I'll be back once we get airborne in case you have any questions."

* * *

Sarah and Hans were selected to go to Cairo. They had the best Arabic, plus Sarah was the only one who had actually seen Nura in the flesh. They flew commercial to Cairo and were documented as husband and wife—her as a Lebanese and him as an Austrian. They checked into a suite at the Four Seasons Hotel, which was just north of the Cairo University campus on Rawdah Island in the Nile and close to the neighborhood where Al-Maadi lived. Sarah tried to change her appearance since Nura could recognize her too. She dressed in plain, traditional Arabic clothing, complete with a hijab and kept her makeup to a minimum. Large, dark sunglasses completed the ensemble, and her appearance was far removed from the glamorous look she sported in Copenhagen.

The first thing they did was check out Al-Maadi's apartment. It was located on Al Mawardi Street a little more than half a kilometer from his office. They staked it out. That first night, they sat outside in a rented car and just observed. They determined which windows belonged to his apartment and searched for any sign of life. After two hours of seeing nothing, Hans decided they needed a better vantage point. They entered a building across the street on the coattails of another resident by dropping the name of someone on the building directory. They were an obviously affluent couple so the man didn't question them. They proceeded to the top floor of the building but found the door to the roof locked. Hans picked the lock, and in a few moments they were on the roof looking down on Al-Maadi's apartment. Sarah had a pair of night vision binoculars in her oversized handbag. A couple of the curtains were open enough to give them a limited view inside, and the window to the kitchen was open a few inches. No one was there. The apartment was dark. Sarah made out some dirty dishes next to the sink in the kitchen and that the bed in the master bedroom was unmade. It was now after 9:00 p.m., and the night air took on a chill. Hans offered Sarah his jacket but she refused. She just kept watching.

Finally, at about midnight, Hans said, "I'm going to try something." He took a burner phone from his pocket and punched in the number for Al-Maadi's apartment. In the quiet night, they made out a faint ringing coming from the apartment across the street. It rang at least ten times before he ended the call. "No one is there. Even if they were asleep in another room, they'd have heard that. I think we should head back to the hotel and get some sleep. Tomorrow we'll hit the university."

Sarah stood up and stretched. "Yeah, that sounds good to me. We'll see what we can find out tomorrow. However, I suggest we bug the apartment in case they come back."

Hans nodded. "Good idea. I'll put in one of those sound-activated sensors. That should at least let us know if anyone goes there."

They cautiously exited the building, being careful to relock the roof access door behind them. They went back to their car and drove east to leave the immediate area. They parked a couple of blocks east and south, and changed their appearance. Hans took off his dark suit jacket and put on a light-colored wind breaker. Sarah put on a striped sweater and a replaced her hijab with a hat. They walked west on Bostan Al Fadel, the parallel street to the south of Al Mawardi, before circling back north to approach Al-Maadi's building from the west. It was almost 1 a.m. The front door to the building was locked but Hans made quick work of the lock. Al-Maadi's apartment was on the third floor. They took the stairs to avoid any cameras that might be in the elevator. The hallway was dimly lit. They walked down the hall to Al-Maadi's door and Hans started to work on the lock. Just as he was about to open it, Sarah stopped him. She ran her fingers around the door where it met the frame. She cautiously opened the door and detected the small, folded piece of paper as it started to drop from above the middle hinge. She picked up the paper and handed it to Hans. "We'll need to replace this when we leave."

Hans wasn't taking any chances and pulled a compact Glock 43 9 mm pistol from his pocket as they cautiously entered the apartment. He quickly and quietly moved through the apartment to confirm it was empty. Once satisfied, he rejoined Sarah in the living room. She was looking for somewhere to put their bug. The device was a flat, compact, cellular-based model developed by one of Travis's companies. Hans pointed to the bookshelf as he handed Sarah his weapon. She nodded her acknowledgment and covered the front door as he went to work. He scanned the books and magazines. He was searching for something more for show than daily reading. There were a number of magazines on the second shelf. They were technical journals like *The Lancet* and the *New England Journal of Medicine*. Even in the dim light, he saw they had a layer of fine dust on them. He took out the bug, turned it on, and gently slid it between two of the magazines. He pulled out the tiny microphone/camera which was no larger than a grain of rice and made sure its tip was facing out from between the spines of the two magazines before sliding them back in their original position. He pulled out his smartphone and opened up the app. He could clearly see the room. He walked in front of the bookshelf and a red dot started flashing on his screen. He whispered to Sarah, "Camera is up and the motion detector is working. Let's go."

Sarah handed him back the Glock and walked to the door. She checked the peephole before exiting into the hallway with Hans right behind her. Before she shut the door, she held out her hand and Hans gave her the folded piece of paper. She replaced it in the doorjamb just above the second hinge and pulled the door closed with a click. Hans used his lockpick to relock the door, and they slipped away into the night, tired but satisfied.

* * *

The Bombardier landed in Kuala Lumpur at about 0800 hours. Alen and Magne went through immigration and customs in their alias identifications. Both had very Russian names—Mikhail Antonov and Alexandre Meknikov—but were carrying passports from Cyprus and Malta. People who flew around in $50 million airplanes rarely were dragged into secondary, and they were no different. They were carrying cash—enough to look rich but not enough to trigger a money-laundering investigation. When asked the purpose of their travel, Alen said they were investing in a local company. No further questions were asked.

They had arranged for a car and driver to meet them upon arrival. It was a black Mercedes-Maybach S-Class and completed the image of power and money they wanted to portray. They gave their driver the address and he sped off into Kuala Lumpur's notorious traffic. When they arrived at MalayVax, Alen told the driver to park right in front of the building. When a security guard approached them to tell them to move, Alen got out of the $170,000 car and approached him. At six foot five and 250 pounds, Alen was already a very imposing person. Now he was wearing what could only be described as a mobster suit and dark sunglasses that obscured his eyes. He had a scowl on his face and barked at the man in Russian. The guard cowered and just shook his head to indicate he didn't understand what Alen was saying. Alen gave an irritated growl and said in heavily accented English, "I park where I want." Jabbing his finger in the guard's chest, he added. "Anyone touches car, I will hold you personally responsible. We are here to see Tuk."

The guard was thoroughly intimidated. "Uh, yes sir. I understand. Uh, just go through those doors. They will see to you. I will make sure your car is safe."

Alen snorted. "Good." He then handed the guard a hundred-euro bill and said, "Keep people away from it." The guard just nodded and slipped the bill in his pocket.

Alen and Magne walked into the lobby of MalayVax like they owned the place. They walked right up to the receptionist and Magne said, "We are here to see Mr. Tuk. Where is he?"

The receptionist was taken aback by the boorishness of his tone. "I'm sorry, do you have an appointment with *Doctor* Tuk?" She added emphasis to the "doctor" as a mild rebuke.

"No, we do not have appointment, but he'll want to see us. Tell him Mikhail Antonov and Alexandre Meknikov from Moscow are here."

The receptionist was clearly intimidated and was eager to extricate herself from the situation. "Let me call Ms. Zhou, his assistant." She quickly dialed the phone and whispered to whomever was on the other end of the line. "Uh, Ms. Zhou will be out in a moment. Please have a seat. Can I get you anything?"

Magne snorted. "No, we won't be here that long." Everyone else in the lobby stared at them but immediately turned away if Magne or Alen glanced their way. A few moments later, the door behind the receptionist opened, and Ms. Zhou walked out with a false smile painted on her face.

"May I help you gentlemen?"

Magne replied, "Yes, we need to speak to Tuk . . . right now."

"May I ask what this is in reference to?"

Alen said, "We are here to retrieve our stolen material—one way or the other."

Ms. Zhou was taken aback. "What? I'm sure I don't know what you are talking about."

Alen scowled at her, "I'm sure you don't, but your boss sure does. Al-Maadi stole it from us and we know your boss has it. It's ours and we want it back!"

Ms. Zhou was suddenly aware that all the other people in the lobby were now listening intently to what was going on. She smiled nervously and said,

"Uh, gentlemen, if you would please follow me, we can discuss this in a more private setting." She led them back to Tuk's office and motioned for them to have a seat, but they remained standing. She walked into Tuk's office and a few seconds later, she returned and said, "I'm sorry, but Dr. Tuk is not currently available. Would you like to make an appointment where you can address whatever issues you might have?"

Alen pointed at the office door behind her and said, "Bullshit! I know he's in there. I'm not going to give him chance to hide our material." He pushed past Ms. Zhou and into Tuk's office. Magne entered behind him and shot Ms. Zhou a menacing scowl as he did. Inside, Tuk was sitting at his desk with his phone in his hand. Alen said, "I suggest you hang up. Your security won't help you and I don't think you want the police to know you are holding stolen property."

Tuk gulped and hung up the telephone. "What is this about, exactly."

Magne spoke with false politeness. "I'm sorry, Dr. Tuk, my colleague is upset. My name is Mikhail Antonov and this gentleman is Alexandre Meknikov. We work for a prominent Russian businessman and philanthropist. Among his many holdings is a pharmaceutical company. This company supported development of a new vaccine. One of the people working on the project was Dr. Khalid Al-Maadi. Do you know him?"

Tuk replied, "Yes, of course. I have known Dr. Al-Maadi for several years. What does that have to do with me and my company?"

"It is our understanding that Al-Maadi came to you recently with new vaccine stock. Am I right?"

Tuk replied, "Well, I am not allowed to discuss my business arrangements with third parties. You understand, I'm sure."

A glowering Alen started to approach Tuk, but Magne stopped him. "I suggest you just answer the question."

Tuk was now frightened. "Okay, Al-Maadi came to me to discuss production of a new vaccine for the Egyptian Ministry of Agriculture. It had nothing to do with Russia."

Alen barked, "He stole that vaccine from us! We developed it and we were going to produce it. What he gave you was stolen goods. I can assure you that our boss does not like being robbed. You don't want to be the one who pisses him off."

Tuk started to feel brave. "Then call the police; we'll see what they say about it. I didn't steal your silly vaccine and I don't know where it is."

Magne leaned across Tuk's desk and said, "Our boss is not the kind of man who calls police. He prefers to handle his problems personally. Do you understand me?"

Tuk said, "Are you threatening me?"

It was now Alen who leaned across the desk. "Yes, we are. That is exactly what we are doing. You can't save Al-Maadi but you can save yourself. Tell us what we need to know and you walk away from this while you can still walk." As Alen leaned over him, Tuk made out the grip of the Sig Saur 9 mm automatic in a shoulder holster under Alen's jacket.

Tuk gulped. "Okay, okay. What do you want to know?"

Magne said calmly, "Al-Maadi came to visit you recently, correct?" Tuk nodded. "What did he tell you?"

Tuk was suddenly sweating profusely. "Uh, he told me he had developed a new FMD vaccine for his government. They wanted to purchase up to ten million doses but first he wanted us to do a sample run of five hundred doses to test our production process. I agreed and we set a price."

"How much?"

"Uh, $200,000, but he wanted it expedited, so it ended up being $220,000. He was supposed to get the money from the Saudis. He said they were funding the project to make sure animals the Kingdom bought to feed people making the pilgrimage to Mecca would be disease free."

Alen asked, "Did he provide the vaccine culture?"

"Yes. He brought it with him."

Alen asked, "How much did he provide?"

Tuk answered, "Uh, 20 milliliters."

"What is the status of the production? How much more virus did you culture?"

Tuk replied, "None. We never got started. We are in the process of selling our company to a German pharmaceutical company. As part of the due diligence, they insisted that all contracts be validated. They apparently contacted the Egyptian government to confirm Al-Maadi's project but they said they weren't aware of it. I guess now I know why. I was unaware the vaccine culture belonged to someone else, I swear! We canceled the project before it even started."

Alen asked, "What happened to the vaccine culture?"

"Well, I held on to it until we were reimbursed for our expenses incurred before the production program was stopped. It was $100,000."

"You said you never got started."

Tuk suppressed a smile. "Well, you know, administrative costs, lab scheduling, planning, and the like. This is a business after all. I told Al-Maadi I'd not release it to him until my company was made whole. I have a board of directors to answer to."

Alen's heart leapt. "So, you have it? It's here?"

Tuk shrugged. "Well, I did, but Al-Maadi paid us so I returned it to him."

"How? How did he pay you? The project wasn't real."

"I don't know but a few days ago we received the full $220,000 for the preproduction run. I kept $100,000 and I am, uh . . . holding the rest for him until he straightened everything out with the Ministry of Agriculture. I assumed it was a legit program. He said the Ministry denying the program was just a big misunderstanding. I had no reason not to believe him."

Magne asked, "The money, the $220,000; where did it come from?"

"Saudi Arabia. Just like he said. The project was supposed to be funded by the Saudis."

Magne glanced at Alen as if to say, "What now?" Alen grumbled at Tuk, "You're not off the hook yet. Where did you send our vaccine culture?"

Tuk was scared. "Cairo University! I sent it to Al-Maadi's office at Cairo University! I swear, I don't have any more of the vaccine culture, and I hope to God I never see it again."

"When?"

"Three days ago! I was happy to be rid of it, too."

Magne said, "Okay. We're going to check out your story and you'd better be telling the truth, or we'll be back, and next time, we won't be so polite. You do not tell Al-Maadi or anyone else that we were here. If you do, that will tell us you were in on it with him the whole time, and our boss will not be happy. And you really want to keep our boss happy. Do you understand?"

Tuk nodded furiously. "Yes, yes, I understand. No one. I will tell no one."

"What about your secretary?"

"I will tell her this was about some contract screwup. She won't ask questions."

Magne replied, "That's good. If all goes well, you'll never see us again—but only if all goes well." With that, they turned on their heels and walked out. They walked past Ms. Zhou's desk and Magne said, "We'll show ourselves out."

Two security guards walked up as they were leaving; Ms. Zhou had called them. They were unarmed except for nightsticks. They stepped in front of Magne and Alen to block their path. The two men were much smaller and they were frightened but also determined to do their jobs. When Alen pushed past them, one of them took out his nightstick but Alen snatched it from his hand before he began to swing. Alen snapped the nightstick in two with his bare hands, sent the pieces clattering across the floor, and continued walking. The other guard froze in his tracks, staring at Magne. Tuk had watched the scene unfold from his office doorway. He ran up smiling awkwardly, "It's okay, it's okay. Our guests are leaving. Everything is all right. You men can go back to your stations." The two guards just stood there as the two big "Russians" walked out, got in their car, and sped away.

In the car, Magne directed the driver to go back to the airport. Alen asked, "Do you think he was telling the truth?"

"Yes, I do. He damn near pissed his pants."

"Yeah, but do you think he'll refrain from calling Al-Maadi? I mean, he probably thinks we're going to kill the guy."

"That's true, but he has 120,000 reasons to keep quiet."

Alen laughed. "True. If the Russians whack Al-Maadi, Tuk can keep the leftover $120,000 and no one will be the wiser."

Magne snorted. "Hell, I'll bet he plans on pocketing the whole 220 grand. He strikes me as a venal little shit."

* * *

Once airborne, Magne and Alen passed on what they learned to the Praetorians at the villa in Cyprus via the jet's encrypted satellite data link. Gunny, in turn, passed it on to Hans and Sarah in Cairo. At least for the time being, Black Sun's bioweapon was in Cairo—somewhere. The plan was to get the rest of the team to Egypt as soon as the jet landed in Larnaca. Travis got on the phone with a broker and rented a large home in the Garden

City district of Cairo. It was short notice and the agent was being difficult until Rusty offered to pay $7,000 per day and a $10,000 deposit. The rental agent would meet them at the airport with the keys. One thing Rusty had learned was that money talked, and the more money you had, the louder it talked. In situations like this, he preferred to shout.

* * *

Sarah and Hans got up early and headed for Cairo University to learn about Dr. Al-Maadi. They came up with a plan and got Steve to give them an online presence in the event anyone checked on them. They walked up to Al-Maadi's office where his secretary, Miriam, was holding down the fort. Sarah approached her and asked, "Is this Dr. Khalid Al-Maadi's office?"

Miriam looked up find a sharply dressed woman accompanied by a European man in a suit. "Yes, it is. Can I help you with something?"

"Yes, thank you. We were visiting the university and thought we would drop by to see if Dr. Al-Maadi was here by any chance."

Mariam wasn't used to people just dropping by unannounced—at least people who were not students. "He isn't here right now. Can I ask what this is in reference to?"

Sarah replied, "Yes, I am Farrah Basara from the Ministry of Agriculture's International Cooperation Committee, and this is Dr. Frederick Weber from the Max Planck Institute for Medical Research in Heidelburg. We have an opportunity to collaborate with them on a new animal vaccine, and Dr. Al-Maadi's name was given to us as a leader in this particular area."

Mariam was impressed but still a little skeptical. "Oh, I see. Did you have an appointment, because I see nothing in Dr. Al-Maadi's calendar."

"No, like I said, we were on campus anyway and thought we would stop by. I would have called, but I left Dr. Al-Maadi's contact information in my office. This was not a planned visit. If you need to verify who I am, you can go to the ministry's website."

"Okay, please give me a moment." Miriam had the ministry's web page bookmarked so it only took her a few seconds to pull up the page. She searched for the International Cooperation Committee and it took her to a separate web page. Listed toward the top were the committee members. Among them was Farrah Basara's name and photograph along with an email address and telephone number. Miriam dialed the number and the cell phone in Sarah's purse started to ring.

Sarah said, "Oh, excuse me. I'm getting a call."

Miriam smiled, "No, that was me. I'm sorry but I had to verify who you were. Dr. Al-Maadi works on a number of sensitive and proprietary projects. You understand."

Sarah smiled. "Oh course. I should have made an appointment."

Hans interjected, "I'm impressed with your security procedures. Most people would not have gone to the trouble to verify our identities. You and Dr. Al-Maadi run a tight ship. That is good."

Miriam blushed a bit at the compliment. "Thank you, we try. Like I said, Dr. Al-Maadi isn't here. Is there anything I can help you with?"

"Do you know where he is or when he is expected back? I have been trying to reach him for a couple of days now but without success."

Miriam responded with an apologetic tone. "Yes, I'm sorry but Dr. Al-Maadi has taken a few days off for personal business. I spoke to him a couple of days ago and expect him back in the office soon."

"Really? When?"

"I'm sorry, he didn't specify. Can I leave a message for him?"

Ignoring her question, Hans replied, "My institute is working on FMD, uh foot-and-mouth disease, and we are seeking collaborators—specifically in North Africa. I understand Dr. Al-Maadi is one of the leading experts in the country."

Miriam wanted to talk up her boss. "Indeed, he is, sir. He's brilliant. And I know he has been researching that disease, that FMD, and has been talking to the Malaysians about it. I'm sure he would like to work with the Max-Planck Institute. I mean, who wouldn't?"

Hans raised an eyebrow. "Malaysia? Which university?"

"Oh, no university, a company—MalayVax. He just received a package of vaccine culture stock from them a few days ago."

Hans smiled. "Well, it looks like I've come to the right place. This would speed things up immensely. Is that a vaccine Dr. Al-Maadi developed?"

"Uh, I believe so but I'm not sure."

"This vaccine. Where is it now?"

Miriam said, "I turned it over to Ahmed, one of the senior lab technicians, to store it until Dr. Al-Maadi returns. It has to be kept very, very cold."

Sarah asked, "Where did Ahmed put it, exactly?"

Miriam shrugged. "I don't know. You'd have to ask him. But he wouldn't even show you the stuff without Dr. Al-Maadi's permission. They are very strict about that sort of thing. Proprietary information and all, you understand."

Hans smiled. "Of course. Excellent security procedures. Very impressive. I will discuss it with Dr. Al-Maadi when I see him. So, you have no idea of when he's expected back?"

"No sir, I do not. But I'm sure it'll be soon. Maybe the next day or so. Do want me to leave him a message?"

Hans pondered this. It would be unusual for him to ask her not to. "Yes, just tell him we dropped by and that we'll be in touch soon. I don't want to interfere with his personal business."

Miriam picked up a pen and started scribbling out a short message. "I know how to spell Ms. Basara's name, but how do you spell yours? I don't want to get it wrong."

Hans replied, "Yes, of course. That's Frederick Weber, W-E-B-E-R."

"Just like it sounds."

Hans glanced at her name plate on her desk. "Well, Miriam, you have been most helpful. I look forward to interacting with you more in the future. Good day." As they left, Sarah made a point of talking loudly about touring other university facilities until they were out of earshot.

A few meters down the hall, Sarah glanced over her shoulder to make sure Miriam had not followed them before retrieving her cell phone from her purse. She punched in a number and after a couple of rings Gunny answered. "Hello."

"It's me. We just visited his office. He hasn't been here for a few days. His secretary doesn't know where he is but was obviously covering for him. She confirmed that a package from KL arrived a few days ago. It was transferred to one of the labs for storage. She said it needed to be kept cold. She doesn't know which lab but it appears that it may still be here on campus."

"Okay. Roger that. I'll let the boss know. Keep hunting for the target."

Sarah answered, "We will. We're going to check out his old neighborhood next. We'll keep you apprised of any developments."

Gunny replied, "Copy. The rest of us will be there soon. We rented a house, I'll text you the address. How did Steve's little ruse work?"

"Like a charm. Tell him thanks for us."

"Will do. Stay safe."

* * *

While Sarah and Hans were on their way to the university, Khalid and Nura were deciding their next steps. Their problem was how to retrieve the virus and get it to Jordan without being caught. Complicating this was the fact that they were not even sure who they were up against. Was it the Americans? The Israelis? The Egyptian government? Whoever was pursuing them had in all likelihood killed Al-Rafah in Gaza, found Andreas and Nura in Denmark, identified and exploited their communications system, and wiped out Trabelsi's Black Sun cell to a man without even so much as a rumor or a news story to say it happened. Governments are usually quick to take credit for such things. *Who are these guys?*

Nura asked, "Okay, what are we going to do?"

Khalid replied, "I'm sure I can get the virus from the university. I just need to avoid Miriam and faculty members. If I can get to Ahmed, I can get it. It's a big place and I know how to get around. We need to figure out how to get it to the West Bank. That's going to mean going through Jordan."

Nura replied, "We have our false identities. I can buy two tickets to Amman in my alias and put one in your name, your alias name, of course."

Khalid mulled this over. "That's good, but flying into Amman might be a problem. I have gone there a lot."

Nura scoffed. "It's a pretty big airport. I don't think anyone will recognize you."

"It's not the people I'm worried about; it's the cameras. If they have a facial recognition system and they are searching for me, they'll find me when I go through customs and immigration."

"Leave that to me. You need to get the virus. How are we going to transport it? I don't want to put it in checked luggage."

"I'll carry it in my hand."

"Are you crazy?"

"No. We'll hide in plain sight. We will put it in a medical transport container in our carry-on. I have the Ministry of Health transit forms and letterhead on my computer at home. We can just fill it out in our alias names and print it. We'll say it's medicine. No one will question it. I need to get to my apartment but I'm afraid they're watching it."

Nura said, "I'll do it. I'll make sure they're not surveilling it. If it's clear, I'll go in, print the forms and a transit letter, and get out. It's your apartment. Odds are they're expecting a man—not a woman. While I'm doing that, you go to the university and retrieve the virus. I'll meet you back at the other apartment when you're done. I'll make the travel arrangements too. We'll leave tomorrow."

Khalid took a deep breath. "Okay, but it's awful risky."

Nura stared him in the eye and said, "Freeing my homeland and avenging my family is worth the risk to me. Is uniting the Arab world for the first time since Suleiman the Magnificent worth it to you?"

"Yes. You're right. Let's go."

Nura and Khaled left separately. He slipped out the back of the apartment building; ten minutes later she walked out the front dressed in conservative Arab garb. He walked northwest toward the university while she walked north toward his apartment.

As Khalid approached the university, he became more and more nervous. He avoided the faculty building altogether. This is where his office was and, if anyone were lying in wait for him, this where they would be. Instead he went to the western fringe of the campus and walked through the Al-Manial Hospital and into the Clinical and Chemical Pathology building. Once there, he found an empty office and called Ahmed, his laboratory manager.

"Hello?"

"Ahmed, it's me, Dr. Al-Maadi."

"Oh, hello, Dr. Al-Maadi. I haven't spoken to you in a while. How are you? Is everything okay with your family?"

Miriam must have made excuses to explain his absence. "Oh, uh, yeah. Everything is fine. You'll understand when your parents are as old as mine. Anyway, the reason I called was that Miriam gave you a sample that came in from Malaysia a few days ago. I understand you put it in one of the lab freezers."

"Yes, it was packed in dry ice so I put it in one of the ULT freezers."

"Great. Thank you. Uh, I need you to get it and prepare it for shipment in one of those foam cold shipping packs, the ones that use dry ice."

"Okay, sure. Do you want me to bring it to your office?"

"No. I'll meet you in yours. I'll be there in twenty minutes. Don't tell Miriam I'm here if you see her."

Ahmed chuckled. "Yes sir, and I'll make sure it's ready."

Ahmed's office was in the next building, so Khalid had time to kill. He found a little alcove with some old magazines to read but couldn't concentrate. He was too nervous. Time crawled, and fifteen minutes felt like fifteen days. Finally, he headed toward Ahmed's office. He ducked out a side door in an effort to avoid running into anyone but was still recognized by a couple of students who greeted him. He entered the next building and walked up three flights of stairs. The elevators all had security cameras and he didn't know if the authorities were actively searching for him or not. As he left the stairwell, he turned right and walked directly to Ahmed's office. He didn't have a secretary and Khalid just went in. Ahmed wasn't there. Instantly panic began to wash over his body. Had Ahmed called his office? Had he been instructed not to help him? Had he walked into a trap? The door opened behind him and he half expected it to be Asim Nader from El Mukhabarat. It was Ahmed and he had a cryo-pack shipping container in his hands.

"Oh, Dr. Al-Maadi. Sorry I'm late. I got cornered by Miriam in the hall. That woman can really talk."

Khalid asked cautiously, "You didn't tell her that I . . ."

"No, sir. I didn't tell her anything."

"Good. It's just that there are some admin meetings this afternoon that I'm trying to avoid and I don't want to put Miriam in the position of having to lie for me."

Ahmed smiled. "Plus she's terrible at it! That woman cannot keep her mouth shut. She did say you had some visitors this morning. Someone from some Ministry and some European researcher from Germany or Austria or somewhere. Were you expecting someone?"

Khalid tried to act nonchalant. "No. There was nothing on my schedule." He immediately recalled his conversation with Dr. Tuk when the vaccine project was canceled. Tuk said he was selling his company to a German pharmaceutical company and they had contacted the Egyptian Ministry of Agriculture. Was this some sort of follow-up to that? He didn't intend to stick around long enough to find out.

Ahmed opened the package to show Khalid that it contained the correct vial. "Here it is, Dr. Al-Maadi, the FMD vaccine culture." Khalid instantly recognized the small vial of Ostergaard's virus he had received from Nura. Though it had only been a few weeks, it felt like a year ago.

"Great, thank you, Ahmed. This is perfect."

"Where are you shipping it?" As he asked this, Ahmed sealed the box with packing tape and put a bright red seal over the opening.

"It's going to Jordan for a field trial. It's very promising. I'm sure you'll hear about it very soon but in the meantime, say nothing."

"My lips are sealed, doctor. Good luck."

"Thank you, Ahmed." Khalid took the box and left. He exited the building the way he came and slipped off campus.

In the meantime, Nura returned to Al-Maadi's apartment on Al Mawaradi Street. She did not simply walk into the building but rather found a vantage point a couple hundred meters away and just watched. She studied every car on the street. Which ones were occupied? Which was out of place for the neighborhood? Most had dark windows so she focused on their exhaust pipes to see if some were idling—a sure indicator that someone was inside. After about twenty minutes she walked down the street on the opposite side from his building. She checked all the vehicles. She stole glances at his apartment windows and those of every other apartment on the street. At the end of the block she stopped and waited again—observing, looking for anything out of place. Finally, she approached the building. She stopped at the corner store and bought a bag of groceries. As she walked, she held it high against her body to obscure her face. As she approached the building, she had her key ready and entered quickly. She walked up the stairs to Al-Maadi's floor. She peeked out the stairway door. In the hallway, two children played in front of their open apartment door. From inside came voices; they were from a television. The woman inside was watching an Egyptian soap opera. Nura eased out into the hall and walked toward Khalid's apartment. As she passed the children, they looked up at her but said nothing. She glanced into the apartment. Their mother was sitting on the couch drinking tea in front of the TV. Nura just glided quietly past. She put her key in the lock, but before opening it checked for the folded piece of paper just above the second hinge as Khalid had instructed. It was still there. She pushed the door open and went inside.

The apartment was just as they had left it several days ago. She fought the urge to make the bed and do the dishes. She had to keep reminding herself that they probably would never come back here. She put the bag of groceries down on the kitchen table and went into the guest bedroom where Khalid kept his desktop computer and printer. She turned on the computer and once it booted up, she typed in the password. There was little of importance on the computer, and Khalid never used it for anything having to do with Black Sun or their operation. He used it primarily for surfing the internet and making reservations. Nura opened up a folder named "travel" and quickly found the forms she was looking for. She filled out Ministry of Health transit forms and typed up a phony letter of introduction on MOH letterhead. Once she was done, she printed two copies of each, folded them neatly, and put them in two Cairo University envelopes she found in a drawer.

She was confident no one had seen her enter the apartment. If they had, the police—or someone—would have kicked in the door by now. Maybe they hadn't been discovered after all? The phony text from Trabelsi hadn't mentioned her or Khalid by name. It may have been intended just to bait them into some activity. It certainly did that, but they had encountered no problems in Libya or afterward. She went into the bedroom and made the bed. She was a little bit OCD, and when stressed tended to focus on establishing order around her. She grabbed the small black suitcase that had been with her since fleeing Denmark and put in it some clothes, toiletries, and the like. If they were going to travel, they had to look like travelers. No one travels without bags.

After packing the bag, she returned to the kitchen. It was a waste of time but she couldn't help herself—she did the dishes. Finally, logic overruled her mania. It was time to leave. She put the two envelopes in her suitcase. Once in the hall, she replaced the folded piece of paper, locked the door, and left.

* * *

As Sarah and Hans were walking out of the Faculty of Medicine toward the Kasr Al Ainy Fountain, Hans's cell phone chirped. Sarah asked, "What's that?"

Excitedly, Hans grabbed his phone. "It's the motion sensor in Al-Maadi's apartment!"

"Shit! Well, open the app!"

"I am, I am!" Hans answered frantically. "I can't see shit!" He fumbled with this phone as he walked to a spot under a tree. Once in the shade, the screen became visible. "Okay, we have an entry. Let me find the video."

Sarah looked over his shoulder as he maneuvered through the app until he found the option he wanted. He hit the replay button and they both crouched over the screen. The video showed a body pass in front of the camera hidden in the bookcase. The person walked by too fast to get a good view. Sarah bit her lip. "Damn it! Could you tell who that was?"

He rewound the video played it again. "No. It's just a blur. A woman? Maybe? Let me see if there's more. He set the playback to show him only that which was motion activated. Again, the camera caught a figure passing in front of the camera but no face. "Goddamnit!" He moved on to the next alert. This time they observed the figure move toward the master bedroom door and disappear inside. It was definitely a woman. A few seconds later, she returned.

Sarah shouted, "That bitch! It's her!" A couple people walking by gaped at Sarah suspiciously. She shrugged and apologized in Arabic, "Sorry about that." Turning back to Hans, she said, "Go back to that image." He did as she asked and she stared at it intently. "That is definitely her. It's Nura. She's there, right now. We have to move."

They ran to their car and drove east. Al Mawara Street was less than a kilometer away but traffic was heavy. They finally got there and Sarah bailed out of the car on Al Mawara. Hans found a parking spot two blocks away and around the corner. He walked briskly to a location a couple blocks south and east of where he dropped Sarah off. As he walked, he checked the phone. There was another alert. Nura walked out of the bedroom with a small suitcase and past the camera toward the door. He recalled the layout of the apartment from the day before; there was really nothing in that direction. She was leaving. He quickly called Sarah. "The target is leaving. Repeat, the target is on the move."

Sarah was standing about a hundred meters west of the apartment build-ing. She was behind a van which provided some screening. "Okay, I see her. She's leaving the apartment and carrying a small black suitcase."

Hans replied, "That's gotta be her. We need to follow her. We need her to lead us to Al-Maadi and the virus."

"I know. I have to stay back so she doesn't see me. Okay, she's heading east on Al Mawara toward you, walking on the north side of the street. She's wearing a black blouse and skirt with a black hijab." She added sarcastically, "Yeah, she won't be hard to spot on the street dressed like that. She's like every other woman in Cairo."

Hans replied, "Yeah, that'll make it tough, but at least she has the suit-case. That makes her stand out a little. I'm westbound one block south of you on, uh . . . Bostan El Fadel."

Sarah followed Nura from the south side of the street and stayed back about one hundred meters. Sarah had put in earbuds to talk to Hans while she kept her phone in her pocket. At the next intersection, Nura turned south. "Shit. She's crossing at Haret Fahmy to the south, to my side of the street. I have no cover. I'm going to have to duck into a doorway or she'll see me." After a short pause, Sarah continued, "She's continuing south on Fahmy on the west side of the street. I'm moving."

Hans replied, "She's headed right toward me." He altered his pace to make sure he didn't run up on her. A minute or so later she emerged from behind a building at the corner a block and half in front of him. "I have visual. She's continuing south. Do you have eyes on her yet?"

Sarah had just rounded the corner. "Yeah, I got her. Moving south on Haret Fahmy."

"Okay, I'm going to parallel her to the east. I'm headed south on Haret El Helaleia." He had a map program running on his phone and checked where they were. "Okay, Fahmy Ts into the next street—she can only go east or west. I'm thinking east since west would be a backtrack. I'm going to hold back."

"Copy that. I'll let you know." Sarah was a full block behind Nura and she had moved to the east side of the street so the cars and trees provided some screening. Nura was casually looking around but nothing blatant. She took a left at the next intersection. Sarah said, "Target is eastbound."

Hans replied, "Copy. Eastbound on El Rashedy. I'll pick her up when she crosses my bow. Okay, there is a children's hospital to the south and a Metro stop to the southeast. If she gets on the Metro, I'll have to go with her. You go back and get the car. The keys are on top of the driver's front tire. It's at the end of Bostan El Fadel—assuming it hasn't been towed or stolen."

Sarah chuckled. "That would suck. I'm going to go west at the intersection and south behind the hospital in case she continues south. If she heads for the hospital, I can enter from the west. If she heads for the Metro, I'll reverse and head for the car."

Hans said, "Roger that. I wish we had more people."

"Me too, but we don't, so it's just you and me."

Hans waited on El Helaleia. He stood behind a van for cover but eyed the intersection ahead through the windows. As Nura crossed in front of him, she peered up the street in Hans's direction but didn't change her pace. Hans said, "Okay, she just passed my position and she took a long look up the street. She's looking for something."

"Did she see you?"

"No, I don't think so. I have good cover here. I'm on her."

Sarah said, "I'm at the intersection and I can see her. As soon as you have her, I'm going west and south."

A few moments later, Hans said, "Okay, I got her. You can go. She's turning south in front of the hospital." There was a long pause. "Damn, there are a lot of people on the street. I don't have a visual."

"Did you lose her?"

"Don't get your panties in a twist. Okay, I've reacquired. She's crossing the street toward the Metro. Repeat, she's headed for the Metro. I'm going after her."

"Damn. Okay. I'll get the car." Sarah turned around and started trotting back toward where Hans had left the car. She had three blocks to cover. She hoped the train would not be arriving too soon.

Hans followed Nura into the Metro station and paid five pounds for a multi-ride ticket. He wanted to follow Nura at a discreet distance, but the Metro was crowded and her clothing made her blend in extremely well. Afraid to lose her, he stayed close. When she committed to a platform, he contacted Sarah. "She is on the southbound platform. That is the Helwan line. The next station is El-Malek el-Saleh and then Mar Girgis."

Sarah acknowledged him. "Copy that. Southbound on the Red Line to Helwan. I'm almost to the car. I'll be moving south in a couple of minutes."

Hans stood patiently waiting for the train. He was on the main platform standing with his back against the wall. There were no seats on this platform so Nura moved toward an adjacent corridor where a number of other women congregated. Hans lost sight of her so he casually walked down the platform past the corridor toward some vending machines. As he purchased some chewing gum, he glanced back. She was standing against the wall behind the other women. They waited at least five minutes until the train arrived. As it pulled into the station, he went back to the vending machine and bought a candy bar while he waited for Nura to walk past and onto the train. "On board southbound train."

"Copy. I'm moving south on El Kasr but I doubt I'll catch up. If she gets off at the next station, you're probably going to be on your own."

"Copy that. I'll do my best." He got on the same car but entered through the doors on the opposite end. Nura took a seat and sat quietly. She didn't glance around but rather looked like a bored housewife. As they approached the next station, the train slowed. As it came to a stop, some passengers started moving toward the door. After a few seconds, Nura stood up and followed. Hans waited a few seconds and exited after her. She moved toward the exit. He whispered into his earbuds, "We're off the Metro at El-Malek el-Saleh Station. She is moving toward the west exit—repeat, west exit toward Qais ibn Saad Street."

Sarah replied, "I'm still a few minutes away. Keep me posted on your location and I'll try to vector in as best I can."

"Roger that." Hans rushed to catch up to Nura. She was only out of his sight for a few seconds but that was enough to slip in behind some luggage lockers. She dropped a coin into the locker and opened it. She removed her purse before putting her suitcase in the locker. She closed the door and pocketed the key. She then immediately moved toward the woman's lavatory. Once inside, she went into a stall and removed her hijab and let her hair down. She took off her black blouse to reveal a white, short-sleeved shirt underneath. She took a pair of sunglasses out of her purse and stuffed in the black shirt and hijab. Her hair was still the light brown color she had dyed it in Tunisia. She was a totally different person. Meanwhile, out in the station Hans was panicking. He had lost her and it wasn't even that busy. After scurrying around the small station for a few minutes he rushed to the street side. He checked the pedestrian overpass to the south to determine if she was heading east over the train tracks. She wasn't there. He then scanned Qais ibn Saad Street north and south. There were a number of women dressed in black but none with a suitcase. He spotted someone resembling her walking north and rushed off after her. As he did, a pretty young woman in a white shirt and sunglasses walked behind him to the south. When he got close to the woman walking north, he discovered she was an older woman in her fifties. He spun around searching in all directions, but Nura was gone.

Hans immediately got on the phone with Sarah. "Goddamn it, I lost her!"

"Okay. Where are you?"

"I'm outside the station. She just fuckin' vanished on me. She must have dumped the bag and done a clothing change. No one, I mean no one with a black suitcase left this station. I checked the pedestrian walkways—she didn't go east."

Sarah checked her map. "Okay, I'm north of you. We have the river to the west and the train tracks to the east. So, unless she's swimming, that leaves north and south. You head south to El Nafuq el Gharby Street and cover any movement south. I'll stop along the Magra El Oyoun aqueduct to cover the north."

"What if she's gone to ground in the neighborhood?"

"Then we're going to be here a while."

* * *

Nura walked aggressively through the neighborhood west of the train station. She wasn't sure if she'd been followed but she did pick up on a couple of suspicious people—the woman in the neighborhood and the man on the train. She had been trained in surveillance detection by Hamas operatives who had, in their day, been trained by Syrian and Russia intelligence officers. She was very good at it but had to admit, she was rusty and didn't always trust that she actually saw what she saw. Before going to the apartment, she made sure she was "clean" by walking an aggressive and illogical route. If she was under surveillance, those following her would know they had been discovered and would likely move to grab her immediately, but at least Al-Maadi and their operation would remain safe. She zigzagged through the area, which included everything from slums to archeological sites to commercial businesses and middle-class apartments. She saw nothing so, after an hour, she felt safe enough to go to the apartment.

When she arrived, Khalid was there waiting for her. She gave him a kiss and then plopped down on the bed exhausted. She asked him, "Did you get it?"

He smiled. "It's in the refrigerator. How about you? Did you get the forms?"

"Yes, they are in my purse. I made copies of everything, just in case." She sat up on her elbows and added, "Oh, by the way, I may have been followed today."

Fear flashed over Khalid's face. "What?!"

"Yes, when I was leaving your apartment there was a woman on the street. She followed me for three of four blocks before breaking off. She was too far away for me to get a good look though. She appeared to be an Arab. Immediately after, there was a man who rode the train with me—a European man. I think I saw him a couple of blocks before the station. He rode in the same train car as me and got off at my stop. I went into the lavatory to change my clothes and when I came out, he was searching for someone or something. He didn't recognize me and he moved off to the north in a hurry. I didn't see him again after the train station. Just to be sure, I spent an hour in the neighborhood making certain I wasn't followed before coming here."

"Well, if you're right, we may be screwed." Khalid was pacing the floor nervously.

Nura replied calmly, "Well, if they don't kick in our door in the next few minutes, I think we're okay, at least for the time being. If it was only two people, then it probably is not the Egyptian security services. They have a lot more people to throw at a problem like this. They would've cordoned off this entire neighborhood and done a house-to-house search. An Israeli team? Mossad is capable but they don't have the luxury of unlimited manpower when operating outside Israel. I have a plan on how to deal with them if and when the time comes. In the meantime, I need to print out our boarding passes and prepare for tomorrow."

Khalid gaped at her in shock. "How can you be so calm about all this?"

"Because one of the things my father taught me was that panicking never improves your situation. If they're there, they're there. If they're not, they're not. You losing your cool will not change that." She reached into her purse, pulled out a pistol, and placed it on the nightstand. "I hope for the best and prepare for the worst. You had better too. Now, get some rest. We have a long day ahead of us tomorrow."

* * *

The Bombardier 8000 touched down in Cairo in the afternoon. The customs check was cursory. Rusty had paid to have it "expedited," which means the customs people were bribed to rubber stamp their papers and usher them through with a smile. The real estate broker met them at the airport with the keys to their Garden City district villa and offered to show them around, but Rusty declined. They had called ahead, and three rented Mercedes SUVs were waiting for them at the airport's executive terminal. Within twenty minutes of landing, the team and their gear were loaded and on their way to the villa that would serve as their home base. The house they had rented was only a short distance from the Four Seasons where Sarah and Hans were staying. It was a standalone building surrounded by a high, vine-covered wall and a parking area in the back. It was nice, but they didn't plan on spending much time there. They had a job to do.

As soon as they got to the house, they contacted Sarah and Hans, who filled them in on what had transpired with Nura. No one faulted them for losing Nura. They didn't have the manpower necessary to conduct proper surveillance, and they were lucky they accomplished what they had. The team immediately deployed to the area to relieve them. The Praetorians set up a perimeter bracketing the neighborhood. It was a fairly confined area and they were confident that Nura, and possibly Al-Maadi, were in there somewhere. In two of the vehicles, Steve set up remote night vision cameras that recorded everyone on the street and ran their faces through the Wise

Owl's facial recognition software. They also had body cameras so they would take turns periodically walking through the neighborhood gathering images of everyone they encountered. These too were fed into the Praetorians' computers in the hope of locating their target. While going house-to-house wasn't an option, they could secure the perimeter and keep Nura hemmed in.

The team stayed out all night. Sarah and Hans joined the others after a quick stop at their hotel to change clothes and grab a bite to eat. Steve set up shop in the back of one of the Mercedes so he would be available should they need an extra body. Rusty and Gunny remained at their rented villa and monitored developments from there.

At 0600 hours, the team was bleary-eyed from boredom and lack of sleep when the alarm went off on Steven Chang's computer. They had a hit. He immediately perked up. He keyed the mic on his tactical radio. "This is Alpha Eight. I think we have something!" Everyone immediately snapped out of their stupors. "I have a possible hit southbound on the street parallel to the train tracks. The bogey just walked past vehicle two. Static cameras got a good image. Wise Owl gives it an 87 percent chance that it's our girl."

The sun was starting to come up, but it was dark enough for the few streetlights in the neighborhood to still be on. Sarah was on the west side along the Nile in one of the Mercedes with Hans. "I need to get in position to see her. I'm the only one who has seen her in the flesh."

Hans replied, "Okay, but don't get out of the car. She can ID you as easily as you can ID her."

"Okay. Go east on Muslema and then north on Qais ibn Saad. She'll be on the opposite side of the street but walking straight toward us. I should have a good view." Hans did as she asked and sped east to get her in position. As they turned the corner onto Qais ibn Saad Street, the Metro station was directly in front of them. "Hurry, get past the station before she gets there. I don't want to miss her." As they approached the station Hans pointed to someone to his right. He slowed down and a woman stepped off the curb to cross the street toward the station. She walked right in front of their car. It was Nura. She glanced in their direction but more like she was checking traffic than looking in the car. She continued across the street and into the train station without as much as a sideways glance.

Hans continued on before saying, "Holy shit! Was that her?"

Sarah used the sideview mirror on the car to check Nura's progress. "Yes, that was definitely her."

Hans keyed his mic and said, "We have a positive ID on the target. She is walking past the train station. She is wearing a dark skirt, a light-colored shirt—white, possibly light blue, a floral scarf, and a dark sweater."

Sarah said to Hans, "Slow down a bit." Sarah turned in her seat. "She's taking the pedestrian bridge to the east over the tracks."

Hans keyed his mic. "Alpha One, she's headed your way on the first pedestrian bridge over the tracks."

Lon answered. "Copy that. I'm in position." There were two pedestrian bridges over the Metro tracks and Lon had positioned himself in between them to cover both, but he was the only team member on the east side of the tracks. He was standing in the shadows under a copse of trees south of the station. He barely made out a figure moving across the bridge and then down the steps on the eastern side. "Okay, she's moving toward the north-bound platform. Alpha One is moving to follow. If she gets on, I'll go with her. Car two start moving north. We don't want her to get away from us."

John answered, "Car two copies. We're moving." He turned to Magne and smiled. "Showtime, Bubba. You may get another shot at her."

Magne nodded his head. "If only. Let's roll. The next Metro stop is just north of Ali Ibrahim Basha."

Lon walked slowly north across Abu Sefain Street from the El Mabara Hospital toward the station. He was dressed in local garb, but he didn't want to get too close. She would tell he wasn't an Arab if for no other reason than he was too big. He had purchased Metro tickets the night before so he was ready to jump on quickly. The Metro was aboveground at this point so he would know when the train was coming. A low rumble was coming from behind him; the train was on its way. He walked through the turnstile and moved to the platform. He located Nura. He keyed his mic twice to indicate he had a visual on her. She was standing at the far-left end of the platform and would get on the last car, affording her the opportunity to observe everyone getting on the train with her while only facing in one direction. He moved to the far-right end of the platform and waited. When the train arrived in the station, he got on the train without hesitation. There were only five or six people waiting for the train, and a quick glance to his left showed that Nura was waiting for everyone else to get on first. Once they all committed, she got on as well. He keyed his mic three times to indicate they were moving. As the train began to roll, Lon stood up and moved through the car toward the back of the train. He stopped at the second-to-last car—one away from Nura's. He spotted her through the window.

Nura didn't get off at the next two stops, but as they approached the Anwar Sadat Metro Station, she stood. Lon texted Alen—*Exiting Sadat Stn.* Alen got on the radio. "This is Alpha Two. Alpha One said the target getting ready to exit at Sadat Metro Station."

Sarah chimed in. "This is Alpha Four. That's a transfer station for Line Two, the Orange Line. We need someone in there."

John responded. "This is car two. We're across the street. I'm putting Alpha Three out on foot. He can pick her up."

Alen responded, "Okay. I'll pick up Alpha One at the south entrance. Did you copy that, One?" The radio clicked once. Lon was confirming.

They continued to follow Nura as she traveled about the city. They weren't sure what she was up to but they determined she didn't have the virus since all she was carrying was a small purse. She stopped at a shopping mall where she bought some shoes and then got back on the Metro. She transferred to the Orange Line and took it to Shobra Metro Station— the end of the line. Anticipation in the team grew since there was a train station there, but instead she went to the Nile Hospital. Hans followed her in, thinking maybe she was there to pick up the virus, but instead she went to the business office to fill out some forms. Afterward, she had a coffee in the cafeteria before getting back on the Metro and heading south. Traffic on the streets was getting busier and busier as the day progressed, and the rest of the team, following in vehicles, were getting strung out, and some were falling behind. At Al-Shohadaa Station, she transferred to a northbound Red Line train. No one was in position to take over for Hans so he had to make the transfer with her. The rest of the team scrambled to keep up.

Nura's travel was not random. She knew exactly what she was doing. She was waiting for traffic to build to a point where following her in a car was untenable. She didn't know how many people were following her but she correctly assessed that she had reduced it down to one, maybe two people on the train with her. The Red and Orange Lines were separated by two large sets of railway tracks which meant there were few ways across them. This was a natural barrier for anyone trying to follow the Metro train from a car. Even if they got on a parallel road, Cairo's notorious traffic made it essentially impossible to keep up.

About an hour after Nura left the apartment and began dragging the team all over Cairo after her, Al-Maadi finished his coffee inside the apartment. He took the package containing the virus out of the freezer and walked to the Metro Station. Using the key Nura gave him, he opened the luggage locker, removed her suitcase, and carefully placed the package inside. He then took the Metro to New El-Marg Station at the end of the Red Line and waited. After an hour or so, his telephone chimed. It was a text from Nura. She would be arriving in a few minutes. Al-Maadi got up and walked outside the station to hail a cab. He told the driver to wait at the north end of the station. A few minutes later Nura walked out of the station. He waved his white handkerchief out of the window of the taxi to get her attention. She walked over to the cab and got in just as Hans walked out of the station behind her. He ran up as the taxi pulled away and got on the ramp to go east on the Ring Road highway toward the airport.

"Fuck!" Hans keyed his mic. "I fucking lost her. When she got off the Metro at New El-Marg, there was a taxi waiting for her. She is east bound on the Ring Road."

Lon replied, "Well, shit. Did you get a license plate for the cab?"

"Yeah, I'm texting it to Alpha Eight. I'm sorry, guys. I fucked up."

Sarah interjected, "No you didn't. She played us. All of us. She led us away and waited for traffic to get so bad we couldn't follow in vehicles. Damn it! She led us on a wild-goose chase chase. This isn't exactly what most of us are trained to do."

Nigel added, "That's true. We were trained to shoot people when we find them, not follow them around."

John got on the air, "Why? Why'd she do it? Why risk it?"

Nigel answered, "She was leading us away from Al-Maadi. I'd bet money she was with him last night. She was the decoy while he got away clean with the virus. She's smarter than we thought. I'm beginning to think she's the brains of the outfit."

Lon reasserted discipline. "Okay, okay. Enough chatter. East on the Ring Road. Where does it take you?"

Sarah replied, "The airport."

Steve chimed in. "Alpha Seven is right. It's about twenty klicks from here."

Lon asked, "Can you access airport traffic cameras or interior cameras?"

"I was working on that last night. Give me a few minutes and I'll have them for you. They have license plate readers so we'll be able to tell if they arrive."

"Great. Let homebase know what's going on. Alpha Seven, you go to New El-Marg and pick up Alpha Four, then head to the airport. Everyone else, move toward the airport. If they show up there, be prepared to move out. All other vehicles confirm."

Magne answered, "Car two copies."

Nigel said, "Car three copies."

Sarah responded, "Car four copies."

* * *

Nura and Khalid arrived at Cairo International Airport about thirty minutes after they left the Metro station. Khalid paid the driver and retrieved the little suitcase from the trunk. They walked into the airport like any other couple. They already had their boarding passes so they went straight to the security line. They had Egyptian passports that said they were Mustafa and Amal Qureshi from Giza. When the security personnel X-rayed their bag, they inspected the package with the virus. Nura provided a letter from the Egyptian Ministry of Health indicating it was a vaccine intended for a hospital in Aqaba. They were waved through.

* * *

As soon as they got off the phone with Lon, Rusty, and Gunny packed up the team's gear and were on their way to the airport, but it would be a while before they'd get there. Because of the time difference with Washington, DC, Rusty contacted the German member of the targeting committee. He told him to issue a security alert on Dr. Khalid Al-Maadi and Nura Ostergaard née Al-Doghmush so if they tried to get on any commercial flight in almost any country, they would be detained. Even if they were fool-ish enough to travel under their real names, it was unlikely the alert would populate through the international airline security apparatus fast enough to keep them from flying that day, but he had to try.

As Nigel navigated the black Mercedes through Cairo's snarled traffic, Steve Chang was busy accessing the security network at Cairo International. Fortunately, he had worked on it the night before to fend off the boredom while they staked out the neighborhood where Nura disappeared. Gaining access to the network was relatively simple. The Egyptian security system wasn't exactly state of the art, but he could work with it. They did have a license plate reader system to tap into, so he punched in the license plate number Hans had texted and waited. After about twenty-five minutes, he got an alert. The security system took a photo of the front and back of every car accessing the airport. He doubled-checked the license plate number from the system photo. It was the car. He zoomed in on the grainy photo. There were clearly two people in the back seat, one shorter than the other but he couldn't make out their faces. "Okay the taxi in question just entered the airport. It stopped at Terminal Two."

Lon responded, "Great work. Can we get eyes inside to see where they go?"

"Let me see. It's awfully crowded in there. We need to link to our facial recognition software but I'm using a cellular data link and it isn't fast enough. When we get to the jet, I can use its satellite uplink, but right now I'm ham-strung. I'm archiving everything from Terminal Two starting from when their taxi came through the reader."

"Well, do the best you can."

Twenty minutes later, they were at Terminal One, where the private jets were parked. With Gil's help, they quickly got through what little security there was and were on the plane. Steve wasted no time connecting to the plane's high-speed satellite uplink. Sarah and Hans were already on board. Gil told Nigel, "I've precleared with the tower and filed a flight plan for Istanbul. It's a placeholder until I know more. We'll be ready to depart as soon as the others get here."

Nigel said, "Roger that. The rest of the team should be here soon. The delay is going to be with Mr. Travis and Gunny. They're coming from downtown."

"Yeah, well, we don't know where we're going yet so until then, it's a moot point."

"Steve's working on that."

Gil asked, "Not really in my wheelhouse, but why don't you just take them out here?"

Nigel replied, "We considered that, but he has a purified sample of that virus we destroyed in Libya. We don't know what form it's in. If it can be aerosolized, we sure as hell don't want him releasing it in a crowded airport if he finds out we're on to him. We need to get to him before he knows what's happening or get him in a controlled space so that, even if he does release it, we can contain it. He wants to infect Israelis, not Egyptians, so he'd only release it here as a last resort."

Gil shook his head. "Too bad you can't just walk up to him and shoot him in the head."

Nigel smiled. "That would make it easier, but I don't think airport security is going to just let us waltz in there with an MP-7."

"Yeah, I suppose not."

After a few minutes, Steve shouted out from the back of the plane. "I got 'em. I got footage of them passing through Terminal Two security about an hour ago. The video isn't the best." Narrating the video as it played, he said, "Okay, security is removing a package from their luggage and inspecting it. The guy is showing them a letter or something. Damn, they're giving it back to them and now they're through. Can you believe that? They gave it back to them."

Sarah quipped, "Well, I doubt they had it labeled 'biological weapon.' Security is looking for bombs, guns, and knives. As long as it's under four ounces, they aren't going to care about a liquid. I'm sure it's labeled as medicine or something."

Hans added, "See where they went next. Let's see if we can figure out where they are headed."

"On it," Steve replied. Sarah, Hans, and Nigel were now huddled around Steve and his laptop. "Okay, they're headed for the Royal Jordanian gates."

Nigel asked, "Can someone pull up their flights for today? We need to figure out how many flights, to where, and when."

Hans shouted, "I'm on it." He sat down across from Steve and plugged in a laptop. After a few minutes he called out, "Only one Royal Jordanian flight today. Flight 504 to Amman departs at 1315 hours out of Gate 9."

Nigel checked his watch. "Shit. We don't have much time then. What's the ETA on the rest of the team?"

Sarah got on her radio and asked, "All cars, what is your ETA at the airport? We think the Tangos are booked on a 1315 flight to Amman."

After a couple of seconds, the radio chirped. "Car One ETA is about five minutes."

There was a short pause. "Car Two ETA about 10."

Nigel was just about to ask about the others when Gunny's voice crackled over the radio. "We are en route now. Driver says he can have us there in twenty-five."

Sarah replied back. "Copy all. We'll plan on rolling as soon as the last two are on board. Just leave the vehicles in the executive parking lot. We'll deal with 'em later."

Gil overheard the conversation. "Okay, I'm going to amend the flight plan for Amman and get precleared. I'll spin the engines up in twenty minutes so we can roll as soon as the boss is on board."

Nigel replied, "Great. Thanks, Gil."

Gil added, "Donny has been listening to the tower frequency, and a lot of these commercial flights are late pushing back today. We might get there ahead of them if we're lucky. At worst, we'll be right behind them."

Sarah addressed the assembled group. "I think we should let my old colleagues know what's going on. They need to be ready to close the border crossings—just in case."

As the senior team member on site, Nigel answered, "I agree but we should run it by the boss. I think he has his own channels and they're probably higher up the food chain. A decision like that would likely have to come from the top anyway."

Sarah replied, "True, but I would still like to reach out to my personal contacts. They are in a better position to provide us with tactical intel—off the books—if they understand the threat."

Hans looked at Nigel. "What she says makes sense." The others nodded their agreement.

Nigel pondered this for a moment. "Okay, but just give them a heads-up. We need them on deck, but not in the batter's box."

Hans laughed. "Did you just use an American baseball metaphor?"

Nigel smiled. "I've been working with these Yanks too long."

After a few minutes, Lon and Alen arrived. Hans filled them in on recent developments while Steve continued to monitor Nura and Al-Maadi. Sarah was in the back of the airplane on an encrypted satellite phone reaching out to her old coworkers in the Mista'avrim counterterrorism unit. Nigel asked Steve, "Status?"

"Still hanging around in Terminal Two. Sitting between Gates 8 and 9. No movement."

Sarah walked forward. "I just got off the phone with Mista'avrim. They're standing by to assist any way they can. They've been alerted to a major threat but don't have all the details. I'm assuming Rusty's contact put the word out. That'll make it easier when the time comes."

Lon looked at Nigel quizzically, and Nigel said, "I gave her the okay. This is no time to stand on protocol. This isn't some Katusha rocket attack we're talking about. We may need their help and if we do, it'll be on short notice."

Lon nodded. "Yeah, you're right. Good call, guys." As he said this, Magne and John clambered up the steps onto the plane. Now they were just waiting for Rusty and Gunny.

The next fifteen minutes were an eternity. They all worried that every minute gave Al-Maadi the advantage. Finally, an SUV rolled up and Gunny and Travis piled out. Gunny yelled for Lon and John to grab the gear from the back. Hans and Magne followed them to lend a hand. Travis tossed his bag toward the back of the plane and asked, "Where do we stand?"

Steve replied, "I have 'em on security cameras. Still hanging around Gate 9. That's Royal Jordanian flight 504 to Amman. They're about to start boarding."

Sarah said, "I reached out to my old colleagues and they are ready to help us anyway they can. Don't get mad at Nigel; it was my idea."

Gunny said, "No, it was the right call. I want to grab them in Jordan as soon as we can isolate them, but there are a lot of variables. This shit can go sideways a dozen different ways. If we need the Israelis, we'll need 'em in a hurry."

The other guys were finished loading the last of the gear and Gil pulled up the steps behind them. "Everyone buckle up. We're getting ready to roll."

Steve interjected, "They're starting to board 504 and our tangos just stood up."

Gunny said, "Let's get this thing in the air. With any luck, we can beat them to Amman."

Gil smiled. "That's what I was planning on."

Rusty said, "Gil, drive her like a rental car."

* * *

While the Praetorians had video from inside the terminal, they didn't have audio. What they missed were the two announcements over the public address system—one for Royal Jordanian Flight 504 departing out of Gate 9, and the other, for Red Sea Charter Air Service Flight 6 departing out of Gate 8. The two announcements came within a few seconds of each other. The attractive couple sitting near the gate, Mustafa and Amal Qureshi from Giza, stood and walked to the boarding line. They presented their boarding passes and were waved on with a smile. They walked through the door for Gate 8 and down the jetway to the Embraer 145 regional jet. Once on board, they slid their small black suitcase into the overhead baggage compartment and took their seats. Once everyone was seated, the flight attendant spoke over the airplane's intercom.

"Welcome aboard Red Sea Charter's Flight 6 to Aqaba, Jordan. We expect a short flight this afternoon and the pilot says the weather is perfect. You have picked a lovely time to visit Aqaba. We understand that your tour group will be visiting Petra and we hope you have a lovely time."

The Praetorians were headed to the wrong city and the head of Black Sun was in the wind.

CHAPTER NINE
ENDGAME

As soon as the Bombardier 8000 took off from Cairo, Steve went to work hacking into the security system for Amman's Queen Alia International Airport. Royal Jordanian Flight 504 was due to arrive at Gate 120 and they wanted to have access to the security cameras before it did. Rusty immediately contacted the Israeli and American members of the targeting committee to let them know what had transpired in the last few hours. Understandably, the Israeli was extremely concerned and advised they would be putting their border security forces on immediate alert.

Rusty called a quick meeting of the team and Gunny spoke first. "Okay guys, this is where we are. We think Al-Maadi has the virus with him but we have no proof. Nura used herself as a decoy this morning while Al-Maadi escaped from wherever they were holed up without us seeing him."

Sarah chimed in. "She must have had surveillance training from someone good. There's no way a novice played us like that."

"Agreed. Maybe the Syrians or even the Russians." Gunny continued, "Given that, Rusty and I are still not convinced that this current excursion isn't just another ruse designed to draw us away from another courier."

Lon jumped in. "I'm not so sure. If they're going to deploy this shit, they'll want to deploy it inside Israel. It makes more sense to do that from the West Bank. Gaza has been all but sealed off since Hamas started lobbing rockets over the fence. The only way to access the West Bank—other than through Israel—is through Jordan. If Nura and Al-Maadi were using themselves as a diversion, they'd be heading *away* from the target area; not toward it. We need to act on what we actually know and not on what might happen."

John nodded, "I agree. Tactically, it makes no sense to draw your opponent closer to where you're going to launch a clandestine attack." The others nodded in agreement.

Gunny said, "I concur but I just want alternate theories."

Nigel added, "They could deploy it from Lebanon or infect a traveler and send them directly into Israel. If we cap this fucker and he *isn't* carrying the virus, then we're in deep shit. Ideally, we need to nab him alive so we can squeeze him for intel if we need to."

Rusty interjected, "We've already reached out to the Israelis. They're on alert and prepared to close their borders on a moment's notice. I talked to our CIA contact this morning before we left the hotel. They're asking Egyptian security go to Cairo University and question everyone connected with Al-Maadi. It should be happening as we speak. I think it's a waste of time but ya never know."

Hans asked, "What about the Jordanians?"

Gunny answered, "I wanted to bring them in on this directly but was overruled. For the time being, we're on our own. The plan is to get eyes on them, follow them out of the airport, and hit them the first chance we have them isolated. We don't want to hit them in the airport. The danger of an accidental release is too great. That shit could get around the world in a goddamn heartbeat. We've called ahead to line up vehicles but I'm not sure what kind and how many we're going to secure on short notice. We may literally have to put a couple of you in taxis if they get out quick."

Magne said, "If it has four wheels and a motor, we'll make it work."

Gunny smiled. "I assumed as much."

Alen asked, "What about weapons?"

Gunny frowned. "That could be a problem, especially in the short term. We have weapons on the plane, and Gil said that, as long as we don't try to offload them immediately, we can probably manage it, but you guys still have to go through immigration and customs. We can't have you standing in line for a visa while you're packing."

Alen nodded. "Understood."

Gunny continued, "On the bright side, it's not like they're flying with weapons either so they'll be just as naked when they get off the plane."

Hans said, "Not to be negative but someone might hand them a weapon as soon as they pass through security."

"Let's hope not. The Jords don't mess around. Anyone caught trying to sneak a weapon into the airport is likely to get his ass shot off. If they are provided with a weapon, my guess is it'll happen when they're away from the airport." As Gunny said this, the jet's engines begin to slow and the flaps started to extend for landing.

Gil got on the intercom. "Everyone, find a seat and fasten your seat belts. We're on final approach."

The jet landed and taxied to a parking spot on the apron reserved for VIPs and private jets. When they stopped and shut down the engines, a Jordanian customs official approached the plane in a Jeep. Gil lowered the stairs and the official boarded the airplane. Gil introduced Rusty as the owner of Praetorian Security Services and explained they were in-country to provide consulting services for the royal family. Everyone was ready with their passports, but when the official eyed Sarah, he was stunned. His attention was focused on her rather than the passports. He finished in a few minutes and was on his way. Terrorists and petty criminals didn't usually fly in on $50 million airplanes. As soon as he left, John quipped, "I'm glad Sarah is good for something. My passport could have said 'Mickey Mouse' and that guy would've let me in."

The rest of the guys laughed while Sarah smirked, flipped him off and said, "Go fuck yourself, Kernan."

Gil came back from the cockpit and made sure the customs official was gone. "Okay, this is how it's going to work. You'll need to go into the VIP terminal where they'll issue you a visa and stamp your passport. Donny will go with you and bring back a baggage cart. I'm going to wait here to do our postflight paperwork and get her refueled. Once the customs guy is busy with another arrival, I'll offload the gear. I have some customs tags so it'll look like it's been inspected. Once we get it outside the wire, one of you can transfer it to a vehicle. I'm not sure how long it's going to take but it might be a little while."

In the back Steve was furiously banging away on his computer. "Our bags have been cleared."

Gil turned around and said, "What? How?"

Steve smiled. "I just cleared them. I marked them in the computer as inspected and cleared."

"By who?"

Steve replied, "The guy who was on the plane. While he was gawking at Sarah, I saw his name tag and put him down as the inspecting official. We're good to go."

Gunny said, "Everyone, grab your passports and don't forget which alias you're using today."

John quipped, "If I do, I'll just claim I have Alzheimer's, like you."

"Bite me, wiseass." After going though immigration, they rented four vehicles that would serve their purposes while Hans, Magne, Nigel, and Lon left immediately for the main terminal. Flight 504 had already landed and was due to arrive at the gate in a few minutes. They wouldn't get to the gate but they would wait outside security to pick up Nura and Al-Maadi as soon as they found them. Steve connected through the airport's WiFi and accessed the security cameras outside the arrival gate for Flight 504. He and Sarah sat in the back of a Toyota 4-Runner and watched as the passengers filed off. The facial recognition software he was running scanned each passenger as they walked through the door onto the concourse and compared them to pictures of Nura and Al-Maadi stored in its memory. There were over a hundred passengers on the plane, so it took a little while for them all to deplane. A full twenty minutes later, the flight crew exited. There were no more passengers on board. There had been no hits.

Sarah turned to Steve. "That's not possible. They have to still be on the plane."

"I don't think so. The flight crew wouldn't leave a passenger on the plane unless it's a continuing flight and this one isn't. This is the end of the line."

"Did we just miss them? Maybe they changed their clothes? Maybe he shaved his beard or something?"

Steven rewound the video. "No. The software is state of the art. It would've seen them. Besides, we were both watching too. I might see one of us missing one of them but both of us missing both? No way. I'm going to run it again. I can speed it up." The video of the passengers deplaning ran again. It was moving faster but paused briefly as each passenger's face was read and compared. Each was framed in a blue box that would turn red when it was determined they were not one of the targets. When it finished, Steve said, "They aren't here."

Sara said, "Well, where the hell are they?"

"How the hell would I know? We saw them sit at the gate in Cairo. When they started to board the plane, they got up with everyone else."

"Did we see them actually get on the plane?"

Steve replied, "Uh, no. We were getting ready to leave ourselves but where else could they have gone? I checked again, once we were airborne, and they were no longer at the gate or in the immediate terminal area."

Sarah yelled out the door, "Gunny, Rusty, we have a problem. You'd better get over here."

The rest of the team walked over the Toyota. Gunny asked, "What's the problem?"

Sarah replied coldly, "They never got off the plane, which means . . ."

Gunny finished her sentence, "They never got on."

Rusty flashed red. "How the hell is that possible? We were on them the whole time! I saw them with my own eyes!"

Sarah said, "We never actually saw them go through the gate. The cameras are pointed at the gate from the concourse to get pictures of arrivals, not departures. We were getting ready to leave ourselves. Even if we had been watching, all we would have seen was the back of their heads."

Rusty was pissed. "Well, goddamnit! What the hell are we supposed to do now?"

Steve called out from inside the 4-Runner. "I think I figured it out!" They all tried to crowd in but there wasn't enough room. John, Alen, and Sarah backed off so Gunny and Rusty could squeeze in. Steve explained, "I checked departures from all the adjacent gates in the same general timeframe. There was only one—a charter flight out of Gate 8. It didn't show up in our original search because it wasn't a regularly scheduled flight and therefore didn't show up on the airport's arrivals and departures board."

"Well, where the hell was it going?" Gunny asked curtly.

"Aqaba. It's a city on the Red Sea near . . ."

"I know where Aqaba is, goddamnit. Details, kid, I need details!"

Gunny was impatient. "Okay, it was a Red Sea Charter that left right after Flight 504. It was an Embraer 145 scheduled to land forty-five minutes ago."

Rusty shouted, "Shit! Can you find out if they were on that flight?"

"Yes, sir, but I need time to access their security system." Rusty moved away cursing at their bad luck and Sarah slid into the van next to Steve. It didn't take him long to gain access since the Aqaba King Hussein International Airport used the same security system. "Okay, this is a much smaller airport. Fewer passengers." His fingers danced across the keyboard. In a few minutes he said, "Okay, the charter landed at 1355. Here's the video feed of the deplaning passengers. Let me run this through the facial recognition software and we can . . ."

Sarah interrupted. "Don't bother. Freeze that." Steve tapped a couple of keys and the picture on the screen stopped on the image of a man and a woman walking through the gate holding hands. Pointing to the screen she said, "That's her, right there. I'd bet my life on it."

Steve said, "Let me confirm, just to be sure." He tapped more keys and blue boxes appeared around all the faces on the screen. A second later, the boxes framing the man and the woman turned green and flashed. "Yep, that's them."

Sarah called out. "We found them. They're definitely in Aqaba—or were."

Rusty and Gunny walked over. Gunny asked, "Confirmed?" Steve gave a thumb's up. "Okay, let's think. Would they try to enter Israel overland from there? Into Elat?"

Sarah said, "It's possible, but the border there is heavily guarded. They would have a better chance farther away from Elat but that would put them in the middle of the Negev Desert and there are no roads crossing the border. Going on foot would be stupid. That's a military training area. Great way to get shot."

Gunny said, "We need to give the Israelis a heads-up; tell them to seal the border down there."

Alen commented, "For what it's worth, I don't think that's where they'd do it. Elat is too isolated. It'd be too easy to quarantine. There's gotta be a hundred and fifty kilometers of nothing between Elat and the Dead Sea and probably another hundred to Jerusalem. It doesn't mean it's not possible but it'd be like attacking New York from Arizona. My gut says they're heading north. I'd fly, personally. Once you're inside the country, there are no more customs or immigration checks."

Sarah said, "He has a point. If you want maximum impact, you need maximum population—and visibility. Most people don't even know where Elat is; and they only know Aqaba from *Lawrence of Arabia*. But we still have to tell Israeli border security. There's too much at stake."

Gunny said, "Agreed. Sarah, make the call. Steve, check outgoing flights from Aqaba and find out if they flew on to Amman. Let's see if we can also figure out what names they're using. See if we can find a flight manifest for that charter and check for last-minute additions. I doubt they planned this little detour too far in advance."

Steve replied, "On it, Gunny."

Turning to Alen, Gunny said, "Contact the others and get them back over here. We have some planning to do."

Gunny whispered to Rusty, "We may have to bring the Jords in on this. We don't have the manpower to cover all the roads between here and Amman—assuming that's where they're going."

Rusty nodded in agreement. "I'll reach out to the committee. Ultimately, it's their call. The Jords aren't in on any of this. If we can find out what aliases they're using, the Jords could at least put out a BOLO on them for drug trafficking or something. Anything to get the local authorities out looking for them would help."

Gunny commented, "That's above my pay grade, boss. I leave it to you."

* * *

Nura and Khalid deplaned the Embraer 145 and went through Jordanian Customs and Immigration along with the rest of the tour group. Afterward, when everyone else went to baggage claim to collect their luggage, they walked out of the airport and hailed a cab. The taxi picked them up and took them to an address just off Al Farooq Street due south of the airport. Khalid paid the taxi driver and they walked toward the front door of the house. As the taxi pulled away, they reversed course and walked to the

house across the street. There was a blue Volkswagen Passat in the driveway. Nura reached under the right front wheel well and found the keys. She
handed them to Khalid, who unlocked the door and slid behind the wheel.
Nura walked around the car, put the small black bag in the back seat, and
got in next to him. She checked under the seat and found a Makarov 9 mm
pistol and an old Webley .32 revolver. He started the car and drove south
through the neighborhood before getting on Highway 65 and driving north
to Amman. Khalid gave her a nervous smile. They were closer to completing
their mission than they had ever been, but they still had a long way to go.

* * *

I dentifying Nura and Khalid's alias names turned out to be harder than
Steve anticipated. The Jordanian immigration computer system was part
of the Ministry of Foreign Affairs, which had high-level network security
provided by the US government to keep terrorist groups from hacking them.
To Steve, it was more than a little ironic that security provided by the NSA
to help thwart terrorists in Jordan was keeping him, a former NSA staffer,
from trying to thwart terrorists in Jordan. He felt pressured to come up with
something. The rest of the team was standing around twiddling their thumbs
waiting for actionable intel from him.

Gunny stuck his head into the Toyota and asked, "Any progress?"

"Yeah, a little. If I'd known I'd have to break into a USG-supplied system, I'd have asked one of my old buddies about a back door. I think I'll get
it soon, but this laptop doesn't have the computing power and the internet
connection is mediocre at best. To be honest, I don't know what we'll find
anyway. Hans did some research. There are several countries whose citizens
don't even need a visa to visit Jordan. If our tangos are using passports from
Egypt, Tunisia, Turkey, Palestine, or any of the Arab Gulf states, they may
get waved through. There may not be any record to find. I think we should
be assuming they're headed north."

A few minutes later, Rusty walked over. "I just heard from one of our
contacts. The Egyptians marched into Al-Maadi's department at the university like Germans into France. His secretary confirmed he received a package
from MalayVax. She gave it to a senior lab guy. He said Al-Maadi got it from

him yesterday, about the time Nura was tripping the alarm at the apartment. According to the lab guy, it contained one vial labeled FMD vaccine stock. I'd say they definitely have it. Now we just need to find them before they release it and kill a few million people."

Sarah walked quickly over. "I just got off the phone with the charter company. It took me a while and I had to threaten them with Mukhabarat, but they coughed up some info. The lady said there were two last-minute additions to their tour. An Egyptian couple—Mustafa and Amal Qureshi from Giza. She gave me their address—it's a fake. She never met them so no description, but I'm betting its them."

Steve wanted to redeem himself in the eyes of the team. "Okay, I can work with that." His fingers started dancing across the keyboard. In a couple of minutes, he had some results. "Okay, no one by that name on any out-going flights today. Hold on." He started typing furiously again. Another five minutes passed. "All right, no bus or train tickets purchased in those names. I'm checking the rental car companies at the airport. Hold on." After another seven or eight minutes, he added, "No one rented a car as Qureshi or Al-Maadi or Al-Doghmush or Ostergaard."

Sarah asked, "Could they still be in Aqaba?"

Lon chimed in, "I'm gonna say no. There's no reason to stay there. I'd bet they're on the road already. They might have hired a car or even a taxi. Hell, we don't know how big this Black Sun group even is. Do they have a cell in Jordan who prepositioned a car for them?"

Steve added, "Hey, got a possible hit. Facial recognition has a 'maybe' outside at arrivals. I told it to pull all couples leaving the airport and then match for height, gait, and build. I'll pull it up. Sarah, you want to take a gander? You're the only one who's seen her up close."

Sarah peered at the screen and the grainy image. It was a man and a woman but they were blocked by other people standing around them. The woman slid into the backseat of the taxi and the man got in after her. "It could be them. Wait! Back it up a few seconds and go frame by frame." Steve did as she asked. She pointed to the screen. "Right there. What's that behind him . . . it just came into view from behind that porter."

Steve zeroed in on what Sarah was pointing to, and enlarged the image. "Well, I'll be damned. It's that little black suitcase. That's gotta be them."

Gunny perked up and asked, "Can you get a license plate on that taxi?"

"No, it's blocked. It's a gypsy cab anyway. But at least we know they're using ground transport."

Sarah said, "Steve, back it up to when the taxi pulled up." He quickly backed up the video and stopped. She said, "On the side of the taxi, that's a telephone number. Someone give me a phone." Lon handed her a phone and she punched in the number before walking away. She stood a few feet away obviously talking to someone in Arabic. After four or five minutes she returned. "Okay, I just talked to the taxi driver. He said he picked up a couple and took them to a house in Aqaba. His description fits our tangos. He said after he dropped them off, he pulled over down the street to call his wife, and they drove past him in a car."

Gunny said, "Well I'll be damned. Did he say what kind of car?"

Sarah smiled. "A blue Passat."

Lon asked, "How in the hell did you get him to tell you all that?"

"He sounded older so I took a shot. I told him the woman was my little sister and she was running off with her married boss. I said we needed to find her before she brought shame to the family. He was more than happy to help."

Gunny smiled. "You are truly devious. I'm glad you're on our side." Turning to Steve he asked, "When were they picked up by the cab?

He checked the time stamp on the video and said, "An hour and a half ago. They have a good hundred-klick head start on us."

"Now that we know what we're looking for, we need to start hunting. We need to get vehicles on the road headed south. Steve, see if they have any traffic cams we can tap into. We need to find these people."

The traffic cameras turned out to be a dead end. There were a few in Aqaba but nothing on the highways outside the city. Six of the team members jumped in vehicles and sped south to cover the three possible routes north from Aqaba. Lon and Alen took Highway 65, which ran along the western border next to the Dead Sea and was closest to Israeli territory. Magne and John drove down Highway 15 to the east. It ran past the airport in Amman and had more traffic into which Khalid and Nura could blend. That left Sarah and Hans to cover Highway 35 which was in the middle. The day was fading fast and they had no idea where Nura and Khalid were. Once it got dark, the odds of finding them dropped precipitously.

* * *

Two hours north of Aqaba the Volkswagen started to overheat. Khalid cursed the vehicle and pulled over to the side of the road. He checked the trunk but found no water. They'd been in such a hurry to leave Aqaba, they hadn't picked up any food or water. The Jordan Valley Highway, as Highway 65 was known, went through some very, very desolate country. It had been over half an hour since they'd seen any sign of civilization and almost two since the last gas station. The closest town was across the border in Israel and that was clearly not an option. A truck driver stopped to give them some water for their radiator. He told them they needed to wait for the car to cool down, add the water, and hope it limped along to the next town.

After about twenty minutes, Khalid used a cloth to open the radiator cap with a whoosh of steam. He was starting to pour in the water when a man in an old Fiat pulled up behind him. The driver was a man in his late forties. He had a scruffy beard and was wearing a dirty white thobe with a red and white keffiyeh. "Hello. Car troubles I see."

Khalid replied, "Yes. It overheated. I was just about to add some water."

The man leaned over and peered at the engine. He pulled on the fan belt and poked around. "I don't think that will help you. See that burned rubber on that pulley? That's your water pump. I think it has seized. Even if you can get it started, you'll be lucky to get another kilometer before it overheats again. And you'll probably ruin your engine in the process—blow a head gasket or crack the head completely."

Khalid asked, "Can you give us a ride to the next town? We really need to get to Amman tonight."

The man said, "I am only going as far as At-Tafilah, but I can drive you there. You and your wife gather your things."

Khalid said, "Thank you. That would be very nice of you. Would you drive us to Amman if we paid you?"

The man mulled this over but said, "No, I have to get back to my shop and my family. I will take you to At-Tafilah. You can figure something out there."

Nura had taken the black suitcase out of the Volkswagen and was walking back toward the man's Fiat. He took the bag from her and walked ahead to put it in the trunk. As he did, she pulled the Webley from her skirt and shot the man in the back of the head. He fell face-first onto the ground. Khalid yelled, "Why did you do that? He was going to give us a ride. He was helping us!"

Nura said coldly, "He wasn't going to take us to Amman and we need to go to Amman. Help me get him in our car before someone else comes along."

Khalid was in shock. While he had no problem planning the murder of millions, it had been almost an academic exercise for him, but coming face-to-face with an actual murder made his blood run cold. Equally unnerving was how it had absolutely no impact on Nura. They dragged the man's body to the Volkswagen and dumped it in the trunk. Before slamming it shut, Nura used the bottom of the dead man's thobe to wipe away the blood that dripped on the bumper. She retrieved the 9 mm from the Volkswagen and locked the doors before tossing the keys into the desert. "Let's go. We're behind schedule." Khalid got in the Fiat, started the engine, and drove.

* * *

Magne and John drove south on Highway 65 for two hours. The farther they got from Amman, the lighter the traffic became. While the decreased traffic made their task easier, that was offset by the dusk creeping across the sky from the east. They had seen nothing so far. They were too far from the rest of the team to use their encrypted tactical radios, so they had to rely on their cell phones to update each other. The area was extremely desolate, and their cellular coverage was spotty. Once they got south of the Dead Sea, they were pinging off Israeli cell towers more than Jordanian ones.

John sent a group text to the others that simply read, "150 klicks—no contact." He looked west toward the setting sun and Israel. "Hey, Maggie. What are the odds that the Shin Bet is picking up our texts?"

Magne smiled. "Oh, probably 100 percent. I mean, I would if I were them."

"Yeah, me too. We're about to hit the halfway mark and it's getting pretty dark. If we haven't seen them by now, they aren't on this road. We might need to turn around."

"Yeah, I hear ya. Contact Gunny. Tell him we'll give it another ten minutes and then we're turning around."

John started to tap out the text when Magne said, "Whoa, hold up. Up ahead, on the left. It's a car."

Magne started to slow down. John looked up and said, "Is that a blue Passat?"

"It would appear so. Seems abandoned."

"Drive past and flip a U."

"Roger." Magne drove past the car, turned around and stopped about twenty meters behind it. Without a word, they exited their car with weapons at their side. They scanned up and down the highway. There were no headlights to be seen. John raised his Sig 9 mm, scanned the desert around him, and then cautiously approached the car on the right side. Magne raised his weapon and approached on the left, being alert to any movement. As they got closer, Magne held back to cover John while he looked into the car. It was empty. He then tried the door and found it locked.

John said, "Clear. Empty and locked." He walked around to the front of the car. The hood was down but not latched. He lifted it. "They overheated; coolant is sprayed all over the place."

Magne was now approaching when he spotted a dark liquid on the ground at his feet. He reached down and touched it. It was thick and a little slimy. "Uh, step back, John. I've got blood."

John immediately raised his weapon and, holding it in front of him, canvassed the desert on both sides of the road. "Warm or cold?"

"Cold. At least an hour." He knelt down to inspect the dirt on the shoulder. "There was another car back here." He followed the tracks in the dirt. "Pulled out headed north."

John walked back to the rear of the car. Blood was smeared on the bumper. "More blood here, too." He checked the trunk but it was locked. He walked to the driver's door and smashed the window with his Sig. He reached in and hit the trunk release button. The trunk latch popped and the trunk lid started to rise slowly.

Inside, Magne found the body of the Arab man who'd stopped to help Nura and Khalid. "Shit. We've got a body. Not one of our tangos. I think they have a new car."

John walked back and stared at the dead man crumpled in the trunk of the Volkswagen. "Poor bastard. Wrong place, wrong time. I'll check the car for intel while you call it in. Let 'em know our tangos are running free."

"Roger that. Goddamn if these assholes aren't the luckiest pricks on the planet."

"Or we're the unluckiest. Either way, someone needs to kill them."

* * *

Nura and Khalid continued to drive north on the Jordan Valley Highway toward Amman but rather than head east toward the capital at the north end the Dead Sea, they continued north to the town of South Shouna less than ten kilometers from the Allenby Bridge connecting Jordan with the West Bank. They drove into the city and pulled over at a gas station. While Khalid filled up the Fiat, Nura found a pay phone and made a call. She returned to the car as he finished. "I have the address for a house near here."

"Is it safe?" a nervous Khalid asked.

"Yes, of course. These are my father's people; the Army of Islam. They are completely trustworthy. Once we are successful, they will come flocking to join Black Sun and we will need people with their experience. We need to find a car park first."

"Why?"

Nura explained calmly, "We need to find a similar car and switch license plates. They are going to find that man's body soon if they haven't already. Once they do, they'll figure out that whoever killed him took his car."

"Yes, of course." Khalid didn't know whether to admire her or fear her. She was clearly better suited to life as a Black Sun freedom fighter than he was. She was ruthless, smart, logical, and totally unemotional. Though he genuinely loved her, he worried about what kind of mother she would be to his children.

They drove east on Highway 437 to a large apartment block just east of the South Shouna Hospital. There were a number of cars parked in front of the building. None matched the Fiat exactly, but Nura found an old white sedan that was close enough. While Khalid stood guard, she snuck behind the car, unscrewed the license plate, and replaced it with the one off their car. After she attached the new plate to the Fiat, they drove to the safe house. It was located in a neighborhood just northwest of the hospital. The houses were on large lots with plenty of distance from the neighbors. They found the address and stopped. Khalid stayed in the car while she went up to knock on the door. A few minutes later, she returned with an older man at her side. He motioned to Khalid to drive the car behind the house. Khalid parked it and Nura removed the little black suitcase from the trunk before the man covered the car with a dingy brown tarp. He pointed to the sky and said, "Israeli drones. We have to be careful. Please, come inside and rest." He reached out to shake Khalid's hand. "I am Issa, Nura's cousin. It is a great thing you are doing. You are welcome in my home for as long as you need."

"Thank you, Issa. I'm exhausted. It's been a very long day."

Issa smiled. "Then come inside. My wife began cooking the minute Nura called."

* * *

Gunny took the news from Magne and John stoically. Getting angry wouldn't improve their situation. He immediately recalled the other two cars—there is no point of looking when you don't know what you're looking for. While the three cars were searching, Rusty and Steve found a villa for rent in Ar-Rawda, a small city west of Amman, so as to be close to the West Bank border crossings. The broker was irked to get a late call but quickly changed his tune when they agreed to pay twice the rent in cash to atone for the last-minute booking. Sarah immediately contacted Israeli authorities to advise them that the two Black Sun terrorists were in the wind. By this time, Steve had sent the Israeli security services all the information they had on the pair, including a number of photographs.

The three road teams finally dragged themselves in to the rented villa around midnight. Everyone was thoroughly exhausted. None of them had gotten any sleep in the last couple of days. Gunny and Rusty called the team together for a brief meeting. He started by saying, "Great work today, guys."

This received a number of snorts and grumbles from the team. They definitely didn't share his assessment of a day where Nura strung them out all over Cairo before losing them and slipping away to the airport. "I'm serious guys. Yeah, they gave us the slip in Cairo, but we regrouped and quickly figured out where they went, how they got there, how many vials of this shit they have, and what aliases they're using. We know they're here somewhere and I'd bet they're pretty damn close to where we're standing right now. We have a good idea as to where they're going and we know which way they have go to get there—over the Allenby Bridge. We haven't failed; not yet anyway."

Gunny interjected, "The boss is right. We're definitely still in this game. Fortunately for us, the bridge is closed from 2200 to 0800 hours, so grab some shuteye. We muster at 0600. It'll take about thirty minutes to get to the crossing from here. I want everyone in position by 0700. If they try to cross the river, we'll take them. Understood?" They all nodded in agreement.

Steve added, "I have some long-range cameras. If I can find a decent place to set up, we can get a picture of anyone approaching the bridge from a good distance. I can run the feed through the facial recognition software."

Gunny said, "That's great, Steve. Maybe you and I should go early to find good vantage points?"

Nigel said, "I'll go with you, in case you need an extra body or an extra weapon. I sat on my arse while these guys were covering the roads from Aqaba."

Lon quipped, "Yeah, we kind of noticed that. We just figured it was your teatime." Nigel just flipped him off.

Gunny responded, "Okay. I want to be on the road by 0600 hours." Steve and Nigel nodded. "Now, everyone, get some sleep. I have a feeling we're going to need it."

* * *

The next morning, Gunny, Steve, and Nigel left the villa a little before 0600 hours. When Steve and Nigel got up, Gunny was already in the kitchen drinking coffee. Nigel asked if he had bothered to sleep at all, to which Gunny Medina just grunted. They packed up their gear into a rented

Mercedes SUV and headed out. The area immediately around the Allenby Bridge was desolate. Both sides of the river contained old fortified positions dating from the time when Israel and Jordan were sworn enemies. The land was also said to hold thousands of land mines that were never cleared, so all traffic over the Jordan River was funneled over the Allenby Bridge. The bridge itself, at least on the Jordanian side, was pretty isolated. There were a couple Jordanian border security facilities nearby but otherwise, there was over three kilometers of empty desert between the bridge and the Jordanians' border crossing station.

The crossing was always busy, with trucks lined up on both sides of the border waiting to cross into the West Bank or Jordan. They carried everything from fuel to cement to foodstuffs. Included in the mix were buses, taxis, and private cars. Crossing was complicated. The Jordanians, Israelis, and Palestinians all had a say in the matter and, just to guarantee congestion, the bridge was the only designated exit/entry point for residents of the West Bank who needed to travel abroad.

Nura and Khalid would have to cross in a vehicle and would have to stop at the Israeli-operated Allenby Bridge Terminal. If they got that far, the Israelis would stop them, but for the Praetorians, this was a last resort. They didn't want to risk a release of the virus in a crowded area where vulnerable people would be present. Steve and Gunny set up their camera in an area about three and a half kilometers east of the bridge at the King Hussein Border Crossing complex. It was the final chokepoint before the border.

The area immediately around the complex was fairly crowded, but there was about three kilometers of empty farmland between it and the town of South Shouna to the east. The complex was on the south side of the road where people entering Jordan had to stop. There was a small village on the north side that included a number of rental car agencies, gas stations, and cafes. This is where Steve set up. He parked the SUV along the road facing west and aimed his long-range camera out the back. The area around the border crossing station was unorganized with cars and trucks parked everywhere. Any vehicle approaching the crossing station would have to slow down, thus giving Steve a chance to get a good picture of the occupants. Someone needed to keep tabs on Jordanian police and border troops stationed at the complex. Of the three of them, Gunny best passed as an Arab, so he took a seat on a bench just outside the border crossing station where vehicles from the West Bank unloaded their passengers. Nigel checked out the commercial truck inspection station a few hundred meters to the west. There was an overflow parking lot on the north side of the road and a number of truck drivers were milling around waiting for paperwork. One more man wouldn't stand out. From there he could easily see oncoming vehicles.

The rest of the team arrived on-site about half an hour later. Lon and Alen in Car One moved to the commercial truck area with Nigel. Magne and John in Car Two parked at a rental car business across the street from the border crossing's VIP Services just west of Steve's position. From there they could support Steve in Car Three or Gunny, who was on foot. Sarah and Hans were in Car Four and took the other long-range camera and parked near a gas station in South Shouna and pointed their camera up King Hussein Bridge Road toward Highway 65. It was the most logical way to approach the bridge. Their hope was that they would spot their targets early and give the rest of the team a heads-up. Rusty didn't want to stay at the villa alone so he jumped in with Sarah and Hans but only after promising to stay out of the way.

The crossing opened at 0800 hours. Mercifully, traffic was relatively light. The cameras and software were working perfectly. The laptop computers took the camera feeds, automatically isolated the faces of the people in the cars, scanned them, and compared them to the biometric profiles of Nura and Al-Maadi stored in their memories. The computers scanned hundreds of faces but with no positive hits.

About 0930 hours, Hans's computer pinged. They had a hit. He immediately pulled up the photo. Sarah leaned over his shoulder. On the screen was a black-and-white photo of a man behind the wheel and a smaller, younger woman in the passenger seat. Sarah leaned in and squinted. "That's her! That's her!"

Hans immediately got on the radio. "This is Car Four. We have a positive hit. An old white sedan heading west on the bridge road. An Opel, no . . . make that a Fiat. No front tag." Hans grabbed the camera and quickly pointed it out the front window. "Okay, rear tag is Jordanian; number is one, eight, dash, zero, six, niner, niner, seven. That's 18-06997. Tangos are in the front seat. No other passengers visible."

Steve replied, "Car Three copies. White Fiat. Alpha Nine, do you copy?"

Gunny whispered, "Copy." He stood up and began to walk closer to the road.

Alen added, "Car One copies."

Magne replied, "Car Three copies. White Fiat, two tangos."

Lon got on and said, "Car Three, call them out when they pass you. Car Two, you drop in behind them. We'll be prepared to move east. As soon as they pass that road to the south, I'll run them off the road. I'll push them into that empty field on the north and we'll converge and eliminate them. Alpha Nine, if anyone escapes on foot to the south, they're yours. Car Four, you contain to the east."

Gunny said, "Nine copies."

Magne replied, "Copy that. Car Two in position."

Hans and Sarah anxiously watched as the white Fiat drove slowly down the road but then turned north while still in South Shouna. Hans called out, "Hold on. They're turning north. Into the parking lot of a small store." He monitored them through the camera from about five hundred meters. "Okay, they're getting out of the car and entering the store. It might be a café. Too far to tell. She's carrying a shopping bag."

Lon asked, "Do you think they made you?"

"I don't see how. We weren't moving." After a few moments Hans said, "Tangos are still inside. We have a vehicle approaching from the west. A red Renault. Driver is a young Arab male. No passengers. He is out and entering the store."

Steve added, "Yeah, the red Renault just came from the bridge. He just passed me."

Hans replied, "Copy that." After long pause, he said, "No movement." A couple of minutes later Hans gave an update. "Okay, someone is leaving the store. Arab male carrying a grocery bag. He's getting in the red car. He's heading west on Bridge Road. Tangos are still inside."

Lon replied, "Copy."

After about twenty minutes, the team was getting impatient. Lon was about to suggest someone drive by when Hans broke in. "Okay, we have movement. Our two tangos have exited the building and are getting in their car. Woman is carrying a bag. They are backing out and approaching Bridge

Road. They are turning east, repeat east, on Bridge Road. They are going back the way they came."

Lon interjected, "Shit! They may be aborting. We need to move. We cannot afford to lose them again. Car Four, confirm they're in that car and then follow them. Car Two, move east immediately. We'll be right behind you. Car Three, pick up Alpha Nine, but stay on Bridge Road in case of a possible backtrack. We need to protect that road."

Gunny replied, "Copy that, One. Headed toward Car Three now." As Gunny crossed the road and trotted up to Steve's SUV, the Range Rover with Lon, Alen, and Nigel sped past.

Sarah got on the radio. "This is Car Four. Confirm tangos in the white Fiat. We are dropping in behind them now." Sarah, Hans, and Rusty drove east on King Hussein Bridge Road. As they approached the South Shouna Hospital, the Fiat turned south into the hospital parking lot. Nura and Khalid parked the car, got out, and walked toward the hospital building. Sarah said, "This is Car Four, the tangos have pulled in at the hospital. They are out of their vehicle and walking toward the hospital building. She's wearing a red shirt over a black skirt. He's wearing a black jacket and white shirt over jeans. Alpha Seven going in on foot."

Hans drove past the hospital entrance and turned right onto the street just to the east. Once out of view, he pulled over and said, "I'll cover the back." Sarah jumped out and walked quickly to the front entrance of the hospital while wrapping a scarf around her head to try to hide her face. She entered the lobby but didn't see Nura or Al-Maadi anywhere. Hans drove into the neighborhood south of the hospital and began working his way back north toward the rear of the hospital.

Inside the hospital, Nura and Al-Maadi were met by her cousin, who walked them briskly to the ambulance bay. There they were met by two more people—a woman and a man. Nura stripped off her red shirt to reveal a black T-shirt underneath. She tossed the woman the red shirt while the woman handed her a black baseball hat with a red crescent on it and a black shirt. Khalid took off his jacket and handed it to the man. Nura's cousin gave Khalid a red keffiyeh to put on and then led them to a waiting ambulance. Khalid got in the back while Nura sat in the passenger seat.

The man and the woman, now wearing Khalid and Nura's clothes, walked to the rear of the hospital and slipped out a service door. They walked into the neighborhood behind the hospital. They didn't walk too fast. They wanted to be seen. They got in a gray Nissan that was waiting there.

Hans and Rusty were parked at a bend midway in the road that ran behind the hospital to cover the whole area. They were about a hundred meters from where the decoys emerged from the foliage at the far end of the street. Hans keyed his microphone and said, "I have two people coming out of the trees behind the hospital. A man and a woman. She's wearing a red shirt over a black skirt and he's wearing a dark jacket over jeans. Too far to get a good look. They're walking with their faces down. Can't get a good shot with the camera. They're getting into a gray Nissan sedan. It's pulling out and they're headed south. We're following. Someone needs to swing by and pick up Alpha Seven." Rusty moved up to the front passenger seat to help Hans spot. Hans said, "They're now headed east and turning south on Al-Fahdi, that's the road just east of the hospital. We're following."

Magne and John had already reached the hospital. John said. "This is Car Two. We've picked up Alpha Seven and are turning south on Al-Fahdi now. We're your number two."

Hans said, "Copy that. Nice to have company."

As Lon sped east to catch up, Alen studied at the map of the area on his tablet. "That road they're on doesn't offer many options for them. If we go south on Highway 65, we can parallel them and probably get ahead of them before they reach the bottom."

Lon said, "Good call. I'm on it."

Alen got on the radio and said, "This is Car One. We're going south on 65 to parallel. We'll try to get ahead of them."

Hans replied, "Copy. Let's squeeze them at the bottom of this road."

Nigel was in the back seat of Lon's Range Rover. He removed an MP-7 from the bag in the back seat and chambered a round. He then double-checked his Sig 9 mm to make sure it was ready as well. They sped down Highway 65 at almost seventy miles per hour. Alen got on the radio and said, "This is Car One. There is a large open field just before Al Fahdi meets the highway. We'll cut them off and block Al Fahdi there."

Hans replied, "Car Four copies. Car Two, move up into the one. You have more manpower than we do."

John answered, "Car Two copies. Our pleasure." Sarah and Magne nodded to each other acknowledging that they would be the first two out the door. Both were armed with MP-7s and Sigs.

Lon gunned the Range Rover to pass slower traffic on the highway. Alen vectored him in. Alen said, "Okay, slow down. It'll be about two hundred meters on your left." Lon slowed the SUV just enough to make the turn without flipping it. Up ahead they spotted the little gray Nissan being followed closely by John's Toyota 4-Runner. Alen pointed out a deep ditch on their left and said, "Let's do it!" Lon cut the wheel sharply to his left and it slid broadside across the road throwing dirt and gravel in front of it. When the Range Rover came to a halt, Alen and Nigel burst out with their weapons raised. The little Nissan skidded to a stop and started to back up but was hemmed in by John's vehicle, which had stopped diagonally across the road behind it. Sarah and Magne jumped out of their vehicle with weapons raised. Sarah shouted in Arabic, "Let me see your hands! Hands on the dashboard!"

The two people in the car complied immediately. "Don't shoot! Don't shoot! You've made a mistake! We're not criminals!"

Sarah opened the passenger door, ripped the woman from the car and threw her face-first onto the ground. On the other side, Alen gave the driver a similar treatment. The driver protested initially and tried to get to his feet only to be kicked in the ribs by the big Serb. The man crumpled to the ground gasping for breath. Sarah rolled the woman over. It wasn't Nura. "What the fuck?"

Alen rolled the driver over too. It was clear, he wasn't Al-Maadi. "It's not him. We've been played—again! These two are just decoys."

Sarah shouted, "The hospital! They're at the hospital."

Lon had walked over by this time. "No. They were at the hospital. I can guarantee they're headed anywhere but south."

Sarah and Hans interrogated the two decoys while the others updated Gunny and Steve. Rusty walked up to Lon and asked, "Well, what are our options?"

Lon was processing everything. He got on the radio and asked, "Alpha Seven, you still monitoring the road to the bridge?"

"Yeah, never stopped."

"Any hits?"

"None."

Lon said, "Well, that's good. That means they're still on this side of the river."

Sarah walked over. "I've got IDs on these two. A couple of locals. Said they were paid a hundred euros each to trade clothes with people in the hospital. They were told the woman was trying to escape her family and elope with her boyfriend. I'm not sure if they're telling the truth or not but regardless, I think they're little fish."

Lon asked Sarah, "When you saw the tangos walking into the hospital, was either one carrying a bag, a backpack or anything?"

"No, they weren't. But they left that little store with a bag."

Lon turned to Magne and said, "Go back to the hospital. Check that Fiat for bags, boxes, luggage, anything."

"Roger, I'm on it." He grabbed John and the two men got in the Toyota and sped back up Al-Fahdi Road.

Lon looked at Rusty and Sarah. "Something doesn't make sense. They didn't come all this way just to drop the virus and run. Nura strikes me as the type who would die trying rather than give up."

Sarah nodded. "I concur. She's a fanatic."

"So, where's the virus? It has to be packaged in dry ice, according to Alen. That means a package of some sort. You can't just slip it in your pocket. If it gets too warm, you ruin it. Tuk in Malaysia said as much."

Rusty added, "Yeah, that makes sense. According to the Egyptians, it was stored in some sort of super freezer at the Cairo University."

Lon asked, "So where the hell is it? They didn't take it into the hospital. I doubt they just left it in the car, either."

Sarah said, "They knew we were on to them. Nura's actions in Cairo yesterday pretty much confirm that. In Copenhagen, it was clear that she assumed I was Israeli. So, if she thinks the Israelis are onto her, she's got to know they'll be waiting for her at the border. There's no way she'd get through security with that virus."

Lon said, "Yeah, but someone else might. Someone Israeli security is *not* looking for."

Rusty groaned, "Son of a bitch. They passed it to someone."

Sarah snapped her fingers. "That store. They passed it at the store." She got on the radio and said, "Car Three. When the tangos were in that store there was a car that arrived just after and departed before them. A red Renault. You said you saw it come from the bridge and pass you."

Steve replied, "This is Car Three. Yeah, I remember it."

"What happened after they left?"

"Let me run back the video. Give me a sec."

While they waited, John called in. "We checked the car. There was a small black suitcase in the trunk. It had some clothes and a couple tooth-brushes but nothing else. Also found an empty shopping bag on the floor of front seat, passenger side. You'll love this. There was an old Webley revolver under the seat. One spent round. Smelled like it's been fired recently. I'm thinking it was used on the guy we found in the trunk of that Volkswagen yesterday."

Lon said, "They didn't want to walk around with a weapon tying them to a murder. Smart. Good work."

Steve called in. "Alpha One, I found that car on the video. It went straight back toward the Allenby Bridge."

Lon asked rhetorically, "Now who travels from the West Bank to Jordan, buys a bag of groceries, and then goes right back? Last time I checked, they had grocery stores in the West Bank."

Sarah said, "Crossing the border is a major hassle. No way you'd do it for something so minor."

Lon keyed his mic, "Alpha Seven, do you have a good photo of the driver of that Renault?"

"Yes, I do. I already ran it through our facial recognition software. I got no hits."

Rusty said, "Sarah, if you get that to Shin Bet, do you think they can ID him?"

Sarah smiled. "Yes. The Allenby Bridge Terminal is operated by the Israeli Airports Authority and they collect data on everyone who passes through. Since we know he passed through today and we even know about what time, it should be a snap."

Rusty said, "Get to it then."

* * *

Nura and Khalid fled the hospital in the ambulance. The driver was one of her uncle's men who took them to a warehouse a few kilometers north of the hospital off Highway 65. Once there, they transferred to a commercial truck that took them to Amman. Jordan's capital was a city of over four million people, and from there they could travel by vehicle to Saudi Arabia, Iraq, or Syria. The last two destinations barely had functioning governments so getting in would not pose a challenge.

As they got into the back of the old Mercedes delivery van, Nura turned to Khalid and said, "Smile, we have escaped."

Khalid was uneasy. He had a number of reasons to feel so. He was now on the run. He had abandoned his cushy job and easy life in Cairo for the hardscrabble life of an Islamic militant with no home base and no real security. "I will only feel comfortable when it is done."

Just before he shut the back door to the van, the driver stuck his head in and said, "We just got a message from Abdullah. He made it across with the virus. Praise be to Allah!"

Nura nestled up against him and said, "See that? Everything is working out. It may not be exactly as we planned but thanks to your foresight, we will still be successful. Once the virus spreads and most of the Jews are dead, Israel will become an Arab state. The first order of business will be to change its name back to Palestine. What Jews remain will beg to leave. We will call on you, as our liberator, to be the first leader of the new Palestine. We will inherit all that the Jews have, including their nuclear weapons. Palestine will go from a collection of refugees to the first Arab nuclear power in the world. We can use that and the Israelis' tanks and planes to push the apostate Shia out of Lebanon and Syria, and back to their Iranian masters. The Europeans will be powerless to intervene, and as for the Americans, do you think they'll be willing to send in their armies when there are no more Jews to defend?"

Khalid finally smiled. "No, I guess not."

"As the man who made all this possible, how would you *not* be chosen to be the leader of the Arab world?"

Khalid contemplated this and his family's storied history—from the Arab League to Al Qaeda. "I will have accomplished more with a virus than everyone in my family have accomplished in all its distinguished history."

Nura beamed at him. "You will be a modern Suleiman, and I will be your Roxelana. And this time, we won't be stopped at Vienna."

Khalid said, "Khalid the Magnificent." Her enthusiasm was infectious. He was beginning to believe it was not just possible, but destined to occur.

* * *

It took the Shin Bet less than an hour to identify Dr. Abdullah Al-Yasuf as the man who met with Nura and Al-Maadi at the little store in Lebanon. He had told the border security people that he was in Jordan picking up medical supplies. They inspected his car, of course, and found the back seat and trunk full of medicines, vitamins, flu vaccine, IV bags, bandages, and other supplies one would expect to see in a local clinic. A check of the records showed that Dr. Al-Yasuf regularly traveled to Jordan in a private vehicle or taxi to pick up supplies purchased in Jordan or donated by humanitarian groups like the Red Crescent. They had no reason to stop him so, after about fifteen minutes, they let him pass on through toward Jericho.

Gunny and Rusty's reaction to the news was mixed. They were glad they had identified their next target but they had missed him. They were so focused on getting Nura and Al-Maadi that they had missed the obvious. Rusty was the first to ask what they should do next.

Gunny took charge. "Okay, we need to figure out how we can get our people—and their weapons—into the West Bank without declaring war on Jordan, Israel, and the Palestinians at the same time."

Lon said, "I doubt the Jords will care. Once we cross the bridge, we're no longer their problem."

Sarah spoke up. "I will make a call. I think we can get past the Israelis, but if they wave us through that would definitely draw the attention of the Palestinians."

Lon said, "Arrange for them to give us a cursory inspection. You know, the kind where they ignore our weapons. That way we got the same treatment as everyone else. We can have Steve dummy up some documents saying we're there under contract to the Palestinian Authorities. IT people or something like that. We should also be ready to grease some palms to speed the process."

Rusty said, "That's great but if they check our 'cargo' we're screwed."

Sarah made a suggestion. "What if we got a bunch of medical supplies. I mean, it worked for this Al-Yasuf guy."

Lon asked, "And where would we get a truckload of medical supplies?"

Sarah shrugged. "We can steal some from that hospital, but I bet if we gave them a wad of cash, they'd sell them to us. Have Steve dummy up a Jordanian Ministry of Health transit letter or something. We pack our weapons under the supplies. I bet it'd work. We work for some multidenominational charity in defiance of the evil Zionist blockade."

Rusty said, "Yeah, I like the sound of that and I bet they would too. Let's do it. Sarah, get on the horn to your old colleagues. Get a path greased for us. Hans and Magne, you come with me. We're going to go shopping. Steve, get to work on the docs and make the charity European. Sounds more believable given the international flavor of our group."

Hans asked, "Do you have enough cash on you, boss?"

Rusty replied, "I have fifty thousand euros in my bag."

Hans choked, "You just happen to have that?"

"I always carry walking-around money. You never know when you might have to buy a round of drinks."

Magne laughed. "I do like traveling with rich people."

It took them just over an hour to buy enough supplies to fill the back of the Mercedes SUV. The hospital's administrator thought they were crazy at first and refused to deal with them but when Rusty plunked five thousand euros down on his desk, he knew they were serious. They bought a hodgepodge of bandages, sheets, IV bags, scrubs, and other equipment as well as a number of drugs nearing their expiration date. They also grabbed a few empty boxes to bulk up their cargo. Rusty paid another ten thousand euros for all this, with the initial payment going to the administrator for his inconvenience.

The team got together in a parking lot to divvy up the supplies. The extra boxes came in handy as they allowed the team to place their weapons in the bottom and cover them with bandages and the like. With the boxes in place, they were ready to go. They were just waiting on the Israelis. It went against their nature to just let someone pass. It took a call from Rusty to his contact to finally get it done. They were ready to go. That's when Gunny said, "Boss, I don't think you need to go any farther."

Rusty was taken aback. He was beginning to feel like part of the team. "What? Why not?"

"Well, sir, it's going to be dangerous and there's gonna be shooting."

Rusty was in trouble whenever Gunny called him *sir*. "I can shoot. I was in the army, remember?"

"And you gave me tactical command, remember? I know you can shoot because I trained you but you've never seen combat. Have you ever shot anyone? Have you been shot?"

Rusty replied, "You know I haven't. What's your point?"

"I know you're willing, but it might get very hairy, very fast. I don't want you—or me—slowing these guys down."

"Or you?"

Gunny confirmed, "I'm not going either. I'm too old, and my knees are shot. I don't want them worrying about us when they need to be shooting bad guys. Besides, if shit hits the fan, someone needs to be on the outside to make the call to the Israelis or whoever. It's hard to do that if you're getting shot at. I know, I've tried."

Gunny was right. "Yeah, I get your point. I just got caught up in all the excitement."

"Don't worry, Rusty, we still have a role to play but it just doesn't include pulling a trigger; not this time."

"Okay. We'll need another vehicle to use as a home base for you, me, and Steve."

Gunny said flatly, "Just you and me. Steve's going with them. They may need the tech support and the extra gun."

Rusty said, "So he gets to go?"

"He's former pararescue, a military jujitsu champion, and about a hundred years younger than us."

"Jesus, man. You don't have to rub it in."

Gunny smiled, "I promise, if we ever go after a bunch of geriatric terrorists, you can go along."

"Gee, thanks."

Rusty rented another Toyota 4-Runner while the Praetorians got started. Their little convoy rolled up to the Jordanian checkpoint. As expected, they were not particularly diligent about outbound traffic. A problem that leaves is a problem solved. They gave the transit documents a cursory glance before waving them on. Lon, driving the first vehicle, gave them a smile and said, "God bless you," as they rolled past.

The Israeli checkpoint was much more intense. Despite their having made arrangements ahead of time, the Israelis at the checkpoint were not in a good mood. It may have been just their nature, or they were mad that senior officials from Tel Aviv had called to ream out their boss for being uncooperative. In any event, they made a good show of checking the vehicles. They were about to drag everything out of the SUVs until Sarah pulled the senior inspector aside and explained to him, in Hebrew, that it would not be career enhancing for him to do anything that might delay or jeopardize their mission. He got the hint and they wrapped up the inspection after about twenty minutes. Now there was just the Palestinian security checkpoint.

Lon's vehicle rolled up to the guard and stopped. The guard peered in and asked for their papers. Hans was in the front seat and said, in Arabic, that they were carrying humanitarian supplies to the people of the West Bank. The guard was dubious, even after they showed him the letter from the Jordanian Ministry of Health. A couple of other guards came over and started searching the vehicles. Lon was starting to get a bad feeling when Sarah walked up. She had been in the second vehicle and got out, ostensibly to stretch her legs. She walked up to the senior guard, and in perfect Arabic asked, "Do you have a cigarette? I'm dying for one."

The guard tried not to stare at her but he was failing miserably. "Yeah, sure. They're Egyptian, is that okay?"

"Sure." Sarah took the cigarette and he lit it for her. She arched her back to stretch it and groused, "Those fucking Israelis crawled up our asses back there." Gesturing to her cigarette she added, "I needed this to keep from killing one of them. Arrogant assholes, aren't they?"

He chuckled. "You don't know the half of it. Is this your first time crossing?"

"No, I'm originally from Ramallah. But this is my first time with a load of medicines. It's like they want to keep us sick."

"That, and they want us to buy their overpriced medicine."

Sarah took a drag off the cigarette. "Like I said, arrogant assholes." She smiled at the man. "Thanks for the smoke. I'll give you a pack on our way back."

He replied, "I work all the time. Ask for Anwar."

She took another drag and then ground out the cigarette on the pavement. "Thanks, Anwar. You're sweet." As she walked back to the SUV, she turned to give him a quick smile; thirty seconds later, they were on their way. When she got in the SUV, Alen just grinned at her. "What?" she asked.

He chuckled. "You. You manipulated the hell out of that guy, and with what? A cigarette? You're fucking dangerous."

She put on her sunglasses, smiled at him, and said, "You don't know the half of it." As they drove past Anwar, Sarah made sure to wave to her new friend.

The four vehicles rolled on into the West Bank. No one, except Sarah, had actually been there before, so they relied on their mapping software to get them where they needed to go. The Israelis provided them information on Al-Yasuf. As Sarah read it, her smile faded. "Jesus. This family is totally snakebit. I can see why Al-Maadi recruited him. Like shooting fish in a barrel. Some of it was us and some of it was them, but I can see why this guy is bitter. Maybe not bitter enough to kill a few million people, but bitter."

Lon got on the radio. "We have an address on this guy in Ramallah. Let's hope he's home."

The convoy rumbled south down Highway 90 before turning west on Highway 1. It was about an hour's drive to Ramallah. It wasn't that far but the roads were narrow and congested. They didn't know what they'd find when they got there. Would Al-Yasuf live in a nest of terrorists? Was he married with children? Did he live in a communal home with multiple generations of family members? All of this complicated any plan of attack, but they still had to attack; millions of lives were at stake.

As he navigated the narrow streets, Lon said to Hans, "This place is a tactical nightmare. These streets are too narrow and too congested. You have almost no vantage point where you can set up an overlook to cover the operational area. This place makes Beirut look like Nebraska."

Hans nodded. "I agree. Getting in is going to be bad enough but getting out may be impossible depending on the amount of noise we make. I strongly suspect these people are not going to be predisposed to cooperate with us. That doesn't even take into account the local gendarmerie."

Sarah got on the radio and said, "His address is up on the right a couple of blocks ahead. What's the plan?"

Lon now regretted being put in charge of this particular mission, but he was happy that his boss was no longer in tow. He'd suggested Rusty stay behind in Jordan and, fortunately, Gunny concurred. He got on the radio and said, "Pull over at the vacant lot up ahead." They pulled over and got out. Lon surveyed the area. The lot was trash strewn and empty. The walls of the adjacent buildings had no windows that looked down on them. Lon said, "Okay, we should be good here for a couple of minutes." He took out a tablet with imagery of the immediate area. "Okay, we're here. The intel says he lives on the third floor of this building here." He pointed to a building up the street. "No elevator in the building. Two stairwells—one in the front and another in the back. John, you get in with Hans and me. Hans and I will go up the stairs while John secures the first floor entrance. Magne, you drive to the next intersection to the north and contain. Nigel, you get in with Sarah and Alen. You go around the back. Nigel and Alen go up the stairs while Sarah secures the back alley. Steve, you contain to the south." He pointed up the street. "That intersection right up there."

They all nodded except Sarah. "Can I make a suggestion?"

"What?"

"Let me go in. As an 'Arab' woman, I'm going to attract less attention."

Alen quipped, "Less attention? Have you looked in a mirror lately?"

Sarah smirked. "Okay, I will be of less concern if there are other tangos in that building. Let me go in with Hans. We speak the best Arabic." They were all dressed in native clothing, and Sarah looked like an Arab anyway.

Hans chimed in. "She's got a point. And if I walk in with her, no one is going to pay attention to me anyway. If anyone asks, I'll just say I'm French-Lebanese."

Lon knew she was right. "Okay. I'll secure the front entrance. John, you secure the back. Are we clear?"

They all nodded. "Okay, let's go."

The four vehicles moved out together but split at the next intersection. Magne was in the lead and continued past the target building and pulled over just before the next intersection. Lon, Sarah, and Hans parked on the street near the building's front entrance. Alen, Nigel, and John turned down the alley and stopped behind the building while Steve parked near the intersection south of the building. Lon keyed his radio and said, "Everyone in position?" After getting affirmative responses from everyone, he said, "Execute."

Sarah, Hans, and Lon exited their SUV and walked into the building. Lon stopped in the small lobby while Sarah and Hans walked up the stairs. In the back, Nigel and Alen walked up the back stairs while John guarded the alley. The third-floor hallway was dim and a couple of the other apartment doors were open to allow for a cross-breeze. Sarah and Hans checked out the apartments as they passed, but seeing no threats, kept walking. As they approached the end of the hall, Sarah picked out Alen and Nigel in the back stairwell. They had stopped at the top of the stairs. Alen stood in the shadows with his MP-7 raised and covering the hallway behind them. Nigel had his weapon ready and was pointing it down the back stairs in case anyone came up behind them.

Sarah stood back away from the peep hole and checked the latch, but it was locked. Hans whispered, "Try knocking." She knocked on the door but there was no answer. She knocked again but there was only silence coming from inside the apartment. Hans knelt down and quickly picked the lock. He pulled the door lever just enough to disengage the latch. As he did this, Alen moved in closer and Nigel moved up to cover the hallway and the back stairs. Hans stood and counted down with his fingers—three, two, one. Then he pushed the door open and burst into the apartment. He immediately moved away from the door, expecting gunfire, but there was nothing. Alen and Sarah moved in after him, Sarah going left and Alen right. There was no sound. They quietly and quickly cleared the apartment. No one was there.

Nigel slipped just inside the apartment door to avoid being seen by the neighbors who were now sticking their heads out into the hall to see what the commotion was about. Hans and Alen started searching the apartment while Sarah walked to the front door. Nigel covered the front door from about three meters to the left. She started to close the door when there was a light knocking. Everyone froze. Sarah put her Sig behind her back and answered the door. It was a small woman, maybe seventy years old. She lived next door. In Arabic, Sarah said, "Hello, can I help you?"

The old woman tried to peek around Sarah and into the apartment but Sarah moved to block her. The old woman asked, "What are you doing here? Are you robbing Dr. Al-Yasuf?"

Sarah laughed. "Why? Do I look like a thief?"

"You might," the old woman replied.

"Well, I assure you I am not. I am Meena, Abdullah's cousin from Lebanon. We were in the city and hoped to visit with him."

"We?" The old lady was suspicious.

As she said this, Hans walked up behind Sarah and said in Arabic, "Is everything all right, my love?"

Sarah replied, "Yes, darling. This lady is Abdullah's neighbor."

Hans smiled. "Well, hello. Maybe you can tell us why Abdullah isn't here. He was supposed to be home, although we are a little late."

The old lady was still not satisfied. Ignoring Hans, she said, "He doesn't look Lebanese."

Sarah said, "Well, he takes after his mother; she's French."

Hans asked the lady, "*Est-que tu parles français?*"

"What did he say?"

Sarah smiled. "He asked if you spoke French."

"No, I don't. Dr. Al-Yasuf didn't say anything about family stopping by today."

Sarah shrugged. "Does he always tell you when people are stopping by?"

"No, of course not. It's just . . ."

Sarah pouted. "Well, I guess we've missed him. I had a letter for him from my mother to his, too."

The old lady said, "You could just leave it here."

Sarah leaned in as if sharing a confidence. "I would, but there is money in it. I really should hand it to him personally."

"Well, it's Tuesday. He's at work."

"At the hospital?"

"No. He's at the clinic today."

Sarah put on an expression of mild surprise. "Oh? I didn't know he also worked at a clinic. My industrious cousin is putting the rest of us to shame. Is it nearby?"

The old lady said, "It's three streets over to the east. It's the Al-Maqta clinic." She glanced at Hans and then back to Sarah. "How did you get in, anyway?"

Sarah reached into her pocket and pulled out a key. "With a key of course. His mother gave it to us."

Her curiosity apparently satisfied, the old woman snorted and padded off back to her apartment. Sarah shut the door behind her and let out an audible sigh of relief after the door closed. "That was close."

Hans chuckled. "Would it be bad if our entire operation was undone by a hundred-year-old spinster?" While they talked, Alen called Steve and gave him the name of the clinic, which Steve located immediately. While Nigel slipped back to the stairwell to cover the hall, Sarah, Hans, and Alen searched the apartment and found no sign of the virus. Hans said, "He must have it with him."

Alen added, "Yeah, I wouldn't take my eyes off of it either." He got on the radio and said, "No sign of the package here. We're about to make our exit."

Lon replied, "Copy that. The package must be with him. We need to check out that clinic. Let's get out of here."

The Praetorians exited the building without raising attention from the other residents. They believed they were away clean but didn't see the old lady peeking out through her kitchen curtains at the alley below. As the two large men exited the building and got into a waiting Mercedes SUV, she mumbled to herself, "I knew something wasn't right about them." She picked up her phone and dialed. "Hello? Is this the Al-Maqta Clinic? I need to speak to Dr. Al-Yasuf right away. It's an emergency."

* * *

About half a kilometer away, Abdullah Al-Yasuf put down his phone and said to the four young men standing in front of him, "That was my neighbor. Apparently, I just had some visitors—a cousin from Lebanon. I don't have any cousins in Lebanon. They're on to me. I don't know how, but I am certain of it. We need to move—now."

The four men were serious and stoic. One of them said, "We are ready to martyr ourselves, Dr. Al-Yasuf."

He was preparing a hypodermic needle with the virus serum. "Don't be too eager, my friend. The whole point is that you must live so you can infect the Israelis. You are of little help to the cause if you are dead. Do you understand?"

"Yes, sir." The men rolled up their sleeves as Al-Yasuf swabbed the arm of the first man and injected him. He didn't know why he bothered to swab the arm—habit he guessed. The odds of any of these men living long enough to die of infection was slim but he did need them to survive—at least for a little while.

* * *

The four SUVs approached the clinic and then split up with one each stopping on the streets that defined the block that included the Al-Maqta Clinic. There was a large apartment building on the south end that ran the length of the block. On the north end, there was a building that housed a grocery to the west and a woman's clothing store to the east. The clinic was in the middle between them. Its main entrance faced west but there was another door in the alley to the east. The team deployed around the building. As they did at the apartment, Sarah and Hans made the initial entry. Sarah strode into the little clinic past the twenty or so people waiting in the dingy little lobby. She walked up to the receptionist and said, "Hello, I am looking for Dr. Abdullah Al-Yasuf. Is he here?"

"Yes, but he's with a patient right now."

Sarah glanced at Hans who took a couple of steps away and keyed his mic and whispered, "Target is in the building. Repeat, target is in the building."

The receptionist perked up. "What's this about?"

Sarah ignored her question and pointed to a door beside her. "Through here?"

The receptionist picked up her phone and punched in a number, "Dr. Al-Yasuf, there are some strange people here to . . ." She didn't finish the sentence because Sarah had hung up the phone. The receptionist started to protest but came face-to-face with Sarah's 9 mm.

Sarah grabbed her by the arm and led her back into the clinic. The people in the lobby were oblivious to what was happening. "You don't want to upset your patients, now do you?" Hans followed behind her and pulled his MP-7 compact submachine gun from under his jacket. Forcefully pushing the receptionist in front of her, Sarah barked, "Which room? Where is he?" The receptionist pointed to a door at the end of the hall but before she said another word, a man with an AK-47 leapt out into the hallway and fired a burst at them. The first two rounds struck the receptionist, who screamed and fell to the floor. The other shots went high and into the ceiling. Hans and Sarah immediately dropped and dove for cover behind a stainless-steel utility cart. Hans rolled out and fired a burst from his suppressed MP-7 that sent the man scrambling back through the door from which he sprang. With the burst from the AK, the people in the lobby suddenly woke up. They started screaming and rushed for the door. Inside the clinic, an old Arab woman peeked out from one of the exam rooms. Seeing the receptionist on the floor bleeding, she darted back inside and slammed the door shut.

Sarah checked the receptionist. She'd been hit in the shoulder and the gut. She was bleeding but still breathing. Hans crouched behind the cart and aimed his weapon down the hall while Sarah moved ahead, ducking into an open door on her right. The room was empty. She rolled out slightly and aimed her Sig Sauer toward the door through which the shooter had retreated to give Hans cover to move up. While he did, he updated the team on what was transpiring.

"We have shots fired! One civilian down. One unknown shooter so far. He's in a room off the central corridor, north side, all the way in the back."

Lon responded, "Alpha One copies. Alpha Two, heads up out back. May be coming your way."

Alen replied, "Copy that. We're in position."

Sarah quickly studied at the layout of the clinic. The waiting room and receptionist's desk were up front. The door to the bowels of the clinic opened onto a long central corridor with exam rooms on either side. The gunman had come from the last room on the left, which appeared to be an office. Opposite the office was a supply room and bathroom. Directly ahead at the end of the corridor was a heavy steel door that led to the alley behind the building. Sarah keyed her mic and said, "Only two exits visible; the front door and a back door. We have the back door covered. The shooter is bottled up in what appears to be an office or something."

Lon said, "Copy that. Alpha Two, can you enter through that back door?"

Alen replied, "Copy. Moving now." He cautiously approached the steel door. He turned the knob but it was locked. "Alpha Four and Seven, stand back. I'm going to have to manually breach it."

Sarah eased back into the exam room she was in, and Hans did the same in the room across the corridor. Sarah said, "Go with the door."

In the alley, Alen fired a burst from his MP-7 into the door lock and kicked. The door burst open. "Alpha Two is in."

Lon said, "Copy that. Alpha Two has breached and is inside."

While Alen kept his weapon aimed at the office door, Sarah and Hans crept up the hallway. The next exam room on the right held a terrified old man and an equally frightened nurse. Hans grabbed the man by the arm, pulled him into the hallway, and shoved the nurse out behind him. Pointing toward the lobby, he said, "Go!" That was all the encouragement they needed. Sarah crept up to the last exam room on the left where the woman was. The door was locked, so rather than try to extract her, Sarah said, "Stay inside, get low in a corner. Barricade the door if you can and wait for the police to come." She continued up the hallway to the bathrooms; both were empty. The only rooms left to clear were the office and the storage room. The office door was closed, and Alen had it covered so they cleared the storage room next. Hans kicked open the door and Sarah rolled in low. It was unoccupied. That only left the office.

Alen cautiously approached the door and tried the doorknob. It was locked, but whoever was inside heard it rattle and put two rounds through the hollow-core wooden door to let whoever was on the other side know that he was listening. Alen signaled to Hans to get ready. Alen eased up to the door and standing with his back flat against the wall next to the door, Alen extended his right leg and thrust it back, hitting the door flush with his big right boot. The door popped open and Hans flipped in the flash/bang. There was another door on the far wall, and he saw at least two men dive through the door.

There was a loud explosion and a blinding flash in the room. Hans burst in to find Al-Yasuf stunned and lying on the floor. There was another man on the floor next to him rubbing his eyes. He had an AK-47 in his other hand, so Hans put three rounds in his chest. Alen came in behind him and Hans yelled, "Check the other door! I think a couple of guys got out right before the flash/bang went off."

Alen kicked the door open. He peeked out onto a dark, dingy passageway. It was a service corridor through which the grocery and the clothing store north of the clinic received deliveries and took trash to the alley without going through their front doors. Alen turned to his left as the door leading to the grocery slammed shut. He then looked to his right. The heavy steel door leading to the alley banged closed. In front of him was a door leading to the clothing store. It was ajar, and a woman was yelling inside the store. He keyed his mic and said, "Heads up north and east. There is an access corridor back here. We have two, maybe three tangos running free through the grocery store, the clothing store, and the alley on the northeast corner. I don't have descriptions, but they were in a hurry."

Lon got on the radio and said, "Copy that."

Hans asked Sarah, "You got this?"

"Yes, go help Alen."

Hans ran into the service corridor. Alen said, "I'll go right, you go left."

John came on and said, "This is Alpha Five in the alley. A guy just came out of a door north of the clinic's back door. He was in a hurry and ran off to the north. I'm going to pursue." Just as he said this, Hans came bursting through the same door. "Alpha Four just exited. I'm picking him up and going after the suspect tango. Okay, T1 went east on Ghassan. We're on him."

Lon replied, "Copy that. Alpha One and Three will check the grocery." They drove up to the corner just as a young Arab man ran out of the grocery. He dashed across the street and then sprinted west on Ghassan Harb Street. They turned left to follow him. Alen exited seconds after and began searching for him. Lon got on the radio, "We have eyes on him, Alpha Two. Be alert for anyone coming out of that clothing store."

Alen trotted to his right down the sidewalk. Ahead of him, John and Hans pulled out of the alley in their Mercedes and turned east in pursuit of the guy from the alley. As he walked toward the clothing store, there was a commotion from inside. Through the window he saw two women in the store hitting a young Arab man with their fists. The young man was trying to fend off the women while making his escape from the store. He ran out the front door with the women in hot pursuit and calling him a thief. When the man reached the sidewalk, he spotted Alen and his eyes got big. The huge Serb didn't exactly fit in. The terrorist ran east past the alley and then cut across Ghassan. Alen had started to give chase and was about halfway to the next intersection when a Toyota 4-Runner approached from the south on Al Yarmouk Street. It was Steve and Nigel. The young man ran right in front of them. Alen keyed his mic and said, "That's him right in front of you!"

Nigel replied, "We've got him. Go see if Alpha Seven needs help inside."

"Copy that." Alen went into the clothing store and, in his rather poor Arabic, asked the women where the "thief" had come from. They took him to the back of the store and showed him the door to the service corridor. He thanked them and exited through the door. He stepped back into the room where Sarah was holding Al-Yasuf at gunpoint. He was recovering from the effects of the flash/bang. He tried to move away from the dead man lying next to him. On a table behind him was a bottle of alcohol, some used cotton swabs, and three empty syringes.

Sarah nodded to the syringes and said, "He's injected them already. It's started."

Alen replied, "Not yet, it hasn't. We have three runners plus this dead one—that's four. I only see three syringes." He looked around on the floor and found another syringe still in its plastic wrapping.

Sarah said, "We interrupted him before he finished."

Alen searched around him and under the desk. "Yeah, but where's the virus. This syringe was never filled. We need to find the shit was supposed to go in it."

"What does it look like?"

Alen replied, "Probably a small, clear glass bottle with a metal top."

While Alen hunted, Sarah put her weapon under Al-Yasuf's chin and asked, "Where's the virus?"

Al-Yasuf smiled. "You don't think I know who you are, you fuckin' Israeli bitch. Nura should have killed you when she had a chance."

"Maybe I should just kill you now?"

"You will anyway. That's what you do. But you're too late. Right now, my comrades are loose in the city, carrying the virus inside them. With every cough and every sneeze, they are infecting more and more people. Sure, the Arabs will get sick—but the Jews will die." He smiled. "You can't stop it now. You can kill me but not before I kill you first."

Al-Yasuf had palmed the small vial of virus. He raised his hand to smash it on her face but she was too quick for him. She grabbed his wrist and wrenched it violently until he dropped the vial. But before she picked it up, he grabbed it with his other hand and threw it at her. The vial bounced off her jacket and into the corner of the office a few feet away. It hit the concrete wall and smashed, spilling its contents on the floor. Sarah recoiled in horror. Al-Yasuf laughed, "You're infected now, you Jew whore." Alen stepped over Al-Yasuf, raised his MP-7, and shot him twice in the chest and once in the forehead.

Sarah took a step back away from Al-Yasuf and stared at the wet spot on the floor where he smashed the vial. "I'm fucked, aren't I? I mean, you heard what he said."

Alen smiled. "I don't think he was a very good doctor. They aren't contagious yet, but their blood probably is. You'll be fine so long as you don't lick that shit off the floor. It's in a saline solution, not aerosolized." He led her out into the hall. "Just wait here." He went into the storage room across the hall from the office and returned with two one-gallon jugs. The first was bleach. He walked over to where Al-Yasuf threw the vial and poured bleach all over the area. "That'll take care of the virus." Then he poured alcohol all over Al-Yasuf's body and the empty syringes on the table. He reached into his pocket and pulled out a cigarette lighter. He grabbed some papers from the desk, lit them on fire, and tossed them on the syringes and the corpse. The alcohol burst into flames and immediately began consuming the used syringes.

Sarah asked, "I get why you're burning the syringes, but why his body? Was he infectious or something?"

Alen poured more alcohol on the body to give the fire a boost. "No, just a prick."

Sarah shrugged. "Fair enough." The first police sirens screamed in the distance. "We need to get the hell out of here."

Alen said, "Let's go out the back." He led her to the service corridor, but as they started to walk toward the alley, a car screeched to a halt just beyond the door. He grabbed her by the arm and pushed her toward the door to the clothing store while he walked quickly toward the grocery.

The female proprietors of the clothing store were just outside the shop's front door watching all the commotion, which allowed Sarah to slip into the store. She walked to the racks of clothes and pretended to be browsing. She was going to just leave, but all the patients who saw her and Hans walk into the clinic were probably now out on the street—the same street where their vehicle was parked. She needed to alter her appearance. When the two women came back in, they were surprised when Sarah approach the counter with a brightly colored scarf and black shawl. "I'll take these."

One of the women started to ring her up as the other one looked around the small store. Who else had they missed? The cashier said, "We didn't see you come in."

Sarah smiled. "Really? I walked right past you, but then, you were looking at the police cars." Sarah paid for her purchases and walked out. As she did, she threw on the shawl, wrapped the scarf over her head, and put on her sunglasses. She was a different person.

Alen snuck into the grocery store, picked up a couple of things, and walked to the counter. The old man seated there was reading a newspaper and oblivious to what was going on outside. He glanced up and was only moderately surprised to find a hulking European standing in front of him. He took Alen's money without question and went back to his paper. Alen hung around just inside the front door of the grocery and took a bite of the apple he'd bought. A couple of minutes later, Sarah walked by, obviously looking for him. He whistled to get her attention and they walked together around the corner toward the clinic. The police were there and directing onlookers to move across the street. Alen and Sarah politely complied and continued south until they came to their vehicle. As they drove away, Alen got on the radio and said, "This is Alpha Two. Primary target is down. The three tangos on the street have been infected. They won't be sick yet but their blood will be infectious. When you catch up to them, suggest you refrain from doing anything that makes them bleed."

Lon replied, "Copy that." Turning to Magne, he said, "They don't make it easy, do they?"

* * *

John drove east while Hans tried to keep eyes on their target, who they designated Tango One. The target turned to walk south on Al-Yarmouk Street. About midway up the block, a taxi sat along the side of the street, idling. He jumped in the back seat and yelled to the driver to go. The taxi pulled out, turned left on Khalil Salah Street, and then right at the next corner onto Palestine Street. Neither the driver nor the passenger paid attention to the black Mercedes that had parked about three cars behind them.

Hans got on the radio. "Tango One just got into a taxi and is now southbound on Al-Yarmouk." They followed the taxi at a discreet distance but not so far that they risked losing him. As they approached Highway 60, the taxi turned south. Hans gave an update. "Tango One is now southbound on 60." John said, "This is a major road. Where does it go?"

Hans checked his mapping software but Sarah chimed in. "That road heads toward the airport."

Hans asked, "He can't get in there, can he?"

"No, the airport is behind the wall." She was referring to Israel's security barrier that separated Israel from the West Bank. "But there is the Qalandia Checkpoint at the eastern end of the airport. It's closed to most Palestinians, but if Tango One is an Israeli Palestinian or has an entry permit, he can get through. They'd check him, but they're looking for bombs, guns, and contraband. He could get through."

Hans replied, "I have a feeling they took all that into account."

Lon broke in and said, "Alpha Seven, reach out to your old friends. Tell them what's coming and that they need to lock down the border until these mopes are corralled."

"I was already planning to."

"Ask them not to publicize the closure. Keep it quiet if they can."

She asked, "Why?"

"I assume they are heading for the border with plans to cross into Israel. If the tangos know the border is closed, who knows what they'll do? Also, see if they can get a surveillance drone or two in the air. I don't want to risk losing one of these assholes because of a flat tire or something."

Sarah replied, "I'm on it."

Lon said, "All Alpha Teams, Since Alpha Two and Seven are not in pursuit, I'm designating them as the central coms link. Seven, you guys keep track of where everyone is."

"Will do, One."

John said to Hans, "We need to stop this guy before he gets to that checkpoint. Even if they shut it down in time, there will still be plenty of vulnerable people there."

"I agree. Let me find a good place along the route to take him down." Hans studied the map on his tablet. "Jesus, this place is a nightmare—people and houses everywhere." After a couple of minutes, he said. "Okay, it isn't perfect, but I think it's our best option. Up ahead about a klick, the road passes through a ravine. There is a rock face five to ten meters high on our side of the road. All houses are above it. There will be a couple modern buildings on the left where the road curves. After we pass them, run him off the road to the right. We can take him there."

John took a deep breath. "Copy that." John had his MP-7 wedged between his seat and the middle console. Hans placed his in his lap. As they neared their attack point, John noted a gas station ahead on his right and the modern office building on his left. The road was dropping down into a small valley between rocky hills. Patting the dash of the Mercedes, John said, "Let's see what this thing can do."

Hans pointed to the buildings and said, "Okay, this is it." John punched the gas pedal and the Mercedes lurched forward and gained speed. The taxi was in the right lane so John pulled alongside him on the left and then cut the wheel sharply to the right. The right front corner of the SUV hit the left rear corner of the taxi sending it into a spin. The driver of the taxi tried to regain control but John slammed the Mercedes into the taxi again, sending it careening backward into the trash-strewn vacant lot below the cliff. The taxi and the Mercedes were now face-to-face and John stomped on the gas again to push the taxi backward up onto the rocks and debris at the bottom of the cliff. As they came to a halt, Hans and John leapt from the car. The driver of the taxi leaned out of his window and let off a barrage of random fire with a Makarov 9 mm handgun. The rounds were intended for Hans, who instinctively jumped behind the SUV's door for cover. Up to that moment, they considered that the driver might have been an innocent bystander— just some poor schmuck who picked up the wrong fare. That changed in an instant. Before Hans shouldered his weapon and returned fire, John put a burst through the windshield of the taxi. The rounds ripped violently into the driver's body. Weapon raised, Hans traversed the vehicle. Two of the rounds had hit the man in the head. He was dead.

John cautiously approached the passenger side of the taxi. Tango One had been in the backseat but John couldn't see him. He had no idea if the man was armed or not, and at this point, he really didn't care. He fired a burst from his MP-7 through the open front passenger door window and through the seats. Tango One had been lying on the floorboard and only one of the rounds hit him producing only a superficial wound to his scalp. Tango One sat up and pointed a Kalashnikov AKS-74U compact assault weapon toward John and yelled, "*Allah akbar!*" But before he squeezed the trigger, Hans unleashed a barrage of rounds from the opposite side of the vehicle. He was killed instantly.

Cars on the street behind them had stopped for the "accident," but when the gunfire erupted, they all reversed madly or hopped the median to get away. Peering at the corpse in the back seat, John turned to Hans and said, "Well, so much for 'no blood.' That *is* what Alen said, right?"

Hans looked at him in mild irritation and said, "You're welcome. Next time, maybe I won't save your ass."

"You saved it, all right, but only after I saved yours first."

"Okay. What now?"

John keyed his mic and said, "Alpha Two, this is Alpha Five. Tango One is down, repeat Tango One is KIA. Uh, that 'no blood' thing didn't exactly work out. What do we do now?"

Alen got on the radio. "Jesus Christ. Can't you follow simple instructions? Okay, you're going to need to destroy the body."

"Uh, we're kinda out in the middle of the shit here and need to move out soon. Any suggestions?"

Alen replied, "Burn him. Cook him. If you can get him over 70 degrees celsius, it should kill the virus."

John replied sarcastically, "Oh, is that all? What are we supposed to do, order an industrial-sized crockpot from Amazon and hope it gets here before the police?"

"Try gasoline."

John replied sheepishly, "Oh, right." Hans just shook his head. "Okay, let's fire it up. Where's the gas tank on this thing?"

Hans replied, "Under the trunk."

John walked around to the rear of the car and fired several rounds through the trunk lid. He peeked under the car. Gasoline was pouring from the holes he had just created. He was about to light it when Hans told him to wait. Hans ran back to their vehicle took something out of their weapons cache.

John asked, "What's that?"

Hans replied, "Thermite."

"That should do it."

Hans pulled the pin on the thermite grenade and tossed it in Tango One's lap. The thermite ignited and immediately started to burn into the corpse. Within seconds it ignited the gasoline leaking from the perforated fuel tank, and the car was soon fully aflame. As they got in the Mercedes to leave, Hans said, "If 2000 degrees doesn't kill it, it can't be killed. Let's get out of here."

* * *

Nigel and Steve had picked up their target, designated Tango Two, at the corner of Ghassan and Yarmouk. When the terrorist spotted Alen, he correctly determined he was one of the people going after Al-Yasuf. Tango Two was so busy focusing on Alen, he missed the fact that a slow-rolling Toyota 4-Runner was pulling up ahead of him from the south. When he got to the next intersection, he turned around and was thrilled that the big man wasn't chasing him. He ran north to Palestine Street, crossed the street, and walked west hoping to be obscured by the trucks and shop awnings lining the thoroughfare. The street was one-way, east bound. Steve was already wearing a keffiyeh and put on sunglasses to hide his Asian features before jumping out of the 4-Runner to follow Tango Two on foot.

The street was congested with both cars and people. Steve kept his eyes on his target as he walked west. The young Arab man stopped periodically to check behind him. He wasn't being subtle. The first time he did it, Steve was unnerved, but Tango Two was watching for a six-five, 250-pound European man, not a five-nine Asian wearing a keffiyeh. In the meantime, Nigel sprinted to find a way to get ahead of them. Ramallah was a rabbit warren of roads laid out with no rhyme or reason. He had to turn east because of the one-way streets but turned north at the first opportunity. He picked his way through the back streets to get to Al Nahdha Street, a major thoroughfare that ran roughly east to west. It was a one-way street too, but it went west—the direction he needed to go.

Just before he reached Manara Square, Tango Two stopped. He stepped into an alcove of a shop and got out his cell phone. Steve slowed his pace and then stopped, pretending to window-shop so as not to overtake his target. He wasn't close enough to hear the conversation, but he saw the panic in the young man's face. After a few seconds, Tango Two ended the call and continued walking toward the square. He walked around the square clockwise until he reached Rukab Street and turned left.

Steve kept his distance and hurried to catch up once Tango Two turned the corner. "Tango Two is westbound on Rukab Street. Repeat, westbound from Manara Square on Rukah." As he rounded the corner, Tango Two approached a blue Nissan sedan and got in. "Tango Two is getting in a blue sedan. I'm going to lose him."

Nigel replied, "I'm westbound on Nahda about two hundred meters from the square. I'll be there in thirty seconds. Be on the north side of Rukab for pickup."

Steve said, "Copy that." Nigel went halfway around the traffic circle and turned right on Rukab where Steve was waiting. "Update. We are west on Rukab in pursuit of Tango Two. He is in a blue Nissan Sunny. Driver is unknown but appears to be another Arab male."

They followed Tango Two for about three kilometers. Nigel got on the radio and asked, "Alpha Seven, this is Alpha Six. We're west on Rukab but we are running out of city. According to my map, this road merges into Highway 463. Any clue as to where this guy is going?"

Sarah thought for a minute and then responded. "Okay, 463 goes west and ends up north of the Modi'in Ilit settlement."

"Is there a checkpoint over there?"

"Yes, Ni'lin Checkpoint, northwest of the settlement."

Nigel said, "Could he get through there?"

"No, they're all shut down now."

"Yeah, but he doesn't know that. Could he get through under normal circumstances?"

Sarah said, "If he had an entry permit, then yes."

Nigel said, "I'm thinking that's where he's headed. We need to stop him before he gets there."

Steve was checking the map to find a good attack point. "Just before this road hits 463, it has to go down over a hundred-meter elevation loss. It's barren hillside with switchbacks—four of them."

Nigel smiled. "Switchbacks, you say? I can work with that." Nigel closed the gap on the Nissan sedan and stayed about four or five car lengths behind it.

As they passed the last cluster of houses, Steve said, "Okay, one more house on the left and then it's down the hill."

"Roger. I see it." As they passed the house, the road curved to the right and the little Nissan slowed to make the sharp left turn of the switchback. When it did, Nigel accelerated and rammed the 4-Runner into the back of the car. The driver of the car was caught unaware but responded quickly and managed to keep the car from going off the road. "Damn it!" Nigel roared. "The bloody little cunt made the turn!" Once he'd regained control, the driver of the Nissan stepped on the gas to get away from the SUV. The little car was much nimbler than the Toyota but had less power. Nigel guided the 4-Runner through the turn and then gunned it again. The driver of the Nissan had twin problems—the desire to get away and need to stay on the road through the next turn—but he only had a little over two hundred meters to work it out. Finally, he started braking as he went into the next switchback. His tires were screaming as they tried to hang onto the pavement. He almost made it but then Nigel caught up with him. The big Toyota banged into the Nissan's rear bumper, giving the car just enough of a push to cause it to break traction. The blue sedan slid off the road sideways and rolled down the hill until it came to a stop upside down and a hundred meters down the hill. Nigel immediately braked to keep his own vehicle from plunging over the edge. Fortunately, the same amount of force that pushed the Nissan forward pushed the Toyota backward, which helped him slow down.

Steve shouted excitedly, "Damn fine driving, Nigel. You got him!"

Nigel smiled, "Let's go see what little fishy we caught." He pulled the Toyota off the road. They grabbed their weapons and scrambled down the hill to where the Nissan came to rest. The car was not as badly damaged as they expected. Because it was in a turn when it left the road, its forward momentum was in a different direction than the direction of its roll. With weapons at the ready, they approached the car. The tires were still spinning and steam was rising from a ruptured radiator. The driver of the car was crawling out from where the now-shattered window once was. Once he was out, he reached back to retrieve an AK-47. This was all Nigel needed and he put four rounds into the man's torso. He collapsed motionless where he was.

Steve moved around to the downhill side of the vehicle. The passenger kicked open the door and came tumbling out onto the ground. He gained his footing and turned to face Steve. Seeing the weapon raised to Steve's shoulder, the man froze and raised his hands. In Arabic, he said, "Don't shoot. I surrender."

Steve approached the man and, with his left hand, patted him down to make sure he had no weapons. Nigel said, "You know we can't take him prisoner. Every minute this guy lives, the closer he is to being infectious."

Steve held the man by the back of his collar and briefly lowered his MP-7 while he responded, "I know but I can't in good conscience just . . ." As he was saying this, Tango Two jerked away from him and lunged for his weapon. In the struggle, Steve dropped his weapon and the terrorist started to reach for it. Steve grabbed the man by his hair, pulled him upright, and struck him in the throat with a quick flat hand thrust crushing his larynx. The man staggered back, gasping for air. Nigel said calmly, "You need to finish him, mate."

Steve grabbed the man from behind, wrapped his arms around his neck, and with a quick snap, broke his neck. Letting the body drop to the ground, Steve said, "We didn't have to do that."

Nigel replied, "Yes, we did. That man sitting in a cell could still kill millions. These fanatics can't be saved; they can't be reasoned with. The sooner you recognize that, the better. There is nothing we can do to them that's worse than what they are willing to do to themselves." Nigel got on the radio and said, "Alpha Seven, this is Alpha Six. Tango Two is down. What do we do with him?"

Sarah responded, "Alpha Four used thermite. That seemed to work."

Nigel said, "Copy that."

"I'll get it." Steve ran back to the 4-Runner and returned with a thermite grenade. Nigel had dragged Tango Two to the back of the vehicle and rolled him under the rear deck. Steve put the thermite grenade on the man's chest and pulled the pin. The thermite glowed white hot and immediately began burning up the terrorist's body. Nigel and Steve stepped back and Nigel put five rounds into the gas tank. The fuel began leaking out directly onto the thermite's fire. Within seconds, the flames spread and the car was engulfed.

Nigel said, "Let's get out of here."

"Copy that." As they walked up the hill, Steve said, "I'm sorry about earlier. It's just that I'm not really used to this kind of work."

Nigel said, "That your first, I take?"

"Yeah. Does it get easier?"

Nigel took a deep breath. "Sad to say, yes, it does."

* * *

Lon and Magne were in pursuit of the last terrorist—Tango Three. He had run west on Ghassan toward Nozha Street and as soon as he turned the corner, he got into a waiting Audi A7. When the car sped away, Lon said, "Maggie, I think we're in trouble." He gunned the Range Rover and went after him. The Audi whipped around the traffic circle at Manara Square and then north on Al Irsal Street. They kept up with the Audi in the city; the traffic was too heavy to take advantage of the car's superior speed and power. However, once they got a couple of kilometers away from the city center, the driver of the Audi started to pick up speed. He was driving aggressively, weaving in and out of traffic and recklessly blowing through intersections. Lon said, "I don't know if he's made us or he just drives like an asshole."

Magne quipped, "At this point, does it make a difference?"

"He's heading due north. Where is this guy going?" Lon asked rhetorically.

Magne shot back, "Lebanon? I hear it's beautiful this time of year." He stared at the map on his tablet and said, "We're approaching Highway 463. Let's see if he turns east." But Tango Three did not turn east; he kept speeding north. When they passed Abu Qash, Magne called Sarah. "Alpha Seven, this is Alpha Three. Tango Three is headed north on what used to be Al Irsal Street. It's uh, Road 4566 now. We have just gone past a town called Abu Qash. The road turns back east after this. Any clue where he might be going?"

Sarah checked her map. "Not a clue, Three."

They followed him for another two or three kilometers, when he began to slow down. Magne keyed his mic and said, "Okay, we're in a town called Bir Zayt. He has turned left on some local road. He's heading north and picking up speed."

Sarah responded, "Copy that, Three. If he keeps going north, he should hit Highway 465."

"Roger." The Audi A7 tore through Bir Zayt with no regard for anything or anyone. As it approached Highway 465, it slowed just enough to make the turn. The Range Rover was struggling to keep up, and when the Audi turned west, the driver stomped on the accelerator and sped away. "Goddamn, this guy is fuckin' flying! I don't think we're going to keep up with him. Why did I get the Richard Petty of terrorists?"'"

Sarah said, "Do your best. I'll let Israeli border security know."

Lon struggled to keep the Audi in sight. Magne was using binoculars but he would often only catch a glimpse of it when it was stuck behind slower traffic. They tried to catch up, only to have the Audi pass the offending truck or bus and speed away again. Lon almost got into a head-on collision with a bus trying to pass a slow-moving truck. He cursed the Range Rover, "This thing has no balls! I can't pass anyone without taking my life in my hands."

As they crested a hill, Magne just made out the Audi A7 as it turned north on Highway 446. Magne got on the radio with an update. "Alpha Seven, Tango Three just turned north on 466, but we're a good kilometer behind him and there are a shitload of trucks in our way. I don't think we can stay with him."

Sarah replied calmly, "If he's north on 466, he's heading for the Rantis Checkpoint. I'll advise Israeli border security."

Lon said, "She's going to *advise* border security? That's it?" Magne just shrugged. As the Range Rover approached Highway 466, an Israel Defense Force Eitan drone passed over them flying above the highway. About a kilometer ahead of it, the Audi was speeding toward the Rantis Checkpoint. As the A7 approached the crest of a hill, the Eitan launched an AGM-114N Hellfire II laser-guided, air-to-surface missile. It took the missile a little over two seconds to cover the distance between the drone and the Audi. When it hit, its metal-augmented thermobaric warhead detonated. The Audi disintegrated in a ball of fire at 1400 degrees Celsius, vaporizing the two terrorists inside. Lon and Magne saw and heard the explosion. They drove on and stopped short of the impact point. There was nothing left identifiable as a vehicle. It was just a burning heap of twisted metal.

Lon said, "I guess that's what they call border security over here." He got on the radio and said, "Tango Three is down. Repeat Tango Three is definitely down. Alpha Seven, any idea how we can get out of here before the locals catch up to us? I don't think they're going to be happy."

Sarah replied, "Yes, head north and go east on 465 until you reach the Rantis Checkpoint. Just give them my name and they'll let you through. They're expecting you."

"And you and the others?"

"We already vectored them in to a safe crossing point. You're the last of us."

Lon breathed a sigh of relief. "Great. See you on the other side."

EPILOGUE

It had been three weeks since Black Sun's attempted attack on Israel had been thwarted. The details of the plot were kept out of the press. The activities in the West Bank were impossible to ignore, but there was a lot of confusion as to who did it or why. The Israelis denied any involvement, as they always did. This time, however, it was the truth—not that anyone believed them. There was also a lot of condemnation. Dr. Al-Yasuf was portrayed by the Palestinians as a victim and a pillar of the community. His family's history of extremist activity and involvement in the Intifada were overlooked. The seven other men killed that day were also lionized. They were depicted both as innocent bystanders and brave martyrs of the war against the oppressors. The obvious contradictions of that narrative were ignored. Also missing was any mention of the biological weapon. Some of the remnants of Black Sun were eager to take credit for the attack, but the existence of the virus had been so secret—even inside the organization—they didn't actually know what they were taking credit for. Of those who did know about it, only two were still alive and they were on the run.

Nura and Khalid had been in hiding ever since they fled South Shouna in the ambulance and went to Amman. They had plans for what to do afterward, of course, but like most plans they didn't survive first contact with the enemy. The original plan assumed they weren't discovered and had them returning to Egypt until the epidemic took hold, after which then they would travel to the West Bank under the guise of helping with a humanitarian crisis. Once there, Khalid was to secretly reveal his involvement in the crisis to Palestinian leaders and leverage it to secure a position of power in the wake of a collapsing Israeli government. Once it became clear he was compromised, however, the plan was changed. When he was named publicly, he was going to claim he was a scapegoat to cover up the fact that this heinous crime had been perpetrated by Andreas Ostergaard, a deranged European Christian. Privately, of course, he would take full credit for the destruction of Israel. He'd no longer have to fear Israeli retaliation, and the people of the West Bank would eagerly shield him against any possible American military retaliation until he engineered his rise to head of state. But that had all gone by the wayside. With his plot in ruins, his focus turned from planning his triumph to merely staying alive.

Soon after the Praetorians disrupted the attack, key details of the conspiracy were shared with security services throughout the region. The Egyptians moved quickly to seize all of Al-Maadi's property and freeze his bank accounts and credit cards. His colleagues and family members were all brought in for questioning that would last weeks. His entire department within Cairo University was temporarily shut down until experts from the CDC and WHO conducted a detailed audit of everything in the department's freezers to ensure that none of the virus still existed. The Jordanians, too, leapt into action. They were embarrassed that their territory had been used to launch the attack and angry that one of their fellow citizens was brutally murdered by the perpetrators. Once they learned that Nura and Khalid had escaped in South Shouna, the Ministry of Interior's Public Security Directorate (PSD) descended on the area like a swarm of locusts. The couple driving the decoy car was arrested and interrogated. They quickly gave up Nura's cousin, and most of his cell was wrapped up, which included the ambulance driver who'd helped them escape. Under interrogation, he revealed where he had taken Nura and Khalid. They escaped only minutes before the PSD descended on the safehouse.

With the help of a couple of Black Sun survivors, the couple was successfully smuggled out of Amman to a farmhouse on the outskirts of Azraq Ed Duruz in eastern Jordan. Once there, Khalid contacted the sheik for help. One of the sheik's men slipped across the border from Saudi Arabia and was escorted to the farm. When he arrived, he found Khalid and Nura in sad shape. Khalid hadn't shaved since he fled South Shouna and was very disheveled. Nura's eyes were sunken and hollow. She was stressed and angry and hadn't really eaten much since learning their plan failed in spectacular fashion.

The Saudi walked in, hugged Khalid, and kissed him on both cheeks. "Brother Khalid, it is good you are alive."

Khalid smiled for the first time in weeks. "Brother Mohammad. It is good to see you as well. How is the sheik? I know he is disappointed that our plan was ruined. Please, tell him I am sorry that his money was wasted."

Mohammad waved off his concern. "The money is nothing, but he is disappointed that the plan has failed. The virus worked, did it not?"

"Yes, yes it did. Just like Kalib Kabir said it would."

Mohammad stroked his beard. "Then he can make more of it, if he has the necessary facilities."

Khalid shuffled uneasily. "Uh, Kalib Kabir is dead."

Mohammad was irritated. "He is? I was unaware. How did this happen?"

"Nura killed him in Copenhagen before fleeing with the virus."

Mohammad was shocked. "Why? Why would she do this?"

Khalid sensed that Mohammad was angry. "Because I told her to. He had been compromised; we think it was the Israelis. He was brilliant but weak. He would not have held up to interrogation. He would have exposed everything."

Mohammad did not appear satisfied with Khalid's answer. "Yet, everything was exposed anyway. Your decision to kill the Dane was rash."

Khalid pushed back. "Everything was not exposed. Your involvement, and that of the sheik, is still secret. She protected you."

"Perhaps. In any case, it is all academic now. So, how can we help you, Dr. Al-Maadi?"

"We need to get out of Jordan and to someplace safe."

Mohammad asked, "Where did you have in mind?"

Khalid replied, "Someplace safe. Maybe with my cousin?"

"Your cousin is not an easy man to find, which is, I suppose, why he is still alive. I can get you as far as Pakistan. Beyond that, you will have to rely on your own people."

Khalid sighed. "That will have to do. If you can get us to Pakistan, we will forever be in your debt."

Mohammad laughed. "We? Surely you understand she cannot go with you."

Khalid was surprised. "Why not? She is my wife!"

Mohammad stared at him in disbelief. "You, the two of you, are the most wanted people in the world right now, except maybe for your cousin. Everyone is hunting for you. They are looking for a couple. Everyone has your photos—every bus station, every train, every airport, every ferry. Your only chance is to split up. I can get you to Pakistan and probably get her to Africa. Maybe, in a few months or years, you can get together but not now. It is impossible."

Khalid hadn't even considered this, but then, he was a pampered academic. "How can I just leave her?"

"The same way your cousin had to leave his family and Brother Osama had to leave his."

"But Brother Osama was with his family when he was martyred," Khalid protested.

"Yes, but he had been without his family for many years. Some would argue, and I among them, that the reason he is dead is because he insisted on having his family with him. Ultimately, that is how the Americans found him. But what do you care? You don't have children. She is just a woman. You will find another, if that is what you really want."

Khalid said meekly, "But I don't want anyone else."

Mohammad said, "That is what the Sheik has offered. I can get you both out, but separately. If Allah wills that you and this woman be together, it will be. Otherwise, move on with your life."

"Okay. I will tell her. You will promise that she will be safe?"

"We will do all in our power to get her to a safe place. We cannot guarantee that she stays safe. I understand she is a very angry and vengeful woman who is not so obedient. If she chooses to endanger herself, we cannot stop her."

Khalid replied, "That is fair enough. Let me go tell her."

Nura was not happy that Mohammad would only help them escape separately but she had no choice. The PSD would find them if they stayed in Jordan. They had to go. She reluctantly agreed to the arrangement. They had one last night together before they left.

Mohammad took Nura southeast toward Saudi Arabia and smuggled her across the border near Al Qurayat. There she was met by another Saudi man and his family. He took her gruffly by the arm and shoved her toward the other women. Mohammad handed the man a wad of cash, which he proceeded to count. "I will get her as far as Al Qunfidah as I promised, but no farther."

"As agreed," replied Mohammad. He said nothing to Nura before he left.

The man walked up to Nura and said, "My name is Abdel. If anyone asks, you are my cousin. Say nothing more." He looked her up and down and asked, "Do you have money?"

Nura replied, "I have some, why?"

"I need four hundred Riyals more."

She protested, "Why? Mohammad paid you already."

Abdel snorted. "Don't argue with me, woman." Nura stood steadfast. He grumbled to himself, "Expenses. We have additional expenses—food, bribes."

Reluctantly, Nura gave him a hundred-euro bill. Abdel took it and shoved it in his pocket. "Let's go."

* * *

About 230 kilometers to the northeast, Khalid Al-Maadi prepared to cross the Iraqi border. It wasn't going to be easy; the Jordanian PSD had been searching for him aggressively for weeks. Now the time had come, and Dr. Khalid ibn Mahfous Al-Maadi—a professor at Cairo University, a man with two doctorate degrees, and the head of Black Sun, the terrorist group that came within a hair's breadth of changing the face of the world forever—was hiding in the trailer of a semitruck transporting sheep into Iraq. The driver of the truck had been smuggling people, money, weapons, and alcohol in and out of Iraq for years. He knew what he was doing.

The border security guards didn't relish the idea of getting sheep shit on their shoes and clothes and usually only gave the truck's cargo a cursory inspection. Al-Maadi had to lie on the filthy floor of the trailer under a layer of straw in a depression along the back wall. The smell was horrendous, and the sheep had no aversion to standing, shitting, or pissing on him while he was among them. Traffic at the border crossing was backed up, and he had to wait for over an hour before it was their turn. The border guards opened the rear door of the trailer and started to wade in among the bleating sheep. The sheep pushed farther back into the trailer in an effort to get away from the guards. Khalid started to panic as more and more sheep pressed up against him, but to speak or move would be his death. Finally, the head guard snorted and jumped down. He scribbled his initials on the driver's bill of lading and said, "Go." The guard thanked him and drove away.

A few kilometers inside Iraq, the driver pulled over and rescued Khalid from his ovine prison. He pointed to a little jump seat behind the cab on the outside of the truck. "You ride there."

Khalid was stunned. "What? There? Why?"

The driver laughed. "Because you smell like shit! I don't want you in my cab. Don't worry, we'll stop in an hour or so and get you some new clothes." Khalid's humiliation was now complete.

It took Khalid a week to transit Iraq. His first stop was Ramadi, then Karbala, Najaf, As Samawah, Nasiriyah, and finally Basra. In each city, he was turned over to someone new, and with each turnover, he was confident that this new person would turn him in for the reward that was undoubtedly on his head by now. But Mohammad was true to his word and at the end of a long week, he was smuggled aboard a small coastal freighter bound for Karachi.

* * *

Nura had been in Eritrea for six weeks. Abdel had gotten her to Al Qunfidah as promised. There she was met by another of Mohammad's colleagues who put her on a small fishing boat. Two days later, she was unceremoniously dumped on a beach near Massawa, an Eritrean fishing village on the Red Sea. She was picked up there and moved to Ginda, a small town on the rail line to Asmara. Mohammad's people arranged for her to move into a small, one-room house half a kilometer northwest of the train station.

Nura was not happy to be there. Khalid was over three thousand kilometers away. He was supposed to be in Pakistan somewhere; she didn't know where and had no communication from him since they left the farm in Jordan. She was stuck in a primitive town in a primitive country where she knew absolutely no one. She did, at least, have a roof over her head, though it was made of galvanized metal and sounded like a drum when it rained and was like an oven when it didn't. She never thought of herself as spoiled, but after living in Copenhagen, Cairo, and even Gaza, she couldn't bear to live as she did. She was in a small house made of mud brick, with a tin roof, no electricity, no running water, and a small lean-to in the backyard that served as a toilet. She never thought she would miss the bunker in Libya, but she did now. She had no friends and no entertainment. She had nothing to do but contemplate her life and plot her revenge. One of Mohammad's people came by every week or so to check on her and give her a little money. Every time, she asked when she'd be reunited with Khalid, but every time, she received the same answer: "Soon, soon."

Nura had been to the market and walked home through the little town. Ginda was quaint, in its own way. The people were nice enough and sort of friendly, but they spoke primarily Beja, a local language. Few spoke any Arabic at all. Children played in the streets, and goats, sheep, and dogs wandered freely. While she considered herself tough and resourceful, she had always lived in cities. Even Gaza had modern amenities compared to Ginda. Most of all, she was bored. There was no television, no internet, no radio, and few newspapers. When she found a paper or magazine in a language she read, it was usually days, if not weeks, old. That morning she had been grocery shopping, a daily occurrence when you have no electricity for a refrigerator. On the way back, she stopped by the train station where she found a copy of *Al-Ahram*, an Egyptian daily she used to read in Gaza. It was several days old but she didn't care. She wanted information on what happened in Ramallah all those weeks ago.

Nura walked home while carrying her purchases in a cloth bag and perusing the front page of the newspaper. When she got home, she put the bag of groceries on the table and opened the front and back doors to allow some air to circulate through the house before sitting in one of her two chairs near the back door to read. A couple of minutes later, a shadow passed briefly across the room. She stood up and moved toward the kitchen area to pour herself a glass of water from the large plastic jug she kept there. As she did, she reached into a drawer and quickly pulled out a Makarov 9 mm she kept hidden under a dish towel. She spun on her heel, raised the pistol, and pulled the trigger. Instead of a bang, it was an empty and disheartening "click." She racked the slide to chamber a round and pulled the trigger again. Another "click."

"I found that while you were out. I took the liberty of unloading it." It was Sarah Rabin. She was standing in the doorway, leaning casually against the doorjamb. "I figured you had one stashed around here. Given the size of this place, it didn't take me long to find it. Kind of a step down from your place in Copenhagen or Al-Maadi's apartment in Cairo, don't you think?"

Without saying a word, Nura reached for a small, cast-iron frying pan and hurled it across the room at Sarah while yelling, "You bitch!"

Sarah just slid slightly to her right and let the frying pan hit the wall and fall harmlessly to the floor. "What is it with you and cookware? First in Copenhagen and now this. It's so clichée. You're making all women look bad when you do that shit."

"How did you find me?"

Sarah said, "Your friend Mohammad? His people are not well trained. For what it's worth, you don't have to worry about that anymore. Anyway, they gave you up pretty quickly. Turns out you weren't all that popular with them."

"What do you want?" Nura spit.

"I want to know where Khalid is. I assume you know." Nura was seething but said nothing. After a few seconds of awkward silence, Sarah said, "You know, I'm surprised. I expected a defiant speech about how you would rather die than tell me anything and would see me dead blah, blah, blah." She took a couple of steps closer to Nura to accentuate the fact that she was almost a foot taller than her rival. "I don't think you know where he is. You don't, do you? When did you guys split up? Amman? After? How long have you been on your own?"

Nura tried to regain some emotional and tactical control. Sarah wasn't carrying a weapon. She may yet get the upper hand. "What makes you think we are apart?"

Sarah looked around the small house. "No guy stuff. No men's clothing, no razor, nothing. He's never been here and never will be. Not now." Sarah twisted the knife a bit. "He dumped you, didn't he?"

"He did not!" Nura answered defiantly.

"Well, I'm sure he didn't call it that. What'd he say? You had to split up for safety's sake? Couldn't risk traveling together? Something like that? Men. They're all the same. Never can just say they aren't interested anymore. I tell you, us girls need to stick together."

Nura spat, "You're a lying whore. Khalid loves me and I love him. After I kill you, I will rejoin him."

Sarah ran her finger along the back of the chair next to her. "A couple problems with that plan, Nura. First, he doesn't really want you to join him. He won't let you find him. And second, you aren't going to kill me . . . little mouse."

Her worst enemy calling her by her pet name sent Nura into a rage. "Don't call me that! You killed my father, my mother, and my sister!"

"I didn't kill any of them, but I would have gladly killed your father if I'd been given the chance. He blew up a school bus full of little kids—a fucking school bus! He was no soldier; he was a murderer. As for your sister and mother, he knew we were after him but he used them as shields. In that coffee shop I heard him tell your mother that the Israelis wouldn't dare strike if innocent people were in the car with him. But he screwed up. You see, no one knew they were in the damn car. He got your sister and mother killed while trying to use them as shields."

Nura screamed, "That's a lie!"

"No, Nura, it's not. Your father was a cold-blooded murderer who wouldn't let anything or anyone—including his wife and daughter—get in the way of his blood lust. Your rage, your whole identity, is based on a lie."

Nura's eyes flashed red. "That's a lie, you evil bitch!" She grabbed a knife from the counter and charged at Sarah. Sarah stepped to the side and deflected Nura's charge, pushing her onto the small bed along the wall. Nura jumped up and charged again, this time with the knife raised high to slash at Sarah's face. As she approached, Sarah grabbed Nura's wrist with her left hand and held it up. With her right hand, Sarah grabbed the hand holding the knife, twisted it toward Nura, shoving it down and into her stomach. An expression of shock and pain spread over Nura's face. The blood rushed from her cheeks and her skin started to pale.

Sarah drove the knife deeper into Nura's gut and twisted it as she did so. "That is for those two boys you killed in Libya."

Sarah stepped back, taking the knife from Nura's hands as she did. She tossed the knife into the corner of the room. Nura clutched her wound and stared down at her hands—they were covered in her own blood. Her eyes grew wide. She was mortally wounded and at the hands of the woman she hated the most in the world. "You fucking whore! You've killed me!"

Sarah said calmly, "Actually you killed yourself, I just helped. Judging by the amount of blood, I'd say you nicked an artery. Maybe even the aorta."

Nura gasped, "You don't know what evil you have done."

Sarah snorted. "This from a woman who just tried to kill millions of people. Excuse me if I don't lose any sleep over this one."

Nura collapsed onto the bed. "What now?"

"What now? I watch you die to make sure you're dead, and then I find your boyfriend and do the same to him."

"Husband."

Sarah asked, "What?"

"Husband, Khalid is my husband." The light was fading from her eyes as the blood gushed from her wound.

Looking down at her, Sarah said, "Well, I guess he's your widower now."

* * *

Khalid Al-Maadi finally made his way to Pakistan. The captain of the coastal freighter he had boarded in Basra was nice enough, at first. Once they got to sea, he extorted Khalid for more money and made him work as a deckhand to "earn his passage." Khalid was not used to physical labor and this was evidenced by his blistered hands and aching back. Conditions aboard the ship were horrible. It was hot and cramped. The food was terrible and the water brackish. He expected a private room, or at least a bed. What he got was a sweaty, greasy hammock the smell of which made him hearken back to his time in the sheep trailer as halcyon days of old. The worst thing was the ship's latrine. It was disgusting; so much so that he would sneak up on deck at night to defecate over the railing rather than risk his derriere touching anything in that shit-smeared cell.

By the time he reached Karachi two weeks later, he had lost ten kilos and had gone almost completely gray with a long scruffy beard. This was actually to his advantage as he no longer resembled the handsome man on the wanted posters that had been circulating for the last several weeks. The posters had used an older photo from the university's website. Now he was gaunt, haggard, and gray. Once he got to Karachi, he spent almost all of his remaining money to bribe his way into the country. All he had left was his gold wedding ring. This he sold for ten thousand rupees—less than fifty euros—but it was enough to get him to Mardan in northern Pakistan. After two weeks there, he was taken to Mingora and then finally, on the back of a donkey, to a nameless village some forty kilometers north in the Hindu Kush mountains.

Al-Maadi fell off his donkey and lay on the ground exhausted. If his weight loss, stress, and recent bout of dysentery wasn't enough, he was struggling to breathe in the thin mountain air. A local man approached him and said in Arabic, "Are you Abu Almawt?" Khalid only nodded. "Good, I am here to take you to your uncle."

Khalid corrected him. "Cousin."

"What?"

"He's not my uncle. He's my cousin."

The man shrugged. "Whatever. I was told to bring you to him." Khalid struggled to his feet and slowly followed the man, who laughed and said, "Don't worry. You'll get used to the altitude . . . or die."

After a short walk, he was led to a walled compound with a large house and several smaller buildings. He was ushered into a sitting room and given tea and nuts. "Your cousin will be with you soon. He told me to tell you that your woman, Nura . . ."

Khalid perked up. "Yes, what about her? Is she here?"

"No, she's dead. They found her in Eritrea." Khalid almost collapsed at the news. The man said, "Don't worry. There are women in this district. We will find one for you."

Khalid was about to say something when a man walked into the room through a door on his right. The man was short and fat with long white hair and a long white beard. He wore several layers of thick clothes to protect him against the cold and a Pashtu-style hat. He walked up to Khalid and gave him a big hug. "It has been a long time, cousin, but I would still recognize you anywhere."

Khalid hugged him back and said, "Cousin Ayman, I can't believe I am finally here."

"Come, sit and relax. You must be tired after your journey. I was sorry to hear about your woman."

Khalid asked, "When did it happen? Who?"

"It was two weeks ago in Ginda in Eritrea, where Mohammad had arranged for her to stay. We don't know who it was or how they found her—at least not yet anyway. But we will."

Khalid broke down and started sobbing. "I have failed her and I have failed you, cousin. Our plan was perfect but we ran into these . . . people. They killed Al-Rafah, they killed Trabelsi and his entire cell, they killed Al-Yasuf and his people, they destroyed my virus—all of it, and I am certain it is they who killed Nura."

"Was it the Israelis? The Americans?"

Khalid replied, "I don't know. Some might have been Israelis or Americans but there were others too. Europeans, I think. What difference does it make now?"

Ayman Zawahiri comforted his cousin. "Do you not recall that when we brought down the infidel's buildings, it was our second attempt, not our first? Your plan was so much bigger. We were reaching for the moon while you are reaching for the stars. It was only your first effort. Our jihad requires patience and perseverance. Rest and regain your strength. There is always another day and another Black Sun rising."